Necessary Techniques
of
Obsession

Mat Murphy

Also by Mat Murphy

Non Fiction

Lucky 13 – Thirteen Foundation Stones for Building Wealth
(ebook only)

Available through Amazon & Smashwords

This is a work of fiction. Names, characters, places and incidents either are the product of the author's imagination or are used fictitiously, and any resemblance to any persons, living or dead, business establishments, events or locales is entirely coincidental.

THE NECESSARY TECHNIQUES OF OBSESSION

Published by Mat Murphy
Copyright © 2015 Mat Murphy
Cover Art by Fiona Jayde Media

ISBN-13: 978-1505217865

First printing: February 2015

Printed by CreateSpace

The Flow

The Tribulations of This Disaffected Teen - 1987

This was Mani Alves's battleground. Here among the war era arch-fronted buildings surrounded by a thousand of the nation's finest young men, Mani absorbed the punishment. He'd been shot at, bruised and wounded in a fight he wanted no part of. But he would endure without complaint. That's what was expected here, embodied by the motto of this stern place.

Sit Sine Labe Decus.

Let Honour Stainless Be.

The famous Chandler Boys College. CBC. A place full of history and fine achievement, but for Mani Alves a test of his mettle as he steeled himself when dropped off by his mum Celia, aware of the travails he would face that day. A 12 year old shouldn't have to go to war like this.

Lumbering out of the family Honda Legend, Mani joined the swelling throng of straw boater hats and striped blue blazers pulsing in the various directions of their house groups. He moved through the crowd, head down, eyes flicking nervously for threats, trying his best to not attract attention. This was Mani's morning routine, high in hope for a better day than the one previous.

Arriving at his classroom, Mani shoved his bag in the wooden racks on the veranda and stood in line at the door. Around him kids were sky-larking, shoving each other and laughing. Gangly vessels full of teen energy and attitude. Mani stood quiet and still. He was different from the other boys in Grade 8. He was larger than most. A thick torso and powerful legs, yet his manner more subdued. His ploy was to avert his eyes, like a little kid whose instinct to keep out of trouble is squeezing their eyes shut. Maybe if he couldn't see them, they wouldn't see him.

It didn't work. Just as Dennis Derwent stepped onto the veranda to start his inspection and roll call, Mani copped an ear-flick. His first of the day. He grimaced. Ear-flicks, crowpecks, deadlegs, nipple cripples. Mani was a regular target.

Dennis Derwent, a 20 year CBC veteran rose to his full height, looking down through his half-moon glasses and prodding out his ample gut as he walked the line to view the young gentleman of his class. He used the wooden metre ruler as a walking stick as he ran the rule over the now hushed line-up, ensuring all students were properly attired for the school's high expectations. Grosby shoes polished to the required private school sheen, socks up, grey shorts, white shirts tucked in neatly, ties straight.

He stopped in front of Mani.

"Everything alright today Alves?"

Mani's ears throbbed, the red-eared burn of his shame and anger as bad as the numbness from the flick itself. Was it that obvious?

"Yes, sir," squeaked Mani. Not a word of complaint. Mani was used to being harassed. At school and at home. He'd heard his Dad call it 'hardening him up' when Mani's Mum had asked Peter to go easy on the youngster.

"And it's Alv-Ez, sir," Mani said.

"What?"

"Alv-Ez. My name. It's Spanish style."

"Oh, yes," Derwent said. "That's right. The old El Toro. The Spanish Bull."

"El Weirdo," someone piped up, prompting starts of laughter.

Derwent rapped his metre ruler twice on the floor, glaring down the line.

"Thank you Alv-Ez," he said.

Derwent held his gaze on Mani's face for a few seconds, then let his eyes drop to continue his morning inspection. The teacher drew his metre ruler back and swung it forward at knee height. Derwent was renowned for his backhand, both on the tennis court and in the classrooms.

Mani flinched, waiting for the impact. He heard it but there was no pain as the ruler clattered into the shin of the boy next to him.

"Socks up, Miller," Derwent growled.

The roll call completed, boisterous scuffling resumed as the boys jostled to get inside. The room was a blend of the historic and modern. High ceilings and ornate cornices and windows, but air-conditioned and filled with the latest school-use electronics. The campus obviously had budget.

Mani avoided the bumping and elbowing, spotting his seat and moving toward it. But the pressure never stopped – he was flat-footed from behind. Some kid had kicked his heel as he walked. Mani's foot leapt forward, banging his shin on a chair, lifting the skin and causing a trickle of blood to soak through his sock.

It never ended.

Mid-morning, the throb of his shin having died down and Derwent espousing his theories on Shogunate Japan, Mani felt the thud of the day's first spitball in the middle of his back. Almost simultaneously, another claggy white lump pinged by his eyeline from a different angle. There were stifled giggles.

Derwent turned from the blackboard, scanning the room for any trouble. Only angelic faces peered back at him.

Mani felt the wetness of the golly on his back. The soggy lump had affixed to his shirt, creating an ever-expanding patch of spittle between his shoulder blades. Despite this, he remained focussed, stoic.

Minutes later came the headshot the class had waited for. Mani's hair fanned out in slow-motion, like splattering blood in a war movie. The spitball struck behind his right ear and the potent mixture of chewed paper and saliva acted like hair-gel on Mani's head, strong-holding his hair in its new bullied style.

Stifled yelps of triumph echoed around. Mani did not turn to see the perpetrator. Last time he wore the inevitable follow-up in the face. Instead he processed his humiliation, lowering his head to the desk as Derwent spun around. Mani had lost his focus.

"Mr Alves. Perhaps you would like to explain to the rest of us how emperors fitted into the shogunate system and who held the power in this arrangement?"

Mani lifted his head. He dare not voice an answer to a question he had no chance of comprehending. He looked sideways, seeing only smug faces. The class waited for an answer.

"So, Alves. It seems odd you can afford to lay your head down during class. Perhaps you require some extra time spent studying this."

Mani fumed. The class had won again, as evidenced by Derwent's attention and subsequent detention. He wondered how he could break away from this, wipe the target from his back. He pawed at his hair, trying to remove the paper and restore some dignity.

****

Though Mani often wondered why his parents sent him to this school, the decision was based on wanting the very best for their only son. Peter Alves was a Western Suburbs success story and indeed many of the parents delivering children to CBC each morning had been coerced, cajoled and caressed into buying their luxury model from Peter Alves. This was a man who had the gift of the gab.

Mani's Dad liked to display his successes, as evidenced by the sprawling acreage home by the river and the jewellery and stylish outfits worn by Celia. Chandler Boys College was how Peter contributed further to his own image. Enrolling Mani into grade 8 at CBC was seen as a mark of Peter's social pedigree and accomplishments. None of this assisted Mani though. He enjoyed the curriculum and was a bright student but he had become more withdrawn since joining the school. All was not lost though as Mani had a support system at CBC.

Jason Sharpe was Mani's cousin, their mothers close-knit sisters. Both being in grade eight, Mani sought Jason out most days at school and he knew precisely where he'd be. Jason was fun and brilliant, an immediate lure for other kids, and he could be found hanging and playing with the cool group.

Mani approached the building under which handball games were in full swing. Squares of concrete were painted for these spirited battles. There was always a buzzing atmosphere with plenty of banter between cocky, confident kids. Jason held sway, in the Ace possie as usual.

Sidling up to Jason's end of the handball court, Mani greeted his athletic cousin.

"Hi, Jas. What are you doing?"

Jason continued playing, sharp-eyed and energetic. "Mani!" he replied. "Just showing these guys how to play handball."

Mani grinned. He enjoyed Jason's company and there was a genuine bond between the two. Jason knew of his cousin's difficulties fitting in at school, though he also knew of Mani's cheeky, exuberant side and the wicked aspect of his personality.

A kid with insane blond-hair won the point, moving him up the pecking order. He celebrated as teenagers do, pulling a striped headband from his pocket, sliding it on his head and doing a fist-pumping run around his vaunted opponent.

Jason laughed during the respite before the next point began. "Where were you yesterday, cuz? I thought we were meeting at lunch."

"Detention," Mani replied.

"Really. You?" Jason baulked. He re-started the ball game.

"Yeah. Muckin' up in class," Mani lied. "Got caught. Just unlucky."

"Bummer."

Jason was being targeted in the game, firstly because he was in Ace but also because he was Jason Sharpe. Everyone wanted to get him out. He paddled a passing shot wide. The game erupted into high-fives and raucous yells as the kids shuffled to their new squares.

"Get ya cousin in, Sharpie," one kid called out.

Mani and Jason lined up for their turn at the bottom of the squares. Jason offered Mani to go in next.

"Hook in there, matey," Jason encouraged as Mani joined the game.

Though he was Double Dunce, Mani was immediately targeted. He held his own for a while. Mani was no oaf. His Dad insisted on both study and physical fitness. Discipline of the mind and body. As a result, Mani was powerful in the legs and quite agile despite his size.

They eventually got him, prompting another round of high-fives despite no-one gaining from getting the lowest square out. Kids just know how to hammer home an advantage.

"So we're coming to your place on Saturday," Mani said.

Jason knew about it. "Yeah. Wish we were going to yours. It's heaps better than our joint. We could rig up that swing over the river."

Mani looked at his feet. "Mum says we shouldn't do it anymore."

Mani's words hung in the air. Both boys pondered them.

"Fine. We'll tell her we are collecting rubbish to beautify the riverbank. She's your Mum. She'll buy it."

Mani laughed. Being around Jason lifted him. He loved his spirit.

The bell went. Kids everywhere ignored it.

Jason gave Mani a playful punch on the shoulder. "I'll badger my olds to organise a barbie at your place next weekend. We'll do the swing. OK?"

Mani was relieved. Grateful that the world let him slide into Jason's slipstream. He felt protected. Having Jason in his corner removed some of the stress of being hassled at school.

"So, what class have you got now?" Mani asked.

"Geography. Then PE."

Jason reached out and picked some leftover spitball out of Mani's hair. Mani lowered his head. Hurt.

"Hey, I'll need you to help me with writing my birthday invites this weekend," Jason said. "You're better at it than me."

****

The Southern Cross transit bus swung off Moggill Road, the main arterial that snaked from Chandler Boys College in Toowong through high-density suburbs to where the acreage properties gradually fanned out some twenty kilometres from Brisbane's CBD. Mani watched as the only other boy on the bus stepped off, leaving Mani as CBC's western-most student.

The ride home, though forty-five minutes long, gave Mani some respite from the degradation he felt at school. It allowed him to choose a seat away from others on the lightly used service and he usually read some of his favourite spy action novels on the trip home.

Once off the bus it was several minutes walk to his driveway. Gum trees waved and slapped their leaves together overhead. Blue skies peeked through. Perfect autumn weather. A cool breeze washed off some of the late afternoon heat.

Mani ambled down the sloped driveway. The Alves house overlooked the river on a couple of usable acres. Yet despite the fine weather and big yard, Mani would typically spend the afternoon in his room, knocking off his homework, reading and tinkering. Except for those afternoons when his Dad insisted on being his physical trainer.

Mani approached the front door. The large deck rolled outwards from the front porch over the sloping block below. Mani could hear the familiar sounds of his home. Magpies warbled in the trees and a powersaw screeched in the distance. But one sound stood out. Unexpected. His father's voice.

He's never home this early, Mani thought.

Peter Alves was his own man. He came home when it suited him to do so. That was his right as he saw it. He earned the dollars so he had the say on how it was spent on the family's activities. He had bought this house eighteen months earlier after the landlord at their inner-city Paddington rental had chased them out of his house, sick of having to pursue Peter for the rent. Peter guarded Celia from the fall-out. It was his own doing, over-spending and living too large while his real estate career floundered.

As always Peter Alves bounced back, and quick. His gift of the gab got him into selling cars and the success was immediate. The bank loved his earning capacity, gratefully lending him the money to buy his acreage dream home. The family also enjoyed the trappings of Peter's run of luck. Holidays, eating out, a nice car, and Celia on a first name basis with boutique owners across Brisbane west, flashing her sparkling fingers as she lunched with businessmen's wives on her personal Bankcard.

But Peter was home early today. Mani sensed something was amiss.

He eased the door open, elevating the volume of his obviously agitated father. Peter was on his feet, walking the living room with the receiver to his ear and the phone trailing out the extension lead. Mani noticed his mother coming towards him as he stepped through the door.

Celia was wearing the stylish floral dress she was wearing when she dropped Mani off that morning. Bare upper arms, her face fully made up, earrings and thigh length dress that had become something of a uniform in her socialite existence. Celia had maintained her looks, her middle-aged curviness having not yet extended to plumpness. She had evidently worn her "uniform" while doing the housework that day.

Corralled toward the staircase by his mother, Mani looked over his shoulder at his father. He felt the anxiety in the room and had an idea of the reason. He'd seen it before.

Peter was distressed, grumbling down the phone line. "Mate, I sell cars for a living and no-one wants cars this week. I'll sell you a sun hat if it's sunny next week. If it's raining, I'll sell you an umbrella. Point is, I can sell. I'll start selling something soon and you'll get your dough."

Gently urging Mani into his room, Celia then closed the door. She appeared on edge to Mani, concerned about the family finances once again. She gave Mani a hug.

"How was your day, darling?"

Mani shrugged.

"Steer clear of your father for a while. He needs some space to sort some things out."

"I know, Mum," Mani said. "I've got some homework anyway."

"You're a good boy," she said. She gave him another hug, as much for herself as for the boy. Celia stood there for several seconds, then let out a nervous giggle and left the room.

Mani waited for a minute, then inched his bedroom door open. He was curious about how things were playing out downstairs. From what he could hear, it appeared Peter was speaking to the bank. Mani managed to grasp where things were at, despite only hearing one side of the conversation.

"So, you invited me to the dance and now you want me to serve drinks and clean up the bloody hall as well."

Despite the impact whatever was happening would doubtless have on the family, Mani felt becalmed. Matter of fact. Life rarely and barely changed when his Dad stuffed things up again. They just moved on to the next house, the next big deal, the next school.

"You're a Bank Manager," Peter growled. "Can't ya give me two months to get my cashflow sorted? Isn't that what banks do?"

Mani heard Peter slam the receiver into the phone. Something got kicked. Then more dialling. Another bank, cap in hand, Peter Alves-style.

"Thanks, mate," Peter said, a hint of sarcasm in his voice. "Let me take your name down. OK. Robert is it? Bob. Rightio. How about I give you a call when I'm back on my feet and I'll tell you to stick it up your arse!" Again the receiver slammed into its cradle with a raucous ding.

Mani giggled silently from behind his bedroom door. He felt there was some excitement when Peter was trying to get the family back on their feet. It shook things up.

Peter dialled again, this time a mate from the caryard.

"Trev, you can have the Honda Legend and I'll take that shitty '82 Sigma you got in the yard. But I need a changeover of three grand, mate." Peter was at his smooth-talking best. He needed something, Mani could tell. "No, I'm not paying you, ya flamin' idiot. You give me three grand! Jesus, you're a greedy prick."

The calls kept coming – more banks, asking for jobs, hustling, trying to get a break. Mani lay on his bed and read a while, interrupted periodically by an outburst from his Dad downstairs. Things would change quickly, he sensed.

Mani drifted off as Peter kept punching out the calls. He knew how to get things done, even if he often over-did things.

"I could start tomorrow if you want. And the first house I'll sell for you will be me own. Bank wants their bloody money back."

****

The evening meal at the Alves house was the typical meat and three-veg affair, eaten as the late afternoon March sun still licked at the dining table. The men of the family sat as Celia delivered their meals with a jug of water and three goblets. Peter had a whisky on ice half dusted.

Mani was quiet, aware that his father's mood could be prickly after his afternoon of negotiations.

"Looks lovely, Ceels," Peter said, giving her a wink.

Mani dutifully responded. "Thanks for dinner, Mum."

They made a start and it wasn't long before Peter brought up the issues of the day.

"I'll be tidying up the last couple of deals at work tomorrow, then that will be it," he said in his deep, almost croaky voice. "The boss has halved his orders, and sacked half the staff – the ones on salary and left us poor bludgers on commission to mop up the last of the sales."

"Business is bad," Celia said cooing in agreeance.

"Car industry is stuffed anyway. Too many cheap imports and not enough dough to be made. Only the loyal clowns will stick around"

Mani could see his father had already moved on. Mani knew the signs. Peter would slate anything that did not work for him and there'd be another deal around the corner. He kept his tongue, listening while eating.

"We'll get a good price for this joint. Should go quick," Peter said. "It's a nice enough place. I'm sure this suits some people but we can get a nice house, closer in, still have a bit of a yard. And save $80 a week."

"Excellent, Peter," Celia agreed again.

Peter continued looking for positives, justifying the inevitable next move. "Stuff paying 15% interest. And why would anyone live out here. It's too far out. It was a mistake to move here."

Mani's stomach grabbed. He liked this house. Liked the river being close and the wind that gusted through his window, flipping pages off the desk in his room. His view out to nothing but green and blue. The enormous gum trees that stood sentry to their comings and goings. The rope swing. It would be gone soon when Peter sold the house.

"The car will go," Peter continued. "It was just a money pit. And Ceels, we will all need to make some sacrifices." He wiggled his ring finger at her, indicating her anniversary ring, bought for plenty in the good times and pawned once already in the bad times.

Mani soaked up the conversation, seeing his mother's head drop in disappointment as she conceded her sacrifice for the family fortunes.

"Chin up love," Peter said. "You know we get it back soon enough."

She smiled sadly.

Peter continued his virtual monologue throughout dinner. The family listened. Peter already had the next plans laid out it seemed. Failure washed over him, unaffecting. He bounced back quicker than most, the remorse brushed aside as he built his empirical plans.

"There's plenty of opportunity. We'll actually come out of this sweet as. Free up some capital, it will. There's some other projects I have had my eye on, and the timing is perfect."

"It's a blessing in disguise...one door closes, another opens..." Peter kept the 'get back on the horse' clichés coming as he mapped out his next steps.

"We'll have to ditch the fancy school for the boy," Peter said. "It's a waste of money, and money better used elsewhere. Saving that much will free up money for the move and to knock over some debts."

Mani stopped chewing. He did not look at his father.

He processed what was just said, initially with distaste that his father thought that money spent on Mani was such a waste. And that Peter spoke so matter-of-factly about their lives as though he were the unquestionable king of the domain, organising two other lives around his own ambitions. Peter had spoken this as though Mani was not even in the room. No consultation. Just orders barked with a positive spin and a cackling laugh at the end.

Peter lit up a smoke after dinner, leaning back and blasting smoke into the air. "Let's get stuck into it, then," he exclaimed. He was pumped up. He enjoyed the thrill of things being shaken up like this.

Then it occurred to Mani that he would be leaving CBC. No more lime shirt. No more Derwent and his El Toro comments. No more bullying...no more spitballs. Mani's heart soared. A blessing in disguise, he thought. One door closes, another opens. His father's mantras.

"Can I pour you another Scotch, Dad?" Mani asked, barely able to mask his excitement.

"Good on ya, boy. Of course you can."

"Excellent, Mani," Celia smiled as Mani leapt up.

"Don't forget," Peter said as he held up a hand toward his son, gesticulating. "Four cubes, two fingers. One perfect Scotch."

Life was going to be alright.

****

Peter stood at the window of the main bedroom, looking out through the trees towards the next home several hundred metres away. He took a sip of his whisky on ice, lit a Winfield Red and kept staring. He was hoping for a glimpse of the neighbour's missus, a good sort who got around in short shorts while doing the yard.

Peter was alone in the room, dressing for the weekend barbecue at Celia's big sister's place. He wore his brown trousers and a thick belt but remained shirtless, displaying his wiry body and thin arms. The short sleeve shirt, ironed by Celia, lay spread on the bed. It was a uniform of his own. Stylish. Perfect dressed down for a barbie, or slide on a tie and tweed jacket and you were ready for business. His chosen look spoke of success. Substance.

Celia was already dressed and downstairs. They would leave soon but Peter was steering clear of his wife. She was dark at him for having to hock the anniversary ring and the past 48 hours had been quite sombre between them.

It would be OK though. Peter knew this. He had been in the doghouse plenty of times in the last fifteen years. He knew how to get back into Celia's good books. He'd been smoothing things over with her since the first night they met in 1972. Even that night saw him having to claw back Celia's favour after offending her and her sister at the Victory Hotel in Brisbane's city centre.

Peter had been a labourer turned real estate agent with an arrogant streak and a quick mouth. Adding Sunday afternoon beers and throwing him into a beer garden amongst fun-loving young ladies and other blokes looking for a triumphant end to their weekend and there was always going to be fireworks.

Celia Benson had urged her older sister to chaperone her for an afternoon out. Celia was the more progressive of the two, Patricia more reserved and observant. Following her sister to the big smoke from rural Nambour as soon as she could, Celia had landed secretarial work and her busty look and sociable nature assured her popularity in the bars and clubs of early 70's Brisbane.

When some beer-soaked skylarking ended with Peter's schooner down Patricia's back on that fateful afternoon, Celia showed her firecracker nature. Introducing herself to Peter Alves by grabbing his mates' beer glass to give Peter an equivalent dousing along with some choice words, 18 year-old Celia piqued her future husband's interest.

Peter had talked his way through that first of many episodes as they firstly courted, soon married and then, with a new son, Peter set them on their see-sawing way through life by making a small fortune flogging cheap land in the expanding suburban sprawl north of Brisbane. Several booms and busts later for the Alves clan – from which they always swiftly recovered – and here they were still living the financial and emotional zig-zag that Peter had made an art-form.

He flicked his smoke out of the window and drew himself away. No sight of said sexy neighbour. Peter downed his Scotch, scooped up his shirt and checked his look in the mirror, dabbing at his mouth with a handkerchief. He smoothed his moustache on the sun-hardened face looking back. Never did a mo find a face more suited.

Bounding downstairs, Peter joined Mani and Celia. He felt the tension from Celia immediately.

"You look good, love," he said.

Cold silence.

"Mani, be a good lad and take the esky to the car, will ya?" Peter said.

Mani lifted himself from the couch and heaved the orange esky toward the door.

Peter sashayed up to Celia. A groovy little half-dance, half-walk to break the ice with his wife.

"Don't try and get in my good books, Pedro Alves," she said firmly. Celia used Peter's full Spanish name when she was annoyed. "It might be best if we just stayed well clear of each other this afternoon."

"Oh, come on, love. Is this about the ring is it?"

Celia gave him a glare. How could it be about anything else?

"Ceels, we all had to make some cutbacks. It's a tough time. I lost my car, Mani changing school. It's all temporary though. You know that. You've seen how I work. We'll be back on our feet in no time."

"But that ring, Peter. It was an anniversary gift. How many times do we have to go through this."

"That ring was $1500 that we needed right then," Peter said, more coldly than he thought. His wife's shoulders sunk. "Life goes in waves, darlin'. You know what it's like when we are on the up. Plenty of parties. Plenty of booze. Nice clothes. We're just in the water waitin' for the next wave. You know it's comin', don't ya. You know Peter Alves always hits back. And when we get on board that wave, you know you'll get your ring back, with interest."

"Forget about my ring," Celia said, wanting to shift the focus of the conversation. "What about Mani, Peter? It's the upheaval. Pulling him out of school is probably very upsetting and it could set him back in his schoolwork."

"Kids adapt, Ceels. It'll keep him on his toes." Peter let his words hang in the air, considering them and then deciding he needed to be less harsh. "How about we look at this as an opportunity for Mani to learn. For all of us to learn. What better lesson than to witness a bit of hardship and see his old man stay positive and jump straight back into getting things back on track?"

Celia crossed her arms and tilted her head. Saying nothing, she maintained a cross face as well as she could. She had thin, attractive lips and her skin was smooth. Her eyes – those eyes that captivated Peter back in the bar in 1972 - still shone, portraying the cheeky, extroverted girl that loved life.

But Peter saw through the act. He saw a hint of a smile cross her lips, and he seized on it, moving toward her. "My sweetheart. I look at you and I see my inspiration for life. There's a lot of beauty in this world, but none as beautiful as you. For you, I do my work, I seek my fortune. For you, I would do anything, my love."

He put his arms around Celia as she let a smile soften her face.

"You're just a smooth talker, Peter Alves," Celia spoke softly, leaning into his embrace. "But let me stay cranky at you a bit longer. I don't want you thinking you're back in my good books that easy."

Peter heard Mani coming back in the front door. "Wait. What's that noise?" he said with mock urgency. "Sounds like a wave coming, Ceels. Sounds like our wave!" He let out his trademark cackle at his own joke. His laugh turned into a phlegmy half-cough. Too many smokes.

Mani walked in the room and looked at his parents curiously. They were hugging.

"To the car everybody," Peter yelled. "Let's go and see how the other half live."

****

Reaching the Sharpe's modest suburban home, Mani untangled himself from the backseat and lifted the esky from the carboot. They had made the journey in silence and Mani sensed he needed to stay on his father's good side. Watching his Dad scoop up the esky and turn away, Mani became aware of how hot the day was as he stood on the footpath, the couch grass neatly mown and perfectly-edged along the gutter.

Jason Sharpe was first to the door to meet the Alves family. He was a thin kid with a moppy fringe and hair short around the sides. He still wore his white shirt tucked into his shorts from his tennis lesson earlier in the afternoon. Mani immediately felt the ease of his cousin's company, like a security blanket as he was beckoned inside with the lure of party food.

With big-sister kindness, Patricia welcomed Celia's family into her home. She was slim, conservative and her tidy home reflected the orderly mind required in her occupation as a book-keeper. Mani gave in willingly to her hug. She emanated a warmth that Mani saw only fleetingly from his own mother.

As Mani dipped his first cocktail sausage into tomato sauce, the rasping voice of his father broke through over the low music and other greetings.

"Trish, darling," Peter said as he gave Patricia a kiss on the cheek. "House lookin' lovely, as always. Graham, old mate. How are ya? How's life on the southside?"

Offering his hand, Graham Sharpe met the gaze of his brother-in-law with a steady smile. He was a wide-shouldered man but dressed plain in a light blue collared Penguin shirt. He maintained his calm nature despite his apprehension around Peter. "Always good on the southside, Peter. How's business?"

Mani watched his father slip into his old routine. And he sensed the whole room was watching this show.

"On the move, actually, mate. Getting out. Decided to pursue some other opportunities. Car business is just too slow. Too much red tape for a fella like me." He popped a handful of peanuts into his mouth. "I've found better use of my talents."

"You are one to make the most of things. What is it you're looking at doing?" Graham asked.

"This and that. You know. Making some big changes, actually. Gonna sell up the house to free up some capital. Got a couple of irons in the fire." Classic evasion. Peter cracked a beer open and made it more than clear that this part of the conversation was over. "Cheers mate. Now, how's that pergola project going?"

Sipping his drink, Mani had kept an intuitive eye on the scene. He had noticed how his mother held her lips pursed while

Peter spoke of their situation, busying herself with arranging the esky contents. But Mani also saw the knowing glances between the sisters.

As Mani followed Jason upstairs, he overheard his Aunt Patricia. She had moved over to Celia and put a hand on her arm.

"It's happening again, isn't it?" Patricia asked quietly.

It was these little details that Mani noticed in his world. Like how he saw, as he followed his cousin up the staircase that Jason, still dressed in his tennis attire, had odd socks. Someone else might not notice. The socks were both white with one blue and one red hoop. But the left foot, Mani observed, had the blue hoop on top. Maybe he just saw the world different to others.

Jason was his chirpy self as they reached his room. "Have a look at this," Jason said, handing a black and white curl of plastic to Mani. "It is unreal!"

Mani looked at the toy in his hand. "What is it?" he asked.

"Rubik's Snake," Jason replied, taking it back. He began twisting the thing so that the triangular pieces splayed at different angles. Within seconds he had shaped it into a dog. "See what that is? I can do a cobra too!"

Mani smiled. He loved his cousin's infectious bubbliness. Jason had brought a bag of chips to the room. The boys would spend much of the next couple of hours joking and laughing, eating chips and making regular sojourns to get more soft drink. Eventually Mani broached the subject that spending time with Jason had briefly scrubbed from his mind.

"End of term is my last week of school."

Jason looked up from his comic. "What?" he asked. "What do you mean?"

"I've got to change schools," Mani replied. "Dad said we need to save money so I'm going to Westside High."

"Why do you have to save money?"

Mani held his hands in his lap as he sat on the carpet, leaning back against Jason's bed. His eyes stayed down. "Something about the car industry is stuffed. We're moving house, too."

"Holy hell, Mani."

"Dad's not worried though. He reckons things will be better."

Jason shook his head in wonder. "Doesn't your Dad own the caryard?" he asked. "I thought you guys were rich."

Nothing more was said about the issue. It would not affect how they related. They would still see each other often, still be mates. Downstairs, another family had arrived and the barbecue was well under way. Through the hum of discussion from the lower level, they could hear Peter Alves giving his advice to others, loud and clear. Four beers down and getting into his stride.

New Boy!

The heat had gone out of the city. Scorched over the summer months, Brisbane showed its lovable side at either end of the summer months. Before the foul heat and violent afternoon storms, the city comes to life in a jacaranda blaze of purple flowers and perfect days hot enough to swim but not to swelter.

Now, at the start of April, the city's finest hours returned once more to soak its citizens in glorious autumn sunshine. There was a feeling of promise in the air. Brisbane was growing up, expanding. It had done so since landing in the international eye through hosting the Commonwealth Games earlier in the decade. New national sport teams were afoot. The embryonic Brisbane Bears AFL side were struggling to gain enough footing to compete with the established southern clubs, the Brisbane Bandits baseball team had groomed several potential stars and were starting to make waves, the Brisbane Broncos were newly-formed though yet to play their first game in the National Rugby League. Now, with the city building its identity, construction was well underway for Expo 88.

Yet its icons remained – the far-reaching fig trees dotted through the suburbs, the exquisite Italianate architecture of historical structures like the Treasury Building, the variegated rock walls of the Kangaroo Point cliffs. The country town jibes were being thrown off as the little cousin grew up. The cultural cringe was dissipating.

The start of the Easter school holidays saw schoolkids and their families across the city packing up their cars to enjoy a week in a caravan park up the Sunshine Coast or partaking in the warmth and fine beaches from a holiday unit on the Gold Coast.

Peter Alves and his family were also packing their car. And a truck. They were on the move from their Karana Downs acreage to move into a rental in suburban Kenmore. And Peter was in a foul mood.

"Worst job in the world," he'd grumbled to anyone who would listen.

Packing up and moving house was not his only issue. He had got what he asked for the house and signed it off within three days. Normally a pleasing experience, Peter saw this as an opportunity missed, seeing only missed profits rather than convenience and certainty. "I could have put an extra ten grand on it."

Now, with Graham roped in to help him do the heavy lifting and Celia inside cleaning and wiping out cupboards with Patricia, Peter had willing helpers and someone to listen to him sprout his plans. He had made things happen quickly, a standard response to the regular occurrence of having to re-shape his family's life when he had overcommitted on his loans, misjudged the market, over-read the demand, misinterpreted potential and sent them broke again.

Peter had slipped into his usual mode of talking up his plans. Finishing up at the caryard, he was in a property management role within a week, his smooth-talking talents angling into the office principal's good books. And the proceeds from the house sale were already ear-marked for the next project.

"Thirty percent in the last 6 months, mate," Peter said to Graham as they constructed the car-boot jigsaw puzzle necessary to ensure maximum use of packing space. "Where else are ya going to get returns like that?"

Peter had found the Australian sharemarket and now relentlessly postulated about being amongst the riches supposedly on offer. Graham listened without judgment or comment.

Peter used this chance to sound out his brother-in-law about Graham and Patricia's recent purchase. "How did you and Trish go about getting another property?" he asked.

Graham, a strongly-built man who had shouldered much of the heavier lifting, responded cautiously to Peter's line of questioning. "Trish has picked up plenty of little tips from her boss. He lodged our tax returns and thought there might be some spare cash to put towards a property."

"But you had to borrow money, didn't ya? Surely you didn't pay cash!"

"Yeah, of course we borrowed."

"There ya go," said Peter, as though he'd pin-pointed the folly of their plan. "It's not yours. And you've got a loan to repay."

"Well the tenant pays most of the costs," Graham countered.

"Most of the cost?" Peter queried. "So, you're going backwards then. It's costin' ya money. How is that a smart investment?"

Graham remained patient. "Because of two things. We'll get a big tax cheque back, and the house price will go up in the future. It's called 'negative gearing'."

"Negative all right." Peter tied a truckies knot to secure the bedposts to the roof racks of the Sigma. "How long's all that gonna take?"

"Trish reckons it's a ten-year plan."

"Ten years? Far out! Who's got that long to wait? Fair dinkum, Graham. You gotta get into the shares. Life's too short."

Graham let a smile cross his face. He was enjoying the banter, unfazed by Peter's negativity. "Sharemarket. Sounds like a Get-Rich-Quick scheme to me," he said.

"Nothin' wrong with a getting' rich quick, mate," Peter said. "I reckon that's the best way." He let himself consider his own words, surmising that he was pretty proud of his insight. He let out his cackly wheeze of a laugh. Graham laughed and shook his head as Peter's cackle faded out to a coughing fit and a spit on the dust of the driveway.

The two men continued filling the car. Peter felt vindicated, as though his logic had achieved some sort of victory over his brother-in-law. Peter considered Graham slow, often showing his disdain for the man. He wondered why anyone would be content with the sort of stable, mundane life that Graham Sharpe had eked out with Patricia.

The reality was they suited each other. Graham was a cautious, conservative man. He had secure employment in a physical job, his thick arms and barrel chest testament to the handyman work he performed. And he was a family man.

Nothing was more important to Graham than raising his beautiful son and providing for the beautiful, cautious, conservative woman he had married 13 years before.

Peter stubbed out his smoke with his foot and pulled his car keys from his pocket. "Rightio. All packed," he said. "Let's get stuck into it then."

As they drove, Peter re-started his rant about his wealth-building prospects. It was a fifteen minute drive towards town, the swaying gum trees giving way to power poles and the odd traffic light as they neared suburbia.

"So how are you going to invest in the sharemarket if you don't have any money?" Graham queried.

"Creative accounting," replied Peter. "Your missus is not the only one who knows how to fiddle the numbers."

Graham laughed. "No fiddling going on in the Sharpe household."

Peter was swift and vicious with his reply. "Don't bullshit me, Graham! I reckon youse have got something funny goin' on."

****

The aging Bedford bus lurched around the final bend towards Kenmore's Westside State High School, emitting grey smoke from its exhaust and the scream and chatter of 44 kids from its windows. Amongst its cargo, Mani sat observant and non-descript.

He did his best to blend into the scene as he watched these unknowns interact around him. He saw two girls huddled into one another sharing a set of headphones. Further up the bus, a boy spat out of the window at passing cars, egged on by his mates. Another kid had taken a Nikko pen to the back of the seats.

Mani had been feeling unusually calm this morning considering he was starting at a new school where anything could happen. He felt positive. Felt this was going to be a good move for him, allow him to start afresh. He said nothing while on the bus, preferring to watch on and bask in his composure.

He imagined himself striding into his new school, young ladies throwing coy glances at him and the guys giving him high fives and backslaps. There are even some teachers standing and applauding. A jazz band starts up. Mani is wearing a tuxedo. Ticker tape falls gently over the scene.

Now, with the bus pulling up outside the school, Mani's apprehension returned. It was time to face the reality of a new world. The butterflies in his stomach evolved into the Butterfly Effect, implementing chaos theory in his guts. Lorenz's theoretical hurricane churned his insides as he alighted from the old bus. He suddenly felt an urgency to poo.

Kids streamed around him, busloads of potential pressure points coming from any direction. The defence expert within Mani, honed in his harrowing months at CBC, quickly categorised these threats. His mind isolated the various groups as they came through his line of sight, assigning a score of how likely they were to harm him.

He saw skegs, swampies, sporty jocks and nerds, Goth types rolling their eyes through dusky fringes, bogans with mullets and stick-thin metalheads mulling around. Each sub-culture maintained their image despite managing to comply with the requirements of Westside High's uniform policy. Mani wondered where he fitted into this conglomeration of fashions, as he had no distinctive style that aligned him to any of these groups. His Mum had made him wear full uniform for the first day of term. He wore his hair short with a straight-cut fringe. And he liked having a little length at the back, particularly giving it a little shake to feel it tickle his neck. Mani's overall style, however, fell into the range of completely normal.

Mani followed these varying groups, and as they gradually dispersed in front of him, he found himself at the main office. He presented himself at the front counter, where a harried receptionist ignored him.

She finally acknowledged his presence. "New student, I presume? Name please."

Mani gave his name. The reception was busy. One staffer was sorting mail, another collating paper from a photocopier. A handyman was in early, repairing a hole in the office wall.

"You would have been asked to bring a birth certificate," the terse woman stated. She barely looked at Mani, snatching the papers from him. She operated from behind unflattering, semi-circle glasses, her mouth puckered bitterly. "Take a seat. We will take you to class when we can."

Great, Mani thought. He'd be paraded into a new classroom, standing out like the proverbial. He wanted to slink in the room with the other kids, unseen and under the radar. But this way, he would walk in the room with a target on him. His concerns started his stomach up again. He had hardly been welcomed warmly into the bosom of the school by the cold counter lady.

A man emerged from one of the offices up the short hallway. He appeared dishevelled, out of proportion almost. His jacket seemed to be buttoned in the wrong holes and one trouser leg shorter than the other. Mani watched his stilted walk as he approached.

On closer inspection, his clothes were actually quite neat. It was just a general awkwardness that gave the impression. His arms seemed to swing unnaturally as he walked, at odds with each other. His hair was plastered down on one side of his head only. His gait seemed to imply that he was about to turn around every third step and retrieve something he had forgotten. He was the principal.

He conferred with reception Nazi, picked up a file and approached Mani. "Good morning," the principal said. "You must be Manuel Alves. Our new student."

"Mani Al Vez," corrected Mani.

"Welcome, Mani. I'm Mr Prendergast, the school principal. So the last name is Al Vez is it? What's that? Mexican?"

"Spanish, sir."

"Oh, right. The Spanish Inquisition. The Spanish Armada. You'll learn about those in your history classes."

Mani smiled, unsure what to say.

Prendergast scanned his file. "I see you've joined us from CBC. And your marks have been exceptional. What brings you to Westside?"

Mani recalled his pre-scripted answer to this very question, implanted by his father. Peter had said that to fit in, you had to conform. "Piss in their pockets a bit. Tell 'em what they wanna hear," was how he put it.

"My Dad wasn't happy with the culture at CBC," Mani said. "Too snobby. He says he wants me to learn about life in a real world school. Reckons the people here are more genuine."

Prendergast smiled proudly. The sentiment registered with him as a pat on the back for the public system. "Let's head up to class, shall we."

They walked along the covered walkways, chatting as they went. Prendergast revealed that he was a private school Old Boy, having gone to Brisbane Grammar. He let the words hang, expecting a response. Mani didn't know how he should react. Should he high-five the headmaster or was there a private school secret handshake that should be enacted at such times? He said nothing.

Arriving at the room, Prendergast directed Mani to wait outside as he entered the room. Mani peered through the two inch gap in the door, seeing the kids sneering at the visiting headmaster. One kid yelled out "Go Go Gadget", prompting hoots of laughter at this stab at Prendergast's appearance.

With a wave of the principal's hand, Mani was summoned into the room. Mani's heart grabbed in his chest as he pushed open the door. His stomach's cyclone re-formed causing Mani to clench once more to prevent landfall and a very public soiling. He put his hand across his chest to try to cover the target he imagined forming on him.

Someone yelled out "New Boy!" as Mani shuffled in to be introduced.

Prendergast put a hand on Mani's shoulder and cleared his throat. "Class. This is Manuel Al Vez." Ridiculously, Prendergast put a little accent on the surname, along with a wiggle of his head as though he were a Spanish bullfighter acknowledging his faithful fans. "He's a straight A student from CBC."

Nooo, Mani thought. Let me be a trouble-maker from the rough side of town. Maybe having had to change schools for torturing bullies. Or biffing the principal. Don't make me a straight A student from a posh private school. Mani knew what would come next.

As Prendergast and the teacher went through the obligatory talk about helping the new student fit in and showing him around, the class were relentless in their cat-calling. Between the authority's words the insults came like rapid fire.

Nerd...

Dork...

Cretin...

Asshole...

Knobhead!

A kid rose from his seat and approached the front of the class with his hand extended. He shook Mani's hand. "Welcome, Manuel," he said. "We look forward to showing you around and being your friend."

Through the howls of laughter, Mani tried to assert himself. "It's Mani."

This created some confusion from the welcoming party. Still shaking his hand with an exaggerated pump, the kid asked, "What?"

"Mani"

"How many?"

"What?"

"Who?"

"My name's Mani."

The kid smiled. "Oh. New Boy!" he said as he turned to his audience, inciting them into a frenzy of laughter.

Prendergast looked on, thanking the boy for being so polite.

Mani looked at the principal in disbelief. Are you serious, he thought? He wanted to slap the daggy little man.

He was shown his seat, mid class. Dead centre. Threats all around. In every direction. This could not have gone worse.

He sat down, keeping focused as the teacher resumed class. Within seconds, the ultimate indignation. A spitball cannoned into the back of his head. A perfectly-aimed shot from the resident sniper. The class celebrated. Mani put his head in his hands.

Here he was at a new school. But things were no different.

A Meeting of Minds

Mani sensed a gradual improvement at his new school, as the ensuing weeks evened out so he could enjoy his new life. A couple of weeks in, the bullying had mostly ceased and now qualified only as typical pecking order treatment. There was the occasional spitball incident, however Mani knew where he stood, and so he bleakly accepted his status.

However, that did not allow Mani to drop his guard. He remained vigilant to the menace that could rear its ugly head at any time. The attacks could be random acts of thuggery, sarcasm, general verbal abuse or physical humiliation by some mean-hearted, but scared kid trying to cement his own reputation.

He had not made any specific friends, but had gained the teacher's admiration and recognition for the quality of his output in class. That was maybe not the best result in a social sense – being the teacher's 'best bud' ensured unwanted scrutiny outside the classroom – but it seemed to allow Mani to slide neatly into his braniac pigeonhole and this kept the other kids off his back.

The vigilance Mani maintained was evident on his typical lunchbreak. While the other kids ate swiftly to allow time for play, Mani read and ate his lunch. Around him, the school sprang to life in lunchbreak. The sport nuts, sandwiches in hand, lined up to get cricket gear out of the sports room, barely able to wait to get a game going. A handball game started up. It reminded him of Jason and the raucous games at CBC, and Mani suddenly felt lonely, missing his cousin.

A group of girls sat in an alcove just off the main walkway. They gossiped and pointed at the boys playing handball and at passers-by.

A lone teacher paraded around, keeping his eye on things.

Spurning the opportunity for play, Mani found himself a place to sit, strategically positioned between the science block and the library building. Some thought had gone into this position, for it ensured he could see all foot traffic in both directions.

He sat, flipped open his lunchbox and ate while he read. His Mum had packed the plain lunch he enjoyed – luncheon meat sandwich with Three 3's pickles, a muesli bar and a nectarine. Routine in every way. Mani kept one eye on his surrounds, like a nervous springbok grazing on the savannah, knowing the lions could appear in an instant.

A group approached – non-lions. They posed no threat. A group of Poindexters heading to the library, discussing arcade video games. Mani relaxed as they passed, moving attention back to his book. One of the kids pulled away from the group and stood in front of Mani.

Ben Pedley had the pasty skin of an indoor-dwelling study fiend and Mani knew him to be top of the class. He had dinner plates for ears, unfortunate teeth and a complete absence of muscle tone. He struggled with the armfuls of books he seemed to always carry.

"So how are you finding the school, Alves?" he asked.

"All right, I guess."

"It's a good place," Pedley said. "The vultures leave you alone after a while and we can get on with what's important."

The change in wording from 'you' to 'we' gave Mani an unexpected jolt of inclusion, almost a sense of brotherhood. And so it proved.

"To that end," Pedley pulled a note from his pocket – "we hold a gathering. Weekly. It's a study group…a meeting of minds, if you like. We think you should come. You will enjoy it."

Mani accepted the note. It contained a room number and a time. The subterfuge excited him. The gesture touched him. "Thanks, Ben," was all he could muster, though his heart was like a supaball in his chest.

Then there was an awkward moment of silence before Pedley reached out toward Mani.

This is weird, Mani thought. He flinched, pulling back, then tried to cover his reaction by pretending to cough.

Pedley recognised the reaction, seen it before. He'd been it before. "Chill out, Alves," he said. "I was just trying to help. You've got some spitball in your hair."

****

The new home that the Alves family now inhabited was by no means a shack. True to form, Peter had found the best house in a fine part of town. It was high on a hill amongst other architect-designed homes, catching the breezes that channelled down from the nearby Mt Coot-tha. The home had a deck out the back and looked over one of the leafiest suburbs in the city.

The room Mani chose was enormous. It had a built-in bunk bed over a funky storage system of drawers and doors. Under the window provided ample space for his large desk, and a fixed wardrobe meant there was still plenty of floor space to spread out.

There was no ladder leading to the upper deck of the bed unit. Instead, it was accessible through a series of rock climbing holds that snaked up the wall and the side of the bed. Mani pretended he was in a MacGyver episode every time he went to bed.

It was a brazen choice of abode for a family sailing so close to the financial abyss. Peter was defiant in the face of the bank's demands, there being debt collectors chasing him down for long overdue credit card payments and outstanding bills from the old place. He'd had to connect the power in Celia's name, his own rating being so poor due to the slack payment history.

Yet Peter refused to be daunted by the state of his finances. "I'm not gonna live like I'm on the bones of me arse," he had stated. "Form is temporary, class is permanent. We'll be back living large in no time." And so he chose a house that chewed into their meagre budget, but was befitting the image he wished to portray to the world. Peter Alves was still in the game!

Mani watched his father deal with all these situations. He felt a pride that his father could shake off the stresses and still maintain the same positive attitude, cracking jokes and continuing to live the type of lifestyle that even a twelve-year old kid like Mani could see as excessive. The lesson was that life was to be lived, but Mani remained tentative. Quiet and withdrawn, unsure if he could mirror his father's brave face.

Mani's favourite place in the new home was the downstairs rumpus room. It had a tiled floor and was brick-walled, so was the coolest part of the house. He loved to stretch out on the divan and watch TV, while the pine-panelled bar was the favoured place for his parents. A couple of nights a week, there would be visitors, friends of his father who dropped in for a few quiet ones.

Peter had the bar well-stocked, the glass shelves displaying bottles of spirits as well as his artefacts collected over the years. A carved hand giving a peace sign, a topless wooden Fijian woman in a grass skirt, a signed miniature cricket bat, an over-sized mug that had a snarling crocodile as the handle. The drinking had increased in recent weeks, Mani had noticed, perhaps as the release for the money pressures, though it had never really abated. Peter loved a Scotch and Celia loved her champers. It was who they were.

And the Saturday afternoon drinks were flowing once more at the Alves' new home. Celia had wanted to put on a 'thank-you' dinner for her sister and the family, a show of appreciation for helping move house. A roast lamb awaited as the four adults enjoyed some heart-starters around Peter's bar.

Mani had been excitable all day long, looking forward to seeing Jason again. Normally a weekly catch-up, it had been three weeks between visits due to the upheaval in Mani's family life. When Jason arrived Mani had been more expressive than usual, throwing his arms around his cousin.

Mani wore surfie gear – some Quiksilver boardies and a green Mango T-shirt. He was feeling pretty cool in his new threads. He had tucked the shirt in though, destroying the potential of his image. It exacerbated his thick body and round tummy, his arms bulging without definition from the short sleeves. It was not Mani's finest fashion moment.

"Oh, dig!" Jason groaned. "Pull the shirt out. Not cool."

Mani hauled the shirt out of his shorts, embarrassed. He had thought the new clothes might have impressed his cool cousin. Mani was clearly a dude in progress.

And an hour later, Mani's hyper-reaction to having his cousin around had not slowed. "And did you see my bed? It has climbing holds. No ladder. You actually climb into bed," he said. His words were delivered machine-gun style.

"You told me that already," Jason said. "Man, what's going on with you? You are buzzing!"

"I am, aren't I? This is just such a great place."

The boys lapped the house once more before settling onto the downstairs divan in front of the TV with Cokes. The parents at the bar behind them chatted as the kids watched a show about surfing. Jason had noticed a change in his normally languid cousin.

"School treating you OK?" Jason asked.

"Better than private school."

"You seem good," said Jason. He could see the surge in confidence in Mani. "So what do you do in your lunch hour?"

"Well, I was sitting by myself mostly. But I got friendly with this bunch of kids who get together to study and read. They're a bit nerdy, but it's heaps of fun."

Mani's confidence was rising and it was due to the Ben Pedley invitation. Arriving at his first meeting with the group, he was tentative. His uncertainty precluded him from contributing anything to begin with. Yet these were kids cut from the same cloth as Mani. Bookish. Inquisitive. Observant.

Gradually, his input to the meetings increased. Mani began offering his opinion on readings and subjects where normally he would keep his mouth shut. He was broadening his knowledge through prolific reading since joining the study group.

"They just like talking about science and books, and we take turns at presenting to see who can write the stupidest story. I've written a couple of stories. Well, they're half-stories. I haven't finished them properly yet."

Jason listened, staring at the surfers on TV wiping out on huge waves in some remote part of the world. Mani kept firing off words, expounding on his new favourite topic, being abnormally exuberant. He'd found his voice to the point where his cousin had zoned out to the constant hum being emitted. It was a speaking feat to match even his father's efforts.

****

Celia threw her drink back, enjoying the cascading bubbles and the syrupy sweet after-taste of her champagne. She was alone in the kitchen of her new home, battling to make friends with the oven and its functions. She had needed to watch her roast like a hawk. A new oven, with its own idiosyncrasies and variable temperature settings, had to be monitored. It could ruin a meal in the time it took for one of Peter's stories.

The others were still downstairs at the bar. The boys still on the couch watching TV. Peter had, as usual, hijacked the conversation downstairs. He was an extrovert, as Celia was. Yet she felt her own flamboyance was consumed by her husband's gregarious ways. So she drank.

Celia knew it was too much. Too often. And she knew it was occasionally for the wrong reasons. She noticed the effect the booze was having on her body too, the curves becoming bulges as her temple shifted to middle-age. She would do something about it, once things were back on track around the new house.

She would go and get her sister soon to help her with the dishing up. It would be a moment of nostalgia for Celia, remembering the times growing up when Patricia would call on her to help with serving a meal for their parents. Patricia, she recalled, loved helping Mum and Dad with meals, housework. She was a born housewife, but smart too.

Growing up in the hills above Nambour on the Sunshine Coast, the girls were always close. Patricia, two years older, would study hard and then help their mother with whatever needed doing, so that when their father came home from work at the town's sugar mill, there would be nothing to do but for the family to spend time together. They'd talk about the machinery their father operated at work, plan their weekend trips down to the beach, listen to their Dad's stories about his youth as a cane cutter in the wild country up in North Queensland.

Celia thought back fondly to this period. Found it baffling as to why she wanted to escape it at the first opportunity. She did escape. Aged seventeen, Celia followed her older sister to Brisbane in the week after she graduated from Nambour High.

But while Patricia had spent the previous year furthering her education and herself at QIT, Celia opted not to go to uni. She landed a role as a secretary in a legal office and lapped up the party life of Brisbane circa 1971.

It wasn't entirely about the bars and clubs. Though she was always immaculately dressed for her job and her lifestyle, Celia was resourceful and had been brought up to understand the importance of a solid life base. She kept regular money aside, applying the lessons of her parents. She built up her bank and was the first of her new peer group to buy her own wheels.

At the end of her first full year in the big smoke, Celia urged Patricia to come out with her for Christmas drinks. The Sunday session at the city's Victory Hotel was her introduction to her future husband. She had boarded the Pedro Alves roller-coaster and was glad that she had. The ups were exhilarating – plenty of parties and drinks, nice cars, mixing in the right circles and the wardrobe that Celia desired. The lows, they came and went soon enough in the world of Peter.

Rightly or wrongly, Celia had realised early in the marriage that she had to weave a safety net. Soon after Mani was born, she had begun to siphon money into a separate bank account, unknown to Peter. The money was not missed amongst the splurges, but had bankrolled some important family needs in grim times. Mani's school uniforms, re-stocking the deep freeze with meat, keeping the power on in winter.

It was a shrewd tip of the hat to Celia's upbringing. This money was never spent self-indulgently. It was always for the family. For her beloved son. It was to grease the cogs, to keep the family motoring.

"How's it going, sis?"

Patricia had arrived in the kitchen on cue. Housewife intuition. There was food to be served, family to be provided for.

Celia eased the door of the oven open. "I think we're ready to go, Trish. Tell me how you think this looks."

"Looks perfect. Now where do you keep the plates? What can I do to give you a hand."

"How about a hug for your little sister." Celia closed the oven and turned it off. "That's what I could do with right now."

"Oh my darling girl," Patricia said, moving towards her sister. She held her arms up and out, placing them around Celia. "You've had a rough time lately. I know it must be hard. So much going on. So much to worry about."

Celia said nothing, just accepted the hug, luxuriated in the supportive arms of her sister. Felt the arms of her mother, her father, imagined the presence of the whole family, protective and loving.

"It doesn't always have to be like this, Ceels. The ups and downs. Peter should be more considerate. Putting you through the money worries, and Mani too. Pulling him from school, turning both of your lives upside down because of his irrational spending. It's gambling! Throwing money away without knowing where the next penny is coming from. Gambling with your lives. You deserve better."

"He always gets us out of it, though Trish." Celia would always defend her husband. Always see the best. Hope for the best. "He's got himself a pretty stable job and he invested the money we made from the other house."

"I know. He's told us. It's all he talks about. The sharemarket. Does he know what he's doing?"

Celia shrugged her shoulders. "Let's get dinner," she said, changing the subject.

The subject bothered Celia, because she had seen Peter go ahead with his plans without consulting her. Admittedly, he was a fast worker. Within a week of collecting his last pay from the caryard, Peter was in a cruisy office job managing the rental book for a real estate office. Low pay but simple work, and he'd already joined the drinking clique with the salesmen and owner.

The money that came through for the sale of the Karana Downs home barely hit the bank before it was swept into a series of share purchases, done through a broker. The sharemarket had welcomed Peter's $12,000 investment. It was blooming. Stacks on the mill as investors poured into the market. Piling money onto the already bubbling stock prices.

Peter had achieved this through some creative accounting. Using his considerable talking talents, Peter had coerced the local bank manager into a debt consolidation loan, gathering his various loans and credit cards into one loan to keep the repayments affordable. Even a swift and shifty operator like Peter was disbelieving of how easy it was, the bank boss happy to waive the normal checks and procedures for a boozy lunch and a bottle of Johnnie Walker. The new loan was even secured using the newly-sold house as collateral, an incredible oversight from a supposed staid and conservative bank.

Peter not only got the money from the house sale, but he was then given a cheque for a further $6,000 to pay out his other small debts. Such responsibility placed into the care of an opportunist like Peter was faith misplaced. The cheque was added to the pile and delivered to his broker for more shares. The existing debts remained.

"Call the men up, Trish," said Celia. "I think we are ready to serve."

Mani and Jason were first upstairs for dinner, famished as pre-teen boys generally are. Peter and Graham followed soon after. They had knocked over several beers each and had replacements.

"Take your seats, darlings. We've got a delicious roast here for you." Celia brought the carved meat and tray of vegetables to the table. "Peter, can you dish the vegies please."

"Too right, my dear," Peter replied. "Let's feed the Sharpes up. Gotta celebrate the new house, right?"

"Not too much for me, thanks Peter," Patricia said. "I'm watching my weight."

"You're kidding, aren't ya?" Peter said. "Have a look at you. You're as skinny as a swizzle stick. Get some of these spuds into ya, Trish. Graham! Don't you feed ya missus at home, mate?"

Peter laughed at his own joke.

Celia smiled. Peter had a way about him. He loved to stir people up. He was brash. She knew that. But she could forgive his occasional condescension, for the flipside was the positivity and constant joking of a man who sought every opportunity in life without fear of failure or rejection. Celia both loved and loathed him for the same reason, knowing Peter's particular brand of maleness was preferable to living with a shadow.

Celia listened as Peter started up his self-promotion after the meal was done. The kids were back downstairs watching a video and the adults had topped up their drinks. Celia had popped her second bottle of bubbles. She had crested the champagne hill, was feeling chirpy but feared the drop down the other side. She chased that feeling by drinking some more.

"I reckon I'm onto a winner," Peter declared. "Me mate the stockbroker got me a packet of shares and they are flying! Cost me one and a half percent brokerage. It's the best couple of hundred bucks I ever spent."

Graham had heard it all earlier in the evening. He replied in a bored fashion. "They certainly have been on a run."

Peter warmed up to his subject. "Haven't they what? Up a grand in my first month. If that keeps up, I'll double my money in a year. You know there's a rule that tells you how often you will double your dough? The rule of 72, they call it."

"I've heard of that," Patricia said. "How's it go? The yearly return divided by the number of years or something..."

Peter had drained his Scotch, sucked on the ice. "Multiply it," he said. "Or divide 72 by the return. Something like that. Anyway, it means I'll double me money every year."

Graham had tired of Peter's gloating and was emboldened by the beer. "Things don't go up forever, Pete," he said. Graham had rarely spoken up to challenge Peter's plans. "It's dropped before. You never know what's going to happen."

"Different this time, mate." Peter was ready for him. "Look at where it's come from, everyone's making plenty of money, business is booming. Can't see it going down. Why would it go down? You guys would be mad not to get some money in there."

"Be careful," Patricia warned, the voice of reason.

Peter bit back. "Careful? What, careful like youse? Slow and steady don't win the race and if it does I want a different race! Get me a new horse, that one's been flogged to death. I want an inquiry! Get the stewards onto it!" He cackled his trademark laugh, raised his glass in a triumphant salute at his own cleverness.

"Come on Peter, that's enough," Celia said.

"No, that's alright Celia, each to their own," Patricia said. It was obvious she did not like the tone of Peter's comment. She turned her attention toward him. "What you've got to understand, Peter, is that everyone has their own choice. Their own path to follow. Not everyone has to do the same thing. Who's to say that what's right for you is right for us. And to use your racing parlance – we've chosen our pony, and we're sticking with it."

Quick as a flash, Peter responded. "Again with the horses, Trish. Was just givin' ya a hot tip."

"You're talking about it as though you have something to gain from us buying shares," Graham said in frustration. "It's not like one of those horrible bloody 'can't lose' pyramid schemes, is it?"

Peter did not like Graham's input to the conversation. He continued his diatribe, biting back at his brother-in-law. "Geez Graham, you're takin' shelter from life, me old mate. Why don't you step out from behind your ten-year plans and your boring property scheme and a have a dinkum crack at things? We'll get you a top hat and a monocle and you can play-act through life as the Monopoly Man. Ha ha ha ha...."

Patricia defended her husband and their choices. She was amazed at the repugnant attack from this man for whom she had little respect, not just for his lack of intuition but for the years of difficulty she saw her darling sister go through with Peter. Her words were sharp.

"We've considered what works for us, Peter. We're happy with our lot. We understand it. Tell me. When your money doubles as you say it will, how much tax would you pay? Have you allowed for that? Have you even thought of that?" she said.

"I'll happily pay a hundred grand in tax, love," Peter said. "That means I woulda made a profit of double that, at least."

Celia had said little during this verbal altercation. Instead she had been downing her drinks. She had nothing to gain from taking sides, she realised. She pushed her chair back and stood, mumbling something about stepping back from the frying pan. Her head was spinning from the alcohol. "I need some air," she said and left the table, leaving the others to their squabbles.

A Princess in a Public School

Everyone remembers their first love. It cannot be forgotten. Neither the feeling nor the object of those feelings is dismissed from your mind. That person, that sentiment remains, hidden away, deeply entrenched within those recesses of your body that can only be reached upon intense self-reflection and recall, but equally can come flooding to the surface when triggered by something as simple as getting on a bus, hearing the first bars of a song or biting into a chocolate bar.

Random events recalling poignant moments of that first sensation. That first stab of emotion for another human that stays with a person, regardless of the scope of that particular relationship in the bigger scheme of their romantic life. It may be unrequited, or even unknown to the object. Maybe an affair that lasts, like the quintessential high-school sweethearts. Or maybe a brief physical encounter that cannot work on an emotional level.

First love is special and irreplaceable.

For Mani Alves, his breakthrough from little boy to teenager came through Love At First Sight. He had been 'shoed' on the way to Grade 8 assembly. Some goon stomped on the back of his heel on purpose and Mani had walked clear out of his Grosby. The shoe was then kicked in amongst the swelling throng of kids crossing the quadrangle to line up for the principal's weekly address.

Mani dodged in and out as his shoe was trampled, kicked again. Reaching it, he knelt on one knee, retying his laces. Through the oncoming crowd, his eye was caught. Maybe it was the pink-trimmed white tennis shoes or the rainbow laces. Perhaps the tanned legs, thin but muscled, sporty, the skirt short, the walk that resembled more of a glide, like a graceful dance move.

Mani's eyes drew up to witness her for the first time. Everything about her jabbed at his heart. Her thin body emanated femininity. Cuteness pervaded her slender face, pure joy flared from her ponytailed blonde hair. She breezed past him, Mani kneeling as her new subject. The girlish whiff of perfume very nearly knocked him out. He turned as she went by, his eyes transfixed, not wanting to lose sight of this angel.

As he spun on the axis of his knee, scraping away skin unknowingly, Mani tumbled onto his bum, his shoe still dangling from his foot, his mouth agape. He did not want to lose sight of her. The crowd parried around him. He copped an accidental knee to the back of his head as people tried to dodge the lovestruck boy on the bitumen. But there was no pain for Mani.

Only love.

Love At First Sight.

A sheer appreciation for the physical beauty of another person. Not in a pervy way, with wandering eyes isolating body parts for his viewing pleasure. It was an entire package, and even beyond the vision of her, it was an immediate feeling of care. Protective feelings, like a lioness for her cub, a mare for her wobbly-kneed foal. Mani wanted to guard her, stand sentry against all the bad in the world.

From that point on, Mani spent night times imagining their union. Days were spent longing for the breaks from class so he could see her, get to know her from afar. Appreciating her voice when he was bold enough to walk near her. The mannerisms, the walk, the smile, all indelibly stamped into Mani's mind.

He would wake mid-dream to recall a moment from that day, the look in his direction that had to be about him. He fantasised of how this inevitable relationship would be reciprocated. His eyes would spring open too early in the morning, thoughts switched onto his muse, wondering if today would be the day.

Mani had seen his future and she was pure elegance. Popular. Sophisticated. All cuteness from her long, brown legs, her ski-slope nose and long, blonde hair. She was grace. She was Grace Kelly. A screen goddess, Mani thought. A princess in a public school.

She was Alison Archer.

Mani's research began almost immediately. Never had there been such a thirst for knowledge from a schoolboy. Alison became his favourite subject. He asked around, seeking knowledge of this gift he had been provided.

Parker, a fat kid from the study group, could reliably confirm that her Dad was the bank manager at the local Westpac branch. He had witnessed Alison and her mother emerge from the manager's office when he was in the bank with his Mum after school. The mother had kissed the manager, Parker said, so he made the assumption the manager was the husband. The father of Alison. Unless the bank was using alternative tactics to drum up business.

Others were forthcoming with information. Pedley said she was good at English but poor at Maths. Bad at running but apparently very good in the pool. Mani lamented the hot months were all but over.

The next several weeks were tough for Mani as his infatuation consumed him. He watched Alison Archer from afar, not daring to approach her or reveal his infatuation. His sleep was compromised, his schoolwork suffered. His mind was elsewhere, focused on one thing, unable to switch thought to classroom tasks.

He imagined many scenarios where they might be united – Mani pretending to drown so that she could save him; her crying over having left her homework at home and Mani coming to the rescue, with Alison falling into his arms in relief and gratitude; them being presented as the King and Queen of Pop by Molly Meldrum on Countdown. Olivia Newton-John and Johnny Farnham, all teased hair, big sleeves and flowing mullets.

He would do anything in his power to make a connection with this wondrous creature. Each day waiting in hope that the seat next to him on the school bus might be taken by her, but she was rarely aboard. He ached to find out where she lived, just to imagine her daily life. Mani even purported to encourage his parents to switch their banking to Westpac.

She touched him once after Alison's friend pushed her into Mani, putting her hand on his forearm in apology. Another time, he was behind her in the tuckshop line, watching her but pretending not to. He had never been so close for such a length of time. He was sweating despite it being a windy day when her blonde hair flicked up in the breeze, briefly sticking to his face next to his mouth.

There it was. A connection, a tether, her hair the physical and emotional bridge between them. A second later, it was over, but the serendipity of the occasion stayed with Mani. Alison's hair had reached out to him. The kismet was overwhelming evidence of their fate. Such moments of meaning for one passing by unknown and unacknowledged by the other.

This became Mani's life. He existed zombie-like as she consumed his thoughts. Days became drudgery, simple minutiae in the bigger picture of his unmanageable desire. A pre-teen boy a victim of adult feelings, a prisoner of first love.

Aware of his plight, Mani deigned to do something about it, practising his lines in front of the mirror. "Alison, you probably don't know me. I'm Mani Alves. New to the school. I was wondering if..." Then, realising more force was needed, he ramped up his attitude.

"Yo, Alison. The name's Mani. You are a total babe! I see a McDonald's burger and a movie in your future and that future is with me." A smarmy smile swathed the cheesy words. Mani pointed at the mirror and winked. He ran his fingers through his wet hair, slicking it back.

He pulled a few more sexy faces in the mirror, self-analysing his looks, his personality. Mani built up his self-confidence, thought he had the words that would seal the deal. Convinced himself that she knew of his existence and was waiting for him to make the move. He would call her, he decided. He'd scoped out her address through his research, was able to find the number. His bravado was sky high.

Before reason could step in the way of this audacity, the receiver was in his hand and he had dialled the number. The phone rang. A female answered, the voice young, fresh, innocent. It was her.

"Hel-ghgggh," was all Mani managed, his throat constricting in fear and disbelief. The words he had practised would not form. He gargled inaudible gibber for several seconds before slamming the phone down, the moment gone. Mani could not believe what he had just done. What was he thinking? He scurried to the other side of the room, relieved he had not muttered his name to her, thus remaining anonymous. He grabbed a book, any book, from the bookcase and slid onto the couch. His mental lapse would soon be forgotten. His moment of madness consigned to history. Seconds later, the phone rang. Mani, eyes the size of floodlights, watched his mother swan into the room and scoop up the phone.

"Helll-lo! Celia Alves."

Mani watched from behind his book, hoping it was a coincidental call from one of his Mum's social coterie. Surely. It had to be.

"Yes, hello Jeff," she said into the phone. "I don't think anyone's been on the phone. From this number, you say? How did you...? Oh. Call return. I see. Isn't that clever? Something new, is it? Well, it wasn't me. My husband Peter's in the shower. Let me check with my son. Hold on a minute."

Mani slunk down low in his chair as his mother turned around, her hand over the receiver. Surely not, he thought. It could not be.

"Mani, darling. Were you just trying to make a call?"

"No, Mum. Wasn't me. I was reading."

Celia flicked her head as she slid the phone under her hair to her ear. "You there, Jeff? Apparently no-one's been using the phone. Are you sure you have...? Yes, that's right. I have a son. Manuel. Mani Alves.

Mani did not like the sound of this. They were joining the dots.

"Grade Eight. He's new to Westside School. Oh, you have a daughter there. Alison's a lovely name." Celia turned to Mani, smiling. "Jeff, I'll just check to see if Mani wants to speak to Alison. He's right here, maybe they are working on a project at school together."

Mani leapt up, waving his arms side to side across his body. His mother cast a mischievous smile, now realising what was going on. Mani was freaked out, the bravado now thoroughly dissolved. He only hoped the parents kept this to themselves as he ran from the room.

****

Little came of his ambitious phone undertaking, which proved to be a good thing, for the more Mani considered the possible outcomes, he saw only prominent clusters at the negative end of the scale. He had finally managed to exert some control over his emotions, allowing himself to compartmentalise his feelings for Alison. He was thus able to get on with some other aspects of his life. It took a lot of energy to maintain such a disciplined infatuation.

At school, Mani and his friends in the study group had started writing stories to share amongst themselves. They had begun collaborating on a script for a short film which drew on aspects of Star Wars, ET and Evil Dead. An alien-slasher film. Mani's moderated behaviour was also on display at home. Gone were the regular daydreams and the lack of ambition that was a constant source of angst from his father. Where once he would lie around for hours in his bedroom, he had now replaced this with dalliances in the kitchen, where he taught himself to cook pasta sauce and banana muffins and with Celia's input he had begun an herb garden.

He was reading more as well, inspired by the study group and their writings. He was finishing Tolkien's Lord of the Rings trilogy, had found enjoyment in sport biographies and developed a deep fascination with science. The encyclopaedia at the school library copped a fearful hammering from Mani's enthralment and he sought magazines and texts to add to his understanding of every tiny aspect of the natural world. He had asked Peter for a typewriter and while his Dad could not think for a minute why a bloke would want a typewriter, he obliged by purchasing a second-hand model from an office supplies next to his office. Mani taught himself to type by re-writing stories and reproducing cricket scoreboards and statistics tables from the 1977 Ashes cricket tour diary. Getting faster and more confident at the keyboard, he began typing up assignments and essays.

There were stirrings of excitement amongst Mani's peer group with the announcement of an open essay competition across Westside High School. It was the major mid-year event, creating a buzz throughout the academically-minded students of the school, though everyone was encouraged to submit a piece with a story themed around the upcoming Expo 88, now less than nine months away. There would be prizes awarded for the story competition, with a 3-day Expo pass up for grabs for the best story from a girl and a boy in each grade.

The study group had spoken about the essay competition and all of Mani's bookish cohorts appeared hell-bent on producing a piece of work to win the coveted prize. They spoke of the requirements of a great story. They detailed the facets of a story that would help it stand out from the grist that would be offered by the majority of the school. Mani soaked up all he could as the other boys spoke of the importance of character depth, multi-layered themes and three-part conflict within the story.

Mani set to work on his story. He had two weeks before the competition closed, with the victors announced a week later on the second to last day of term. He weaved a magical tale – a love story between a girl from a past age and a boy from the present. Mani channelled Alison Archer to bring his female lead to life, the easiest of tasks in creating this humble anecdote of love. He referenced their joining at Expo 88, her bringing a global worldliness from the previous century to connect with the young man, the analogy being the maturation of the City of Brisbane. The story was joyous, heart-wrenching and triumphant, eking every last piece of creative energy from Mani as he wrote.

The piece completed, Mani read it to his parents. Peter and Celia sat quietly, letting him finish.

Peter was first to comment. "I thought my son would write a shoot 'em up action story, not a love story. You know. Guns and weapons and explosions."

"It's about Expo, Dad," Mani protested.

"Well, it's a bit of a shock. I wasn't expecting you to go all lovey-dovey on us."

Mani's head lowered. He said nothing.

Peter saw his disappointment. Felt the stare from Celia burning his temple. "It's good, mate," he tried to console him. "Just a bit poofy, that's all."

Mani was shattered. In that instant he had decided he would not hand the piece in, a fear building that if his father could criticise the work with such disdain, then the backlash at school would be more significant.

Mani looked at his mother. She had not said a word in support of either Mani or Peter. She could not speak. Mani could see she was crying. Tears welled in her eyes and ran over her cheeks, creating little silvery streams across her make-up. Pride was evident as she clasped her hands together and her jaw trembled, touched by both the beauty of her son's work and the callousness of her husband's words.

That night, Mani went to bed but could not sleep. He lay flat on his bed, staring up to the ceiling, repeating the earlier scene in his mind and analysing his story. He had told his mother he would not lodge it, but she encouraged him and begged him to ignore the criticism.

"But it won't win, Mum," Mani said.

"It's not about winning, darling. If it means only one other person gets to read that beautiful story, then that is reason enough to hand it in. You can be sure that you won't get the sort of feedback you got tonight from any normal adult."

It lifted Mani to hear his Mum defend him like this. He dwelt on his options after she left, still in two minds as to his decision to lodge or not. Still sleepless after an hour and on his second trip to the toilet, Mani overheard his parents in their bedroom. He stood at their door to listen, soon realising his mother was mounting a defence on Mani's behalf.

"What sort of man would you like Mani to become?" Celia asked her husband.

After a brief silence, Mani heard his father's answer. "I just want him to be happy."

"Really?" Celia responded. "Pretty stock standard answer, that."

"It's an odd question. Maybe he'll grow up like his old man."

"Well, if you want Mani to be like you, what sort of man are you, Peter?

"What sorta bloody question is that?"

Celia pulled back the quilt, straightened her side of the sheet. "How do you see yourself?" she asked. "What is your son learning from you?"

"He can learn plenty from me, Ceels. I'm a good provider. I work hard. If he does the same - works hard, uses his brain - he'll be alright."

"How about girls? Women. How will he learn about that?" Celia asked. They stood on opposite sides of the bed.

Mani smiled at the door, unseen. He was enjoying hearing his father being grilled, could sense his discomfort.

"When he's old enough, he'll get to know what he needs to do around women," Peter replied.

"Based on what?"

"What's this all about, Celia? What's with the third degree?"

"It's not a third degree, Peter," she said. "I just want to know how you will handle it if your son turns out different to you. What if he's not rough and tumble and one of the guys? He might be an artist or a writer or a dancer. He might not like beer and sport."

Peter turned his back, doing up the buttons on his pyjama shirt, shying away from the challenge. "Well, he's my son. I'll support him," he said.

"I didn't see that tonight," Celia said. "You cut him down, Peter. Our beautiful son pours his energy and his heart into a lovely story, beautifully written and you called it 'poofy'. How is that supportive?"

Peter was squirming. "Well, it was a funny thing to write about, wasn't it?"

"It shows he is sensitive, and because he's sensitive your words stopped him in his tracks. He doesn't want to hand it in now!"

Mani only heard silence, dared not look in the room.

Celia continued, knowing she was getting the message through to her husband. "You've got a big responsibility, Peter. You have the power over Mani. You have to support him, not discourage him. You said you want him to be happy, well accept him how he is. He's a wonderful kid. You know that."

"I know he's a good kid," Peter stammered.

"And I know you love me," Celia said coming around the bed to touch her husband. "You give me lots of care and I feel wonderful most of the time. But the way you talk to me sometimes is harsh. A son learns from his father. Mani watches everything you do. And the way he sees you treat me will be how he treats me. And if my relationship with my son is poor, then that will affect how Mani relates to women when he's older."

"Rightio Ceels, I get it," Peter mumbled. He wanted the lambast to stop.

"It's critical, Peter and I will do anything to make sure Mani gets the best start in life, despite all our ups and downs."

Mani felt a swell of love for his mother as he stood at the door. Knew her support would always remain and felt comforted by this. He felt suddenly tired and he knew sleep would now come easily. Something in him relaxed, as though he had changed, grown from hearing his parents' exchange.

****

It was the last week of term and across the school optimism was in the air. Everyone seemed playful, unstressed. Even some of the teachers had relaxed their hardline stance in this final week. The vibe in these last few days before school break was of high anticipation. Excitement was freely coursing and a person felt they could handle any annoying thing that got thrown at them because they had just days to wait. To holidays. To freedom.

The entire school gathered in the Westside State High Great Hall for the principal's end of term address where he would announce the winners of the essay competition. There was much sky-larking, as there had been all week with the frisky mood of the students. Mani had copped a spitball to the side of the head early in the day and having managed to scrape most of the muck from his hair, he joined his friends from the study group, forming a small contingent amongst the crowd.

Mani eventually opted to enter his story into the competition. His mother had reassured him of its value and the importance of being proud of your effort regardless of the results. He was pleased with his work but knowing the overall vocabulary and descriptive writing style of Ben Pedley, Mani held little hope of his name being called. It was unanimously considered that Pedley would take out the coveted prize, around which there had been much discussion as interest in Expo gathered momentum.

Though entrenched within his faction, Mani ensured he knew where Alison Archer sat. She was his muse, the story he entered based on the emotions he felt when in her presence, so it was fitting to keep her in his frame of view while the announcements were made. There might be a glance from her which would confirm her interest. Mani lived in constant hope.

The principal, Prendergast was on stage, groaning on and on about the extremely high standard of entries. The mood in the hall became restless until he spoke of the prizes on offer for the winner of the essay competition, immediately setting off a wave of back-straightening through the assembly as potential winners snapped to attention. He resumed his waffle about the meaning of Expo 88 to the City of Brisbane, again losing the crowd.

Throughout the headmaster's monologue, Mani day-dreamed about dating Alison. Taking her to Expo. Eating out, having milkshakes, holding hands as they strolled through one of the grand displays in the exposition pavilions the principal spoke of. The perfect couple. The perfect scenario he built in his mind – two winners enjoying the spoils of their victory. The magical Expo pass, the 'his and hers' versions. But he knew this to be as far-fetched as any of his day-dreams got.

Then Mani heard his name and he snapped back to reality, thinking he had been busted by a teacher for day-dreaming. His confusion was further enhanced by the cheering and back-slapping from the Pedley crew. The study group acknowledging him. He had won the competition. Now, with his brain still returning from the dream-state he had let it slide into, he understood that he needed to go up on stage to collect his prize.

But this was not possible. Mani knew this for certain now that his mind had re-joined reality. He could not stand up. He had been slumped in his chair, his Expo fantasy nearly causing him to nod off. His eyes crossing as he hovered on the edge of sleep. Touching the void of public slumber, Mani had grown one of those spontaneous erections that teen boys often get.

Now, with his synapses fully functioning, he had to make a quick assessment of the situation. There was little chance of it receding before reaching the stage by the standard route, so Mani tried thinking unsexy thoughts, but realised that focusing on his stiffy would ensure it remained.

"Come on up, Mani," the principal called over the PA system. "Congratulations! Come and receive your prize."

Mani had nothing to cover himself with. No folder. No book or bag to sling across his front. When this had happened before, he could always casually cover up as he left class using his texts or workbooks, always walking with his bum out and his hips pulled in to conceal his embarrassment.

A plan of attack came to mind. He would hunch over, struggle over the knees and feet of his schoolmates as he shuffled along the aisle of seats, taking the long way up toward the stage to buy himself precious de-erection time. He stood, tugged his shirt down over his groin and started moving, his arse sticking in people's faces as he bent forward at the waist.

It worked.

He waddled along the main aisle towards the stage. As he mounted the stairs, he could feel the bulge had gone down sufficient to stand in public. He felt a great sense of achievement at his plan and his handling of the situation.

He even began feeling pride as his bigger achievement sank in. He had won. He was now vindicated. Mani imagined his father's jaw dropping open in complete surprise. Then his thoughts switched to Alison. This would get her notice. This might be the impetus that seals their union.

Only one thing could make this better, Mani concluded as he neared the podium.

"Alison Archer!" the principal announced. "Female winner of the Grade Eight essay prize. Come on up, Alison."

And there it was.

Joint victors. Equals. Peers. Forever now, joined in this achievement – Mani & Alison. An unbreakable bond had formed, like when Mick met Keith, or ham joined pineapple on a pizza, he Rum and she Coke. John & Yoko, fish and chips, Clayton on bass with Mullen on drums. Peanut Butter and Jelly sandwiches!

These fantasies Mani concocted in his mind as he stood on stage, award in hand. Their lives would now be one, he thought, as he awaited her arrival into his echelon. He positively beamed, as his juvenile mind registered he and Alison as 'fellow academics'.

Then...

Rarely has there been such a public failure as the one that Mani Alves was about to perpetrate. Perhaps on a worldwide scale, there is evidence of other chronic misreads. The head of Digital Equipment Corporation saying that there would be no reason anyone would want a computer in their home just a few years before the personal computer launched. Or the Patent Office Commissioner who allegedly stated in the 19th Century that everything that can be invented has already been thought of. Possibly the decision of Greg Chappell to instruct his brother to deliver the ball underarm to win a game of cricket for Australia.

Mani shifted weight from foot to foot, fidgety as he waited for his dream girl to join him on stage. Alison, all femininity, received her prize with a smile for the audience and a shake of the principal's hand. She then acknowledged Mani.

He glowed proudly, watching her as if viewing a slow motion replay, wishing the scene was being taped for posterity. Her hand extending for the congratulatory handshake. Mani felt her hand in his own. The handshake was limp. Fish-like. But it did not matter. It was the third time they had touched. A goofy smile smeared across his face. He was drunk on love, like an infant who had overfed on breast milk.

Mani saw Alison reach out toward him, touching his hair. This is the natural evolution, he thought. A handshake was never going to suffice for such a moment.

In a flurry, too quick to be natural or normal to an onlooker, but still in slo-mo to him, Mani stepped in, arms encircling Alison Archer. His lips puckered as they prepared to consummate their victory and their new status as the "it" couple of Westside High.

Then the world changed, the course of history and Mani's future altered. There would be no mutual delight here. In a series of smooth movements, Alison Archer evaded the intended lip-lock. Mani's lips smeared over her cheekbone as she ducked and pulled back under his circling arms, escaping the hug. Simultaneously, and with martial art efficiency, Alison brought her knee up.

It crashed into Mani, groin height. A direct hit. Almost in the same motion, her hand was across his face. An open hand slap to remind him of his place. It was a smooth combination of moves, impressive, as if choreographed.

I always liked the way she moved, Mani thought in the instant before the pain hit home and he collapsed to the floor. His damaged balls throbbed, the ache swishing through his mind, fuelled by the ignominy of being beat up on stage by a girl.

"You disgusting boy!" she screamed. Her first actual words to Mani. He did not look up, clutched his groin as he lay in a crumpled mess at her feet. The nerdy Mr Prendergast looked on, inactive and speechless. "You had a spitball in your hair!"

Life on the Alves Roller-Coaster

Peter Alves had an appointment at the bank, finishing early with the boss's blessing. He knew what he wanted from the bank, but wasn't certain he would get it. But a man steeled into action and with energy and ambition such as Peter possessed could achieve almost anything.

The bank visit had been prompted by an unusual occurrence for Peter Alves. A review. An assessment. A meditation on the ups and downs of his life and his year to date. Here he was in mid-September, so he reflected on his fluctuating fortunes. He thought back over the previous six months. How things had moved through the peaks and troughs which had punctuated his life to this point.

He had been blitzing car sales earlier in the year. Forty-four vehicles in six months – a record for the business. But as soon as things slowed down, Peter had been shafted. The boss dried the leads up on him. Apparently no-one wanted Beemers or Mercs in Brisbane anymore. Peter had been surplus to requirements, and since he had been splashing the cash thinking the good times were here to stay, there was no safety net. That's when the bank came knocking.

He'd got the bank off his back the best way he knew how – flapping his jaw. He could talk up a pretty convincing argument when needed. A bit of creativity on the cashflow front, as well as some high-level verbal persuasion had got him back in the bank's good books. And making a priority of repaying the pawn shop for Celia's ring had got Peter back into her good books too. The new job was laid-back. Simple work with reasonable money, and Peter discovered how little you really need to live on when you made some cutbacks. Still he was seeking the big financial breakthrough as always. With close to 30% growth on his share investments over the past four months, he was certain that he had found the avenue to build his fortune.

The boss and his salesmen in the real estate office, Peter discovered, were not only property nuts, they were nuts about making money, willing to re-direct their allegiances to wherever they sniffed opportunity to turn a dollar. The owner of the business, Phil Patrick and one of his better-performing salesmen nicknamed Wilko, were keen to tap into Peter's success. They listened to him crowing about the returns he had made and both now were delving into share purchases themselves. Wilko particularly had gone hard at the opportunity, being inspired by Peter's immediate success.

Phil Patrick was a gambling man, Peter discovered. A man after Peter's own heart. Always looking for prospects to make a quick buck. He'd been so appreciative of Peter's work in straightening out his rent book, as well as the hot tip on the share bonanza that Phil paid Peter a bonus after only four months in the role. A lazy grand never went astray in the Alves household. One afternoon, over drinks with Phil and Wilko, Peter asked him how he got started in real estate.

"It probably all started about seven or eight years ago. I was having one of those years. Lots of ups and downs," Phil said. He put a ciggie in his mouth, flipped two cigarettes halfway out of the pack and offered them to the other men. He sparked up his own smoke and drew deeply, before continuing. "I'd been selling ad space for the Courier Mail. Business packages. There was nowhere else to advertise other than in the paper, so there was plenty of sales to be made. But long hours. Shit pay for the hours."

"Like here, hey Phil!" Wilko laughed.

"You'll keep, Wilko!" he said, smiling.

"I was a single man at the time. The old missus had caught me shagging around a few months before, so she flew the coop. I had plenty of spare time and more than enough cash, so I was on the punt regularly. The horses on weekends, dish-lickers at night and this was before Jupiter's Casino opened, so the nearest place for a legal game of cards was bloody Tasmania. But I could always find a reasonable size game most weeks. In the middle of the worst run of my life, I got involved in a big game of poker in a room under a restaurant in the Valley. I don't think I'd won anything for a few weeks and I had chewed through a few grand of my savings."

"Mongrel luck," Peter said. "I know what you mean."

"Anyway, this game was big. The stakes got ridiculously high. I was half-pissed, out of my depth. I wasn't sure about the blokes I was playing with and my mind started going to all sorts of funny places. You see, these guys had a look about them. Difficult to explain. But they were, to a man, hard looking bastards. One of them was very heavily tattooed and had scars all around his eyes, like he was some sort of street-fighter. Another bloke kept scowling at whoever won, intimidating like." Phil leant forward with a scowl on his face, acting out the characters in his story, warming to his task. "And there was a Chinese guy, very calculating and he went by the name Luk Kee. Always calling out "Luk-kee, very Luk-kee". So I started getting worried about losing and worried about winning at the same time. Not wanting to take dollars off these blokes, just in case. What if I wasn't able to pay these fellas? I imagined me getting my legs broken, or my body being dumped into Moreton Bay."

"Thugs, were they?" Wilko asked, captivated by the story.

"Never found out," Phil continued. He was comfortable being the centre of attention. A stocky man with a beer gut and red highways of capillaries across his cheeks, he lounged back as he drank a beer, telling his story. "I never got invited back to that particular table. You see, soon after my mind started wandering, it got brought back to attention quick smart. The Hand of Heaven, I still call it. An all-in opportunity on a straight flush. Queen high. Never before and never seen one since."

"You're kidding," Peter cried out, cackling. "That is one hell of a hand. So you cleaned 'em up?"

"I did. Had a few nervous hours afterwards though, as I felt I had to stay in their game, give 'em a chance to win it back. But they were very wary of me then and I could pick and choose my hands to go after." Phil had his story down pat. He'd drawn in his two companions with the yarn, like he knew the story would. He stubbed out his smoke and lit another, then continued. "Anyway, I'd turned around my year of misfortune in one crack, and I was liquid again. Let me tell you - walking through the valley in the early hours with nearly twenty-five grand in your pocket, it's a frightening experience."

Wilko nearly sprayed his beer in shock. "Twenty-five thousand dollars!" he exclaimed.

"What'd ya do with it all?" Peter asked.

"The next week, I'm selling some ad space to a guy who's trying to offload his marine upholstery business. Said he had his eye on a fish and chip shop down by the water that was up for sale because the owner was retiring with ill health. It was going dirt cheap and the books were saying it was a goldmine. This guy told me as soon as he off-loaded his business, he was doing a deal and getting himself in there. So, not being one to miss an opportunity, I looked up this fish and chip shop and bought my first business – The Pelican Bar."

"Bit sneaky, but why not," Peter said laughing.

Phil shrugged his shoulders. "That's business. I spent the next five years flipping businesses. Buying them run-down, dressin' them up, selling at a profit. Eventually, I'd bought and sold so many businesses that I thought it'd be good to find one I could hold onto. What better than the real estate game? People always need a place to live, so I set up an office. Now I've found my very own money-making machine," he smiled.

Peter had a new hero. He imagined himself doing what Phil had done. Could see himself running a big show, raking in the dollars. Phil had hinted that there might be a spot in his sales team eventually. "Get back in the game" he'd said, knowing Peter had sold land earlier in his working life. Peter felt he was mixing with the right crowd to get his long-awaited breakthrough. The sharemarket was flying and he now had a mentor who had done exactly what Peter saw himself doing. Building up a passive cashflow and getting rich.

Phil had some more words of wisdom to complete his story. He liked the limelight. "The important thing I've found is that when an opportunity arises, you jump all over it. Don't let it slide by. There might not be another." He accepted another drink from Wilko who had returned from the fridge. "And if you believe in it, do everything you can to pursue it. Beg, borrow or steal. Matter of fact, borrowed money has been one of my best returning investments in business. If you know you can get a 50% return on the deal, what matter you pay 10% interest on your borrowings. I love them odds! Leverage, it's called. Borrow off your Mum, your Nan, your neighbour. Sell your right nut if you have to. It's worth it to get into the right deal."

Phil's words had a profound effect on Peter. The several beers he'd drunk had removed the inhibitions from his mind and he knew what he needed to do. All became extremely lucid to him. He had seen opportunities come and go. Some he had missed, others he had stuffed up. Yet now, it was obvious what was required to reach his goals. A surprising determination leapt forth from Peter.

And this was the reason for his working through his lunch hour so he could arrive at the bank in time for his three o'clock appointment. He strutted across the carpark looking all business in his brown slacks, short-sleeve patterned shirt and white tie. Approaching the door, he took a deep breath, smoothed down his moustache, steadied himself and pulled the door open.

A familiar face met him as the door opened. Two familiar faces. It was Graham and Patricia, arm in arm, with Cheshire Cat grins on their faces as they exited the bank branch.

"Afternoon Mr and Mrs Sharpe," Peter said, exchanging the customary kiss on the cheek with Patricia and shaking Graham by the hand. "Imagine seeing you here. What are you two looking so happy about? Looks like you just got away with robbing the joint."

Graham answered. "Just some basic business to sort out. What about you?"

"Entering some negotiations with my financier," Peter said, trying to sound important and evasive at the same time. "Looking to lift up some 'leveritch' into some things I have had my eye on. Forging ahead and all that."

Graham and Patricia flicked looks at each other, wondering if Peter realised what he had just said.

"You crazy Sharpes aren't here to buy another house, are ya?"

"As a matter of fact – yes!" Patricia said with slightly too much excitement, causing Graham to tug on her arm.

"You're kidding," Peter said. He'd thrown it up there as a joke. They were doing much better than he thought.

Again Graham spoke on their behalf. The voice of calm, downplaying their plans. He knew Peter would not want to share their excitement. "We found a little renovator, 3 bedrooms, in Ashgrove. Worst house in a good street. Needs some work but the rent should be strong once we fix her up," he said.

"Another house, hey," Peter shook his head in disbelief. "Bloody hell, ya getting yourselves in deep. I hope you know what you're doing."

Peter bade the Sharpes farewell and entered the bank. The manager was a thin man, conservative, with a short haircut and he wore short sleeves and a tie like Peter. In fact, with their dual moustaches, he and Peter could have passed for brothers. He welcomed Peter into his office and they got straight down to business. He asked Peter for the relevant financial figures to help him make his decision.

"Impressive earnings last year, Pete," the bank boss stated. "Do you expect something similar this year?"

"Of course," Peter lied. He knew there was little chance of his current job matching the dollars he made selling cars. "Coming up summer, things always pick up nicely."

The manager scanned the numbers, his mind working out the necessary sums. "So, with this good income, why the debts?" he queried.

Peter had an answer ready for him. Quick thinking was his forte. "Abnormal expenses," he announced. "Had one of those years, you know. The missus had to go to London to bury her Gran, so that cost a bit. Kid going to private school, had to replace the car. You know how things bank up. Good and bad news comes in threes, they say."

He peeled off a thread of lies like a hungry fisherman peels a prawn. But the manager saw through it.

"Lucky the cat didn't need to get braces too, hey Pete?" he said.

Peter didn't know how to take that one.

"So you're looking to borrow to buy more shares. I'm afraid to say it doesn't look good. Without decent security, it's going to be difficult, particularly with the existing loans."

"There must be a way," Peter said in protest. "Look at those shares..."

"Well, there may be one option, seeing it's for investment purposes," he said. "You're in luck. Our financial advisor is here today. He might be able to offer something more suitable. I'll check if he's free."

The manager left the office and arrived back a minute later. In tow was the slick advisor, Harley Spitz. He brought a new level of professionalism to the meeting, wearing his jacket and tie. A confident swagger and powerful handshake complemented his wavy hair. He had Peter's immediate attention.

Harley whizzed efficiently through a disclaimer then proceeded to fire questions at both Peter and the branch manager.

"Financial assets?"

"Eighteen thousand in shares. All Aussie market," the manager replied.

"And you want to get more into the market?"

Peter nodded.

"Best option, no doubt, is a margin loan. No repayments, capitalise the interest. Borrow more than your stake. It's for serious wealth-builders, Mr Alves. Those who want to get some serious traction in these markets using leverage."

That magic word again. Leverage. Peter was sold.

Harley provided a whirlwind explanation of Loan to Value Ratios, margin calls and purchasing power, but there was a distinct heavy focus on the upside potential. "If the market keeps going up, you magnify your gains," he stated. He showed an example where using a margin loan increased the return on capital from 10% to 33%. It was the easiest sale Harley ever made.

"What's the most I can borrow?" Peter asked.

"75% of the holding," Harley replied in a flash of white teeth.

"Let's do it, Harley. Balls and all."

And so Peter walked out of the branch most satisfied, with a loan of sixty-eight thousand dollars and an order placed to buy a parcel of blue-chip shares at the next market open. It seemed the Peter Alves gravy train was back on track. He had found his own money-making machine.

****

Locals acknowledge October in Brisbane as the finest time of year. Drenched in warmth, the foul winds of August having dissipated, the city accepts the graduation from its mild winter to its sweltering summer. With the jacaranda trees waving gently, littering the footpaths with a purple rain of petals, citizens step out of their homes to regain their summer bodies with exercise and to enjoy the public pools and parks. October remained an overwhelming favourite month for people to refresh and recharge their lives.

Peter had chosen a mid-October day to call in sick to work and pull Mani from school for the day to have a man's day out. Peter's diligence to his property management role had drizzled away as his share success added to his feeling of wealth and well-being. He felt he did not need the job so desperately and may even be able to give it up entirely if things kept motoring in the markets. A sick day, knowing he would be paid anyway, played little on his conscience. And, he argued, Mani would learn more about life from a day with his Dad than he would from a day in class.

Parking in a side street just behind the iconic Regatta Hotel, Peter and Mani crossed the busy Coronation Drive and waited for the ferry on the Brisbane River. It would be a short ride that Peter had planned but would be poignant for it would take them past the nearly-finished site for Expo 88. It had been all over the news and things were hotting up for this massive Brisbane event, now less than six months away. Peter then planned a nice lunch at a restaurant in the City.

As they motored downstream, Peter was surprised by the perspective he got of his home town. He'd lived here for nearly forty years and this was his first time cruising the river. He was more excited than Mani, leaping from one side of the deck to the other, towing Mani along to point out sight after sight. The riverside floating restaurant, the distant city skyscrapers and the grandstands of the famous Lang Park footy ground.

Peter sat with Mani beside him. The ferry was slow-moving, but swift enough for father and son to feel the breeze through their hair as they lounged on the sunny front deck of the boat. Silvery flecks of sunlight danced on the water's surface where the swirling eddies and currents of the river reflected the rays. Peter leant back into his seat, his arm flung around Mani's shoulders. He thought of how good life was at the moment. Sun on his face, Celia in a constant good mood lately, feeling positive and of course the shares going nicely, creating a feeling of security. They'd kept rising since the additional purchases and Peter felt blessed with good fortune.

"How do I get a job?" Mani asked, springing Peter from his self-congratulatory day-dream.

"Why do you want a job?" Peter answered the question with another question.

"When I'm older, I mean. How do you get jobs?"

"There's usually an ad. Or you just talk to people."

"How do you know it's the right job?" Mani pressed.

"You get a feeling about it," Peter said. "If it's something you love doing, or a good place to work."

There was a short pause, but Peter sensed Mani had more questions. He was processing.

"Do you love doing your job?" he asked his father.

"No-one loves their job, mate"

"Then why do it?"

"For the money. Finding a job you love is like trying to put pineapples into a plastic bag. Near on impossible."

Mani smiled at the analogy. Thought some more. Peter knew more questions were coming.

"What's the point? If only for the money."

"You need money to survive, son. Makes the world go round, it does. Gotta pay bills, buy food, pay rent, bankroll your Mum. One thing you'll learn is women love spending money."

"You spend all day at work. How many days a week?" Mani asked.

"Five days a week, sometimes six if I have to."

Mani did some quick mental sums. "If you spend about a third of your whole life at work, isn't it dumb not to love it?"

Peter smiled. His boy was getting an education and Peter didn't even need to try. Kids are naturally inquisitive, it dawned on him. They'll ask what they need to know. "Good point, son," he replied.

There was silence between them then. The ferry crossed underneath the William Jolly Bridge, rounded the point allowing the still under construction World Expo site to come into view. Launch bridges jutted out into the river every fifty metres or so. Seagulls swirled above the dusty site, cranes reached skyward. Enormous white sails had been erected, attached to cantilever framework. Bronze-shouldered workmen in Jackie Howe singlets and hard hats graced the chaotic construction zone. Away to their left, the Riverside Expressway hummed with traffic.

Peter was next to speak. "Anyway, you don't want a job, son."

"Why not?"

"You're better off runnin' the business. Then you have people working for you. Making money for you. Or have your money working for you."

Mani cast a confused look at this new concept. "How does money work for someone?"

Peter laughed. "It's a turn of phrase. You invest it. Buy something that is going to go up in value or make more money. Like me with my shares. Or Auntie Trish buying houses."

Peter changed the subject, pointing out the man-made rainforest in the central area of the Expo site and the boardwalk taking shape at the eastern end. "This will all be here for you to explore next year. With your free pass."

"Are you and Mum going to Expo?" Mani asked.

"Too right. Reckon we'll spend a good amount of time there. Tell me, did you end up clearing the air with that girl?"

"Not really," Mani said.

"Do you like her?"

"Dad! I don't even know her."

It occurred to Peter that Mani wasn't yet at the age to be chasing girls. Not like his younger self. He thought back to his teenage years, to how important girls were when he was Mani's age. He couldn't recall being thirteen. Recalled only his later teen years when he found scoring with the ladies a cinch and was just about a sport for him, so dedicated was he to pursuing the ladies. Reckoned he could still pull a few even now. Wondered, though, if it would be lame for a nearly forty-year old married man to even try.

"Not far from the city now," Peter said. "Thank God, I need a drink. I'm sweating like a Pygmalion."

They alighted at Eagle Street Pier in the heart of the city's business district and found a restaurant. They snacked on chips, giggling that these had been served by a waiter in full regalia, while Mani drank a milkshake before ordering their main meal.

"I'm off to siphon the python. We'll order when I get back," Peter announced, rising to go to the toilet.

While he was gone, Mani finished the chips while watching a news article on the TV over the bar. Peter returned just as another beer arrived for him.

"What would it mean for a 'sharemarket wipeout'?" Mani asked, his straw dangling from his mouth as he spoke.

Peter thought for a second before replying. "Well, it would mean we were up shit creek in a barbed wire canoe..."

"With a paddle pop stick as a paddle," Mani completed his father's well-known saying.

"Exactly!" Peter said, wheezing his trademark cackle. He switched to full financial expert mode. "For the sharemarket to drop would mean that businesses were less valuable. That the public had lost faith in big businesses like banks and supermarkets. Pretty unlikely to happen and only temporary if it did. Why do you ask?"

Mani did not say a word, just pointed. The TV told the story.

Peter's face drained of colour. Lost all expression. The face of a dead man. The grabbing in his chest may have been all that kept his heart going. His eyes bore witness to the distress, his mind conjuring a rising sense of doom, thoughts racing. A prolonged involuntary moan of "Nooooo..." escaped his mouth.

He was no mathematician, didn't know his loan-to-value ratios, margins or anything about securities. Peter's mind flickered back to the meeting at the bank with Harley Spitz, trying to recall anything that might help him comprehend what was happening to him now. He wished he'd listened and understood. He knew in his deepest parts that a 25% drop was ugly. He saw the graphic of the day's market activity that the TV statistician had cobbled together, looking like someone had dropped an inky stone off the cliff and the ink had traced its fall. Straight down. No pauses, pure gravity. And the market still had three hours before it would close.

"C'mon, we're going!" Peter growled.

"But what about lunch," Mani protested. "We haven't eaten."

"We're going!"

Mani sculled down his milk as his father flipped two green $2 notes onto the table. Macarthur and his sheep stared back glibly as Peter grabbed Mani roughly by the wrist and strode out.

****

This car needs to go, Celia Alves thought as she steered the blue Sigma into their street. Peter had been saying it would be the next upgrade to their lives. They both could see that it was not representative of their street or their preferred status.

Celia was feeling pleased with herself. It wasn't so bad having just the one champagne while enjoying lunch and a fashion parade with the ladies. As rostered, Celia had been designated driver for the other west-side women. She would have her chances to imbibe her favoured bubbles at numerous events over coming weeks, her taxi obligations now fulfilled. It was coming into the busier period of her social calendar. Spring always seemed to be when it picked up, labels were launching new lines for the warmer months, racing carnivals and the obligatory marquee functions abounded. People were out and about more.

She straightened her dress before opening the door. Entering the lounge room, she saw Peter on the couch. "Afternoon, darling. How'd lunch go?" she asked cheerily.

There was no reply, just a slow shake of the head from her husband.

Celia scanned the scene, a detailed eye joining the dots. Peter was slouched back on the couch. His skin was grey, his eyes bloodshot and red around the rims like he'd been trying to dig them out of his skull with his knuckles. His shirt dangled out, shoes kicked off. The phone had been pulled from the wall. A half empty bottle of Scotch sat next to a glass on the coffee table before him, a circular puddle under the glass.

"You started early," Celia said.

Peter started to say something, then stopped. Just shook his head again.

"What's the matter?" she asked with urgency.

"Bloody shares have hit a wall. Haven't you heard about it on the radio, the news? Dropped off a cliff. Just about worthless." He stood and walked across to his wife. She was just staring, soundless. He grabbed her by the upper arms, facing her. "Don't you get what this means?"

"No, Peter," Celia said, seeing only her comfortable life being torn from her once more. "Not again! How bad is it?"

"The worst. Couldn't be worse."

"Where's Mani?" she asked.

Peter released his limp grip on her shoulders, turned away, waving his arms up the stairs.

Celia hurried to her son, emerging minutes later with a bag for each of them while Peter was back on the couch, staring, a fresh pour in his glass. She was taking Mani to her sister's house. He didn't need to see the mess Peter was in, the mess their lives were becoming. She announced her departure, leaving Peter pinned to the couch by his sorrowful funk like a beetle in a bug display.

"Straighten yourself out, Peter!" she admonished him.

The Girl with the Rainbow Laces

"I need it to leap off the page. It has to sell me," Jason said to his cousin. They were in Jason's room and Jason had scribbled his idea on a sheet of paper for Mani.

"And you reckon people will go for this," Mani asked. "You really think you can make money doing odd jobs for people?"

"Absolutely," Jason said. "Dad's got all the tools I need. A little bit of labour and I get paid. I just need you to do up the words for my flyer. You have a gift for writing that I couldn't hope to match. Your words dance off the page. You're the boss of words. Who's the boss? You are! You're Tony Danza!"

"Settle down, idiot," Mani laughed, shoving his cousin. "How much will you charge?"

"Ten bucks to mow, another fifteen to do gutters. And I'll let you in on a secret. Getting the customers is the first step. Once I have my regulars, I'll get someone else to do the hard labour, pay them a little bit less and pocket the profit. It's the jobs no-one else wants to do, especially now with how hot it is. Actually, put that on the flyer, that I'll do their hot, crappy work."

Mani shook his head at his cousin's ingenuity. He himself had often thought that to have his own money would be cool, it just hadn't occurred to him to pursue it. Parents paid for stuff. Mani quickly tried to imagine himself working, but couldn't think what he would do. "I'll do your words, but I'm not getting sweaty. Even though I could do with some pocket money for the holidays."

Knowing his family had been through a financial calamity, Mani had some deep-seated concerns about how he could contribute to the household. He wondered if he should find a job, bring in some money. His Dad had not handled the initial shock at all well but had bounced back in typical positive fashion. Without grasping the full extent of his family's money worries, Mani sensed the tightening of the belt and the tension between his parents when a bill came in or Mum needed money for the shops.

In fact, there had been all manner of financial manoeuvring in the six weeks since the sharemarket plunge though Mani was largely immune to the details. The bank had moved swiftly in response to the plunge, selling Peter's shares when he couldn't spring for the $35,000 he needed to meet his margin obligations. His $70,000 loan stood despite the portfolio having dropped to $44,000. He should have known the risks but, swooning over the potential fortune he saw, he ignored any safeguards or fallback positions. Should have known that if the loan ratio dropped, he needed cash, which he didn't have. Next step was the shares being liquidated and at the worst possible time.

As he stated when he went in – it was balls and all. Brain turned off, bravado on after-burners. He now held the title of the bank's shortest tenure for a margin loan. Less than a month from hopes high to hopes dashed. Harley Spitz with his big smile and wavy hair was nowhere to be seen.

And so his hole was dug. Once everything was wound up, Peter had a $30,000 investment loan with no investments to show for it. The earlier consolidation loan remained. His low income couldn't hope to meet the bank's demands. He had a wife who didn't work. There was only one option. Peter filed for bankruptcy.

Mani did not see much change in his own life. He still went to school, there was still a meal on the table at night. His Dad went to work each day and spoke of the next big deal in the evenings, optimistic as ever.

Jason sympathised with Mani. Having heard his parents discuss it, he'd looked up bankruptcy in the library. Jason saw the gulf in attitude between his own parents and those of his uncle Peter and was drawn to the excitement of risk versus return.

"This could be our first business collaboration," Jason stated to Mani who had gathered up Jason's flyer notes. "We could do this sort of thing our whole lives. Work together, have a business."

Mani shrugged. "I guess," he said, not grasping Jason's point.

"We're not just cousins Mani, we're mates. Our families are so close we're almost brothers. You're a different sort of guy, low-key and not too crazy. But I love you man and I like hanging out with you."

Jason gave him a brief awkward hug. Mani stood with his arms by his side, dutifully accepting it. He wasn't used to being hugged.

"So what do you think you'll do when you leave school?" Jason asked.

"I don't know. I haven't thought about it."

Jason was upbeat, despite Mani's lack of exuberance. "I'm going to make a lot of money. Start a business, or buy one. A real business, not like this pocket money mowing thing. There's something about having money that excites me. I see your Dad and how much fun he has. Always happy, having parties, going out. That's the life!"

Mani was living that life and it didn't appeal to him. "A lot can go wrong. A lot has gone wrong," he said.

They walked from Jason's room, down the hall through the Sharpe's modest but immaculate home to the kitchen.

"So what do you think you'd like to do after school?"

"A teacher maybe, or sales like Dad," Mani replied.

"You're not like your Dad. I mean in the way he is when he's selling things. You know what I mean."

"I'm not sure what I'll do. There's plenty of time."

"That's true," Jason said, pouring them each a cold cordial. "But we finish grade eight next week and we probably should have some idea of what we want to study."

"You finish next week, private school boy," Mani joked. "I still have two weeks to go."

"Well, you should have stayed at CBC."

"Like I had a choice," Mani said, smiling wryly.

They sat at the kitchen table. Jason put his feet up on the chair beside him. "So what subjects do you like?"

Mani rattled off his favourite subjects. "English, Maths, Geography, History."

"Well that's pretty much all of them. And you get mostly A's. CBC must have been sorry to see you go."

"Westside High has been good, though," Mani said.

"Plenty of time, as you said. You'll find your calling. It might be writing or palaeontology or you might be a trapeze artist," Jason joked, before turning serious once more. "Remember, what I told you. We're best mates. OK?"

"Thanks Jas." Mani was touched by the care in Jason's words. He hadn't received much praise from another male. He was eager to please. "When do you want these flyers done?" he asked.

****

Jason did up four hundred photocopied flyers, delivered locally and within no time had a full week of customers. Mani on the other hand found reason to be pleased that his public school stayed in a couple of weeks longer. The most meaningful interaction occurred with his fancy - one Alison Archer.

Unperturbed by her assault, Mani still held his metaphorical candle for the blond-haired beauty. Though not as intense or engrossing as his feelings from earlier in the year, his admiration still ran deep. Her physical allure, from her face to the way she flounced and bounced along the corridors of the school, complemented her popularity and brains. Alison and Mani were on an intellectual par in his opinion and Mani felt great pride when he heard she was organising a fundraising event to support victims of a Central Queensland flood. He felt a bond, a sense that there could be a future for them despite the current impasse which suggested she did not know he existed and their previous horrid history on stage.

Their interaction was once again in the tuckshop line, reprising fond memories of when Alison's hair had flicked across his face. Mani now felt daft at his excitement for reading anything into such an unremarkable event.

He was behind her in line, this time not by his design. Alison had ordered a sausage roll, Samboy chips and a Sunnyboy. Cost - $1.85. She counted out her coins on the counter. She was twenty cents short and needed to make a decision between the chips and the frozen treat.

"I have some spare coins." Mani spoke before his mind could register the implications. "How much do you need?"

"No, no. It's alright," she said.

"I don't mind. I have enough." Mani expected this to feel different, for his face to burn red with embarrassment, for his knees to wobble or stomach to churn. But his words came out right. He heard himself saying the words and he sounded cool. He was speaking to her and it felt normal.

Alison accepted the coins with a smile and a sheepish half curtsy, paid and left the line. Mani ordered his hot chips, turning to go to his usual lunchtime meeting point. But she was waiting.

"You're Mani, aren't you?" Alison stated. "You won the essay comp. The boy I kneed."

Mani nodded. Was she going to knee him again, he wondered. She was wearing her rainbow-laced, pink-trimmed tennis shoes with little blue pom pom socks. Maybe those were her kneeing shoes.

"Look, I am so sorry about that. That's not what I'm like."

Mani knew she was not like that. Not his Alison. "Forget about it," he said.

"I feel bad. That was shocking what I did."

"It's OK. No hard feelings. They took your prize off you, didn't they?" he said.

"And gave me detention." She smiled and pulled a face like it was her one and only detention.

"Are you still going to Expo?"

"Definitely!"

Mani saw her face light up. It lit him up. "I might see you there," he said.

"Maybe. Thanks for the money." Before turning to leave, she gave him a smile. Mani noticed that the smile came with a slight tilt of the head and a momentary raise of the eyebrows. He watched her walk away. That walk.

It was a mature interaction.

Underneath though, Mani was like one of those lovelorn cartoon characters whose loveheart beats out of their chest, tongue protruding from the corner of their mouth, eyes spinning like a poker machine.

Re-Mounting Peter's Pony

Peter strolled into the kitchen where Celia was covering two trays of hors d'oeuvres with alfoil to keep them warm. He eyed the spicy meatballs before helping himself to a mini vol-au-vent with seafood mornay filling. Celia slapped his wrist playfully. "They're for the guests, Peter."

He reached up to pull a Scotch bottle from the cupboard. "They're not coming for the snacks, Ceels! By the time they hear what we've got to say, they'll be too excited to eat."

Peter and Celia had five couples visiting this evening. But it was not a social visit, despite Celia's efforts to cater. It was to be pure business. These ten acquaintances were hand-picked as the potential core of Peter's new venture – Bettalife, a weight loss company from the US, new to Australia, growing quickly and, of particular importance to Peter, a true money-spinner. Millionaires had been made in the States using this system. Ordinary folk making extraordinary amounts of money.

The evening's presenter, Ronan Walsh had got involved on the ground floor in Australia and was already making five thousand dollars a month within half a year. He had shown copies of his recent bonus cheques from the company to impress Peter. All Gold Coast glitz and salesman charm, he attracted people with his smile and suits. With his squint, he seemed to always be happy. And in his line of business, attracting people was the key. To Ronan Walsh, Peter Alves was a door waiting for his opportunity to knock.

It was a chance meeting at a New Year's Eve party that opened up this new path for Peter. Ronan presided over a crowd and the ladies gathered around as he told his stories about business on the Gold Coast during the property boom of the early eighties. He was a good-looking bloke in his early forties, constantly smiling and people were flocking to be around him. When Ronan made the effort to introduce himself, it may have been because he saw the similarities between him and Peter.

With a few drinks in him, Peter could maintain a crowd with his tales too.

Ronan had his story down pat. When meeting someone new he would start by showing interest in their background. Lots of questions, get the other talking. Inevitably, the conversation would come around to the question he loved to hear. "What do you for a crust, Ronan?" His opening.

He told Peter about the business he was in and how the products helped his overweight brother to lose his excess baggage and helped to reduce his asthma. He spoke with passion of the profound effect this had on him, knowing from that point on that this would be his life's work. He would tell people about these incredible products. It was purely a bonus to him that there was so much money to be made, he told Peter. And it just so happened that they needed more people to help spread the gospel.

Hook, line and sinker. Every time.

A whirlwind two weeks later, Ronan was in the Alves' lovely rented home in Kenmore about to tell his grand story to a room full of people. The invitees were not here because they needed to lose weight, they were here to make money. If the evening went to plan, Peter would have a new business underway and be back on track despite his new status as a bankrupt.

He had hand-selected the guests. Wilko from the real estate office got a start only because Phil Patrick was busy. Wilko arrived with his fiancé Cath, a lawyer. Rob Lewin, a car salesman Peter once worked with brought his overweight wife June. At least they'll buy something, Peter thought. Derek Wagstaff and his wife Cheryl were both accountants, as well as being family friends. Colin Farley, another real estate agent to whom Peter had sold a car a couple of years previously and whose wife Denise did the society circuit with Celia were there. Last to arrive was David Berry, a bank home loans specialist whose card Peter had kept from when he had bought the Karana Downs house, with his eye-catching wife Jolene.

They had been selected for their common traits – they all had large circles of influence or business connections and, based on the jobs they did, they would know how to seal deals.

Introductions all around were completed before the guests took a seat in the quasi-boardroom that Ronan and Peter had established in the living area.

Peter began his introduction of Ronan as though they were old friends when in fact they'd met just two weeks prior. With Ronan being a quick talker and Peter inclined to make swift decisions, particularly when there was money involved, the meeting had been slickly arranged. "Ladies and gents, thank you for accepting the invitation to come to my humble abode. We have a very exciting presentation for you tonight from a dynamic speaker and a successful businessman. I want you to know that you were invited because you were the first people I thought of when I saw this incredible opportunity. Without further ado, please put your hands together for a great friend of mine and a great success story, Mr Ronan Walsh."

There was polite applause, an apprehensive welcome befitting the general feeling of uncertainty as to why they were there.

Ronan stepped forward with a hearty handshake for Peter and knowing he needed to win over his crowd and ease their scepticism, he threw in a joke accompanied by his ever-present salesman smile. He began his introduction, telling his background before explaining why they were listening to him. He used clichéd expressions like "Money isn't everything, unless you haven't got any" and "The problem with working for someone else is that JOB stands for Just Over Broke" to murmurs of approval and muffled starts of laughter.

He then launched into the Bettalife product and business opportunity. He outlined the product line, some success stories of phenomenal weight loss using the tablets and powdered shakes, and rattled off statistics of overweight Australians and the subsequent health problems and costs to society. Weight was a national problem and people had run out of ideas. They were floundering with their weight issues and needed some answers.

That was where Bettalife answered their calls. Ronan's presentation was convincing to the ten people in the Alves loungeroom, this being the expected result. Peter sat watching the routine, studying Ronan's moves, his mannerisms, his voice pitch and his jokes. This was important for him. He needed the people in his home to buy into Bettalife's potential. He looked around at the attendees. Positive signs. They were mostly sitting forward in their seats. Attentive. Ronan had captured their imagination. Now he needed to blow them out of the water.

"So let's look at the other side of Bettalife," he cooed, great concern and heartfelt altruism pouring out through his gestures and connection with his audience. "Obviously, where there is a possibility to help so many people, there lies the prospect of making a lot of money. Bettalife is priceless to the people who benefit from it, but of course there is a cost. And someone has to introduce this product, it has to be delivered and explained. And those who do such great deeds ought to be rewarded for their compassion and humanity. That is why Peter Alves has invited you here tonight. He believes in you as someone who can help a lot of people."

Peter smiled. There was a palpable sense of implied importance and responsibility in the room at that statement by Ronan Walsh. It looked good for Peter, particularly if everyone had emotional buy-in to what he knew was about to follow.

What followed was a thorough sales pitch of a money-making opportunity that stood out as being exceptional.

"Now I know this sounds too good to be true," Ronan said. "And you are probably sceptical, thinking it can't be this easy. I know how you feel. I felt the same way when I first heard about this. But what I found is that people are doing this every month, making good profits by helping people lose weight."

Ronan then went into detail of the reward system, squeaking it out on the whiteboard, showing the potential remuneration, whereby payments were made to distributors on multiple levels based on the people they introduced to the products and the business opportunity. The crowd shifted in their seats, excited. Peter had dollar signs rolling in his eyes.

It was an evangelical delivery. Peter expected people to levitate off their seats and ask where they could sign. He felt so close himself to the God of All Riches that he saw nothing but the magic of multi-level marketing and instant, ongoing wealth. But a dissenting voice in the crowd called out to pop his balloon.

"It sounds like a pyramid scheme," David Berry offered.

Ronan pounced on the voice of rebellion, shutting it down, boxing it up and leaving everyone in the room in no doubt as to the veracity of the scheme he had just spruiked. "It's not a pyramid scheme. Pyramid schemes are illegal. This is network marketing, also known as multi-level marketing and it is perfectly legal, valid and accepted internationally. I agree with you. Pyramid schemes are nasty bits of work. They base themselves on this type of marketing, but the key difference is they do not have a product. It is all about money changing hands, so that someone is always left holding the poisoned chalice. Let's compare that to Bettalife. Someone only gets paid when someone buys and sells a product to another person. If there's no sale, there's no money to be paid or made. It's a big difference. But thank you for your query. I'm glad we were able to clear that up."

There were several other questions about how quickly they could make that sort of money and how to get started. Peter's business was underway. Ronan schmoozed with the invited guests, making them feel important, integral to the success of Bettalife. They ate Celia's meatballs and vol-au-vents. They drank wine and beer. All but Derek the conservative accountant signed up to get involved, and he simply needed more time to consider it, despite his wife's urging to get started immediately.

After all the business was done and the guests had left, Peter swung Celia in his arms, dancing her across the tiled floor of the room where the presentation had been held. He was back. The Alves train was on the rails and the good times were around the bend. Like a phoenix, Peter had risen once more from his well-acquainted ashes.

Bandaged Hand in Hand

A new year always held such great promise. A chance for a fresh start, to atone for last year's ills, to aim for a year of achievement. In the early months, resolutions were still intact, as were the good intentions behind those resolutions. Mani had much to look forward to and, as his mother pointed out, at least he would be starting and remaining in the same school for a full year.

"And I'm not in the junior grade anymore," he said. "There will be smaller kids than me to pick on."

Celia was shocked. "You'll be doing no bullying! If I hear that..."

"Not me doing it, Mum. The others. They'll leave me alone. That's what I mean."

"And you'll know most of the kids from last year. That's the important thing," she said.

It was Expo year – 1988. Mani had his three day pass to enjoy and the way his Dad spoke, there'd be many more days at the massive exposition parklands. Now that Peter was enjoying success with his latest venture, he'd flagged plans for regular visits to the city's biggest event in years.

However, all the potential positives faded into obscurity when weighed against the largest of Mani's back to school excitements. He would be seeing his fancy once again. Being back at school meant being back in Alison Archer's stratosphere. In her midst. This gratified him immensely, considering their heartening interaction as school ended the previous year.

Harrying his mother to get him to school early, Mani kept a careful eye out before the bell, scanning the milling throng of attitude and uncertainty that was the first day of school. There was no immediate sign of Alison. Perhaps she was late, Mani wondered. She would surely be with her clique of pretty girls hanging out near the handball courts. He would check, knowing that if he found the posse, he would find Alison.

No joy. She wasn't with her typical cohorts of cool. A mild concern rose in Mani. He conducted a reconnaissance back past the front gate, passing by the heaviest concentration of students. The bell tolled. Again, he had no luck. No sign of Alison.

Class was purgatory that morning. He could not concentrate, his mind drifting to the possibilities explaining her non-appearance. The explanations were at either end of the limits of probability. Quite simply, she was away today and would be back tomorrow. The thought settled Mani's frayed sensibilities. Or she was dead and he would never see her again. A bilious dread stirred in his chest. He filled the gaps between these extremes with fanciful thoughts of alternate scenarios.

A different school maybe. Maybe.

She had got famous over the holidays and was now entrenched in Milan striding the catwalks, having been recruited by some eagle-eyed modelling talent scout.

She was being home-schooled, or had dropped school altogether.

She was now a teen Mum caring for her newborn baby. No, physically impossible and just ridiculous. The school holidays had only been six weeks.

Suffice to say, nothing new entered Mani's learning sphere that morning. At lunchtime he might be informed of her whereabouts. One or two of the study group had noticed her absence, for like Mani they had designs on the prettiest girl in grade 8. It became a focus for the group to ascertain whether Alison Archer was returning to Westside State High to resume her title by being the prettiest girl in grade 9.

It took three days of intense research for the answer to come back via the jungle drums and grapevines of high school hearsay. Alison would not be returning. Her father, the bank manager, had accepted a transfer with his job to the Sunshine Coast. The family had packed up soon after Christmas and were now living by the beach. Caloundra State High School was the fortunate beneficiary of Westside State High School's loss. The look on the faces of several of the young men in his study group confirmed for Mani that his loss was not to be felt in isolation. She was a popular girl.

Mani could not accept this.

His year was in ruins. His first foray into the world of love had ended before it had a chance to flourish. A hollowness settled within him. Pain wracked his body like a car crash, feelings - those pesky feelings - tearing at his insides. His disembodied mind clouded over with loss, with hurt. Over days, his appetite failed, his sleep suffered, yet the image of her held strong. His mother noticed he hadn't been near his typewriter in days. Mani Alves. The empty shell - absorbing food, light and education but barely subsisting without the nourishment of those tingles of love. Of hope.

She was gone from school, but not from his heart, his core or memory. He would see her again. He felt it. One night, days later, Mani dreamt that he injured his hand on a piece of wire. He was building a fence, a long fence that he could not finish. Alison was there. She stopped the bleeding and applied a dressing. Her eyes met his as she wrapped the bandage for him, rolling it around his hand and when she finished she had bandaged her own hand together with his. Joined, hand in hand.

The Hedonism of Heavy Hitters

Ronan Walsh was not only a sharp dresser, slick talker, successful businessman, possessed of a maturity and worldliness, good with the ladies and sported a fine head of hair. He was much more than that. He was also pretty good on the drink and knew how to have a good time.

Peter had developed quite a man crush on Ronan these past weeks since having tagged his trailer to Ronan's swathe-cutting prime mover and he felt future success was assured. Celia didn't mind his constant talk about Ronan and the excessive praise. "I shouldn't be worried that you are going to leave me for Ronan, should I?" she joked.

Peter knew it was business twenty-four hours a day with Ronan. "He doesn't want me for my body," he replied, a mischievous grin across his face. "He only wants me for my contacts." Peter, under no illusions Ronan would ditch him if he wasn't producing.

Celia was grateful to see her husband bounce back and be so positive. It was far better than the self-pity that followed Peter's meltdown after the shares went bust, though that black period lasted for all of two days before the entire incident was consigned to experience, replaced by the confidence and enthusiasm she had seen numerous times before. Nothing like a good failure to launch a drive to succeed. Peter was a past master at the art of re-invention.

There had been several opportunities for Ronan to display his party prowess in recent weeks. As Peter's commitment to the business was proven, he was accepted into Ronan's inner circle which included the overweight younger brother who so inspired Ronan. The parties were regular, the drinking increasing and the standard of decadence improving upon the previous outing, as though trying to prove that the rising rich can have more fun.

Peter's Bettalife downline had launched from that first meeting and he did what he did best in the ensuing weeks – he flapped his gums to anyone who would listen. He was not afraid to receive a knockback. He set himself a daily target for knockbacks on the advice of Ronan, who was blazing a trail for Peter to follow. Every knockback gets you closer to a yes, was Ronan's theory. They perennially tried to outdo each other by boasting of their failures as well as their successes. Things built quickly.

Peter directly recruited all those at the original meeting plus another four keen business builders. He'd assisted these nine frontliners to recruit at least 2 people each to get themselves out of the blocks and onto the path to eventual riches. Ronan was thrilled, stating that it took him three months to get the same quick start that Peter had achieved in just one month. And because all of this activity got Ronan paid, he was more than eager to make himself available for whatever assistance Peter and his fellow newcomers needed.

They established weekly recruiting seminars. Competition between the distributors was healthy, driving one another on at the meetings to inspire the next generation. The partying started in earnest when Peter's bonus cheque for the month of March 1988 arrived in his letter box. Aside from the $600 he had made from retailing the products directly, his bonus had jumped to $1,187 for the month, up from $365 in February. A bonus he got paid for the efforts of others. He had stared at the cheque for more than ten minutes when it arrived, curling it in his hands, his fingers feeling the texture of the bank's cheque paper. He read over every line of words several times, double-checked the date, added and re-added the numbers behind the dollar sign. He tried to decipher the code of the computer-written numbers of the account number on the bottom line of the cheque, analysing the meaning of this gratuity.

Tripling in a month and things were so young and raw compared to where he envisaged taking this. A broad smile spread across Peter's hard, tanned face. He was making more from Bettalife than from working with Phil Patrick, though he would keep the job for the steady stream of contacts it provided.

Phil would be on board soon enough too, when he saw the cheques rolling in for Peter.

Saturday nights were the chosen nights for the Bettalife team to get together to let their hair down. Ronan Walsh had spread his business to total over fifteen hundred people spread across Australia with satellite groups in Europe and the US. Here in South East Queensland, he had nearly five hundred people in his downline, with his band of close confidants, the team he called his 'heavy hitters', numbering around twenty.

The Saturday night parties were rotated through the homes of the 'heavy hitters' and this week Peter & Celia had been honoured to be hosts. People started arriving at the Alves house at six in the evening, just as the dusk sky started blackening into night. Swirling shapes of light blended with the clouds. Colours melded into one another. Oranges, pinks and blues formed waves in the sky, a visual spectacle. Though typically warm for an April evening, the first round of cocktails were served on the sprawling back veranda that offered breezes from the surrounding hills.

Invitees were festooned in dinner suits and cocktail dresses, as dictated by the invitation. Ronan and Peter had created this event, chipping in equal amounts to bring this extravaganza to life. They planned to achieve a triple benefit – to reward those who were having a red-hot go at the Bettalife opportunity, as an encouragement and an example to those who were ambitious, and as a lure to the high profile and well-connected guests who might get involved in the business.

Little expense was spared. Two waiters worked the room with trays of food and drinks, another filled orders for cocktails or spirits. Two enormous eskies full of ice, in which bottles of Swan Premium, Crown Lager and West Coast coolers chilled, were on either side of the main room. A DJ filled the sound gaps with funky and refreshing tunes. Champagne flowed. The place reeked of success. Of money. These were people attuned to the excesses of the rich, the element of society to whom unadulterated profligacy was a way of life. The rich got richer in these circles.

Peter noted Celia was in her element. She was mixing with her society friends as well as her new acquaintances, proud to be the hostess of such a classy event. She swanned wall to wall, kissing guests on the cheek, clinking glasses and filling the room with her devilish charm. Her regular greeting of "Darling!" and her trademark "Wonderful!" rang over the general din. She was an easy conversationalist, extroverted, at ease in such an environment. Peter could tell it was where she belonged and was gratified that he was able to provide his wife's preferred lifestyle so swiftly after the lows of bankruptcy.

Celia had played her part in their resurrection. Peter freely acknowledged this. He leant on her for moral support. She provided encouragement and belief in spades. Socialising was critical in spreading the Bettalife gospel and being an easy talker, Celia could easily discuss the product or the business opportunity with strangers and friends alike. Planting the seeds then deferring the prospect to speak with Peter for more detail. A recruiting super-team.

Her sister Patricia had shown no interest in getting involved, as much from her and Graham's conservative natures as from having their own plans for building their wealth. Patricia did not want to mix blood relations with business, considering Peter's track record. Celia hadn't pushed it.

"We don't need any extra money, Celia," Patricia had said. "We've got our own plans and our own investments. Good luck with it though." She divulged to Celia that she and Graham were hoping to buy a third investment property by the year's end once the tax returns had been processed. They expected a windfall from the deductions and depreciation write-offs on their other properties. Enough to provide a deposit on another 'renovator'.

"It's security, Celia. Something to fall back on if anything else might go wrong," Patricia had said, urging her sister to consider doing what they had done. She highlighted the passive nature and simplicity of it. "Set and forget. The real estate collect the rent, the accountant does the books. Hang in there and the property will go up in value."

It occurred to Celia that Patricia was doing precisely what Peter had done to them. A reversal of roles. "I can't see Peter going for it," she admitted. Celia had invited her sister to their parties, but she had not accepted for any of them. Parties were not Graham's scene. Renovating homes was his hedonism.

The party was in full swing and Peter, enjoying his fourth Swan Premium, eyed Ronan Walsh working the room. The guy was good. He could speak to anyone at any level, whether it was the local newsagent or a concreter's labourer. A solicitor at tonight's party, a guest of Wilko's lawyer missus Cath, was the evening's major target, meaning Ronan would be shadowing him through the night. Landing a big fish as a distributor was critical to Ronan's plan for swift reproduction of his downline. Recruit, convince, sell them on the prospect of quick earnings and overseas expansion. Add to his array of 'heavy hitters' then provide guidance. Show them how to replicate the recruitment throughout their own list of connections. Get them making money in their first month, exhaust the contact list of each individual who displays promise. Rinse and repeat.

Ronan was impressive. Peter trailed Ronan around the party, listening, learning, joining conversations where he felt it suitable. It was not as though Peter had a problem talking to people. Yet he remained in awe of Ronan's smooth demeanour and his ability to promote his business and himself. In awe of how he was able to direct the conversation to his own needs, effectively getting another person to come around to his way of thinking and to join Bettalife. Doing this without pressure and all the while making it seem as though it was the other's idea.

"Give them what they want but make sure you get what you want too," Ronan said. "Make them feel like their opinion counts, agree with them, plump up their egos – everyone wants to be the expert on everything – then guide them with facts to your way of thinking."

"Ah, piss in their pockets," was Peter's crude summation of the strategy.

"Control the direction of the conversation," was Ronan's more apt description.

Either way, it worked, and Peter was learning some useful strategies he felt sure would make him a lot of money.

The party was proving a success, the perfect warm-up for the six-month binge that would be Expo 88 which started in a fortnight. Peter and Ronan had garnered interest from their target, a partner in the law firm. It so happened he was looking for ways to wind back his involvement in the legal side of things, a semi-retirement, but needed to keep his wealth flowing in. A meeting had been arranged for the following week.

The drinks were flowing, the music getting louder and dancier, the crowd loosening up. The children, who had spent the evening downstairs with party food and a video to watch, had long since crashed out. The adults began their debaucherous slide. Tequila Slammers were demanded as the Bettalife party people shifted into overdrive. One of the young guys, a mover and shaker around Brisbane, started doing a strip tease to Joe Cocker's 'You Can Leave Your Hat On'. It ended tamely when he chickened out. He, along with everyone else at the party, felt uncomfortable when the wife of one of the Gold Coast team under Ronan started getting worked up, wanting to join in the cabaret and get a bit hands on.

Peter knew her form. She'd cornered him half an hour earlier on the balcony and made her intentions obvious. Sidling up to Peter seductively, she had under her arm the remains of the Tequila bottle and the other ingredients needed for a Tequila Lick, Sip, Suck. "You're Peter Alves and I hear you're quite the success story," she slurred.

"It's a great business," Peter said. He was smoking despite having come outside for some fresh air.

"Not everyone has been able to do what you've done, though. You've got tongues wagging, people are interested in you." She wore expensive jewellery and her dress must have cost the equal of the party's budget. She came from money, her husband a prominent businessman on the Coast. Her face was tanned and had the smoothness of youth, but her eyes revealed her age, not helped by the alcohol. Her body was lithe, defying time. "You're a star in the making," she said.

"Well, I know Ronan likes what I'm doing. If I make money, he makes money. Your hubby does alright out of it."

"He does," she smiled. "He makes it, I spend it." She cocked an eyebrow, tilted her head with an arrogance to suggest she was in a league of wealth that Peter had not yet reached. A power play. "Tequila time!" she sang. She had set two shot glasses on the railing of the balcony along with a small dish which held sliced lemon and a salt shaker.

She reached for Peter's hand, brought it to her mouth and licked his hand in the V between his thumb and forefinger, then sprinkled the salt on the dampness. "He makes money," she said in her sexiest voice. "But he's not as much fun as you. Sometimes, money can't replace what a woman really wants."

Peter knew exactly what she meant. He watched her pour the tequila, pouting lips and wiggling in front of him. They locked their eyes together as they performed the Tequila ritual - licking the salt, downing the fiery liquid and sucking the juice from the lemon. The music inside was still loud enough to reach where they stood. It pumped steadily. Peter smiled as she leant forward, moving to the music, her arms squeezing in to enhance her ample cleavage. He knew Celia was passed out downstairs. He wouldn't be missed if he chose this option that had been offered to him.

Still smiling, eyes on her eyes, he leant closer to her. He said one word.

"Lamb."

"What?"

"Lamb," Peter repeated. He paused, still smiling, looking for her reaction. "There would have been a time when you were lamb. It's hard to tell how long ago though. All I see is mutton, love."

"You bastard," she said, shrieking as she swung a fist which Peter easily ducked, causing her to stumble. "No-one talks to me like that. You're screwed, mate! I'll tell your old lady you were hands all over me."

"My missus wouldn't hear a word of it. I think she'd see she has no competition."

The fury on her face changed her. She now looked her age. Mutton. The years of surgery now seemed obvious as she scowled. "She's fat!" she scythed. "And you're a loser."

"I'll pass on your sentiments, sweetheart," Peter called after her as she waddled inside. He followed up with his trademark laugh. The Peter Alves cackle that he made sure she could hear as she strode off.

Not a chance, he thought to himself as he grabbed the bottle of booze. No way would I do that. Not to my Ceels.

Bloodlines

Peter Alves smiled with deep satisfaction as he sat down at the breakfast table. He couldn't recall a time when everything in his life had aligned as it had at this moment. He'd seen some great times, but his successes were often short-lived, often brought down by some unexpected failure. Looking at the family scene before him – Mani smiling and full of chat with his now-longish hair bouncing across his forehead, Celia serving up a breakfast of bacon, snags and scrambled eggs while she smiled and listened to her son – he sensed the evolution of himself and his life.

Peter's business was strong; money was increasing month on month. He was being cherished in the bedroom of late. He was being feted by men and women on all levels throughout the Bettalife organisation for his business-building prowess. And Expo 88 was finally on. Like the new maturity of the city in which he lived was hauling Peter up along with it, leading to a deep self-awareness in him.

He straightened his back as Celia trailed her hand across his neck and shoulders as she passed him to sit down. Her touch still did wonderful things to him even after their nearly fifteen years of marriage. She remained the cheek-filled country girl from that afternoon at the Victory Hotel. Celia wore one of her selection of stylish floral dresses. He watched her smooth her skirt then tuck it under her as she sat. In that moment he wanted to squeeze her close.

They were off to Expo today, to use the third day of Mani's 3-day pass. Peter and Celia had lost track of the number of visits they'd already had. Peter and Celia had each purchased a season pass for $160 at the urging of Ronan Walsh. "Well worth it," he'd reasoned. "Lot of people there, lot of opportunities to promote the business. And, come on. It's Expo. There won't be another event like this in your home town in your lifetime. Live it up! Spend big. It's a tax write-off anyway." The place had only been open for eight weeks and here they were in mid-June wondering, like many Brisbane locals, how they had utilised their time before Expo was there.

Mani was talkative this morning. The kid had come out of his shell of late. Peter could not be disappointed that his boy wasn't the sport-loving, easy-talking high achiever that he envisaged when Mani was born. The Sharpe boy, Mani's cousin, fitted that bill. But something was awkward about him, Peter thought often. A false front or something.

Peter saw none of that in Mani. Verbose, but at times withdrawn as if deep in thought, Mani surprised Peter with some of his conclusions. How on Earth he came up with some of his thought processes, Peter had no idea. But looking at him today – his body maturing and thickening across the chest, the baby fat having melted away in recent months, promoting his strong jaw, and Mani nattering away with hypotheses and queries to keep the family talking – Peter could see Mani in the future. As a man. Then saw himself as a boy, then himself again, older. Calm, greying, maybe bouncing a grandson on his knee while Mani spoke in his man voice about the ways of the world he knew. His successful, bright, amazing son. He hoped he'd been a good Dad. There would be judgment, he knew.

Peter watched Mani struggle with his cutlery, hampered by the splint on his ring finger. A dislocation and small bone fracture, courtesy of a playground accident at school. Building human pyramids in Phys Ed class. The big kids, like Mani, on the bottom row. Bearing the brunt of the weight and of the inevitable collapse.

"You need me to cut your brekkie up for you?" Peter enquired as he tucked his napkin into the front of his collared polyester casual shirt. He was dressed up for their Expo day out, matching the blue shirt with brown corduroy slacks.

"Nah, I'm alright." He continued to fumble, a sausage sliding across the plate. "Have you ever broken a bone, Dad?"

"Yeah, actually," Peter replied, a dreamy reminiscence streaking his face. "Broke my hand fighting when I was in my twenties."

"Yeah! Really?" The thrill of hearing of his Dad in a fight had Mani eager and excitable.

"Taught me a lesson. Don't fight!" Peter said. "And if you do fight, make sure your fist is closed when you connect with another blokes head." He guffawed and winked at Mani.

Celia said, "Good lesson. Why don't you teach him something useful?"

"What? Like how to build a human pyramid?"

Celia shook her head at him. Peter just smiled. He knew how to press her buttons.

"What actually happened to break your finger?" Peter asked as he stirred his coffee.

"Someone's knee. I was still on all fours, my hand was out like this when he landed. Bang, right on my hand."

"What lesson can we get out of that, Ceels?" Peter said, teasing his wife. There was no response as she kept a smile while eating. "How about this for a lesson?" Peter continued. "When you build a human pyramid, make sure you're at the top. You fall on them rather than them falling on you."

"Or stand to the side and watch. Don't get hurt," Celia suggested. Mani cocked an eyebrow, considering this alternative.

"What's that teach him?" Peter said. He picked up a piece of toast and pushed his plate away. "Not gettin' involved is the sure way to fail in life. You don't learn unless you get hurt along the way."

There was silence. Peter had spoken, given his point of view and there was no use disputing it.

Mani spread some Vegemite on his toast and asked, "What about you, Mum? Any broken bones?"

She pointed at her nose. "Over the handlebars," she said while contorting her face.

"Ha. Bike riding," said Peter. "Now there's something that's better being watched than being involved. Why ride when you can drive?"

"Are you scared of bikes, Dad?"

"Scared? Nah-ooo! Just that four wheels are better than two."

Celia rose, collecting the plates. "When you grow up in a little country town like I did, you rode your bike all day. Up hills. Plenty of hills in Nambour where I grew up. All weekend cruising around to your friend's house, finding bush tracks and going faster than you felt comfortable doing. I had some good accidents, saw many worse than my own. But the biggest and best was over the handlebars, face first into the dirt. Blood and dust and snot, my mouth was full of all three. Very embarrassing for a young lady to crash like that."

Mani enjoyed his parents' banter and after some thought said, "So, don't ride a bike because you might get hurt, but get involved in building human pyramids because you learn more by being hurt."

"Father's logic," Celia stated.

They all exchanged glances then laughed together when they realised that Mani had de-constructed their twisted reasoning.

Peter paddled his hands on the table in a swift drumroll, as though he had hit on the answer to all their queries. "Riding bikes is like wearing one of those full-length yellow raincoats when it rains. It serves a purpose, but you lose all dignity doing it. You don't see the CEO of a company riding a bike. It's a poor man's transport."

"You don't see CEO's making human pyramids," Celia jumped straight in, giving as good as she got in this cat and mouse with her beloved husband. It kept their marriage fresh. Kept the love alive.

Mani, of course, trumped them both. "But being the CEO and having people under you is like a pyramid. The boss at the top and all the people underneath him."

"Wacky-doo!" said Peter, clapping his hands together. "You've got it. That's my boy!"

"Does that mean that the boss crushes his workers underneath him when he finally falls?" Celia was trying to stay in the game.

"You can't have the boss at the bottom, Ceels. The boss is at the head of the organisation because he's the brains."

"You're the boss in your business, aren't you Dad?" Mani asked. "You always say you have people under you."

"Yeah, similar," Peter answered. "But it's not a pyramid!" He was firm with his answer. He held a finger up to make his point as though somewhat defensive on the issue.

"What is it then?" asked Mani. Always with just one more question.

"It's layers...levels." He was struggling to quantify it.

"Right," Mani said, examining his finger splint. "Layers."

"It's a business system. We're suppliers. Middle men supplying the products. Simple as that. Definitely not a pyramid." Peter was fumbling for the right words. When he found them, he clicked his fingers and pointed at his son for effect. "A hierarchy!"

Peter slumped back in his chair. Even for a world champion talker like himself that was an exhausting conversation. How did my son get so switched on without me noticing, he wondered.

"Enough talk," Celia announced. "Whether it's a pyramid, a cone or a box of lies, it won't matter if we get stuck in those Expo queues. We'd best get going."

The Alves were picking up Jason for the excursion to Expo. The cousins could keep each other company. Celia and Peter would focus on the things they wished to see and also on the supplementary reason they were visiting the event. Peter had found it a fertile recruiting ground for the business. Bettalife was an international affair and, with Ronan having explained how worldwide business could be done, Peter had been forging contacts among the international visitors in Brisbane for Expo.

Peter would hang around the various pavilions of the participating nations, the large display halls that highlighted and promoted that country's virtues. He would spend most of his day saying "G'day" to people. If they responded with any hint of a foreign accent, Peter would strike up a conversation. Consider them ambushed. Utilising Ronan's teachings, he would then swing the conversation around to his business. He'd say he was run off his feet and so was enjoying some leisure time at Expo, which was great for business because he got to meet people from all over the world and that was helping him make a lot of money because it just so happens that his business had opened up recently in 'Insert Country of Origin of Target' and they needed some key people with contacts in that region to help them expand. And did they know anyone...

It was guerrilla marketing at its best. "They come here thinking they're having a nice quiet holiday and they go home with a new business underway," Peter boasted.

Regardless of the underhandedness, it was working. He'd garnered interest from more than a dozen people, each of whom had asked for contact when they got home to New Zealand, the US, Malaysia, South Africa, Ireland or wherever. The results flowed in. Peter officially recruited four people – two Kiwis, one Pom who had already bought in and had signed six of his friends to the scheme as well, and an Aussie ex-pat now living in Japan who reckoned he could single-handedly destroy the Sumo wrestling industry with these weight-loss products and was keen to make some serious Yen.

Peter had confided to Celia his mixed feelings of excitement and dread. "This is so easy for me, Ceels. Talking to people and teaching them how to do what I do to make money. It's going so well, I'm just waiting for someone to jump out from behind a pole and yell 'We got it wrong! It's not meant to be this easy. You need to pay back those cheques!' Put an end to me like what's happened before."

"Darling," Celia had replied with deep empathy. "You deserve this success. The Gods are smiling on you at last."

"You're one hell of a lady, Celia. Knowing you believe in me just makes me wanna get stuck into it."

"Don't be concerned. You're looking after me and you're looking after your son. Keep thinking that you are doing it for Mani. For his future. Doing it for the right reason."

Peter nodded, letting that sink in. Maybe this one will last, he thought. All those other screw-ups he'd put his family through were the learning he needed to achieve eventual success. Like that saying he'd heard once. Every time you fall, pick up something. He felt a new empowerment. A certainty.

"Let's get moving," Celia called to the house in general. "We've got a big day ahead of us." And then to Peter, with that familiar playful look on her face, "Remember, we are meeting the

Farley's for dinner at Picasso's. And I get a feeling there might be some surprises tonight."

"Whattya mean?" Peter asked.

"Just a feeling. We'll see."

There it was again. Keeping the love alive.

****

The first impression you get as you approach the Expo gates is of the mass of people. Throngs of them, surging towards the parklands on the south bank of the Brisbane River, pouring off buses, streaming off the trains, building in strength as they funnelled toward the entry points. The Expo site stretched for nearly a kilometre along the river's edge, so the two gates, one at either end, choked up as patrons hustled to get close for the ten o'clock opening. It provided one of the true iconic memories of Expo for which the celebration would become synonymous. Queues.

It became the quintessential Expo experience – lining up to await the opening of the gates, the familiar gliding sound overhead as the lapping monorail whooshed by, while quirky street performers provided eccentric diversions. Characters on stilts strutted by, with painted faces and bright outfits flaring behind them. Jugglers, mime artists, clowning posses, the robot-impersonating 'Mechanical Man' and the turquoise-adorned marching band. All employed to help the many visitors forget they were standing in line, barely moving, and would be for some time.

Peter, Celia, Mani and Jason spent the day traversing the avenues and boulevards of the complex. The kids urged the adults to let them visit the theme park, but obediently trailed Mani's parents in trying to see as many pavilions as possible, getting their Expo passport stamped at each entry point as if they were travelling the globe. The colours, the crowds, the noise, the sound, all melded with a general feeling of goodwill as the city celebrated its coming of age. The shackles of the little country town were being thrown off to reveal the bulging, rollicking cutting-edge city it had always hoped to become.

Celia flipped up a red umbrella to ward off the late morning sun. Her vibrant dress and umbrella added to the stunning kaleidoscope of colour and movement as they strolled the parklands. The Ayers Rock outline of the Australian pavilion beckoned them inside to their home expose. The Sky Needle stood eighty metres tall as their point of reference, a compass to guide their wanderings. Tourist groups muddled past them, trying to stay close together. Peter tried to pounce on the stragglers for a chat, like a big cat picking off the infirm prey on the savannah. Whimsical plaster cast characters looked on, silent witnesses to the thousands of wide-eyed visitors, in turn providing fascinating spectres to grab the tourist's attention - dangling astronauts, the family crowded around a campfire, a busking violinist, the farm kid riding on a galloping emu. All come to life while standing stock still and always entertaining. Expo was that sort of place.

The day disappeared. Time for the kids to go home so that Peter and Celia could play. Mani and Jason were collected by Patricia and Graham. Sundown was Peter's favourite time at Expo, as the crowd seemed to alter from the sensible, staid tourists to more of a party atmosphere, a younger crowd, though the Alves were no youngsters. They did however like being out when the cool people were at play.

Expo had proven to be an ideal fillip for the couple, providing them a new lease of life. Combined with the plentiful cashflow, the fun of regular visits to Expo ensured that Peter & Celia's relationship had never been better. The fun was back, their love rekindled.

It was June 14th, the day before Peter's birthday and Expo's designated Spanish National Day, being celebrated in the European section of the Expo around Times Square and European Boulevard. They had their pre-dinner drinks at the Plough Inn before moving on Picasso's Spanish restaurant, which was full. Rarely was it not, for it was recognised as one of the city's finest eateries.

This was Peter & Celia's third visit to Picasso's. It became their regular haunt not only for the magnificent cuisine and its ideal location central to the bustling walkways, but also because they felt it a suitable way to validate and honour Peter's Spanish heritage. They had become known to the head waiter, a short, wide, ever-smiling rock of a man named Fernando, to whom the Alves were recognisable from their previous rowdiness during late suppers.

Fernando was welcoming. Celia dealt with him in her typical flamboyant way, which the Spaniard enjoyed. He welcomed a lady with style. He had seen more than some individuals lacking Euro sophistication during the exposition. One late night arrival, a lady who was part of a group having come for supper from the nearby theatre, wore a magnificent fur coat with her thongs. Ooh la la!

Peter and Celia were the first of their party to arrive. They sat and ordered a jug of sangria while waiting for Colin and Denise Farley to arrive. The Farley's had also invited Colin's brother Keith, a new Bettalife member, and his wife Antoinette. The sextet had secured a table on the much in demand balcony which provided the perfect view of the restaurant's happenings, the wandering crowds of the European Boulevard as well as the exquisite, intricate matrix of neon lights that dazzled in lines and squiggles around the ceiling of the Times Square structure. Seats were difficult to secure, but Celia had persuaded Fernando to reserve this spot for the special occasion of Peter's birthday. She wanted a special night, which, she told Fernando on the side, included a surprise.

Dinner was a mixed tapas plate and skewers of marinated meats, enjoyed with several rounds of drinks, with the soundtrack being the outspoken exuberance of the socialite friends Celia and Denise. The men laughed and joked, sharing stories of business, life and times past. Peter was sharing his story about the time he went pig shooting out west when his yarn was drowned out by the sound of Spanish guitar.

The music was accompanied by the click of castanets. All eyes sought out the source of these lush sounds, and were soon transfixed by the flamenco dancer threading her way through the restaurant, hips shaking as she moved between the tables, her musician in tow. Sultry eyes, pouting lips, glorious mocha-brown skin and her hips wiggling in a most sexual way.

"Dinner and a show!" Peter enthused too loudly. He watched her, eyes moving from the hips to the lovely face, over her brown skin of her bosom, but always drawn magnetically back to those hips. That movement. The colourful dress, a gypsy-inspired traje de flamenco, reaching to her ankles and adorned with ruffles. The aural and visual treat before him, of a beautiful woman moving.

He felt Celia's eyes on him, feared her castigation. But he glanced over to see his wife smiling at him. OK, he thought. What's going on? Sprung perving and I get a big smile.

The dancer moved through the appreciative crowd, trailed by her guitarist, all busy fingers and intense concentration and passion for his music. The musician was dressed for the part in his laced-up silk shirt with layers of ruffles down the sleeve. He glanced up and forced a smile every few steps as the duo snaked through Picasso's, attracting the attention of all the patrons.

Next thing Peter knew, Celia was standing behind him, her hands on his shoulders. This is strange, he thought. I hope Ceels isn't getting worked up here. Could get embarrassing. He tried to figure out what Celia was up to, as the dancer and guitarist were at their table, completing the final flourishes of their display.

Fernando arrived immediately with a sparkler-enhanced cocktail, placing it in front of Peter. "Harpy Bort-day, Mr Alves," he crooned in his thick Catalan accent.

The crowd was applauding. Peter laughed, and bid cheers to them all as he took a sip of his drink. He felt Celia's hands give a loving squeeze on his shoulders. He turned to her, saw her smile. She had a piece of paper in her hands.

"*Mi esposo querido, te amo immensamente y amar nuestra maravillosa vida juntos. Este es un regalo para demostrar mi amor eterno.*"

It was a fumbling effort in Spanish.

Repeated in English, for the Aussies in the room. "My darling husband, I love you immensely and love our wonderful life together. This is a gift to show my everlasting love."

She produced an envelope and, planting a big kiss on Peter's lips, saying "This is to commemorate your glorious heritage and to celebrate your fortieth birthday. Let's enjoy the spoils of our wonderful life."

Peter accepted the kiss and the envelope. Faces peered at him, smiling. He edged the envelope open. Airline tickets. Brisbane to Barajas airport, Madrid. "Spain? We're going to Spain?" he croaked, emotion cracking his voice. "You bloody beauty, Ceels!"

Fernando clapped. "Congratulations, Mr Alves. Beautiful, my friend Celia. Just beautiful. Viva Espana!"

Raucous applause sprung forth from the other diners on the Picasso balcony. There were handshakes, back pats and hugs for Peter and Celia, from their own group and from total strangers caught up in the moment. Peter even got a kiss from the Spanish dancer. And one from Fernando.

****

"I'm going?"

"Yes, darling."

"You for real? I'm going overseas? Me, you and Dad?"

Celia, having just informed Mani of the surprise she had sprung for Peter at the restaurant, reached forward and swept her son into her arms. "Of course you're coming. The three of us are going. We couldn't leave our darling child at home. Couldn't have you miss all that food, the paellas, the seafood and olives, and the scenery, the beautiful beaches and the glorious mountains, or the people."

Mani pulled back from his mother's clutches, his brown eyes large on his face. He was maturing in his looks, his face thinning to look more like his father, though it was apparent he would be thicker in build than his wiry Dad. His eyes stared beyond the room while he processed – Mani, always processing - this superb morsel of information. "Will I need to learn Spanish? I mean, do they even speak English over there?"

Peter rollicked into the room, bringing a waft of cigarette smoke with him. "You've got three months to learn it, boy," he said to Mani. "We'll get you a dictionary and a phrase book to translate."

"We'll learn the basics," Celia said. "I think we could get by. They would get loads of English-speaking tourists in the parts we're going. And if we have trouble with the language, your father can be our translator. The reason we're going is to celebrate his Spanish heritage. You'll know how to speak to your Spanish brothers, won't you Peter darling? It's in your blood." She flung him a cheeky smile.

"Spanish brothers! Have you got brothers over there, Dad? Like, family?"

"Not actual brothers, lad. Your Mum's a stirrer." Peter smiled back at his wife. She was playful, and he was willing and up for her games. "She means a brotherhood of Spanish men. That's my history. My bloodlines."

Mani was wide-eyed with excitement. He could not absorb this news. Could not believe he was included. He had never expected he would ever go overseas for anything. He'd never even been out of Queensland. The furthest he had travelled was up to the Sunshine Coast, when they had a day at Coolum Beach and travelled home to Brisbane after fish and chips for lunch, going home via Nambour to go past some of Celia's old favourite places from her childhood. The home she grew up in was now in different hands and overhauled by renovation since her father died and her mother moved to beachside Caloundra. Mani saw the emotion and youthful excitement in his Mum that day as she reminisced over her simple childhood in that country town.

Now he was going travelling farther than he could have conceived, and on a jet airplane. His excitement bubbled up as stood in the kitchen with his parents.

"But you could have relatives over there, Dad."

"Maybe, you never know."

This planted a seed in Mani's mind. "I'm calling Jason to tell him. I can't believe I'm going overseas. Can I use the phone, Mum?"

None of Mani's friends had been overseas. Jason hadn't. One kid at school went to Fiji one school holidays and another girl's family had gone to New Zealand to attend a funeral. But now Mani's mind was being opened to the wider realm of global life. Expo had helped with this, having brought thousands of tourists from dozens of countries to Brisbane. It was becoming more regular to see Japanese and Vietnamese families and groups throughout the city, immigrants now calling Brisbane home. He had visited the Expo pavilions of countries he could identify by name but had little idea of their location or culture. Nepal, Pakistan, Yugoslavia and Hungary. And of course, now Spain edged to the front of his cognition, more important and real than just a stamp in his ersatz Expo passport.

His mind drifted to his future. His past scrambled to keep up, not wanting to be swamped by Mani's new awareness. He thought of Alison Archer, wherever she was. Up at the Sunshine Coast, maybe back in Brisbane, who knows where she might now live. He would see her again. She would hear his stories one day, of his enjoyment of Expo, his tour of Spain. Had she been overseas? Often he would think of her, keeping her image alive in his mind. She would be different now; it had been close to a year since he last saw her. But the vision was powerful, the feeling of fate conspiring to bring them back together was all too real, tangible enough for Mani to maintain his vigil for Alison. He would keep his memories for her, to share at the inevitable time in the future when they met as friends, soul mates, forever.

Mani rang Jason. He could not believe it. "Man, you are lucky. Your parents must be loaded to be able to take you to Spain. Do you even know where it is? It's like, over the other side of the world. In Europe."

"I know it's in Europe, but that's all I know. Mum said there are olives, which doesn't excite me. And bullfighting, I know they do that there. Now, Jas, keep Saturday morning free. I've got an idea. Get a leave pass from your Mum. I need you to help me with something."

Mani spent the entire following week reading everything he could about Spain. He leant on Ben Pedley to let him use his library card to borrow some additional books which would have been beyond Mani's borrowing limit. Mani read excerpts from these numerous varied books – histories, travel reviews, he garnered an understanding of Spain's political position, read of the island beauty that is Majorca and of the rolling hills beyond

Barcelona that undulated all the way into the city before crashing like waves into the sea.

He learnt that Spain was about to hit the world stage with Expo 92 at Seville and the Olympics at Barcelona. He read of the rich sporting history of Spain and the legendary sportsman who hailed from these ancient and historical lands – Ballesteros, del Bosque and Aragones. And of the one of the great rivalries in sport, that of FC Barcelona and Real Madrid and their battles in El Clasico. He ingested the history of Columbus's travels, the art of Dali and Goya, the Spanish Armada's challenge on England, the dictatorship of Franco and the 15th century religious cleansing by the Spanish Inquisition.

Mani became, in the space of a few short days, an expert on all things Spain. He daydreamed of his impending visit. Sometimes Alison Archer was there with him, though occasionally it was a brown skinned Spanish version of the girl he knew. Yet the feelings remained, the inevitability of their union in place as before. With all his reading, all he'd seen and learnt in the past year, the natural maturation and growth of a young teen, his body and mind stretching toward its predestined capacity, Mani maintained his emotional vigil for a girl he had shared words with just twice. As though all this was for that moment when he met her again, as the man he wanted her to see.

****

The week flew by for Mani with all this study. On Saturday morning he met Jason near the Expo grounds on the Brisbane River's southern bank at the State Library. Mani wore multi-pocketed long cargo pants and carried a back pack containing notepads, sheets of paper in a clipboard and several pens. He carried a pencil behind his ear. He'd planned his day during the bus ride into the city.

Jason was already there, sitting on a step by the bland, concrete walls of the library and art gallery building. He was rugged up against the chill wind, not freezing, but as bad as it got in Brisbane. "So, I assume this has to do with your Spanish trip.

You want to find out more about the country. What are we doing?"

"Research," Mani replied. "Lots of it. And I already know just about everything there is to know about Spain. This is something different. Let's go in. I'll tell you on the way."

"Great. It's the weekend and you want me to spend it studying."

Mani ignored that and strode up the stairs. By the time he had reached the main counter of the reference library, he had explained to Jason what he'd planned.

They approached the counter. A thin librarian lady with glasses – was there any other kind – fussed behind the desk. She put aside a pile of cards and straightened some encyclopaedic-sized volumes before looking up and smiling glibly. "How can I help you boys?"

"Good morning, Miss," Mani started. "My Dad is Spanish. At least his grandfather was. I was wondering how we could find any relatives still living in Spain. We're going there soon for a holiday."

The boys watched in quiet amazement as the lady tapped at buttons and the computer before her spat back menus. Jason elbowed Mani in the ribs, nodded his head in the direction of this modern marvel of convenience. Mani nodded back in acknowledgement. They watched her press 7 from the main menu, which took her to a sub-menu. She chose 6 – Family Name Searches, 6 again for Family History, then 2 for Births and Deaths. The grinding from the box seemed to lag for half a minute before lines of green text on black popped up on screen.

"OK, gents. Family reference, section 3. " She jotted some numbers onto a card. "Over by the windows to the far left. Here are the numbers you will need to find. Work along the aisles from the left wall. Ref number is 180-220, then it is alphabetical to search by name. Registers of births, deaths and marriages are the large volumes. If you need more dates and history, I can fetch a store of microfiche slides once you have narrowed down your search.

The boys squeaked their thanks and as they walked off, Jason said "How good was that? A computer tells us where we need to look."

"I know!" Mani said back. "And so quick too."

They spent the next two hours flicking through books, jotting notes, trying to reference the Alves name as far back as they could but it was proving quite difficult. They found themselves side-tracked by stories of their local suburbs when they were meant to be linking timelines of Mani's history.

Jason was getting bored. "You've got three months before you leave. That's plenty of time to find what you need. Let's go."

Mani was determined and pleading. "But we've only found my Grandad. We've got to find his father, then it gets hard. We have to switch the search overseas to Spain then. Come on, stick it out with me."

"What? More research? I'm out, Mani. Let's go get Cokes and listen to the screams from the theme park rides."

"You're not bailing on me, are you?"

"Sorry, mate. Why don't you just tell him his Great Grandad is the King of Spain and get them to go past his castle in Barcelona."

"It'd be in Madrid," Mani corrected him.

"OK, Madrid. You know you're not related to the King of Spain." Jason laughed and gave his cousin a little playful shove.

"Yeah, I know," Mani shot back, giving Jason a jab in the ribs. "Because if I was any kind of royalty, you wouldn't have your head."

Mani was determined. He felt the trip needed to have more context than simply being a tour to Spain because some old bloke that no-one in the family knew had originated there. He needed more meaning. And this meaning was being sought through genealogy. He would trawl back to the figure emerging from the primordial sludge if he needed to.

It became an obsession over the next weeks. Searching these volumes, all along imagining life for his father in the fifties and sixties growing up. His father's father living through the war. Afternoons for Mani were spent reading articles on microfiche about life in Brisbane and North Queensland in the seventies and earlier, working his way back to references of the Alves name.

Eventually he found his man. He discovered his father had been christened Pedro in 1948 (he hadn't known this, it made him giggle but he knew he was on the right path, Pedro being a very Spanish name.) Pedro's father was Carlos, whom Mani knew to look for from his father's information. He was born in 1930 but died a young man before Mani was born. Mani's readings uncovered that Carlos was a very good footballer, a regular fighter and worked up and down the coast including in the Central Queensland mines. He had remarried after separating from Peter's mother but had remained close with the teenaged Peter.

Peter had also told Mani to seek out the name Stani Alves, Peter's grandfather. Carlos was born to Stani, but the birth certificate officially listed Stani as Stanley Alves. His curiosity raised by this decidedly un-Spanish name, Mani kept his search up, keeping his findings confidential until he had firmed the trail. He wanted answers, thinking 'King Stanley of Spain' lacked a certain something.

He dug deeper.

The breakthrough came when he discovered the overseas link. Stanley's father had landed in Australia in the year of our Federation, 1901, curiously on a boat from Britain. His name – Alastair Alves. Mani's head was exploding. There would not be one single Alastair in all of Spain. The search had become murky; there was mud in the water nourishing his family tree.

Alastair must have had a lonely boat trip out to Australia for it appeared one of his first acts upon docking on Aussie soil was to knock up a local Sydney girl named Millie. More research indicated Millie was Aboriginal. They married and moved to North Queensland, after which the trail blurred. So the pure Spanish bloodlines of the Alves family were not so Spanish. Mani had Aboriginal blood coursing through his veins courtesy of great-great-Grandma Millie. He suddenly felt a pride, a connection. He was an indigenous Australian man.

He needed clarification, but could not let this very large cat out of the bag to his parents. His alternative source of information to fill in some gaps came from Carlos' second wife. He wrote to Alice Alves at her Mackay address. Weeks passed, hopes faded until one day the response came. Call her, Alice wrote. It's too complicated to put in a letter.

Mani was on the blower the first chance he got. Peter and Celia were out for a Friday night dinner. He was supposed to be doing homework but instead called Alice in Mackay, North Queensland.

"You're the boy who sent me the letter. We're not family you know, we just got the same last name," she said, most straightforward.

"I know. You were married to my grandfather."

"Yes, he died a long time ago. I used to see a lot of your Dad. How is he? Still a wild thing?"

"Pretty much. He works for himself now."

"How old are you boy? And what you doin' chasin' around after dead people, ay?" Alice spoke directly, no crap with her, Mani could tell. Her voice was drawled, the words delivered a smidgin slower than city voices.

"I'm thirteen and a quarter," Mani replied. "Just doin' some research." Mani slipped into speaking as Alice did.

"Well, I don't know how much I can tell ya. He was a good man, your grandfather. He died before you were born. Was a bit like your Dad turned out. Liked a good time, liked a fight. He worked hard, did Carlos, but he could tell a story, that man. Spin a yarn that would make your head spin off its shoulders, roll around the room with stupidity and then tie it all back together with your head back in place. Incredible stories, you know."

"My Dad talks a lot, too," Mani said. He listened to more background on Carlos, writing down all he could. Alice got him giggling with her anecdotes of Carlos. Neither the old woman from Mackay nor the young city boy realised how cathartic it was for them both. Ten minutes passed.

"Alice," Mani said. "I can't stay on the phone too long. What I really need to find out is about Carlos' Dad, Stani. Stanley. And his parents too. Where are they from?"

"Stani spent his life as a bullshit artist, from what I can tell. He denied his blackfella heritage. He was born to a Scotsman and a dark lady. It explains the dark skin he had. But he didn't wanna identify with either – not Scottish like his Dad or Abo like his Mum. Decided he wanted to be seen as Spanish for some stupid reason, concocted a story to win the attention of some lady so he sold himself off as a suave Spaniard and went by Stani for most of his adult life."

"So I'm Scottish and Aboriginal," Mani mused, putting it all together in his brain.

"There ain't no Spain in your background, let me make that quite clear," Alice resumed. "I don't know enough of the whole story. It only got told here and there in the time I was with Carlos. But the short version from the start was that Alastair's ship landed in Sydney, he and Millie moved to Cairns for work in the cane-fields. He married her but he nicked off when Stanley was six, back to New South Wales. Like he wanted to reset himself and start his Aussie trip over again. Married again and had more kids and never was heard of again. So Stanley grew up in Cairns with Millie, who never re-married but had more kids herself."

"Carlos told me that Stanley moved to Townsville. He made a fair bit of money selling cars I believe, based himself in Townsville after all that, got married and had Carlos and his two brothers. Carlos was the youngest and the hardest. But as all Alves men seem to do, Stani died young, before your father was born and Carlos had him when he was only eighteen, so Carlos lost his father at a very young age for a boy to lose his Dad."

Mani absorbed these discoveries, assessed the meaning of all this and the impact on his own identity. Manual Alves was a distinctly Spanish name, as was Pedro and Carlos before him. How would this revelation be accepted within his family, particularly as the Spanish trip was only eight weeks away? He checked with Jason the next day.

"Don't tell anyone," Jason advised. "It'll freak them out. Tell them you lost the trail."

"I just don't think you can keep that sort of thing from a person. They have a right to know."

"Mani, your Dad has based his whole life around being a Spanish man. A bullfighter, a Latin lover. He named you with a

Spanish name. You can't destroy a man like that. He'll change your name to Jock and start wearing a kilt if he thinks he's Scottish. You'll start having to eat haggis for dinner and your old man will be 'Och Aye, Jimmy-ing' all over the place."

Days passed with Mani thinking. He needed to decide if this secret stayed with him. Sleepless nights were spent mulling over whether to put an end to the Spanish lie or to kill dead the Scottish lines. Mani's young face gradually showed the stress of the weight he was carrying in his family's name. Tired eyes on a drawn face. Finally, three days of internal conjecture later, he rang Jason with his decision.

"I can't live with the secret myself. I have to tell him."

"Ah Jesus, Mani," was Jason's forlorn reply. It was as if he might be losing his cousin to cancer not to Scotticism. "Tell your Mum. Then get the hell out of there while she tells your Dad."

His decision made to announce his findings, a weight lifted from Mani. It was enormous news – like announcing the findings of a Royal Commission or the dingo baby court case. All evidence tendered and considered, assumptions made and conclusions reached and now ready to announce the blockbuster results to an eager audience. Mani though, could not see this ending well for anyone, thinking the response from his father would be much as Jason anticipated. It would rock his world to its very core.

He had heard the saying 'Fact can be stranger than Fiction', however the richness of his family's ridiculous background story made Mani smile. Made him feel part of a unique sideshow, a life of vagaries and semi-truths that would stretch the mind of the greatest author. Yet these stories were his, of Mani's finding. He wrapped himself up in the Alves history, Spanish pride, black pride and Celtic pride holding him in.

****

"You will need to sit for this, darling. There have been some interesting developments."

Celia, immaculate at breakfast with her hair up and her face made up, came into the kitchen with Peter in tow. His mind was racing. Celia was on a mission this morning, and Peter felt a surge of anxiety bother his spine, tentacles of gravitas hollowing out his stomach. He wondered what he'd done, what Celia had found out. Mani hovered to the side of the kitchen as they entered, close to the door. Peter thought this strange.

Peter watched as Celia took a binder from Mani and lay out before him an array of photocopies, documents, certificates and a sheet of butcher's paper with a Nikko-ed family tree.

"What's goin' on?"

"We need to talk," Celia said.

Peter's mind galloped through his recent indiscretions, touched over the larger ones from further back. He was empty. He readied himself for the shock. Peter looked to Mani for clues, who cowered further against the wall. Celia's face was stolid, giving nothing away. That was the thing with Celia, Peter knew. She projected the ditzy image of the socialite housewife mother, but bubbling away underneath was the stoic, hard-edged and serious side that seemed to know how best to handle every situation. Peter had seen it at the Victory Hotel in 1972 and every day since and she was easy to love because she always had everything in hand. Under control. Her face now gave kind reassurance while still portraying that this was about to become a serious conversation.

"How well did you know your grandfather?" she asked.

Peter let out his breath, knowing this wasn't going to be anywhere near as bad as he thought, wherever it went. "Oh, geez, old Stani died when I was a boy. I don't remember him at all, but apparently he was well off. He visited me and bought me a budgie for my third birthday. He died soon afterwards. He was only fifty. That's the thing with us Alves men, we die young. In ten years I'll be the longest living of the lot of us, touch wood. Must be the fiery Spanish blood."

Celia glanced at Mani and pulled a sorrowful face, a satirical grimace. "Mani's been doing some research as you know, and he's uncovered something. Something pretty big."

"Don't tell me he's still alive," said Peter. "Couldn't be. He'd be eighty-seven years old!"

"He's not alive, darling."

"You're not gonna tell me he's not my grandfather, are ya? Or he was really a woman and was actually my grandmother."

Mani snorted at that one before restoring his serious demeanour.

"Spit it out love," Peter urged her. "What's up?"

So Celia spat it out. Peter sat wordless as she ran through the trail of evidence and supporting documents. "Carlos is your father. No doubting that. He was, as you knew, a good footballer and a bit of a lad about town in his younger days. I know you are very proud of your Dad's background."

Celia rubbed her husband's shoulder before continuing.

"And Stani is your grandfather, as is stated here," she highlighted and pointed to a photocopied sheet of paper, "on the birth certificate that he is Carlos' father."

"So I don't see any issue. What are you getting at?" Peter said.

"Here's where it gets clouded, darling. You see here it says 'Child's Father' on Carlos' certificate. It says Stanley, not Stani. His name was Stanley Alves."

"Stanley?" Peter mouthed, processing, linking, evaluating. "Not the most Spanish of names, but so what?"

Celia pointed out the next document, the birth certificate of Stanley. "Your great-grandmother was Millie, born on Palm Island, North Queensland. She was Aboriginal, Peter. She moved to Townsville, then south to Sydney. She met your great-grandfather Alistair, who was newly arrived to Australia on a boat from Glasgow via Southampton."

"So he was the one who brought us to this country," Peter enthused, before pausing, evaluating some more. "Hang on. Glasgow? That's Scotland. What was my great-grandfather...Alastair...doing in...Scotland...?" He stretched the words out as the realisation washed over him.

Celia cast a pensive look at Mani. They didn't need to say anything more. Didn't need to fill the gaps as Peter caught on. He ticked over these facts in his mind to arrive slowly, reluctantly, at his conclusion.

Peter had spent half a minute just looking down at the papers on the kitchen table. He leant back in his chair. He looked across to Mani, then to his wife. His face gave away nothing, inside, he was frenetic. "So, I'm Scottish. Alastair Alves. Stani, Carlos, Pedro, Manuel...we're actually from Celtic blood."

"I believe the Scottish pronunciation is simply Alves. One syllable." Mani spoke up at last, no longer a spectator.

"Alastair never professed to be Spanish," Celia said. "Stani chose to be Spanish."

"Holy Christ, I'm not Spanish! So it was Stani who changed the course of our family tree. He would have had the brown skin. And the name Alves would easily transfer to Al-vez." Peter shook his head in bewilderment, looked at his sympathetic wife and his newly British son.

"Sorry, Dad," Mani said. "I didn't mean to..."

"Don't worry, mate," Peter said to reassure Mani. "It's all right. It had to come out some time."

Mani squeezed out a nervous smile in response and took a step closer to the table.

"The silly old goose," said Peter. "He musta thought he could make more of himself as a debonair, exotic Spaniard. Here we are, we all thought we were El Toro and all along we were just tight, wee Scots with a bit of blackfella thrown in." He laughed, cackled. "Betcha he changed so he could win the affections of some young lady."

"It doesn't change a thing, Peter. We are still Al-vez. We are still going to Spain for a brilliant holiday. And we now have a funny story to tell others at parties." Celia putting the positive spin on things.

Mani chimed in too. "Means we'll have to have another trip next year to Scotland, I reckon."

Peter laughed along with them but underneath he bubbled with shame and anxiety. He suffered the family banter for a few more minutes, re-assuring Celia and Mani that all was fine and then went out for a smoke. "What the hell," he said. "It's only history. Only family. Doesn't make a shred of difference what those nutty fore-fathers did half a century ago. We're still us and we've still got our lives to get on with."

His eyes belied the hurtful truth though, and he kept them turned from the ever-alert Celia. A man has corner-stones on which he can lean, a history, a knowledge of who and where he is when he's lost his way. If circumstances yank at his fabric, he should have a family philosophy to fall back on, or to blame if things are unfavourable. The Alves way. The Spanish blood. That's the way us Alves men do things, or it's the European in me coming out. He'd said all these types of things at different times. Now his past was crumbled at his feet like the flaky shale rock of the Scottish Highlands. Here they were in a country settled by convicts and crooked lords, a country where they deified bushrangers and mistreated the indigenous inhabitants and Peter felt shame at the lies of his family's past. The lies that swooped in to diminish his beliefs and shred his internal composure.

Barcelona Dreamin'

The rise in the Alves family fortunes over the past eight months was best portrayed by their life during October 1988. Peter's monthly cheque from Bettalife had exceeded Ronan's for the first time, his downline flourishing and deepening to create a solid continuous flow of royalties. Final preparations were completed for their European trip and the final month of Expo 88 was a crescendo of celebration, spending, socialising, splurging, large living and more spending. The family had each collected the full complement of Expo passport stamps as well as having christened every restaurant with their presence.

This lavish and hectic period was given the ultimate exclamation mark when Mani, Peter and Celia arrived in Madrid, Spain with nearly empty suitcases. Then, led by Celia's eye for fashion and flair, they embarked on a spending spree throughout the local mercado. They began their sight-seeing tour decked out in the latest vogue of Spanish-influenced Euro fashion.

Mani felt ridiculous. He didn't mind the lime Ralph Lauren polo shirt with the mauve popped collar. It was the rest of his ensemble that bothered him. His Mum had insisted he wear his newly-purchased clothes for this day's excursion. He objected to the straight-leg tan knicker-bockers. He argued against the two-tone leather loafers. He tolerated the Le Specs mirror sunglasses, but battled hard against the hairdo. As mothers do, Celia won out and Mani had his hair greased back with BrylCreem.

Self-consciously, he walked behind his parents as they ticked off their list of must-see attractions. Just because they were in Spain, he thought to himself, why did they have to try to look Spanish, particularly when they were Scottish Aborigines? His father had even grown his moustache long over the past three months and he'd used the BrylCreem to twirl it into a crazy little Dali-esque mo. Why couldn't they just be themselves – Australians on holiday?

During the morning though, Mani began noticing some unusual happenings. He saw other teenage boys dressed like him, but doing it with some panache. With confidence. Not tiptoeing along tucked in behind their parents as Mani had been, trying his best to stay out of view. He also noticed something else. This had never happened back home. No-one at Kenmore did this – either at school or at the shops. This never happened! Mani noticed a girl looking at him. Not just once. Twice!

Initially he thought they had to be laughing at his unusual stylings. When it occurred a third time, this time a double look from a pair of teenage girls just older than Mani. They giggled and when Mani looked over one of them gave him a nervous smile while the other unashamedly looked him up and down, nodding and raising her eyebrows as she smiled at him.

Emocionado!!

Mani's back instinctively straightened, the head began nodding ever so slightly as he walked. The chest out, a slight wiggle in his stride. All of a sudden he didn't mind these new threads. Why shouldn't he look good, he decided. His old man had made him suffer through regular exercise sessions and he was strong through the torso, no fat on him despite his bulk. He was big and with these clothes he was handsome. The chinos accentuated his strong thighs and buttocks. His biceps filled his sleeves. His body was maturing – he'd discovered that in no uncertain terms in recent months – and all of a sudden Mani felt good about himself.

He was Mani Alves, a descendant of Scottish/Spanish/Aboriginal Australian heritage. No-one was like him. He could have been a local, a kid from one of the wealthy families of the Spanish aristocracy, a high-born Madrid incumbent, royalty even, dressed in his casual finery to impress the gentrified local ladies.

He wasn't Mani, the kid from Kenmore with spitballs in his hair anymore. He didn't need to be that. He could choose what he was, who he was. This was his time. A time of discovery, a tour of fulfilment and awareness. He would be whoever he wanted over the next three weeks; he could build a new Mani, one of his own making and his choosing. He could construct him, perfect him, box him up and deliver him back home to Kenmore, a worldly, stylish sophisticated version of the young man who left town after Expo.

"Mani," Peter growled. "Stop dawdling and keep up. And why are you walking like that?"

His Dad, trying to burst Mani's bubble. This was the test, the moment of truth. Could his new persona withstand the scorn? Would the structure hold?

"Because I'm an Alves, Dad. I'm a proud Spanish man on holiday, enjoying the sights at my own pace."

Mani could see his father was taken aback. He waited for a dressing down, maybe a clip behind the ear for his backchat. It didn't come.

Instead, Peter laughed. "That's my boy. That's the spirit!" He put a hand on Mani's shoulder, looking into his eyes with a proud smile.

Peter then turned to Celia. "Well, Ceels. Whattya reckon? I think the boy's onto somethin'. No need to scurry around like Aussies on a quick holiday. Let's embrace the local feel, the culture. Take our time. Dawdle if we wanna, and let's get some of Mani's swagger into us."

From then on it was holidaying Alves-style. No panicked rush to visit every historical relic or see every museum, lining up in the hot sun with the other tourists. There'd be none of that. They tread their own path, sat where the locals congregated, ate the local food, drank their coffee. They ventured north after several days in Madrid. Pamplona, in a basin valley at the foot of the Pyrenees near the French border, stunned them with its medieval feel, the narrow cobbled streets on which they retraced the footsteps of Hemingway. They followed the footsteps of grand tourists from centuries before as they swooned east to Barcelona, then south to Granada with its cavernous Gothic renaissance cathedral and on to Seville, where the 1992 Expo would be held.

It was in Barcelona that Mani had an interaction that would forever alter both him and the Alves family. It was their first day in the city, having caught a train from Pamplona. They had booked into their hotel in the old city district of Ciutat Vella. It was late afternoon, so to stretch their legs and get their bearings, the trio went for a stroll. As they wandered, they inevitably separated, spread out amongst the stalls of a street market.

It seemed to have sprung up on a whim – tents and tarpaulins of various ages and states of repair leant against one another along a laneway. There was fresh food being sold. Sweet potato, eggplant with its aubergine skin, the reddest tomatoes on the planet, cobs of corn, red and green chillies of all sizes, an array of spices, fruit of all varieties. In another tent, a man grilled pancakes, which he sold dusted in sugar and with a line of honey, filling the street with a crispy sweet aroma. Other stalls offered books, cassette tapes, potted seedlings, trinkets and handmade jewellery. A man dressed as a 'torero' sketched mug shots for just 600 pesetas, which Mani gleaned was about $5 at home. Another stallholder made his living selling Barcelona snowglobes.

As Mani dawdled through the market he hugged his money belt close to his chest under his shirt. His Mum and Dad, now ahead of him and finding their own interests in this jumbled collection of goods and local salesmen, had warned him about pickpockets, so that his paranoia was piqued.

Mani ducked under an awning as he entered a metal-framed stall with a grimy green canvas tarpaulin over the top. As he browsed the piles of merchandise – stacked books written in Spanish, boxes of hand-made leather wallets, notebooks, leather belts, hats, wristbands and armguards of pressed leather etched with patterns and scenes – the stall owner emerged, almost magically, from behind a makeshift counter. Mani jumped in shock.

The stall owner was a large man with a bald pate. His face seemed to have dripped down from his bald head like melted wax. His brow had a deep V-ish furrow above and between his eyes through which his face seemed to have channelled and spread. His long flat nose swayed down his face like the boxer he must once have been and the waxy skin of his cheeks cascaded down his face in lines and waves and rolls, breaking into thick jowls above the white collar of his shirt.

Mani smiled nervously and nodded a greeting. He picked something up to look at, anything to stop himself staring at the strange Spaniard manning the stall. Mani's hands held a leather-bound journal.

"Good price," the stall owner said, in Spanish.

Mani shook his head in confusion and gestured to his mouth.

"Good price." In English this time. "Hemp pages. Bound strong and leather to protect it. A beautiful piece and only 600 pesetas."

Mani mumbled something about just looking. The man had come in front of the table of books now. He was heavily-built, Mani saw, and his body arched to carry his enormous stomach, out of shape in his post middle age. Despite this, he retained formidable forearms, rippling and bulging as if built. Mani stared, imagining he had robotic hydraulics installed under the skin of these noticeable canisters below his elbows. The arms and stubby fingers of his powerful hands were the result of years as a stallholder, lugging his treasures from truck to tent on a daily basis. The rest of his body was testament to his love of the rich market food.

"Oh, no, it's alright," Mani said. "I'm just looking."

"Your accent. You're not English. What is that accent?"

"I'm Australian."

"Holidaying. Very good. You're very young. Are you travelling alone, no?"

"With my parents. They're just up there." Mani put the book down, suddenly wary. "I'd better see where they are."

"Wait boy," the big man demanded. Mani flinched. "This book, this journal. You wish to buy? Very good price."

"No, I haven't..."

"On holidays," the man interrupted. "How do you think you will remember all you see? All the sights and sounds, the smells, these little things. You must write them down. You record it in a book like this. A journal, what you say...a chronicle. Very good memories."

"Like a diary?" Mani said, becoming interested.

"Exactly! A diary. Memories. No regrets. Come on, boy. Very good price for you."

Mani ran his fingers over the leather cover, the etched pattern. He was thinking he'd buy it, a very adult decision, made on his own, for himself. The new action man Mani.

"Deal!" he said. "600 pesetas!"

"No deal," the stall-owner growled.

"What?" Mani said. "But the sign says..."

"Very silly boy. Yes, it says 600 pesetas on the sign. Never pay the price on the sign." He smiled then and gestured with his meaty hands. "You must haggle. Always in life, haggle. Negotiate. Don't pay me 600 pesetas, tell me you only pay 400 pesetas."

Mani hesitated.

"Go on!" the large Spaniard said.

"I'll give you 400 pesetas for it."

"No deal. Sign says 600."

"But you said to haggle. You said to offer 400," Mani said in protest.

"I cannot sell for 400 pesetas. 550, my best price."

Mani caught on, the lesson sinking in. "450 pesetas. That's as high as I will go."

"Price is 550."

Mani reached into his wallet. "500 pesetas, it's all I have on me."

"Done," the salesman said. "500. Good price, sold. Well done, young man!"

"Are you nuts? I was going to pay you 600, but you talked me down to 500."

"Never pay 600 in life. Haggle always. I don't need the extra money. I am already rich, because I haggled when I was young. And I wrote everything down. You should write this down in your new diary, so you don't forget."

Mani smiled. "I will. I'll write it in my new diary. Thank you, sir."

"What is your name, boy from Australia?"

"Mani."

The man held out his huge paw and shook Mani's hand. "Have a good holiday, Mani."

He would faithfully record everything from that point on, the remainder of his holiday documented to the finest detail so he would not forget. He kept his eyes sharp and his pen handy so he would always recall the smells of street-side barbecuing, the name of the store from which he bought turrón -a Spanish nougat - or their visit to an olive oil farm and factory in a wonderfully preserved 15th century mill on the outskirts of Granada. He noted the chants and music of a street parade in Seville, the atmosphere of the bullring, the fans waving their white handkerchiefs in appreciation of the torero's bravery. On their last day before flying out of Madrid, they witnessed an unruly soccer mob on their way to a game at the Bernabéu Stadium.

It was a tour that Mani could not ever forget. A teenager's privilege that would shape a man, instilling in Mani the love of detail, words and vision. And through it all he would remember the lesson of the large, bald, wave-faced stall-owner and wonder what kismet allowed their paths to cross.

Divergent Fortunes - 1989

"Have a look at this, Mani. See this cheque here?" Peter said showing his son the slip of printed paper. His Bettalife bounty had arrived and he now received cheques in multiple currencies, reflective of the international spread of his downline. "This cheque is for £350, that's something like $800. I got this cheque because I talked to one man at Expo and told him how to do business."

Mani nodded his head in appreciation of his Dad's skills. It was school holidays and the new year promised much for the invigorated Mani Alves. He would start year 10 at Westside State High School in two weeks. He would begin the year as arguably the top student in his grade after thoroughly acing all his end of year exams for the end of grade 9. The European trip had enhanced his coherence of life and the larger world, broadened his mind so that the concepts of the year 9 curriculum seemed quite basic for this worldly young man.

The upcoming school year also held a particular intrigue for Mani. Just as the previous year's return to school had yielded the agony of loss through Alison Archer's move to the Sunshine Coast, so Mani hoped that a new year might deliver her back to Kenmore. Back to him. Maybe beach life hadn't agreed with her mother or the Caloundra finance industry was in the doldrums and the powers that be at the bank saw better use of the bank managerial skills of Mr Archer back in Brisbane.

Mani knew anything was possible but his hopes were low. Mani was flanking that age when little boy hopes and dreams crash into the truth of reality. He doubted the world would be so kind to him. Yet he held fast to the Alison dream – imagining her, visualising her, recalling her bouncy walk, her smile, the brown skin, her fit legs, pony-tailed blonde hair and the pure cuteness of her rainbow-laced tennis shoes. He clung hard to the mirage, the memory.

"And look Mani," his father continued as they sat together at the table. It was lunchtime, Celia was making sandwiches for them while Peter flipped open the mail. "French francs! I haven't even been to France and I'm getting a cheque from 'em. Think I'll go buy me some frog's legs."

"Pretty amazing Dad. But how do you get a cheque from France when you don't even speak French? Who wrote the cheque out to you?"

"France is one of the offices for Bettalife. Paris, I'd say, but I'm not certain. But the fella I yabbered to in Madrid has obviously spread the word. There's no office in Spain so he would have to place his orders through France or London. I suppose that's how it come around, but in saying that, coulda been anyone who had a Froggy mate who signed up. That's the beauty of the business. It spreads itself. A bit like cow dung, hey. Who knows where the cow's gonna poop!" He cackled and coughed, such a familiar routine. You knew when Peter had finished speaking – it always ended with a joke and his phlegmy cackle.

"France is next to Spain, isn't it?" Mani's mind was ticking, putting it all together.

"Right next door," Celia answered as she delivered the cold roast lamb sandwiches.

"That's what I find incredible. These amazing countries right next to each other. Like Queensland is next to New South Wales. But these are crazy, historic countries that you read about in books and in the news, like they are so far away, but they are right next to each other. France and Spain and Italy and Germany. All so close."

Celia nodded her head, seeing the expansion of her son's incredulous mind. "It's a fascinating part of the world. So ancient and wondrous!"

"I just hope they're all close enough to spread the word about Bettalife. Keep them wondrous cheques rollin' in, hey Ceels." Again with the cackle. "Don't forget, we visited all those countries. We've got proof. They're stamped in our Expo passports."

"Yeah, good one Dad. I haven't even been to Victoria but that's like a Spanish kid going to Italy. Or a kid in London going to Paris. Just so close. I think I'd like to go and live there one day."

The wise fourteen-year old, his hair still slicked back with Euro style and his baby face hardening and showing more definition.

They all reached for a sandwich as Celia sat with her men. She too had mail and as Peter crumpled his used envelopes and collated his cheques neatly for his personal viewing pleasure, Celia flicked open her own envelope which was addressed in a flamboyant hand. It was a card. "Oh," she said with a song in her voice. "This is nice."

"What is it Mum?"

"It's a card from the Marlows. Remember I helped Laura with planning her own trip to Europe. I just gave her a few ideas and tips. It's a thank you card and a gift voucher for $100 from Myer. Isn't that nice?"

When Peter heard money, he glanced up, his attention grabbed. "A hundred bucks! Geez you must have made an impression, Ceels."

"Apparently so. She says they had such a wonderful time and it was like they had got professional help."

"Did they go to Spain?" Mani asked.

"Yes, Spain, south of France and across to Italy. I put together a list of to-do's, helped her with the accommodation and connections. Found her a couple of tours."

"So ya pretty much did everything for them but pack their bags," Peter summarised.

"I just thought I was being helpful, seeing we had just got back. I wasn't expecting all this."

"Well, I'll give ya a lazy hundred if you wanna plan another trip for us, love. I hear Greece and Italy are beautiful at this time of year."

"Dad! It'd be snowing over there right now. It's the middle of winter."

"Well your Mum will organise the best time to go, seeing she's so good at it. I'll give you the hundred bucks, sweetheart and how about I pay for your trip as well. You know I'd go nowhere without my beautiful wife and everywhere with her. Plus I'm already bored being back in Brisbane."

"There you go, Mum. You're in business. Getting paid to take holidays." Mani was joking along with his Dad, but through the lunchtime mirth, Mani saw a contemplative look cross his mother's face as she eased out a proud smile.

****

Mani smiled to himself. Around him the hustle and bustle of Brisbane airport played out. Worried faces trying to make sense of the flight list boards, the joy of people about to embark on a long-awaited dream trip, other smiles from returning travellers seeing family again. Middle-aged men trying to put their backs out heaving suitcases for which they'd over-estimated their strength. Reckless Asian tourists slamming over-filled trolleys into already swollen ankles. Messy hair on their way back in to the country, fresh expectant faces on their way out.

Mani's smile reflected the paradox that just once had he been over the Queensland-New South Wales border and not having set foot in any other Australian state, he was about to jet off for his second European tour in eight months.

'Celia Italia' had launched in mid-January and if anything, Mani's mother had usurped her husband's prowess in spreading the word. Her new venture would run tours of the Mediterranean nations with everything organised – just pay your dollars and pack your bags. She had begun research the day after their lunchtime discussion, slept on the idea and woke up invigorated and supremely motivated.

Mani had been a key plank in her research effort. She dragged him to libraries and travel agencies where she picked the expert's brains by pretending to be a prospective customer. She'd studied the tourist hot-spots in Western Europe and decided she would focus her business on the Mediterranean trio of France, Spain and Italy, her designated first trip. By digging through travel guides and tour brochures she found the name of a bus company in Milan and after some expensive ISDN calls, she had gained the trust and friendship of Roberto, the fleet manager of VerdeBiancoRosso Bus Company, who said if she ever needed a bus, favourable rates would apply.

Hurdle number one cleared. She had transport.

With the help of Roberto, she had gathered the names of villa owners in the countryside and further scrutinised the attractions that would be the foundation of her tours. *Celia Italia*, the international brand funded by Peter Alves' Bettalife efforts, laid out a tentative date of June 7th, 1989 for its flight from Brisbane to Milan. The itinerary would include Milan, the northern Lakes district, Venice of course, Bologna to Florence to Pisa, then south through the Tuscan hills finishing with three days and nights in fabulous Rome. Seventeen nights in total. Her strategy to minimise costs was to house her guests in villa accommodation on the outskirts of the major cities. With lower prices than large city hotels, the tour could add value with another day of sightseeing in each area by using the train system to enter the cities.

Celia read voraciously, aiming to be a most knowledgeable guide despite this being her first trip to Italy. Living with Peter, she had an expert to teach her the art of 'fake it until you make it'. She studied the food, the wines of the Barolo region and the excellent Chianti, learnt of all the major artworks they would visit, the magnificent architecture and the history of all the great artists. The Duomo in Florence, the statue of David, that marble marvel, the Pantheon in Rome, the medieval fortifications of Lucca and of course the fresco of the Sistine Chapel.

After all the itineraries were set, her accommodation contacts secured and the group flight prices guaranteed, she needed to find some clients. She worked out that she needed a minimum of twelve paying customers to make a small profit while also covering the costs of Celia and Mani to travel.

"Best way to sell something is to talk to people you know," Peter offered as advice. "Everyone knows someone who wants what you've got to sell. That's what worked for me and look how quick Bettalife has grown. Get out and talk, Ceels. Flap the ol' jawbone. Surely some of your society girls will be up for a quick flit over to Europe."

Still, Celia felt she needed a brochure to give *Celia Italia* credibility. Mani and Jason teamed their creative skills to design a beautifully worded and attractively illustrated brochure for Celia to flaunt. She needed just a fortnight to close the bookings for this voyage, it being over-subscribed with those on the waitlist suggesting they would love to be on the next one. From little things, big things grow. *Celia Italia* confirmed a second European summer tour of Italy for September 1989, even before word had come back on how the inaugural tour went.

So here they were, Celia and Mani along with the sixteen guests of *Celia Italia*'s maiden expedition, tickets in hand. Mani watched his mother fuss over her charges. He had slung over his shoulder a single strap carrybag and in his hand, also making a return journey to Europe, he had his trusty and partially filled journal. Bought from Barcelona and now making its way to Milan. Storied of the sights of Seville and Granada's toreros and soon to include the grandeur of Tuscany and the ruins of Rome. It was a precious and inspiring artefact leading Mani into adulthood.

The image of teen Euro cool had been restored in Mani's image and he had decided the look would stay. The girls of Kenmore had ensured this with their reactions being similar to the young ladies of Madrid. He would take Milan by storm, filling his journal with wonderful memories. He would certainly require a second journal before it was all over.

Mani Alves, who had spent most of his fourteen years turned inside out with fear of being the centre of attention, paralysed with uncertainty as to how he should act, now craved experience, yearned to be amongst the action, to be noticed. He felt he belonged. He felt invincible. And this second trip to Europe would help to etch out his true self.

****

Peter had opted to stay home. Though he enjoyed Spain, the hassle and hustle of walking all day, packing, jumping on buses and trains with suitcases, all the functions of being an overseas traveller had lost their shine. He couldn't lift himself for another effort so soon knowing he would be a drag on Celia's high energy outlook. He could also use a little man-time, around which a very important event had to be squeezed in.

Bettalife were having their health symposium on the Gold Coast and they had invited Peter to present his secrets of recruiting to the assembly. There would be distributors from across Australia and this being the only conference this year in this part of the world, there would be representatives from Asia and New Zealand in attendance as well as selected big wigs from the company headquarters in California.

With Celia gone, Peter was officially 'bach-ing it', an instant, effortless flip to a hard-drinking, slobbish, schnitzel-eating single man. The house was his domain for close to three weeks and its deteriorating condition in Celia's absence divulged the extent of her regular housework. Peter saw no need for clean-ups. There were no visitors expected so he could clean it before the family came home.

He had prepared a talk, practised his lines, re-worked his jokes. It was important he aced this presentation because though he was performing brilliantly – his earnings now pipped even Ronan's at more than $6,000 per month – he was well aware of the need to build the skills of his downline as his organisation grew. He was a member of the Bettalife Success Team now and apart from presenting, Peter was included in a strategic offsite planning session to drive the success of the business.

It was at this session on the first day of the seminar that Peter saw Ronan who had been decidedly low-key.

"Ronan, me old mate. Good to see you here. Let me introduce Geoff Penman, one of my new guns. Not directly under me in the business but we're working closely. Geoff - Ronan's one of the heavy hitters, introduced me to the business and knows all there is to know. Stick close and you might learn some tricks."

The men shook hands.

Peter kept talking excitably. "I tell ya, Ronan, this is a great event. It's pretty bloody exciting thinking how big it could grow and where it can go. Seeing the international guys here, too. I'm more excited than a fat kid in a pie shop. I was tellin' Geoff here how you were sayin' how business spikes once everyone gets fired up by these conventions. Tell him, Ronan. How rich are we all gonna get?"

The response was lukewarm. Ronan looked tired, Peter thought, his face drawn. Something was on his mind.

"Just keep the lips moving and tell the story one more time," he said grimly. "Look Peter, I've got someone I need to meet. I'll catch ya later."

"Yeah, no worries mate. I'll be round like a rissole. See ya in the big show." Nothing was going to dim his enthusiasm.

With a nod of his head to Geoff, Ronan was gone. Peter thought it was the most subdued he'd ever seen his normally effervescent salesman friend. He erased the odd encounter from his mind. He was buzzing with anticipation about being on stage as one of the company leaders. He elbowed his way into the free coffee table, dumping three heaped sugars into his third cup of the day.

The AM session went without a hitch as the dignitaries acknowledged some outstanding local performers. Peter imbibed another coffee and found a bar to slip a beer into his system to calm his nerves before presenting a 45 minute session on recruiting to a highly-charged crowd. They bestowed a rock-star reception, Peter lapping up the adulation, firm in his place as one of the rising stars of Bettalife. Lunch break was spent in the resort's a la carte restaurant enjoying a steak and another beer before the Success Team breakout session.

It was then that Peter's world leant in upon itself, bowed, then buckled. It is said that man must go down to ashes to discover himself, to know his true self. This process is often one of loss, grief driven by the death or displacement of a loved one. Peter's descent was not borne of bad news from Italy of Celia or Mani. It was delivered by a white-toothed, perfectly-groomed salesman with a clip-on hairdo and a five-thousand dollar suit.

The words dug at him like an intruder with an ice pick. 'Accounting irregularities. Funds frozen. Trumped up charges. Payments withheld. Enforceable undertaking.'

"We can assure our investors, distributors and customers that we will be doing everything we can to clear our good name. We totally refute the myriad, mythical claims of the SEC. We are a legitimate business system. We acknowledge that pyramid and other Ponzi schemes are illegal and maintain that our products as well as our unique reward system are both legal and of the highest quality. Regrettably, as we deal with these allegations, payments to business owners and distributors will be put on pause. We expect this process to take no more than six months."

The murmurs of discontent welled up in the room. Peter slumped in his chair, devastated. He was grateful he'd just banked his cheques. He would now need to make it last. Remorse set in over the cash splash of recent months – the parties, the splurges, holidays, the costly drinking and eating out. The gravy train had limped into the station for long-overdue remedial work.

Peter did what he did best when confronted with such shocks. He drank. The next two days were spent drowning his proverbial sorrows, bending alcoholically out of shape in various bars and clubs of the Gold Coast before making his way back to Brisbane to continue his marathon binge. The grog helped him forget, anchored him to the time where he was still the rising business star. When he was hammered, he could maintain the image of wealth with cash to flaunt, finding drinking buddies to whom he could relate his tale of woe. $1000 in two days. So much for regrets, he had never produced a performance like it.

Things fell apart swiftly. With no family contact for four days, which was expected, and with this latest financial calamity, Peter lost grasp of his functions and faculties. His diet atrocious, the drinking, hygiene ignored and the house a mess. Bettalife gave supervisors a week's grace period to advise their teams before public disclosure, so Peter had just a day to gather himself.

It seemed that word had already filtered down among the teams. Peter's alcoholic fog lifted enough to start making calls. The message became clear and it wasn't pretty. He targeted his top ten producers to call, to discuss strategy and to reassure. Each time, the conversation went the same way.

"Peter Alves here. How did you enjoy the convention? Look, there's been a revelation. Bettalife is facing some ridiculous accusations and they are voluntarily putting a hold on doing business until they clear their name. No sales, no payments for a short while."

Oddly, the response was uniform. Across the board, the reaction was, "I understand. It's a real shame. What happens next?"

"As soon as we are open for business, I will let you know and we can run some meetings to re-focus, get things back on track."

"Sorry to hear the bad news. We're fully committed to the business and will await word from you."

The precise response from each of the first nine members he called. The answers as though scripted. His final call to Wilko had one difference. "Sometimes the kennel needs a good cleanout," Wilko said, "and that can mean a new top dog. We're all fully committed to a fresh new kennel, we hope Bettalife sorts this out and we will wait to hear from you."

Odd thing to say, Peter thought. He could see how it related to Bettalife cleaning up its act and addressing the allegations, but in combination with the stock answers, something didn't add up. It triggered some deep thought. He rang his mate Colin Farley."What's going on, Colin? I spoke with you and nine others and amazingly, you all came up with the same answer. The same wording. Is there something going on I should know?"

Colin's reply was delivered with a grim firmness. "It's not looking good for you, Pete. Business-wise, there's just been so much going on. I'm afraid it's going to end badly."

"Bettalife will straighten all this out. It'll be sorted in months, weeks maybe."

"Wrong, Peter! It's over. Your business has shot its load, mate. There's a reason everyone gave you the same answer and mine was the only genuine word you got."

"Whattya mean, Col?" Peter tugged at the curled telephone cord in distress, a bilious burn in his gut.

"Wilko's screwed ya, mate. Dunno how he knew what was coming, but he's been signing up your whole downline behind your back for weeks. A new business, a similar product but a better 'rem' plan. Everyone's gone over. Everyone except me cos I didn't want to rag on you, mate. God knows I shoulda signed, looking at how much better the rem is. Lucky for you, Pete, I'm two things – loyal as hell and already rich enough not to worry about an extra few grand here and there. Sorry to be the one to tell you, mate."

Peter bade farewell, dropped the phone cold and went to the bottle of Scotch in the kitchen. The realisation sank in. Even if Bettalife cleared its name, Peter would be left to start again. He would be left with the stragglers and non-performers in his decimated downline – the multi-level marketing flotsam and jetsam that Wilko did not desire to poach. And Peter knew deep down he had never been one to stand and fight, opting universally to move on rather than rebuild.

Sketchy details emerged over the following grog-fogged days. Wilko had been pressing the flesh with all new recruits in Peter and Ronan's downline, getting tight with them and asking them to look over the new plan he'd happened across. It was an easy sell – same work, better pay. All behind Peter's back and on his watch. Wilko could not have known that Bettalife was going to strike problems – it was just plain dumb luck that all the cards fell into his hand, the antithesis of the mongrel luck hand that Peter had been dealt.

The Writer

Grade Eleven for Mani had begun with its usual anticipation for it represented another chance that Alison Archer may arrive back at Westside State High School. She remained an absent fancy, a fading but not faded memory for Mani as he went about his life, still in her hold and at her service if she ever were to return. It hadn't stopped him living though. He had cemented his friendships among the Ben Pedley-led study group and they continued to collaborate on stories and short film scripts, as well as entering writing competitions.

Mani's size had seen him mix in other circles at school, encouraged and welcomed into the rugby team. He was no longer among the taller boys of his age, usurped by the growth spurts of beanpole kids, but he was of a formidable build, having thickened through the hips and buttocks yet still fit from his father's compulsion to exhort fitness. Mani's low centre of gravity made him an ideal metre-eater through the mid-field, difficult to tackle as he ploughed his bulk forward. His lamentable ball skills and lack of variety however made him useful to the team as little more than a battering ram. The novelty of getting lined up and belted soon wore off.

Pedley's crew were his main protagonists in the story of Grade 11 at Westside and Mani as a ready contributor to their projects, often at intellectual loggerheads with his firm friend. They would challenge each other with hypothetical scenarios based on world news.

"Which side of the Wall would you like to have been on?" Pedley asked once when the Berlin Wall was the enormous news story of the day.

Mani could maintain a highbrow conversation but often instilled some stupidity to re-direct the flow. "I am neither fascist nor communist nor necessarily capitalist, but I do know that Pink Floyd album sales are going to spike with this latest development."

"They should play 'The Wall' album on the Wall," Pedley stated.

"No chance. I think all the band members hate each other. Plus, how could a filthy-rich capitalist rock band slide into Germany and please either side of the political spectrum?"

"Speaking of capitalism, I read there were a lot of souvenir hunters chipping of chunks of wall to sell. 'Wall Woodpeckers' they call them. Do you think there'd be a market for chunks of the Berlin Wall?"

Mani leant down and picked up a rock from the footpath. "I haven't been to Berlin on my travels but here you go. Genuine artefact, a piece of the Wall from the pillar next to Checkpoint Charlie. It's yours for $50."

Pedley's look confirmed the no-sale.

Mani's experience had grown with his third - and *Celia Italia*'s fifth - European trip in the Euro summer of 1990. Celia's business had gone from strength to strength, increasing her clientele numbers and the size of the bus Roberto needed to provide. Her latest tour took in Rome, Florence, glorious Genoa, the Cote d'Azure in the south of France, north through the Loire Valley before flying out of Paris. A full subscription was now the business' expectation and two tours a year were fully booked for the foreseeable future. Celia had found the goldmine with a long-term lease that Peter had sought after and failed at for so long.

Peter had not felt emasculated because his woman was the main breadwinner. On the contrary, it suited him nicely to be a kept man enjoying two trips a year to the wine regions of the Mediterranean. It allowed him to indulge in the good life for which he aimed and to undertake hit and run missions on various sales jobs around Brisbane, making some quick dollars, burning through the customer base and departing the company in time for *Celia Italia*'s next sojourn, and before disgruntled customers had time to bog him down for falsities and failed promises. Six months at a time, long enough to keep the job fresh and be out before the drudgery set in. It was a classic semi-retirement. One could excuse Mani for buying into the oft-quoted mantra that 'Success is a Journey not a Destination', so often did his family land right way up plotting their volatile course through life.

He could not help but mature in this environment. By watching the up-up-ups and downs of his father and the craftiness of his mother's steady business acumen, he was learning from both their example and their mistakes. He was becoming a knowledgeable, well-rounded, confident and very likable young man, yet still maintained his candle for the worthwhile Alison Archer. There were no other romances on the horizon.

His experiences – through life, study and travel – scribed as memoirs in his journals, now reflected in the expanded stories he wrote. Travel reviews of exotic destinations, anecdotes, ruminations and random scenes, each a connection with a time, place or person from a different culture that impacted him. His style sprung forth as magnificently descriptive, florid even, and his scenes and characters easily visualised. Overall it was very readable work, except that no-one ever read it.

This changed one chilly July night. Not long after a *Celia Italia* tour, the Sharpes were invited to view the photo albums that Celia had constructed. Patricia and Graham had politely declined to commit to a European holiday despite Celia's urgings. Having seen the business form and grow, Patricia was proud and excited for her little sister, but the Sharpes were watching their pennies.

"Money's a bit tight. Graham thinks it a bit extravagant to go overseas. Maybe down the line when we've got on top of our loans," Patricia explained. This despite being mostly free of debt on their principal home and being well in advance of their repayments on their four investment properties. In fact, their houses were increasing in value and the in-flows of rent covered all but $80 each week of their costs. Celia made it known she thought it a shame they could not splurge a bit when in essence, they could qualify as wealthy. Nevertheless, the Sharpes enjoyed the stories, the photos, the vicarious living through her adventurous sister's travels.

It was at this modern version slide night that Jason coaxed from Mani his opinions on his travels, extracting something more than the prevailing shoulder-shrugs and muted responses. He pressed further once he got Mani talking. "Tell me. What are you doing with your journals. Are you going to make them into a travel book? A coffee table book or diary?"

They were in Mani's room, a blend of chaos and calm. His desk was tidy, pens aligned by the typewriter and all things straightened. Contrasting, as though a second person shared the room, the remainder of the room had bits and pieces heaped up, a stack of magazines on which a cassette recorder rested, a pile of clean clothes on the bed, some dirty socks at the foot of the bed; shoes, skates and old toys forced the wardrobe door open and tumbled forth.

Mani was subdued in his response. "Doubt it." He was proud of his musings, but they were for him, a cathartic dalliance he felt no other eyes would wish to view.

"How many have you done?"

"I've filled three now. The first from Barcelona, I only half filled and it made do for most of the second trip to Italy. I bought a new one, like the first one it was sort of handmade looking. It was in Bologna and I filled it pretty quick. So when I landed in Paris I needed another one so the first thing I did was hunt down a new journal."

"Just a friggin' minute! Have a listen to you. Barcelona, Italy, Paris, Bologna. You're fourteen years old and you've been everywhere. New York, London, Paris, Munich, everybody talk about Pop Musik!"

The refrain from the late 70's hit song prompted the duo into their laughable rendition. "Pop, pop, pop musik, pop, pop, pop musik," they sang, clicking their fingers and kick-drumming their feet as in the song's video.

Jason kept it going past its use by date, "Wanna be a gun-slinger, don't be a rock singer, eenie meenie, miney, mo..." before fading out. "Seriously, Mani. It's just outrageous. Do you know how lucky you are?"

"I know, Jas. It's mad! It doesn't feel like we're rich but we're living this jet-setter lifestyle. You should come on a trip one time."

"Yeah, as if. My parents don't spend money on holidays unless it's camping. Europe? No chance." Jason scanned the books in the low varnished bookcase. "So have you let anyone read your journals?"

"No."

A pause. "Well, can I?"

"Nah. It's just stuff I noticed and liked. Nothing worth reading really."

"Well, let me look if it's nothing."

"There's hardly anything there."

"It's three books! There's not weird stuff is there? Like, you didn't meet some chicks and get busy, did you?"

"No," Mani said shocked, as if meeting some girls were some heinous crime. "Just a bunch of crap I wrote down. I probably won't even look at it again."

Jason tried a different tack. "If you show it to me, then I'll know what to expect, so I can talk my folks into letting me go to Europe. You know, I'll talk about the cultural benefits and the worldliness that I will gain from going overseas."

Mani showed some excitement. He leapt from the edge of the bed. "So you reckon your Mum might let you go one day?"

"If you show me your stories."

"Well, OK then. But I would have to find them. I don't know where they are."

"Isn't that one of your journals there?" Jason said, pointing. "On the desk. Open. Next to the typewriter."

"Oh. Yeah."

"Come on. Give it to me."

"Well, these are just the scribbles. I've fleshed them out a bit on the typewriter, so maybe read one of these." Mani removed a stapled document from a neat pile at the top corner of the desk and handed the paper to Jason. "It's just a summary of everything really."

Mani watched his cousin read, feeling like he wanted to rip it back off him. His mind spun over what Jason would be reading, cringing as he imagined his words been judged, feeling unworthy of having his work read and critiqued. He knew the article word for word, had poured his heart and full effort into producing the story, doing it justice. Mani ached for a glimmer of endorsement as Jason read of his market interaction in buying his first journal, his accounts of all the wonder he had witnessed on his travels – the gory Granada bullfights in the imposing stadia filled with people, the white handkerchiefs that were waved when the torero triumphed, his garlanded costume now dusty, and how Mani lined up with the local boys for an autograph from the victor, even though the spectacle had disgusted him; the article spruiked the highlights of Barcelona, including the cathedrals and architecture, and the Ramblas, tree-lined avenues filled with street artists and tourists; and he told of the unruly soccer mob in shirts of red and white bars celebrating an Atletico victory in Madrid.

Jason gave nothing away. Mani guessed he was either fully absorbed or being polite in finishing Mani's paper-based dribble. Soon, Jason broke into an expressive smile, shaking his head side to side as though lost for words.

"Mani, man! This is brilliant, incredible. How did you learn to write like this? It's just fantastic, the way you describe things. Like I'm actually there seeing this happen before me, I can really imagine it."

"Well, it was a good trip." Mani being understated as usual.

"A good trip? You didn't tell me half of what you wrote in this. The way you portray the things you saw and expand upon it. You make it sound so real. Do you have anymore?"

"There's these three others," Mani offered, encouraged, emboldened even. "Do you wanna see?"

Jason spent the next quarter hour consuming Mani's second, third and fourth reviews, equally brilliantly written with Jason equally effusive in his praise for each. "You have to send these in. You have to get these published."

"I wouldn't know how."

"I'll help."

And so another Jason project sprang to life. The two of them spent the next fortnight researching travel magazines, seeking an appropriate vehicle for Mani's masterpieces. Without even knowing what to do, they found magazines that printed articles of the same length and style as Mani's, found the editor's name and address, sending in two stories to each of two different magazines. The Hail Mary offering.

A fortnight passed with no word. Mani kept writing and the potential publishing slipped from his mind, until his mother gave him a message to call back Anton Farrugia from "Abroad' magazine. Mani was on the phone immediately.

"Have you had any luck getting your stories published?" the editor asked. "And how many have you done?"

A shell-shocked Mani offered monosyllabic answers.

Anton continued. "Don't say yes if anyone else calls. I will definitely publish these two stories you sent me, with a couple of minor changes if that is OK with you, and I want to see any others you have written. I'll send a cheque post haste. The going rate is $250 an article. Is that suitable?"

Mani's mouth hung open and a grunt emerged.

"How old are you by the way?" Anton asked.

Making a Mint - 1991

Mani's new-found success, leading on from Celia's success triggered a competitive instinct in Peter Alves. Initially content to allow Celia's flourishing business to support their basic needs, he had recently felt perturbed in his role as house husband. Perhaps it was his masculinity being challenged by his wife's success, or a hunter-gatherer instinct kicking in, a need to be the provider. Whatever it was, it prompted him to seek his 'next big thing'.

Half-yearly hit and run sales jobs had become more difficult to find. It was 1991 and employers wanted previous job history and demanded resumes and references. It was not a good look to be in and out of work so frequently, though Peter went to some pains to point out that this was of his choice. He didn't need to work, he chose to. Cosy sales jobs with good pay and little responsibility were thin on the ground, so this fact combined with the manful valor of needing to be his family's big shot, had led Peter to the offices of RayGun Enterprises and a meeting with its CEO, computer guru Ravindra Gunasinghe.

Ravindra had established a business system and now sought to franchise territories not just across Brisbane but around Australia. A veteran of early computer networking technology, Rav had been at the forefront of industry expansion in the United States, London and Australia as a specialist in big business networks, engaged by banks or consulting. Most recently he'd been focusing his efforts on personal computers for home use.

Peter listened to his presentation, saw some potential and moved enquiries to the next stage. "Twenty K, you say? And that includes some stock and all the setup costs? What else do I get for me dosh?" he asked.

Rav was a quiet, mild-natured Sri Lankan man, widely experienced in business, management and particularly computers. Peter saw him as a pushover despite the gulf in their experience and qualifications.

"Mr Alves, you are buying exclusivity. A ground floor opportunity, a proven system. I have sourced PC systems, fully-integrated and ready for homes. You order, computer arrives boxed up within three days, you deliver and install at a profit margin of 55%. It is a turnkey system and you have exclusive rights to all orders placed within the confines of this area." He handed Peter a list of postcodes which designated the suburbs that he would be responsible for servicing. "It is your area. A very generous offer, as it is early days for the industry."

"But, I don't know a thing about computers, Rav. How do I install 'em?"

"Mr Alves, at these prices and profit margins, you can do what many franchisees do. Outsource. There are many very intelligent university students who would leap at $50 to deliver and install the systems."

"Or I could pay 'em $40. Even better." Peter's mind was ticking, dollar signs rolling cartoon-style in his eyes. "So do you do finance?"

"No, Mr Alves, but if you can arrange the finance, I am more than happy to accept your application. I think you are exactly the sort of person RayGun is looking for to grow our business."

Rav considered he had his franchisee. Peter reasoned he had his business opportunity. He had checked out other options – a pool shop, book selling, coffee lounge, a take-away food store, handyman business, car paint touch-ups. This prospect sat neatly in his skill set and his work ethic. Namely, sit back and watch the cash roll in.

Peter smiled, satisfied. "I'll get my lawyers to look over the papers," he bullshitted. "But provisionally, I think we have a deal. You'll be hearing from me, Rav."

****

So mud sticks. Everything you've done in the past, all the upside potential of a man with drive and ideas, ambition and impetus, an individual who wants to achieve, who aims high. It can be brought down by one error of judgment, one stroke of poor luck, a swipe of the hairy hand of fate. Just one insignificant little bankruptcy. As a result, the bank had fobbed him off. Barred him from borrowing, struck him from the register. Black-banned him.

Peter had stormed from the branch, leaving both the manager's door and the external door open to show his displeasure at the decision. He had only needed $25,000 to get the business rolling but now had his tail between his legs. As he had become increasingly prone to do, he eased his frazzled nerves with a beer at the local. A second beer gave him time to think. Clarity.

A future in a job. He used to mock people with jobs when he was flying high with Bettalife. It simply did not appeal to Peter. He had one final card up his sleeve and it was time to slide it out and put it in play.

First stop – the post office, where he set up a post office box.

Second stop – home. Celia was meeting with a travel agent, drumming up interest in *Celia Italia*'s tours. She had four planned for 1991. Peter utilised the empty house to collate some of the papers he required. Receipts, bank statements and customer lists.

Third stop – the bank.

"As you can see, Celia has her accounts with your bank, and the cashflow has been excellent."

The branch manager tilted his head back to look down through his square spectacles. "I can see that. Things are moving along nicely for her business," he stated.

"Our business," Peter corrected him. "It's proving quite successful. Celia's a natural with the tour guide thing. It's her strength. Mine is more the strategy side of things. Bigger picture stuff. And as you know, there's more than one way to skin a cat, so I've been looking at ways to cut costs, make the tours more profitable through working on a larger scale."

"What did you have in mind?" His head was now turned to the side facing his ear to Peter. Eyes turned, eyebrows raised, lips pursed, the odd mannerisms of a man who'd spent a quarter of a century listening to people begging for money.

"There's an array of things. Bulk advertising brochures rather than the smaller runs. Offering our own source of travel insurance. Buying policies en masse and then incorporating them into the price of the tours, at a profit obviously, but then more simplistic for our travellers. Down the line, investing in a bus based in Rome. Also, looking at taking on staff to do multiple tours at peak times of year. Eventually buy our own villa in the Italian countryside. One that's big enough to house the whole tour group. Save paying some other greasy I-ti sod to rent us his joint."

"Quite a vision." The manager was sitting back now, fingers crossed at his midriff. Relaxed and open.

Peter knew he had him. "Absolutely. Baby steps at first. That's why we need the $25 grand. We'd have it cleared within twelve months based on the four trips locked in for next year. Can we get something organised for drawdown next week?"

"Can't see why not. We would need Celia to sign the papers though, as the accounts only have her name attached."

"Absolutely not a problem," Peter said. He scrabbled together his paperwork hurriedly. "Listen, I gotta run. Important meeting to get to. Here's the PO Box address. Just do up the applications, send 'em here and I'll get Ceels to sign when she's about the place next. Hard to catch her these days, now she's a high-flier."

The men each gave one of those polite half-laughs, shook hands and Peter high-tailed it out of the bank, unencumbered by any guilt or concerns about what he was undertaking and confident he would soon resume his place as the eminent business owner in the Alves household.

****

Peter Alves was back in business. The bank had come good with the funds, with all forms issued to Peter's pernicious PO Box. A quick scribble to replicate his wife's signature and a cheque arrived in a few days. A simple process from checks to cheque and Celia remained unaware of her husband's desperate deception. Peter's conscience was clear, knowing he had the smarts to make a success of his new venture. The loan would be paid back in a matter of months.

It had been arranged to sign for the new business at the Alves home. Peter now sat opposite the man whose business system would propel Peter back to the life he knew best. The businessman flicked open his briefcase and withdrew some forms.

"Mr Alves, I am certain you will discover you have made a most acumenical decision, my friend."

"Rightio," Peter responded. "Let's get stuck into it then."

Before he signed, the phone jangled. Peter excused himself.

"Hel-lo, Peter Alves speaking."

"Good morning Mr Alves. It is Ravindra Gunasinghe. I was awaiting your arrival this morning. I expected we were signing the agreements for your computer franchise business. I have my lawyer present to witness the paperwork."

"Oh, Rav mate. Yeah, sorry about that. A bit of a change of plans mate. Something's come up. You might hafta give me a couple of months to get it sorted. We'll talk then, hey. Sorry, mate."

With Rav off the phone, Peter returned to sit with his new associate.

"Now, where do I sign?"

The supplier, a thin man in a baggy suit, pointed to the agreement on the coffee table. He had a sparse beard on a pointed face that culminated in pronounced buck teeth. "It's the future, Pete. Education is the new growth industry. You're gonna make a mint. Everyone wants a set of encyclopaedias in their home. It's satisfyin' for 'em, you know. Parents feel like they're doing the best for their kids. A status symbol too. You can't go wrong," he said through his rat-like mouth. "You're gonna make a mint," he said once more, just to re-iterate.

Peter signed and handed over the twenty grand cheque. A moth to a lamp. He had kept five grand for some pre-Christmas spending money. "So when do I get my books?"

"You'll get a set of your own to show and tell," responded Ratman. "And all the advertising material. But, remember no stock and no storage. You make a sale, collect the dough and the books are delivered by Brittanica in five days. This deal qualifies you for sixteen sets – one a week for four months – at a 50% profit. How good's that, hey? You're gonna make a mint!"

Been Caught Cheatin'

There is little doubt that the final year of school marks the cross over from child to adult. Though there is still physical and emotional growing to do, and not yet legally an adult, the final year demands big decisions to be made about career and the direction of future study. It insists upon personal reflection as the workload of a senior high school student prepares the child for the potential realities of their working life – hard work and drudgery for some; the doors to the world of possibilities swinging open for others.

Mani felt the beginning of Grade 12 was an ideal time to take stock of where his life was right now and where it was going. He made a checklist to self-assess.

Career – this one was a fait accompli. He was churning out stylishly written articles which were being snapped up to produce a steady journalist's income for a teenage boy. Grasping the joy he gained from describing his view of the world, he knew his future lay in the written word. He had scoped out an array of university courses that would help him make this his permanent career, with the only decision left to be made being whether that career was non-fiction or creative in essence.

Personal – this sector was best broken down to:

Family – this would get the tick. His Dad was full bore with no rear view mirror to learn from his past. But the Alves house was full of fun and love, and Mani's Mum was the exuberant glue that held them together.

School – a definitive tick. Steady marks, which kept him near but not quite at the top of the grade. There were obvious high points where his achievements far exceeded those around him, notably History, English and his chosen language subject, Italian, though Mani acknowledged his natural advantage over the other students in these subjects. Not Many 16 year olds had travelled as extensively as Mani Alves.

Health – this tick experienced a mild delay. Mani maintained a powerful build, but he had been less inclined to submit to his father's exercise-cum-torture sessions and he'd let his fitness slide. A thickset body needed to keep moving. He purported to do something about his widening girth, earning himself a tick on his checklist.

Travel – gold-lined, cream-filled, diamond-encrusted, chocolate-coated TICK. This tick came with white truffle sauce, Beluga caviar and demanded its own launch where a bottle of Krug champagne would be smashed on the side of the tick, and it was delivered in a Michelangelo-designed box lined with cashmere from the Himalaya's handsomest goat. It had rows of those cool flashing light-bulbs that light up in order so it appears a glow worm is edging along. The tick had its own fireworks display, came with sparklers and had a cherry on top. It was indisputable, certain and it belonged. Most adults never experienced the travel that Mani had enjoyed in the past three years and this tick was testament to his adventures.

Friends – again a tick. Mani knew his place and he knew how to read people. Consequently, he didn't try to mix with the self-appointed cool crowd, preferring to analyse them rather than socialise with them. He enjoyed the ongoing friendship of his study group. Ben Pedley remained his intellectual sounding board and closest ally and Mani's Grade 8 struggles seemed an eternity ago.

Love Life – unfortunately, a cross. A big red one. And not the internationally-recognised Red Cross that saved lives and alleviated suffering, though Mani's love life could do with some resuscitation. The reason for the cross? There was no Alison Archer.

He was holding on, honouring her, convinced he would see her again. His life decisions were being influenced by her. She drove him on; he was becoming a better person for her, because of her. In the hope of her return, he would be ready to present to her the finest version of Mani Alves. He had witnessed the physical development of the other girls in his grade, many of whom he was spiritually close to. They were like-minded young ladies who enjoyed Mani's charming take on the world and appreciated his knowledge and ability to express himself. These interactions however, never threatened to spill over into anything physical or sexual.

Seeing the obvious physical traits of these sixteen and seventeen year old girls, he occasionally pictured in his imagination how the maturing Alison Archer might present, but her image remained of the pre-teen who was cuteness personified. When Mani tried to imagine her as anything other than this virginal version, the expanding curviness morphed her uncontrollably into the ballistic-breasted vixens in the porn mags that teen boys share. It disgusted Mani to think of her this way.

Overall, Mani rated his existence quite highly, his prospects firm and his life in general – stable. So it came as a shock to hear the vitriolic argument emanating from his parent's bedroom one evening. It recalled past challenges of Celia to Peter at times when Peter's judgment had let his wife down. Mani wondered what might be the cause but the noise soon died down and he became lost in his op-shop copy of James Joyce's Ulysses.

The following morning there was silent tension in the room as they each made their own breakfast. Celia, her every motion forceful and exaggerated, closing drawers loudly but not quite slamming them, cutlery pushed not placed, her jaw clenched. Peter sheepishly sipping his coffee, eyes averted, his usual joviality concealed. Mani discerned these behaviours, knew it best to keep his mouth zipped. He noted his father was denied a farewell kiss before he scuttled out the door. Dad in the doghouse again.

His departure sprung Celia into action. As Mani ate he watched her drag her trusty suitcase from the hallway cupboard and haul it upstairs. After twenty minutes of hearing drawers open and slam shut, Mani's curiosity won out. He ventured upstairs. Celia had two bags and the suitcase by the stairwell and was sweeping her bathroom items into a small case.

"What's happening Mum?"

"Mani. My darling boy. This has been coming for a couple of years. Something's happened." She drew a deep breath, let her eyes close briefly as she found the words she had practised, shook her head to bring her back to this place, her son before her, an explanation required. "Your father loves you. So do I. Don't ever forget that and you will always have both of us."

Mani noticed the strain on her face, and despite her usual impeccable morning make-up, he could see his mother's age for the first time. A tiredness, a sense of defeat. Despite the success of her business, the richness of her life, full of travel and social interaction, Mani saw a weariness cloak his mother, as though worn down. He sensed his own childhood being confined to history. "What's happened?" he questioned, not caring to know the answer.

"I can't do it anymore, Mani. The drinking, the bad decisions, the absolute deceit. I never minded when he would bomb out. He was trying to get ahead and he made his own decisions on his money-making schemes. But this now, this is unforgiveable, putting at risk everything I worked for, everything I built. I just can't be a party to this level of contempt, this complete disdain for the ethics of right and wrong."

"The bags. Where are you going?"

"We are going to stay somewhere else for a while. I want to go while your father's out."

"You're leaving Dad?" Mani said, shocked. A pain shot through his left eyebrow, causing him to wince as the realisation moved to his parents separating. "Mum, you can't do that. Whatever he did can't be that bad."

"Oooh, it was. Grab a bag, muscles. To the car. Don't worry, you will still spend plenty of time with your father. I'll tell you what you need to know in the car."

They drove, Celia talked and Mani only heard bits and pieces. He thought of his future. The stigma. Only half a life with his parents, like being an orphan, but not quite. A semi-orphan, he thought. How often would he see his father and how would Dad cope? The cruel details emerged, or as much as Celia was willing to disclose. The old man had screwed up royally as far as Mani could tell. Mani thought about his feelings for his father. The ups and downs were anathema in each of their lives and while he revered his father's drive and purpose, his desire to better his and his family's future, Mani loathed the recklessness of his failures. And so, finally, did Celia.

Mani looked out the car window as they drove, and while he thought. He recognised the streets. "Are we going to stay at Auntie Trish's?"

"For a while. Auntie Trish has offered her place until we work out what we're doing."

"What about my stuff? My writing and all my clothes and other things."

It seemed incongruous to Mani that the separation would be permanent. For all his foibles, for his polarising ability to rise and fall like nausea on a theme park ride, Peter wasn't, at his core, a bad man. Mani knew that, knew the good in his father. Seventeen years of marriage surely couldn't be flushed away so simply.

****

It was known by Peter Alves and those close to him that he did not fight fate. And as he moved on from previous business and professional failure, so he would let this personal calamity play out the way the world wanted it to. Peter loved his wife and was happy with the state of his marriage, politely sexless as it had become. Deep inside, he sensed the marriage would eventually resume, but for now he had the licence to explore his options, to maybe play the field and, to use business parlance, check his value on the open market. This new freedom situated him at city pick-up joint 'Someplace Else' for the second time that week.

He eyed the room from his position seated at a high bar table. He sipped a Scotch on ice, positioned for ideal views of the foot traffic through the entry door and from the ladies toilets. His years of experience allowed him to scan the best position in the room for optimum visual surveying. The Saturday night crowd was building as people poured into the club from the afternoon races – the club was situated above Brisbane Central train station – and diners from surrounding city restaurants made their way to the popular club. Eighties dance music throbbed over the din of chatter. Someplace Else was notorious for its age-based clientele, a nightspot for those beyond their twenties and the hipper nightclub scene. The club didn't try to be something it wasn't and knew its place in catering for divorcees, cruisers, loners, cougars and late-thirties ladies who had worked hard in the gym and were now determined to get the male recognition for their hard work and sweat. The entire scene fitted Peter's target market.

This was his vengeance for Celia leaving him. The wedding ring was off, the best threads pulled from the wardrobe and his old confidence coming back. The chat-up lines were showing some promise. A couple of nights back he was all but over the line, until the lady he was wooing had to retreat to look after her overly-drunk friend. So Peter was back for more, eager to cash in on this period of liberty he had been granted which he would maximise until Celia came to her senses and came back to him. It wasn't his fault she chose to leave, so Peter felt justifiably free to play.

Deep down he knew Celia's decision was warranted. It had played out messily and looking back, it was a cruel manoeuvre on his part.

He'd received the first set of books and they had sat proudly in a display case he'd picked up. He had glossy brochures, all the order forms and leads were being supplied by the company. Sales had come easily to start with, two in each of the first two weeks and in classic Peter Alves style, he pocketed the cash for his personal expenditure. Then, three months had flown by, most of his stock had been depleted and he hadn't yet made anything more than a single minimum payment on the ill-gotten loan. Sure enough, the bank came knocking and the game was up.

Celia pulled him aside one afternoon and asked how he bought the encyclopaedia. Peter's mind had to work quickly. Should he pile up another level of fibs? If Celia was asking then she must know something, he reasoned. He tried to bluff. "Just organised some short-term finance. Easy payments, I'll knock it over soon enough. No big issue."

"Except that you used my business as collateral for your loan. And the bank's after me because you haven't been paying it!"

"I've been making payments. I'll sort it out."

"You'll sort it out?" Celia screamed. "What about the fact you have put *Celia Italia* at risk for another of your hair-brained schemes? My business – built from nothing but my own ingenuity and you have the gall to jeopardise that!"

Peter was squirming then. He had pulled out a smoke, tapped it on the packet, lit it and drew the smoke in deep. Unsure of how to counteract his prickly wife, he chose to diminish and demean. "Come on, Ceels. Let's look at what it really is. Your business is just a bit of fun to let you go travelling. Yes it makes some money to help the family, but I'm the real breadwinner here. I borrowed some money and out of that I'm making money. So what? It'll get repaid!"

"A bit of fun, hey! Peter Alves, you have done it this time."

Peter had underestimated Celia. She was quite serious and had now followed through on her threat to leave. She imposed a strict set of conditions that he was to follow if he wanted to maintain contact with Mani and this involved paying back the loan and providing money for their day to day needs to prove that he was the breadwinner he purported to be. She allowed him to see Mani on Saturdays.

Depressive at first, Peter began enjoying the solitude of an empty house and the reduced responsibilities. He'd treated the separation as a game, toying with Celia playfully when they spoke on the assumption she would relent and move back after a short hiatus to prove her point. Peter was making the repayments decreed by Celia to reduce the illicit loan, he had kept up his day job on the phones flogging ad space on calendars and sold his remaining encyclopaedia in the evenings after which he often hit the pubs and drank to midnight some nights.

Occasionally these nights would turn into alcoholic splurges, rendering him incapable of functioning the next day. This Saturday, too crook to meet his commitments, he'd rung to say he couldn't meet Mani. The disappointment in Celia's voice was palpable. When Peter had rung back late afternoon to speak to Mani, the boy was too busy to come to the phone. As his nature decreed, Peter turned again to the bottle.

And so on to 'Someplace Else'. Peter had trimmed the mo, slicked back his hair and slid on tight brown slacks and a brown, paisley-patterned short-sleeve shirt. He remained wiry despite his forty-two years, with a muscular back and arms but the hard drinking of recent years had begun to show in the tell-tale pot gut. A skinny man with a gut was an unattractive look. He spent the night with his stomach pulled in and his shoulders back. He hovered close to that tipping point where drinking for Dutch courage segued into slurring then eventual incoherence. He'd tried conversation with several ladies at the bar, hung around the fringe of the dance floor, resorted to dancing solo and grooving with some older birds as though he was part of their group, but to no avail. It was not to be his night. There would be no easy company for him. He cabbed it home soon after 2am.

He had drunk hard since three o'clock the previous afternoon, and had absconded from dinner in his haste to hit the town. The hunger pangs demanded attention and he surmised the perfect remedy to be a late night schnitzel. Peter wobbled through the front door and into the kitchen, poured a heavy-handed Tawny port, threw a schnitzel into the frypan and then sat on the couch to take off his boots. He flicked the TV on. A U2 song played on Rage. He drank deeply from his port glass and let out a moist sounding fart.

He sat leaning forward, loosening his bootlaces. He had another deep drink, lit a smoke and waited for the U2 song to finish. It was followed by some long-haired soft-rock band singing about love letters in the sand. He put his cigarette down, hauled off his shoes, exhausted. One eye blinked shut, the screen blurred. Peter shook his head, trying to straighten his vision. He sipped again at his port, his head heavy, deciding 'I'll just wait to see what the next song is before I...'

The Gift

It could have been a house perfectly suited for Batman's Two Face, Mani decided. One side horribly scarred, where bad things happened, the opposite side untouched but for the water damage from the fire hoses. The lounge room as though they all still lived there, encyclopaedia in the bookcase, magazines under the coffee table. Mani saw a maroon-tinged glass on the table by an ashtray and his father's shoes by the sofa.

Despite its two faces, the house was condemned, gutted by combustion started in the kitchen from an unattended hotplate. The entire northern end of the home, including the upstairs section above the kitchen where Mani's room was situated, was caved in, destroyed, charred black by the licking flames. They were silent enough to not raise Peter's drunken slumber but deadly enough in conjunction with the thick black smoke to have killed him if not for an insomniac neighbour wary of the flickering light from next door. Flames. He called the firies, broke down the door himself and dragged a groggy, smoke-affected Peter from the house.

"How could you not hear me smashing your door down?" the neighbour quizzed.

Peter just drooped his head, shamed, bleary from booze and shock. If the flames had reached his grog-soaked body on the couch, it would have taken days to extinguish the fire. He watched the commotion around him as fire engines roared into the street, drawing the eager eyes of neighbours to the spectacle.

When Celia and Mani arrived as daylight broke, summoned by a neighbour, Peter was barefoot and bare-chested, still staring at the work of the fire brigade. The hangover had kicked in. Mani watched his father bum a smoke off a bystander, and noted the distance kept between his parents. The disgrace of his Dad, the coolness of his mother and her distaste at what she was witnessing. It struck him that this was another sheer rock face on the impenetrable mountain that now stood between his folks. They would not be getting back together.

It was days later when they were allowed into the home. Mani could not even make it to the door of his bedroom, so badly damaged were the floors above the kitchen. The room was cordoned off with plastic tape at a safe distance up the hall by the fire department. He could see in the room. It was as though a grenade had been tossed inside. The charred remains of his wardrobe and desk could be made out amongst the devastation, water damage evident through the house, streaky smoke stains climbed the remaining walls to the ceiling and the awful over-arching, acrid stench of burnt wood and plastic.

Jason stared over Mani's shoulder as their fathers worked downstairs to retrieve what they could. "Your Dad's lucky to be alive, Mani. That looks like a seriously mad fire."

The smell of the room and his distaste at the scene before him drew up anger in Mani. "Maybe that would have been better." He spat the words, getting them out of his mouth as though they were coated with bile.

Jason grabbed his cousin's shoulder roughly. He was shocked by the outburst. "That's a shit thing to say. He's your Dad. You don't mean that."

"Just look at what he's done. All my things, my clothes, my typewriter, journals. My stories, Jason! My stories are gone. The old fart's wrecked everything I own. He did it to Mum and now he's done it to me."

It was a harsh assessment. Jason could not respond.

Mani shook his head, disconsolate. The litany of misdemeanours his father had managed to rack up – debts, sharemarket screw-ups, bankruptcy, defrauding his own wife. Now the fire. The silence let Mani's mind assign a negative score to each event, tally them up, apply a degree of difficulty and calculate the lowest common denominator. His father, the man a mathematical mess.

"All that writing, all my memories gone," he lamented. Jason had loosened his grip on Mani's shoulder but his hand remained. Mani suddenly felt a torrent of loss overwhelm him. All the events of recent months piled into him, filling his mind with a raw screech of white noise, his stomach a hollow ache. His eyes lulled, he felt faint. He reached a hand up to steady himself against the wall of the hallway. It was becoming too much for a kid to handle. His parents removed, the solidity of childhood torn as though his own flesh was being ripped, a boy de-limbed. Now the house, his things. He spat on the floor. A dribble remained over his chin.

"My typewriter too," he said wiping his mouth. "There'll be no more writing, no selling any more stories. All this, gone to shit. That's it...

****

It was a gift that may have saved a future. Mani's dramatic statement about his writing career ending before it had gained traction became self-fulfilling. He had spent the next several weeks moping about at the Sharpe's house – he and Celia would be renting a unit after Celia returned from *Celia Italia*'s mid-year tour – a veritable shadow of the interested, inquisitive sixteen-year old he had shown himself to be. Going through the motions at school, no socialising, an all-pervading melancholy parked within him yet exposed for those close to him to see. Even Jason couldn't raise his cousin from the depths. He had shown no interest in replacing the typewriter.

"What's the point?" Mani whined when Jason asked him when he was going to do some more stories. "Nothing to write about, my journals are all gone. Mum's going on tour soon and I've got school work to do." It was a horribly defeatist attitude. The words fizzed on his tongue, rendering him aware of their acerbity.

And so, the gift – a timely impetus to a young man floundering with the world on his shoulders. Aunty Trish had arranged for Mani to join some of Jason's CBC mates, as well as some of their social group senior girls from other private schools to meet at the sprawling riverside New Farm Park to celebrate Jason's birthday.

The autumn weather in Brisbane was an advertisement for the city, brisk mornings giving way to mid-twenty degree days, a sweep of blue sky, a crisp breeze off the river and the flower beds in the park abloom with May flowers. Locals milled about the park – heavy-footed toddlers chasing balls with their Dads, some hipsters from the nearby Valley precinct stroking their goatees as they recovered from gigs and clubbing with lunchtime drinks on the shaded lawns. Joyous shrieks carried from the children's playground. A soccer game had sprung up between teens, another group celebrated a Nanna's 80th birthday, cyclists circumnavigated the park while others strolled in the sunshine, there simply to watch.

Jason and his mother had marked out a prime section of grass for the gathering. A badminton net was strung on the grass next to the picnic blankets, fold-up tables and chairs. Everyone had brought a plate. Mani knew some faces but kept to himself. A game of touch footy had been arranged, any excuse to instigate interaction between the boys and girls, for the lads to display their machismo and skills, the girls to show their willing nature. More than a game, it was an important social ploy, children well aware of the stakes from their parent's urging, being the opportunity to impress a potential suitor or to maintain the private school network not just for future business but also for breeding.

A film of sweat on his brow from the football, Mani slumped on the picnic blanket and popped a can of TaB while he watched the game continue. Patricia joined him. She had been keeping a close eye on things under the pretence of organising the drinks and food. The consummate organiser, efficient in her dress and her manner.

"Have a good run around?" she asked.

"Yeah, it's been a good day. Thanks for the lunch, Aunty Trish."

"Don't mention it," she said, then in her motherly way queried Mani. "So how are you coping?"

"OK, I guess. This is good fun, but I'd rather be in Italy with Mum."

"But you're spending some quality time with your father. That's a positive. I'm sure he quite enjoys seeing you this much."

Mani crossed his legs and drew his knees up close to his chest, closing himself away from the question. "It's only because I have to. He's not that interested in what I do. And he drinks too much."

"Your dad needs you. There's no doubt he loves you. And remember, blood is thicker than water. Family has to stick together, and you can learn both good and bad from the example of your parents. It's up to you which example to follow, knowing where it might take you."

Mani stayed silent. He analysed Aunty Trish's words and it soon became obvious what she was alluding to.

"You enjoy your trips with your mother, don't you?" she stated.

"Absolutely, it's a different world over there. I never feel more alive than when I'm in Europe, seeing all that history, all the vistas, the beauty." He'd uncoiled from his protective cocoon, letting his knees drop and his hands now gestured like a true Italian orator. "I feel more mature, like I am no longer this dorky teenager from Brisbane. It's my world. Everything is grander and older and more...poignant."

"Poignant?" she blurted out, incredulous at her nephew's term of expression. She held an interested smile.

Mani noted his aunt's surprise at his use of this word. He rushed into an explanation, feeling a tinge of embarrassment but also warm to his subject. "Yeah, more meaningful. You can stand in front of a basilica that's 500 years old and compare that to Australia being only 200 years old. This country is a baby compared to the cities of Italy. The English were on their Grand Tours discovering the secrets of art and architecture, the Medici's were commissioning incredible buildings like the Duomo in Florence, Michelangelo was chipping away at the David, and meanwhile my Aboriginal ancestors were living in bark gunyas and throwing sticks at kangaroos. It's not to denigrate the Aborigines. It's just that when you are amongst all that magnificence, that pure history about which we still fascinate, all the art and culture that makes people spend their life savings to travel the globe just to see it once, well, we are talking about something completely different. You're not you when you witness this stuff. It changes you, and you can feel the change while you are there. And I don't know about everyone else but I loved that change, that point of difference. I loved being the European Mani."

Patricia sat stunned. She had not seen her nephew like this. She knew immediately she had done the right thing with the gift. "Sounds amazing. I should go."

"You should," Mani replied. "Jason should go."

Patricia gave a prolonged blink and a nod, acknowledging his point. A girly scream rang out from the touch football game, which had turned into a playful wrestling match. She continued. "When I see you come to life talking about your travels, all the things you see when you're abroad, it makes me wonder why you've stopped writing your stories. Jason says you're very good."

"Well, I've lost my journals, haven't I? There's nothing else to write of. All my story fodder is gone. I can't really write about the exquisite architecture of Kenmore or the grandeur of miniature Mt Coot-tha."

"There are interesting aspects to every place. You don't think someone in America wouldn't be interested in what Brisbane has to offer?" Patricia said. She eyed Mani, challenging him, seeing where he was at mentally. "Not just its tourist sites, what about its history, its stories, the convict past, all the secrets buried in Toowong cemetery?"

"It just seems like that's all over now," Mani countered. "All my journals are gone, all my ideas. I'd have to start from scratch."

Patricia was exasperated. "You're here for the rest of your life. What else will you do, give up after one setback? Is that going to get you anywhere?" She paused, thought about her next line. She tightened her face, proceeding with a harsh tone. "Where do you think you learned that example?"

Mani shot her a filthy look, his bottom lip out. It didn't take him long to see the sense in what his auntie was saying.

"Just because those journals from when you were thirteen or fourteen years old are gone, doesn't mean you have to stop seeing the beauty in the world, wherever you are. I got you something Mani. Here, open it." She handed him a wrapped box.

"What is it?" he asked.

"Open it, dear."

Mani fiddled with the box, thinking about the things Auntie Trish had said. He knew he was being childish, knew that stopping his writing was an excuse, a tantrum, something else to prolong the blame on his father. As he held the box, contemplative, he noticed a child chasing a butterfly across the lawns, an elderly man walking alone stopping to peer at the city skyline visible beyond the trees, taking it in. In the rotunda, a man had stooped to one knee before his future wife. These things Mani saw in an instant. The beauty in the world. He started pulling gently at the paper around the box.

"You can blow out a candle, Mani," Patricia said gently, touching his shoulder. "But you can't blow out a fire. If you try to blow out a fire it only makes it stronger. There's been a setback. So what, use that ill wind to stoke the fire in you."

Mani pulled the paper off the box. "You should have been a writer, Auntie Trish."

"Maybe I will one day."

"That was deep."

She smiled. "I may be simple, but I'm not stupid."

He held the plain blue box, now unwrapped. Slid the lid off to reveal the gift. It was a dictaphone.

"A verbal journal Mani," Patricia said with a soft smile.

"Wow," he said. He tried the buttons, gripped the recording device, feeling its weight in his hand. "Now that's poignant."

****

As the temperatures rose, easing towards Brisbane's legendary spring warmth, Mani made some changes and the motivation soon returned. Inspired by his aunt's gift, he spent weekends and afternoons with his dictaphone, self-conscious at first, feeling like an idiot savant, talking to himself. He gradually adapted though and the device became an important tool in his writing armoury. He recorded bits and pieces of useful information, conversation grabs, turns of phrase that came to mind, descriptions of sights and scenes that he then scrawled in his journal at home. It became an essential part of his daily routine, keeping the dictaphone close to hand, never missing a thing.

It was yielding results too. His proposal for a column in the free weekly suburban newspaper was accepted. The 'Best of Brisbane' column was a look at events and options for locals to experience the side of Brisbane they may not have seen and highlight some less-publicised events. It was Mani's brainchild, his passion. Low pay but high satisfaction, promoting the bayside, the forest parks, art events, free gigs and historical excursions such as the Maritime Museum and Fort Lytton.

The new maturity had shown through in one other area of his life that needed fixing before he could feel rounded. The efforts he had recently made with Peter had them back on track as father and son. He spent more time with his Dad, encouraging him to be positive and healthy. They played mini-putt, went for walks for the sake of it and barbecued by the river while watching the rock-climbers suspend themselves from minute cracks and ledges in the Kangaroo Point cliffs and appraising the joggers scuffling by.

Most importantly, Mani became the example. He drove the behaviour he wanted to see in his Dad, encouraging him to be a better person, to take better care of himself and get out of his rut. And no alcohol was to be consumed while Mani was in the house. Mani could almost see his old man's tongue dangling from his mouth at times, such was his desire for a beer, particularly after some physical exertion. But rules were rules and the discipline along with the activity brought man and boy closer.

So noticeable was the return of Mani's zest, his mother made a promise that would drive the ambition in him. Seeing his disillusionment with missing the 1991 European summer, Celia promised that he could join the tours as long as his marks remained high. Assuming her son would go to university, she would align *Celia Italia* trips with the breaks between university semesters, so Mani had the choice to travel if he wished. Mani saw life's experiences, he saw culture, beauty, charm and authentic adventure swaying before him. A glorious future of sophistication and insight. But most of all he saw story fodder.

Graduation Night

It was his first time in a suit and because it was a hire suit, Mani didn't want to risk crumpling, soiling or marring it in any way. He was a smart dresser, renowned for his European style and sartorial flamboyance, even if his personality still lagged behind his dress sense. Yet, buoyed as he was by the euphoria of reaching the end of school and loosened by a heady mix of cheap wine and UDL cans, Mani Alves was not going to be persuaded by the withered charms of his graduation date. And not solely for want of keeping the suit in good order.

The date with Carly Grimes was not of his doing. Nearing the end of Grade 12, the big ticket, must-have item was to be paired off with a partner for graduation night, and the higher profile your partner the better. The shallowness of teens ensured all the finest-looking ladies were snapped up by eager male pursuers. Handsome, confident young men staking their claims. Likening this to the stones used to build a pyramid, Mani stood back from this flurry of social self-preservation, too hesitant and impotent to make his mark. He watched the social pyramid's base being established by those with the brightest prospects, the best looks or being the coolest. The building blocks of society, the cornerstones of success. As the pyramid ascended and narrowed, the number of stones thinned as opportunities reduced. Mani, whose size long ago ensured he would be the base stone of a human pyramid, now found himself nearer this less-appealing apex as the final desperate scrambling for positions played out.

Not interested in any of the available options, Mani seriously contemplated seeking out an external candidate. Some of the more mature girls had older boyfriends with cars and jobs escorting them and every school also had that one cheeky bloke who would try to hire an overtly hot female escort, only to have it vetoed by the staid school authorities.

Mani's thoughts were to invite a very special long-lost friend. How he thought Alison Archer would ever make it back to

Westside High he did not know. He didn't know where she was, let alone entertain hopes of her recalling him. He weighed up the possibility of an ad in the local pages of the Sunshine Coast Daily, even called for pricing. He would be able to afford it, but even he could sense the absolute desperation in that. Even if she did come, it would probably only be so she could knee him in the nuts again. For old time's sake. His spirits flagged.

So when Carly Grimes popped the graduation date question, Mani thanked God for small mercies and mumbled a resigned 'yes'.

And so to this night. Having weathered the awkwardness of the photo sessions, arm in arm with his date, his cummerbund riding up over his belly and the baby's breath in Carly's fascinator constantly poking his eyes and tickling his nose as they stood close, Mani needed only to negotiate the after-party. It was not that he didn't find Carly acceptable from a looks perspective – she wasn't the best looking girl in Grade 12, though she had a pretty face despite her and Mani having similar builds – or that she was lacking in personality or intellect. Carly was quite gregarious in her own way, emanating the famed big-girl jolliness. She was thought-provoking in her conversations, intelligent and had a wicked sense of humour. It was more that she assumed that their agreement to frock up and socialise together at the graduation meant they would undertake a deeper, more permanent relationship.

The party was free-spirited, being the rite of passage for under-age school-leavers to imbibe sly grog. Some kids had saved up sufficient to buy quality spirits and cases of beer. Others saw no need to include taste in their criteria when purchasing alcohol. Cheap made sense when its sole purpose was to get these teens out of their heads. The host, a popular long-haired kid with extremely liberal parents who owned acreage verging the Brisbane River at Fig Tree Pocket, had offered up his place to an open invitation for Westside State High School graduates. The sloping terraced block provided several levels over which the party could evolve.

The house poured forth into a wide pergola-covered patio, which during the day revealed superb views along a winding stretch of the river. The polite pergola area was where finger food and punch graced a table. Steps led down from the house through flourishing gardens of ferns and hardy flowers to a flat section of the slope with a paved courtyard. It was of such a diameter that twenty or so hired plastic seats could be utilised and two tables had plastic bowls, snack food and plastic cups. A bathtub filled with ice flanked these tables. Further down the slope, out of view of the house and close to the river on a flat, grassed area, a mini marquee had been erected with tarpaulins as side walls to block the breezes off the river. This area was predicated as the serious party zone where dancing, hard-core drinking, passing out and arguing between lovers occurred and as the sun rose, for crashing out and sleeping off the night's excesses.

At any time, one could assess the state of the party from any of these points to aggregate where the action was. From the house and pergola, the courtyard could be seen. A quick analysis of the bodies present would reveal if the best spot to be stationed was the courtyard, the pergola or, if numbers were lean in these two areas, the marquee would be pumping. The party migrated numbers through these areas and the crowd followed so a fluid line of party-goers seemed to be constantly flowing up and down the slope, like ants on a fence pole. Meeting, stopping, acknowledging the other, busily scurrying on, not wanting to miss anything.

With one hundred and fifty grade twelvers drinking, feeling immortal and trying to impress not only their own dates but those who were their preferred dates, there were bound to be incidents. Late into the evening, someone had lobbed a beer bottle from the pergola area only for the stubbie to come crashing down and shatter on the paved courtyard some forty yards below, narrowly missing a group of girls. A drunken hero who climbed the pergola proved his fallibility by tumbling awkwardly off the structure, luckily having his fall broken by a shrub, which unluckily for him was a sword-leafed agave. Not a serious injury however the scratches and bumps rendered him a bloody, superficially-wounded mess and he succumbed to the combination of shame and pain, his night done before the clock reached 1AM. The school captain flattened the vice-captain after his schoolyard subordinate played a superb game of one-upmanship by consummating graduation night with the captain's date. Girls cried, men roared, eyes were opened, behaviours altered unexpectedly.

The romantic pairings once alcohol was added bore little resemblance to the actual pairings for the graduation ceremony. There were beer cans being shotgunned, vomiting from inexperienced kids trying to play drinking games, confessions of true love from unlikely sources to even more unlikely recipients and the obligatory skinny dip in the muddy Brisbane River. Mani maintained his reserve, only once everyone seemed to have written themselves off and paired up did he step up his drinking. He didn't mind the taste of beer and wine, but when his tongue first felt the sweet burn of bourbon, he knew he'd found his nectar.

Carly Grimes came and went throughout the night, variously standing close to Mani or being unsighted for half an hour or more. Mani at one point walked from the courtyard to the marquee to join a dance when he spotted Carly coming back from the river's edge with another boy and a couple, prompting an unexpected pang of jealousy.

"Hey, I saw that look," she whispered to him. She must have picked up on his possessiveness. "Don't worry. I was just helping the boys look after Tracy. She's drunk and emotional. It was completely innocent."

This confronted Mani, and his denials rang forth. "What look? I don't know what you're talking about." Tracks covered, or so he thought. Her smile suggested she saw his nervous schoolboy excuse and she spent the following hours by his side, unnerving Mani as to her intentions.

Later, alone, drunk, emotionally drained and tired beyond belief, Carly and Mani sat on a blanket under the marquee. Around them, the music was soft and people either slept or chatted quietly and just the diehards continued any semblance of partying. A gentle breeze still carried across the river, bringing the smells of the riverbank to them - lantana, eucalypt and fresh-dug soil. The pre-dawn air had a crispness to it, despite it being the start of summer. Mani offered Carly wine.

"Enough," she replied. I'm too drunk."

"I'm not as think as you drunk I am," Mani joked.

She gave him a playful shove.

"Hey, I'm not your punching bag."

"Oh, you big softie. You're the biggest kid in grade 12 and you can't handle a little nudge from a girl?"

"I'm not in grade 12," he said. "I'm...unemployed! Not a student, don't have a job. I'm a bum."

"Nice observation," she replied with a laugh. "We're all just drunken unemployed bums. Can you believe that we are the future? Look at us. Passed out, drunk, shagging each other. I mean look at that guy there, he's wearing his undies on his head and his socks tied to his wrists. You think he won't regret that when he's applying for his first job. And we are the CEOs and politicians of the 21st century."

Mani enjoyed her witty banter, as removed from his more serious self as it was. "I have no desire to be a CEO," he announced. "I'm going to be Jack Kerouac, hit the road and write wanderer's stories. Follow in the footsteps of Hemingway and Henry Miller."

"Nice ambition. You'll get there, Mani Alves. Something about you tells me that." She edged closer to him, resting her head on his shoulder.

He felt himself flinch. Her touch alerted him to the possibility – the probability – of a romantic liaison with Carly. It confused him but before he could analyse his thoughts, her lips were on his, her tongue playing around his lips. His drunken mind was reeling at the meaning of this and the prospect it represented. It felt so good, he let the moment linger, letting her mouth move on his as he sat rigidly with his lips slightly parted. He dare not move or change lest it might stop. He hardened. She noticed.

Breathing heavily into his ear, she whispered, "It's your grad night. Let's make it your lucky night. We'll move the rug down by the river."

"No," he said, shocking himself with his volume which caused several people to look over. He felt their eyes assessing him and Carly but soon enough they returned to their own endeavours, drifting off in their own space like users in an opium den.

"What's up?"

"Nothing. It's just I..." He didn't know himself what was up.

"You don't like me," she accused.

"No Carly. I do. And I enjoyed that."

"I could tell."

"It's my suit. I don't want to ruin it."

"Your suit will be fine. You won't be wearing your suit."

Mani's mind was not functioning. Here he was being offered the grandest of nightcaps, the ultimate exclamation mark to his school years. Though he was inexperienced, he listed sexual relations with the opposite sex as a major life goal. But so soon after his first kiss? No courtship? A rushed affair, messy, unfulfilling. Dirty. And what would that mean to Carly, her giving herself to Mani? Was it right, did he deserve her? Did she deserve him? And what would Mum say if she found out. He could just imagine. He couldn't believe his mother came into the decision. He thought of his Dad to get his Mum out of his mind but that was worse! Then Ben Pedley came to mind, and it was getting weird. Why did he not want to have sex when he really did? Sure, being scared and nervous was normal. And that kiss was something.

He was seconds from relenting when his mind bent in a kaleidoscope of drunken clarity, phasing in and out of his past and future, seeking meaning, reason, purpose. The music hummed through him, the air cradled him and he could smell the perfume of Carly Grimes, still leaning into him, the remnants of her baby's breath arrangement still in her hair. The moment reigned over him, pulsing. The music created a vision of a beach and on that beach the long brown legs of a girl. Not Carly, not here by the river at the graduation after party. The girl had ponytails, rainbow laces, tennis shoes and she was walking towards Mani, that bouncy walk bringing her into focus and him to attention. It was clear what was holding him back.

"I've got a girlfriend. I shouldn't have let you kiss me. I'm sorry."

"A girlfriend? I've never seen you with anyone at school."

"She doesn't go to our school. She used to though."

"Do I know her? Who is she?" Carly asked, somewhat indignant and a little embarrassed at the rejection.

"I'd rather not say. We're just keeping it low-key. We don't see each other all that much."

He said nothing more, nor did Carly ask. She soon enough crashed off to sleep next to Mani, while he lay awake hoping the loyalty of his abstinence would not be washed away by a distant tide of regret.

The Statistics of Obsession - 1992

"Okay, on three, we open them together," Mani said. "Ready, one, two, three..."

Mani and Jason were together for a ceremonial opening. Figuratively, they were opening the way to their future, but literally they were the envelopes sent to them by QTAC, the Queensland Tertiary Admissions Centre. Inside, their future direction would be dealt to them, be that their preferred choice of course and university or if their ambition outweighed their talent, their third, fourth or fifth preference of a different course or a lesser university. Futures hinged on these envelopes, hence the sense of ceremony.

They each tore at their envelope at the command, flipping open the folded letter inside, scanning over it for the information they sought on their tertiary futures. The boys' eyes met. Mani gave nothing away, his eyes solemn and narrow.

Jason on the other hand let his eyes sparkle with excitement. "I'm going bush," he announced. "Business. Southern Cross Uni, Lismore. My top choice." He shadow-boxed in celebration, flaying his fists around with the letter still in his hand.

Since the beginning of the year, Jason had begun building an ambition to do at least one year of university rurally. He'd lived in the city all his life and despite his mother's protestations he built a case based on bricks of logic. "You're a country girl, Mum," he'd pointed out as argument number one. "It's basically me getting back to your roots."

He was maturing, becoming a prime example of the upside of private schooling. Jason had broadened across the shoulders from the regular sport he undertook and his face was handsome, blemish-free, with the sensible conservative haircut of both his peers and idols. Sharp of mind and open to opportunity, new learning and experiences, he was also a marvellous orator, having honed this in the CBC debating team, hailed as a most glorious private school undertaking, the highest embarkation of a spritely mind.

His argument for why he should go bush strengthened and focused though the second half of the year. He was determined, there would be less distraction, he would get a different perspective, experience bush life and doing a business degree would assume a small economy context. There would be less crime, it would be more laidback, he'd be meeting different people, there is less drinking in a country town (they both saw this for the lie it was) and there would be less chance of getting beat up or attacked by city-dwelling vagrants.

The arguments came back – where will you live, you won't know anyone, you'll miss your family.

He rejoindered each one. "You and Dad can buy a house in Lismore for me to rent. What a great investment! I won't know anyone at a Brisbane uni either. There'll be hundreds of country kids coming to the city for uni, what's the difference with me being a city kid going to the country? You can come and visit me as often as you want and I can drive home on weekends and holidays. It's only three hours away. I've got my licence now," he mock sang knowing it was a sore point for his mother.

"Don't remind me," Patricia said.

It all culminated in Jason growing in determination to select the Bachelor of Business at Southern Cross University and as top of his class in all but History, he had guaranteed himself his top choice of uni.

"What about you, Mani? What'd you get?"

Mani's low-key approach to his envelope's contents reflected his emotions. He understood the gravity of the decisions they were now making. This was his life, his future. The next fifty years hinged on the decision of a sixteen-year old.

For some, this was too much to expect. How was an immature, unworldly teenager supposed to grasp the meaning of a career, the decision to indisputably direct his life in one direction or another not knowing whether the reasons for this choice of study – be it family expectation, a passing interest, delusions of grandeur or an obsession for a member of the opposite sex was the catalyst to pursue pet psycho-analysis, marine biology, bovine dentistry or witchcraft philosophy - were going to be the right reasons and enough to satisfy a 30 year old in future decades. Too many qualified lawyers preferred designing bridges, too many accountants made great electricians and there were school teachers who found that kids annoyed them and mending broken bones was the zenith of human accomplishment.

But Mani's stare was built on quiet confidence and intense inner pride. He knew. He'd known since he met the market stall owner in Barcelona, scribbled his travel thoughts in that journal, even as far back as his essay on Expo88. He was meant to write and his preferred vocation was delivered by QTAC.

"I got in!"

****

Mani had every reason to be confident and indeed the trip in to the Queensland University of Technology campus on Brisbane's city fringe had him feeling poised and calm. Alighting from the bus on George St a hundred yards from the main entrance to QUT, the law and finance sector of Brisbane where the heritage Victorian buildings of red brick and sandstone housed some of the state's finest minds and biggest success stories, Mani drew on his inner power of confidence to guide him for his first day of uni. His assuredness came from having travelled France extensively over the previous few weeks of the New Year with *Celia Italia* and the knowledge that he had been accepted into his chosen Bachelor of Arts creative writing course. His writing ambition could not be quelled.

He had spent considerable time choosing his 'look' for uni, a change from the regimented school uniform of Westside High. His wardrobe boasted some fine Euro style incorporating the latest grunge look with an urban twist. He would be composed, confident for his coming out day, moving to the flow of his surrounds, dovetailing to the city environment. He pictured himself ambling onto campus, sure of himself and able to mix with his peers and instigate new friendships in a mature urbane manner. Like-minded scholars eager to spread their wings as they soared towards adulthood.

The reality was quite different. It was his first day at Westside High all over again. Swelling throngs of kids from differing social sectors, Mani feeling like a pimple on the nose of a TV presenter. The cool kids frolicked and strutted while Mani bumbled along awkwardly like he'd forgotten how to walk. The buzzards as butterflies in his stomach from that fateful high school day also returned. Nerves disabled him, his churning stomach loosening his insides so he walked with clenched buttocks to prevent freefall.

There were further similarities to his Westside experience, one in particular that he expected. He had tried to eliminate from his conscious mind the possibility of Alison Archer also attending QUT. It was not a stretch of the imagination, he reasoned. She was among the cleverest in her grade eight classes - a high achiever. Surely in the subsequent four years since he'd last seen her she could not have gone off the rails to the extent that she could be denied her choice of university or career? If indeed she was to make something of herself she would certainly go to university, and most likely in Brisbane. The two largest universities in Brisbane were University of Queensland on the southwest fringe of the city and Mani's selected QUT smack in the city centre. Mani, having chosen QUT by factoring into his decision where Alison might choose to attend if she were picking a university, albeit with his limited knowledge of her potential decision-making criteria, had put too much thought into it. This was evidenced by his allocating a percentage likelihood of them meeting at uni, which sadly for his forlorn hopes of love resurrection was only 24%.

He had used a top-down view to come to this figure. The potential that Alison Archer would attend university he reasoned would be a 73% chance which seemed reasonable in accounting for other possibilities. She might choose a regional university rather than hitting the big smoke. However Mani's logic that Brisbane had the best and biggest universities would mean that Alison would most likely want to come to the city, thus a 76% chance of her coming to uni in Brisbane.

There were three main universities in Brisbane and Mani again broke down the averages to calculate his chances of seeing the girl. Griffith University, not one of the larger campuses and nestled on Brisbane's southside, would have just a 14% chance of receiving Alison Archer. University of Queensland, quite prestigious but being out of the city, further away from Alison's last known whereabouts of the Sunshine Coast, had it a slight outsider at 42% to QUT's 44%. The favourite. Mani's choice.

44% of 76% of 73%.

24%. A one in four chance.

It was enough to keen his senses. As at school for grade nine, he obsessed over every passing girl, scrutinising their faces for that spark of familiarity. The blonde hair, the ski-slope nose, the recognisable walk. How had Mani changed in four years, he wondered, so he could apply proportionate alterations to his mental image of her. One in four. Every third girl of unequivocal non-Alison Archer features had his heart leaping for the next girl he saw, statistically, might be her, however flawed his logic.

His fixation would remain for much of the first few days of uni, before the search simply became a manageable ritual. If only Mani had been able to set aside this Alison mania, he would have noticed the surfeit of trees as he walked through this campus forest. And he might have twigged to these trees also noticing him, despite his inner turmoil as he gangled through the university's walkways orienting himself with his spiritual home for the next several years. Female eyes following this college enigma. His Euro-influenced style was being noted.

Several weeks into university life, Mani's Alison Archer cravings receded. Without ever fading from his thoughts, his engrossment with the muse he once knew was swallowed by the thorough gratification in his studies. He was soon involved with the campus newsletter, a left-wing rag employing the talents of an array of interesting gents with funky facial hair and intellectual, po-faced hippy chicks with heavenly bodies. The articles Mani contributed were contrite opinion pieces not aiming to ruffle feathers – comical observations of uni life and relevant issues. They gradually became more antagonistic and opinionated at the urging of the editor, an angry third-year rebel taking written pot-shots at seemingly everyone.

Mani's final seismic shift away from his infatuation with Alison occurred by accident. He realised he was letting her go, allowing his own life to flourish in his new world. He attached a certain guilt to this, his final leap in moving on and so shielded her memory from his unfaithfulness.

It was a mid-year party, the week of Mani's 18th birthday and the week before the June break. One of Mani's interactions in the first half of the year had been with a lanky, charismatic kid named Crispian Childs who, apart from being in Mani's classes, contributed to the campus newsletter his thoughts and reports on the local music industry and provided gig reviews. He was a musician and was soon to switch his course to his real passion - Music. His look was direct from the pages of Rolling Stone magazine – wispy goatee beard, long hair and the grunge-look flannelette shirt with knee-length shorts and Doc Martens. He had organised a jam in the unit of one of his muso mates and Mani was invited.

"Well, I guess I could come," Mani replied with hesitance. He wasn't aware of 'jams', his socialising had consisted of pubs and clubs up until then.

"You guess? You're eighteen, on the cusp of the greatest period of your life, though you don't know it yet, and you 'guess' you might come to a party with some extremely cool guys, where you'll listen to some organic, out-there music, drink a little, smoke some, and get tranced out. A party where some of the most beautiful and liberal-minded university queens will gather to receive idolatry from us men."

Crispian and Mani shared an interesting bond, both being intellectual and each considering themselves to be deep thinkers. They often shared spirited and verbose moments of silliness. Crispian though, particularly liked the sound of his own voice.

"Well when you put it like that," said Mani, "I should come. I mean, I'm coming. It sounds rad. I mean, it sounds like a good time." He fumbled over his words this time, trying to control his nerves. He wanted to be himself but there was pressure to be cool and hip to his peers.

"Oh the enthusiasm! No really, maybe sit this one out. Stay home, Alves and leave the lady-loving and tripping out to us pros. Stay home and write a magical piece of prose for that girl you never knew, or wash your Mum's back in the shower, maybe rub some anti-fungal cream into your dear old Dad's Athlete's Foot."

Crispian felt he had some sort of guiding hand in Mani's life, at least an upper hand. He could be dismissive yet still Mani found himself drawn to Crispian's Svengali appeal.

"I swear Alves, you are a funny critter. This party might be too much for your brain. You'd be popping synapses. Pop, pop, pop, everywhere. There'd be serotonin shooting from your eyeballs, squirting out making huge puddles on the floor. People would be slipping over in your serotonin mess and injuring themselves and their clothes will fall off, and there'll be an orgy at your feet and you'll just be buggin' out like a first-year uni student at his first jam. Best you don't come. I'll let everyone know you can't make it."

"No, Cris. I'll be there. I'll bring a bottle of Jim Beam."

"Make it Jack Daniels, Alves. Let's not be cheap."

Mani's home life had changed little. He still lived with his mother and still visited his Dad on weekends. He may have experienced global travel and incorporated this into his writing. He may have had a brain wired to see the minutiae of everyday life to reproduce it in description that sang from the pages and painted a picture for people who read it. But he still lacked street smarts. Socially, he had been stunted by his nervousness, uncertain of his place in the world and content to minimise the drinking and social mingling in favour of home-cooked meals, television and his study books. Crispian changed that. This party broke Mani from the constraints of his childhood, his mental barriers busted apart and a new freedom settled over him like a snug-fitting suit.

What began as a standard frat-room party – drinking games, grunge music, witty banter from competitive guys and demure looks from ready chicks – soon found its rhythm as a jam session. Crispian was the obvious ring-leader on bass guitar.

Three others had their guitars, two acoustic and one amped up. There was a set of bongos, a human beatboxer and a variety of percussive instruments which switched hands as the group traded melodies and alternated roles.

A gorgeous flaxen-haired Joni Mitchell look-a-like crooned a mixture of her own and known lyrics over the sounds as an appreciative crowd danced, cuddled and swayed. Others watched on, heads spinning from the smoke and drink, going to whatever place the music was taking them. The party varied through the night as people came and went according to their grand plans for a Friday night. Finally, well after midnight, it was Cris, Mani, a guitarist, the unit's tenant and his girlfriend and three female uni friends of the musos.

Mani had never been aware of this type of life. He was drunk but not paralytic. Drinking was fun but getting drunk was not his bag; maybe he'd seen his father on the turps too often to cherish getting hammered. What opened his mind was the pot. Joints had been passed around freely, weak stuff that relaxed rather than retarded the mind. Mani had variously danced a slow shimmy, a butt-shaking dance to the mellow tunes, or lounged back in his own world on the Indian cushions on the carpet. Candles provided the sole light in the room and the music took Mani to unexplored fantasies, trips down to a vault of thought that he had previously ignored. Revelations spun together as he found the ultimate state of relaxation. All the tension and inhibitions gone. In their place, just pure enjoyment and open stream of ideas, cognition and pleasure.

Mani barely noticed the crowd thinning as time slid away. It occurred to him only after the fact that he had spent much of the evening close to one particular young lady. She leant into his chest, Mani's arm around her as the musos chased a groove, changing tempo and rhythm to suit their eclectic fancies.

Mani saw Crispian smile at him as he played a reggae jam. "How you enjoying the party, Mani mun?" he said in a poor Jamaican accent, grinning widely. "Looks like Jacinta likes the cut of Mani's jib."

And she did. The relaxation moved from leaning back together on the cushions, to her kissing him, her hands touching him, sinking her hooks into him before they disappeared into a vacant bedroom. From that point, Alison Archer ceased to exist for Mani. He found in this moment the ultimate in physical expression, a world prior unknown as Jacinta took him on a journey unparalleled to anything he had known. The sensations swept the vagueness from his altered mind, he was alert to the here and now and the future and all its possibilities. He was awakened.

The following morning, his eyes sprung open at the ninth hour. His initial moments of panic, not knowing where he was in an unfamiliar room soon gave way to a wave of pain and acrimonious guilt. He was thoroughly busted, damaged from the drink and smoking. A pain in the back of his skull had him questioning if he had not been operated on as a party trick the night before. The foulness of his mouth assaulted his tongue as he swished it around his mouth and over his furry teeth to get the saliva flowing. His eyes fluttered, unable to fully open against the multiple streams of white light sliding between the blinds.

He went to move his hand to check his aching head, but couldn't move his arm. It was under the girl Jacinta, who stirred. A fresh wave struck him, of exhilaration that he was no longer a virgin, but he was soon swamped by the guilt. He had broken his vow. He had not saved himself.

She spoke, reaching an arm across his stomach so he was aware of his nakedness. "Good morning, big boy."

"Morning."

"So how was your first bonk? You're not a virgin anymore."

"You tell me how it was. It was good for me."

"You were pretty damn good for a first-timer. And you'll only get better. Now you've started you won't want to stop. That's what uni's about."

And here Mani was thinking it was about study, futures, careers, but in reality it was about drinking, music, parties and sex. It was about letting go of the past, locking onto a lifestyle, discovery, experimenting, finding what worked for you as an emerging adult. Meeting people like Crispian Childs who threatened his comfortable life but challenged and excited him with this underworld he had not known about. All these realisations tumbled together in Mani's mind. He wondered if he could purge the Alison Archer desire through having launched into this limit-testing debauchery. He doubted it.

Jacinta had been talking through his thoughts, her voice a lo-fi drone typical of the cool hippy-chick art student trying her best to be ironic, intelligent and apathetic all at once while emanating a stream of consciousness ramble. Mani had been grunting in response - a tactic he'd seen his father employ – until she thumped his arm.

"Hey. Are you listening to me?"

Mani's nebulous mind mustered a reply. "Oh, yeah. What?"

"Now that we've done it, are we gonna do it again?" Her face seemed more austere this morning than he recalled of last night.

"Um, I don't know. Should we?"

"How about I leave it up to you. You know where I live."

He didn't, so they never did 'do it' again.

This became Mani's modus operandi for the remainder of his first year of university, as it was for many students. Get wrecked on the weekend, right yourself enough to force some learning inside throughout the week, only to write yourself off again come the weekend. Music, house parties, gigs, jam sessions, clubs, cheap drink nights, picking up. Mani met, impressed and bedded a steady stream of attractive art students, proving popular for his obvious wit, charm, intellect and worldliness as he found his feet and built social confidence and conviction in his own ideas and opinions.

He had filled out with the change of lifestyle and grown into his image. His thick teenage frame carried some weight from the drinking, but he covered this with big jackets, baggy shirts, trench coats, scarves and long hair. The Brylcreem, so long abandoned, had re-appeared to add that grunge edge to his shaggy mane. The European holidays were paying double dividends for him as he experienced an intense period of growing up, getting off and going out.

He saw less and less of Crispian Childs once the quirky musician switched courses from Creative Writing to Music Theory. They caught up at parties on occasion but it was always fleeting. Cris always seemed to be on the move to a better party, focused on music or joining a jam somewhere. It was OK by Mani. The guy was too intense, but he had fulfilled his role in Mani's life as the portal to this mad, brave, hedonistic new world. Mani had seen the other side and he was well ready to see how far he could push into it.

Empire Building

Having given up to the universe any hope of ever seeing Alison Archer again, Mani's motivation turned to the rules of the art of writing. His course was intensive, covering a range of critical analytics on story structure, characterisation, genres for novels and short stories, as well as professional writing for articles, poetry and writing for children. There were segments on the important aspects of the business of writing and how to get published. He dabbled, he practised, he absorbed like a gigantic literary sponge, voracious in reading the recommended texts and masterpieces that others in his class suggested.

The year hurtled by with all in its place and the serene calmness of Mani's life both satisfied and un-nerved him. He was progressing well at university, while the money continued to roll in from his articles so that he was better-funded than the average uni student. He continued to holiday with *Celia Italia* in semester breaks and his relationship with his father was also on the up and up. He had spent a weekend with Jason at Lismore, seeing the university view of NSW country towns, this being the cousin connection he would never let fade.

The old man had smartened up his act and, hilarious in its warped interpretation of Zen, fate had delivered Peter Alves to the computer industry as he latched onto the very money-making opportunity he had scorned just two years earlier. He was killing it, making the 'mint' so promised elsewhere. Perhaps he was settling down, Mani reasoned, and now making sensible decisions. Life teaches you that.

Celia had expanded *Celia Italia* and would run five tours this year and was already fully booked for six tours in 1993. She had taken her sister's advice and spent her profits from the travel business on a home unit in Paddington, a traditional worker's suburb now gentrified just a hop and a skip from Brisbane's CBD.

Mani felt un-nerved by all this surrounding good news because never before had his life been so aligned and aimed pleasurably in the right direction. There always had been issues – Peter's business worries, his drinking, fights between Mani's parents, the earlier bullying at school and being outcast, a general feeling of awkwardness, the house burning down, his heritage being in question. Things just seemed to go wrong for Mani so enjoying a period of relative stability had him so wary of the next calamity that he couldn't enjoy the smooth times for what they were.

It was during this purple patch that Mani and Jason struck on an idea that could utilise the studies and talents of them both. Mani had been jotting ideas down and whispering plotlines into his now indispensable dictaphone with a view to his future writing. Jason meanwhile, in studying business, was grasping the concepts of money-making, finally seeing the sense in his parent's investment plans. Between them they hatched an idea and now, nearing the end of their first year as uni students, the ambitious duo sat with Jason's mother, with a steamy mugaccino in front of each of them.

"You're suggesting I write a book? Why would people read anything I'd write? It's not like I'm an expert," Patricia stated. She was eyeing the teenagers suspiciously, curious to their motivations.

"You're more of an expert than most people," Jason countered. "And look at what you've achieved. You're a success Mum, you know what works and what doesn't. People want to know this stuff."

"I'm only small time, boys. Don't people want to read about millionaires? Real rich people."

Jason looked at his cousin. Mani seemed more interested in removing the chocolate froth from the side of his cup than this business proposal. Jason continued. "You're on the road to millions, Mum. You're a housewife made good. You and Dad have got how many properties now?"

Patricia fired off her answer without even having to think about it, her sharp mind swift to account of her own situation. "Six, including our own home."

"That's insane Mum," Jason said. "Six times you've done it. I'm sure there are some little tips and tricks you've learnt along the way."

Mani joined the conversation, his choc-exploration completed. "I know I always wondered why you did it and how you did it, Auntie Trish. Like, how can one person own so many properties? If you write a book, then people like my Dad can learn about something that works."

"A guidebook Mum. A roadmap to wealth."

"Aren't there already hundreds of books about getting wealthy?" Patricia said, putting up early roadblocks on this proposed roadmap.

"We've looked into that already Mum, haven't we Mani?"

"There are a ton of get-rich-quick books, shysters and hucksters trying to flog off their ideas to make a quick buck," Mani replied. "Pyramid selling, share trading, precious metal speculation. You name it. All the stuff my Dad was into. But there are virtually no books on getting rich slow and steady through property, especially by Mum and Dad investors like you and Uncle Graham."

"I can't write a book. What do I know about writing?"

"Hello?" Jason moaned. "Mother, what do you think Mani is studying and what has he been doing for the last five years? He's a writer, Mum. He knows how to set it all out and how to get published. All you have to do is write down your stories and then expand it out to address the things to consider." He was leaning forward and counted on his fingers as he listed the considerations. "Loans, interest, deductions, renovation costs, type of property, location. Easy!"

Mani piped up then. "Actually, no need to write it all down." He held up a box. It was a dictaphone. "I got you a gift. You can record it."

Lessons in Living Large

In sharp contrast to his cousin, Jason Sharpe did not need time to find his feet at uni. He in fact, by virtue of his extroverted personality was the one who helped others to find their feet. Southern Cross University was a melting pot, as most universities were, of kids from differing backgrounds and social sectors. Pre-formed alliances amongst kids from their previous high schools remained and cross-integration shook up their cosy existences as SCU became the college of choice for the Gold Coast, Byron Bay and an array of regional towns like Grafton, Ballina and the uni's base Lismore. Jason took on the mantle as the social glue, a conduit through which these disparate groups could set aside their parochial differences and get on with enjoying uni life.

Jason's move to Lismore in 1992 was more than just a random choice of university, more a carefully orchestrated grand plan to arm himself with the best possible all-round education he could garner. It was a short-term move. He knew that. The personal growth he would gain by stepping away from the supportive, loving but staid environment of his home would allow Jason to prove himself away from the protective wing. Then, as planned, he could return to Brisbane a well-rounded package and apply for the larger universities in the city. The challenge was to ensure he was an irresistible lure for these establishments and that meant being a high achiever – top of his class.

His goal of a triumphant return to his hometown was the major focus through that first year of university, as he alternated between hard study and every conceivable extra-curricular activity including his favourite pastime tennis. He lapped up country life, attending rodeos and festivals. He drank with the locals, chased hippy chicks from Nimbin, joined a band punching out rough covers of heavy rock songs and got kicked out of all of the pubs in town with the typical harmless pranks of a teenager on the drink. He secured a job at a local real estate agency part-time, running errands and filing, but managing to pick the brains of all of the senior team members.

Best of all, he was involved. Jason was at every community event, joined the sport clubs and ran their canteens and contributed to their fund-raising efforts and was socially over-active, the quintessential everywhere man proving popular with the local girls with his clean cut good looks, brains and ambition. He lived the life of a local, savouring the learning on offer, the memories, drinking it in, knowing in two years he would be back to Brisbane then on to the world.

He kept in regular contact with Mani and admitted his feelings on country living at the start of his second year at SCU. "I love it but it feels limiting," he said with a sense of languor. "I reckon two years is my absolute limit."

"What's different?" Mani asked. "They're still kids after an education whether they're from the city or country."

"Yeah, I agree, but in some way these country kids have lower targets. Not across the board of course, but I sense it. Not low ambition, don't get me wrong, just that most of them plan on getting their degrees and heading back to their home town to settle down as lawyers or accountants. Not many think bigger, no one thinks global. I swear, if I spent five years here, I'd be the mayor of the joint."

"Oh, Jas. How much for one of those tickets you've got on yourself."

"I'm not being big-headed. It's true."

He wasn't being arrogant. It was more a reflection of Jason's drive, ambition and maturity. He could see a bigger picture, better ways of making things more efficient, more profitable or easier. And he dripped with popular charisma. People loved having him around and he got things done. Lismore would have been well-served to make the most of Jason Sharpe's presence for the remainder of the year. The city would soon welcome him home.

Soon after the start of second semester, he was on the phone once more to Mani with some good news. Patricia's book was ready to print and they had secured retail exposure in Angus &

Robertson bookstores. After being convinced during the conversation over coffee, she had made extensive notes. These were delivered to Mani who fleshed them out and collated them into readable order, while Jason had been negotiating printing and marketing costs. It had materialised quickly, driven by the ambitious project managers Jason and Mani who had negotiated themselves a tidy percentage deal on profits. Getting it professionally typeset and edited, they had opted to go down the self-publishing path and locked in their distribution. The book was simple, informative and its title told readers what to expect. 'Building Wealth Through Investment Property'.

Mani hollered when Jason rang with the news. "Whoo! Your Mum must be stoked. A published author! Now we just need to find someone to read it."

"No issue there, I'm certain of that. The bloke I dealt with in sorting out distribution says that these wealth and self-improvement books fly off the shelves. People wanna know how to get rich. They send 'emselves broke trying to learn how to get rich."

"So you think this could be pretty huge. How many books did we end up printing?"

"1000 copies. RRP $24.95. Angus & Robertson take a fair cut and there are other costs to cover, but I reckon the profit will be about $8 a book. At the 12.5% share each for you and me, we make roughly $1 a book. That'll be a lazy grand each on the first run alone."

"Have a listen to you, finance boy!" Mani chuckled. "Hilarious! Whoever gets you working for them after uni will hit the jackpot."

"Books aren't my thing, though. Business, finance, making money. That's my calling. I'll leave the book stuff to you."

"Funny you should say that," Mani replied. "It just happens that your Mum's not the only one with a book on the go."

"Whattya mean? Are you...?"

"Yeah, man. It just came to me. I was helping Mum research an Egypt tour and the book on pyramids and pharaohs had fallen down the back of the TV cabinet. So I had to pull out the VHS to reach down the back to get the book out when the VHS pulled loose and fell on top of me along with some old movies, one of which was, of course, Indiana Jones, you now the one where Harrison Ford stares down the Well of Souls at the snakes. Temple of Doom, or was it Raiders...Anyway, I'm there with a book about ancient Egypt, a video about a high-octane archaeologist adventurer and I'm in mortal peril with things all over me, stuck down the back of a TV cabinet in a little nook and maybe just maybe there are snakes there too, or at least spiders. So I think, this could be a guy. A character, an idea for a story. So I started scribbling down some ideas. It went from there. It's going to be epic. An historical thriller."

"Wow! If it's as crazy as that story you just told me, it'll be a best-seller. When will it be finished?"

"Finished? Who knows. I won't even start writing it for a year. There's a lot of planning involved. Build the characters, sketch out the scenes in my head. This is going to be some mad story!"

"Let me know if you need help with the printing?" Jason offered.

"Nah, mate. Focus on your Mum's book. By the sounds of it we'll need a second run."

****

"I just feel it is best I pursue the next phase of my study and start my career here in the city. It was a conscious choice to experience country life and while it has been a worthwhile two years, I am now ready for my future path to blossom."

Jason was in a suit, looking good and feeling confident, impressive on all counts.

"Why not complete your studies before seeking employment?" the interviewer asked. "There would be better opportunities available for a fully-qualified graduate."

"It's because I have the capacity to work and study. If I only studied I would feel I was wasting the additional hours available to me each week. The subject matter I'm studying, I'd be reading that anyway. It's my passion. I figure it's either fill those extra hours in the week with another uni degree or get a job in the industry in which I know I belong. And I could use the money. Money makes me happy." He was seeking a graduate role with one of the major banks, a part-time role to learn the ropes of the company. Jason was now back in the city, temporarily staying at his parent's place. He had been on the 12-day pre-Christmas *Celia Italia* trip to France and Spain – his first overseas trip – and he had confirmed his enrolment at University of Queensland. The graduate bank role was a money-making ploy so he could get income to resume his solo life. Though he loved his parents, living at home was an immediate drag. He'd lined up several job applications, an ambitious undertaking for a third year student, but this role could give him experience in finance with a view to learning all aspects of the bank's business. He oozed confidence and charm. There was no contest.

The interviewer, sensing he had struck recruiting gold, leapt at the opportunity to have this go-getter on board. "Jason, this is normally for final year graduates, however as you have proven yourself an exception, we will make an exception. We'd like to welcome you aboard."

From this start Jason cemented his knowledge and made the most of his opportunity, working in the many departments of the bank - how the branch worked, how lending criteria was assessed, spending time in their Treasury department watching traders spot miniscule differences in currencies or interest rates to seize upon to create income for the bank. In his 24-hour work week scheduled around his continuing Commerce degree at university, he learnt all about customer service, sat with a financial planner, processed cheques and daily transactions, even spending time in the marketing department to learn how to make the bank sound like they cared even though the entire operation was directed towards the pursuit of profit and a burgeoning share price.

Where others had jobs delivering pizzas or in the Regatta Pub bottleshop, Jason traded his casual uni clothes for his suit four days a week. Being new to UQ in Brisbane he had not formed the close friendships with his student friends, though there were some CBC Old Boys still on campus at UQ. As a consequence,

Jason's social life was geared more towards having Friday afternoon drinks with the bankers at Friday's bar overlooking the river in preference to the cheap drink nights and house parties of his less affluent uni acquaintances. This triggered a mild case of pretentiousness that didn't fit well with those in any of his social sectors. He soon had it told to him that he might want to pull his head in, a similar message to that delivered by his Dad, Mani, one of the bank's trading managers and a mate from his high school days who was in the same course at UQ. He only needed to be told once – yet to be castigated multiply brought him back to earth like a solemn stone. It never needed doing again.

The extra money was a luxury yet Jason felt that he was not making the progress he envisioned for himself. Renting a flat near the train line in Toowong was very convenient for getting to work in the city, but equally convenient for hitting the pubs. It also suited his housemates, a string of whom thought it a great idea to move off campus into a furnished unit for which their name did not appear on the lease. Jason found out the hard way that money wasn't everything to those who rarely had any. He was left paying the rent wholly by himself several times as broke students skipped out on their obligations.

When 1994 was halfway done, Jason took account of his situation, realising that while his study and work were blooming, he had barely a cent to show for half a year's work, a most un-Jason like outcome. He bit the bullet, swallowed his pride and moved back home to Mum and Dad. He drew on his readings, having consumed a multitude of books about building wealth and investing. The core belief around which he decided he would base his future was the key to riches exclaimed by the old classic book "The Richest Man in Babylon". He would put aside a portion of his pay for him to invest. Religiously. Not to be touched but for the purpose of building his fortune from this day forth.

It was just the first step towards his goal. The second step came from one of the bank's analysts, a young gun who had been with the bank for six years named Adrian Toms. Adrian was mid-twenties, well-regarded in the bank not just for his success but his work ethic. His quiet word to Jason led to the positive change in his manner.

"You were loose the other night, young Jas," Adrian pointed out on a Monday morning. Jason was again spending time in the Treasury trading rooms. "I think you might have been crowing too loudly about your position in the bank, and the world, and your importance."

Jason was sheepish. What he thought was high confidence and joviality had come across as arrogance and brashness. "I didn't realise," he said.

"Sorry to be the one to tell you. I like you mate. You're a good young lad. You're smart, you're clever, you're just not focused. Everyone needs to let loose occasionally but just remember who you're around and that what you say will be noted. Step on the wrong toes and it could take you years to win back your rep."

Jason thanked him. The kind criticism prompted his personal re-assessment.

Later that month, after pulling back on his socialising, he saw Adrian again. Jason sought approval from this ambitious finance expert. He was what Jason wanted to be. He espoused the changes he had made, having quietened down and moved back home with a focus on building his bank.

"Good for you. Let me know when you get a few bob together. I'll show you some of the ropes on how to invest. The markets are looking like they're hotting up. Have you ever bought shares?"

"I have tried following the markets, but I haven't had the capital and to be honest, I can't really pick what's going on."

"Do you wanna learn how to trade directionally?"

"Directionally?" Jason replied, unfamiliar with the term.

Adrian sparkled to life as he spoke about trading, making money. "The trend is your friend. How to recognise patterns in the markets. People who say fundamentals are the only thing to follow are just guessing. Trends set the pattern, patterns set the direction, directional traders make the real money. Everyone else is just throwing darts."

It was jargon to Jason. He thought that being three-quarters through a finance degree meant he would know this strange language that Adrian spoke, but it was as foreign as if he were eulogising in a regional dialect of the mountain tribes of Afghanistan. Over the following weeks he and Adrian become inseparable as they watched markets, studying these mythical trends of which the experienced man preached.

The Efficient Market Theory he knew, but Jason learnt of moving averages, oscillators, volume, support and resistance lines and the Fibonacci wave patterns that could be seen in all walks of life from the human body to nautilus shells to flower petals. He learnt to recognise head and shoulders patterns and simpler versions – triple and double tops and bottoms, the hallmark of an uncertain stock. Jason had found a mentor and in the spring of 1994, he felt confident enough in his learnings and his bank balance to buy his first share on the live market.

"Don't get attached to the company you buy," Adrian warned. "Take your emotions out of play. If it doesn't do what you expect it to do, dump it. If it does, take your profit, weigh up whether to keep some of the stock and move on."

"So sometimes you hold your shares?" Jason asked.

"Yeah, why not, as long as they've paid their way. If you make your profit target but you like the long-term view of the company, pull your stake, maybe offload some for extra capital. I still have bank shares that I bought three years ago and sold enough to secure my profit. They are like free shares and I know they'll go up in the future. That way you keep a little security to back you up, sort of like a superannuation for your trading job."

After months of tutoring, practice trades and back-testing supervised by Adrian, Jason had saved enough for a trading kitty and was ready to place a live trade. Adrian completed a final checklist, re-inforcing his mindset and reasons for wanting to trade.

"Well, I want to get rich and you offered to show me how," Jason said.

"Good enough reason. Get deep though. Deep down, give me the reason."

Jason gave it a moment's thought. "Well, my Mum and Dad are pretty rich, quite successful through their own ideas and toil. I don't want to rely on them. I want to make my own mark, create my own destiny."

"Perfect," Adrian responded. "It sounds like you're ready. Don't lose that motivation."

"I won't."

"So what did your parents do to get rich?"

"Invested in property. Loads of them. Mum wrote a book about it."

Adrian took a few moments to absorb this, before realising who they were talking about. "Your Mum's Patricia Sharpe? She's the talk of the town."

"I'm proud to say that writing a book about it was partly my idea. We published 1000 copies, they sold in under a month and she got picked up by a major publisher. Her book's gone national, in its third print. And you know what she did with her first big royalty cheque?"

"What? Bought a car? Took a holiday?"

No, she put a deposit on another house. She's a machine, my Mum."

The pride was obvious, the causal ambition evident. Jason was driven to succeed, witnessing for himself that success came to those who conceived and believed.

Bleeding at the Keyboard - 1995

Hitting upon the idea for a larger-scale story and beginning the research and planning for his novel, something became very apparent to Mani. He had words in him. That was beyond doubt. His descriptions rang from the pages, of beauty and vivid intensity, his words succinct in their use yet with a fullness that painted the mood of his scenes. He was prolific in his story-telling. The revelation that shocked his system was one of self-understanding and of unleashing his potential. He realised that to become a writer – a real writer – he required discipline.

It would not do to simply sit at his computer and start typing. He had to plan the story, winding and binding it around deeper themes, select scenes and imagine them in detail, understand and develop his characters and then release their voice. To do this, he needed to dig deep inside himself, understand his messages and draw on his and others experiences. He had to do what Hemingway once famously quoted – 'There is nothing to writing. All you do is sit at a typewriter and bleed.'

The parties and drinking would have to be curtailed. Not ceased altogether, for a writer needs to hear voices, witness scenes so as to take little bits of each of the people he sees and know them, know what drives and motivates them. He knew he needed to be around people, in the vicinity of the many crazy situations that spring up in the mad journey of life. Sometimes, he admitted, this was best achieved by being drunk amongst the group he was studying, but more often clarity, sobriety and a keen eye was required. He doubted his companions knew they were his subjects playing out their lives under the watchful eye of a writer.

Mani also realised he needed solitude, peace and quiet times in which to disappear within his own thoughts, go deep into his own psyche and spend time questioning the actions and reactions of humans other than himself. He had to journey into the sewer system of thought, those cavernous chasms where evil lurks disguised as benign creativity and genial intention. This a writer needed to explore and Mani found it cathartic to consider the disparity that two human minds each might consider normal behaviour. His characters flourished, the planning of his story blossomed. The agony of being a writer settled within him alongside the beauty of artistic expression.

His course was going well, his marks were up and his work was being critiqued by his lecturers, among whom were published novelists, providing inspiration for Mani. Knowing he needed to focus his efforts, he advised the student newspaper that his three years of contributions would end, claiming he needed to pull back on his commitments to the publication to work on his own projects.

By the end of his final year at university, Mani had a fully planned scene list and character studies so thorough it was as if he had known these people from a past life. Here at the end of 1995, all that was left to do was to write his novel, weave together the numerous scenes and lines of dialogue that had come to him throughout the year. There was one other thing that needed doing. He was ready to graduate. With honours.

His mother fussed over him. Celia had to instil in Mani an understanding of the gravity of his achievement. He was a scholar, an academic, a graduand with a glorious future before him in his chosen field. Sensing Mani would prefer to skip the recognition ceremony and continue working on his novel, she intervened. "I think you can put aside your project for a day or two and enjoy this, Mani. It will still be there, but without these memories, feeling the crowd applaud your achievement, it will seem like a lost opportunity in a few years' time if you miss it. Plus, there'll be contacts that you will need to work with in the future. You might not know it yet, but cementing these relationships is what helps business along."

"I'm not in business, Mum. I want to write."

"Well, no-one gets to read the book by the man who doesn't know how to get it published. It's a business, Mani. I'm sure they taught you that." Celia helped to straighten the Cambridge gown he had hired for the occasion as he tried on the mortar board headwear. "See," she said. "You look wonderful, darling. Take a couple of days to enjoy this."

Mani saw the sense in it. Mother was right again.

With the graduation complete, Mani enjoyed the celebration of his success. Two nights of parties ensued as he criss-crossed the suburbs to attend gatherings. It culminated in a lunch with his father at the Breakfast Creek Hotel, a majestic century-old Brisbane icon near where the creek joins the Brisbane River.

"I'm surprised you'd be up for a pub lunch the weekend after graduation," Peter said. "I remember how you were after your Grade 12 party, mate. I've never seen a kid so green around the gills."

"Barely touched a drop, Dad. Actually, that's a lie. I had a few, but I'm not so into boozing as I was a couple of years ago. Too much to do to be crook."

They sat at an outside table in a courtyard under a large shade cloth that allowed speckled drips of summer sun to settle over them. The busy nearby roads built a steady hum around their conversation. The crowded hotel was coming to life with lunchtime revellers. The men each had a schooner and the order number was on their table. Sparrows bounced around between the tables, picking at crumbs.

The two men looked about, sipping their drinks, enjoying the November warmth. It was an easy silence between them, the teenage fear of his Dad now replaced by a man to man resoluteness, in company as equals.

"You look good Dad. You look healthy."

He did. The pot belly was gone, as were the smokes.

"Feel good too mate. You get to the point where you realise you're not twenty-one anymore and you have to look after the old temple. You can't drink and smoke yourself to death."

"Not a bad thought. How long have you been off the ciggies now?"

It's gettin' on three years now. Pretty much when I started this job."

"And the job's going well?" Mani asked.

"The job's a ripper. Never underestimate the value of a job. A good job, I mean. Good employer, the benefits, the resources available to ya. You might be all right, as a writer you might not need a boss. But there's a lot to be said for a good job."

"You've changed your tune a bit Dad!"

Peter pouted, as if confused. "How so?"

"Didn't you use to bag people with jobs. I remember you saying a J.O.B. stood for Just Over Broke. That you're better off being your own boss." His tone was accusatory.

"I stand by that. There's not many wealthy employees."

"Auntie Trish is wealthy," Mani countered.

"Fair enough, that's true. If I found the right vehicle it would still be the way to go for me. But that's the hardest part, finding the right vehicle for your talents. It just so happens it suits me right now to have a job."

"I never got it, Dad. Why were there so many bust-ups when I was young? It seemed every year we were going broke for some reason or another."

"What about the good times, mate. Don't forget those, hey. The holidays. You go every year now because I worked hard to take us on that first one. Nice home we had, nice cars. Life weren't too bad for you, young fella."

"You burnt the house down, Dad. And look what it cost you." Mani saw his father's quizzical look. "Mum!" he whined in frustration at having to remind his father. "And now you have this great job in computers but you could have been the owner."

Peter drained his beer, contemplative as if weighing up how to respond to his son's gripes. "Hey, are we here to have a steak and a beer or are we here to take an axe to your old man and cut him down?" he joked. A waitress was on his empty glass, whisking it away.

"I guess we never talked about it. You never told me what was going on even though it always affected me. I'm just curious, Dad. I'm not here to cut you down."

Peter flipped a $20 note onto the table. "Get me another beer, boy and I'll tell you some stuff you mightn't know."

Obedient, Mani went to the bar and returned with two beers. An odd feeling was welling up in him, as if now that he was being released officially into the mad, bad world he needed some sort of blessing. Approval from his father. And taking stabs at his

Dad was his way of eking this validation from him. He was unsure of what he was about to hear, hoping only it would be a sign of love from his father.

He returned to the table and Peter continued.

"Life wasn't all that easy for me growing up. My old man, your Grandad Carl, he was a drinker and didn't provide real well for his family. He loved us and was a ton of fun, but we moved a lot, we had the power cut off a lot and Dad would nick off for days at a time. But it was all a bit of a joke. Mum would laugh it off as if it was a game they played, so when Dad lobbed home it was like a big welcome back party."

"It was only when I was fifteen or sixteen I realized how poor we were, how crap our life was. So I went to work and making my own money made me feel like a big man, like I could provide for Mum and be my own bloke. A big guy in town. So money was important to me. But you and I, Mani, we know it's not, hey? Unless you don't have any!" Peter snorted his laugh at the old joke.

Mani smiled with his father, still unconvinced, still not placated. He kept his beer in front of his mouth to cover his tension.

"Me sending us broke those few times," Peter said, "that was me trying to make something of myself for you and your Mum. Push the envelope a bit, you know."

"There's the problem, Dad. No matter how far you push the envelope, it's still stationery."

Peter laughed. "That's a good one, mate. Mind if I use it?"

Mani bowed. "Most welcome," he said. "But you always had jobs though. You always provided. You sold cars didn't you? I remember the sign with your face on it outside the caryard. You were an eighties celebrity."

"Yeah, I had jobs but I always looked to go one better. Making good money wasn't enough. Anyone could do that. I wanted to go one step further. Be the boss, make more money, get the..." He paused looking for the word and gave a grandiose hand gesture when he found it. "...the adulation of being a success. But it came back to bite me."

"Why's that, do you reckon, Dad?" Mani watched his Dad draw deep from his beer, the froth lining his moustache before being sucked away with the expertise of a life-long mo-wearer. "Working for yourself takes discipline and effort. I think I had the effort all right, but I couldn't control myself to get it right and keep it going. Not easy being the boss, trying to get rich. It can get competitive. You lose track of what's important to ya, and what works. You gotta stand out and appear different to every other mug trying to do the same. It's like trying to make love to a porcupine. You're just one prick up against thousands."

Mani giggled at his Dad's analogy. "That's a good one, Dad. Can I use it?"

"Most welcome, son." He smiled back at his boy. "I've tried some things, Mani, had some success, screwed some things up, but I never did the wrong thing by you, mate. And I've always tried to do the right thing by your mother, though she'd argue the point."

"She never says a bad word about you, Dad. She has a laugh about some of what you and her got up to when you were married."

"She's a good woman, your Mum. Yeah, I stuffed up, but my intentions were good. I'm glad she's happy."

An attractive waitress, in white shirt and short black skirt arrived with their steaks. The men stopped talking and smiled, both watching her leave.

"Have a listen to me," Peter said. "I've been waffling. Here's cheers to ya graduation, mate. Best advice I can give ya – find what you're good at, I think we all know what that is, stick at it, appreciate it and don't get bloody sidetracked like I did. Don't jeopardise that one thing until you're absolutely sure there's a better option."

Mani raised his glass and nodded his head. "Thanks Dad."

Here's somethin' I heard that I wish I'd listened to when I was your age. One of my early bosses said 'Find your obsession, make it your profession and you'll never work a day in your life'. There ya go. Dad's advice. Now, this steak isn't gonna eat itself. Say Grace, boy.

"Grace," Mani replied with an obedient smile, knowing the joke.

"Wacky-doo," his father said. "Let's get stuck into it then!"

****

The lunch with his father cemented something for Mani. He did not want to waste the start he'd been given. He thought back over his writing – the essay competition that started it all, that meeting with the stall-owner in Barcelona, his first clunky articles, the exaltation of his first sale and being published, the newspaper column, the degree course and now his planned longer work. It was a privilege to be able to write, an absolute joy. It was not to be frittered away or disrespected. As his father might say – this book's not gonna write itself.

He resolved to throw his full effort into his novel, let the research and the writing consume him. It had been two years since he conceived the story and formulated the plot and characters. Over past months he'd conjured the details of the story, yanking in the threads and pulling them tight, adjusting them here and there so as to close any possible gaps, so that the story was as tight as a bodice on a buxom broad. Mani now had access to the internet to nail down some of the more difficult research parts and had two foolscap spiral notebooks full of notes, these pages overflowing with pictures, sketches and diagrams, so that on Christmas Eve 1995, he felt ready to begin his novel.

It flowed from him, this story of a legendary archaeologist adventurer, trained in weapons, martial arts, war tactics and ancient mythology who teamed with his motley crew of ex-pats, discommunicants and soldiers of fortune to seek out the mysterious links of artefacts based on the Seven Ancient Wonders of the World. It was a mythical, historical adventure thriller and due to Mani's precise planning and deep knowledge of each character, the words came easily. Three thousand words a day for most days. He broke only for Christmas lunch, again at midnight on New Year's Eve to share champagne with his mother and Auntie Trish and for the odd day to attend graduate lunches through the university, a writing workshop or book launch in the city. Otherwise he was at his keyboard, bleeding.

He fretted while away from his story for any length of time, feeling the guilt that he might not be doing enough to justify his study, his future. That he might not be working hard enough or fulfilling his potential. He even felt that this was his one big moment, a one-time opportunity to break through, failure at which could mean having to go and get an actual job.

Like the spiral of water sucking down a drain, the story funnelled from Mani, picking up pace as it reached its conclusion until, in mid-February of 1996, a drained Mani emerged from his room in his mother's Paddington apartment with a printed pile of papers.

"Mum. Look!" He held up the stack of paper, his first draft of his first novel. One hundred and fifteen thousand of his finest words. He smiled broadly at his Mum, accompanying this with a small fist pump. "I've finished!"

****

"Get side on, bend your knees and swing through the ball. A gentle arc. Eye on the ball."

"Easy for you to say," Mani puffed. "My legs are gone. If I bend my knees, they'll collapse under me. Honestly, who does this stuff for fun?"

Mani had sought a meeting with one of his lecturers, Tony Morwell, a fit, middle-aged man, himself a published novelist and one of Mani's closest mentors. The older man had suggested they meet for a game of squash followed by coffee.

Tony, thin and muscular thanks to his regular exercise of squash and jogging mocked his younger, tubbier protégé. "Easy for me? I'm fifty-eight years old, Alves and I tell you my body doesn't find this easy. But I do it anyway. It's good for the mind too. And I say if you are going to be a writer, would you prefer to be handsome like Grisham or have a body like old Tom Keneally? You could let yourself go and grow one of those little leprechaun beards. Might be good for your writing career."

Mani cleared the sweat from his eye sockets, his face red. He held the little black ball with its yellow spot. He held it up as he offered a deal. "Realistically, I'm not going to take a game off you. How about we stop if I win another point?"

"It's only been twenty minutes!"

"Well you don't want me having an aneurysm, do you? You would be responsible for robbing the world of one of the 21st century's greatest literary voices."

Tony dabbed at the thin film of sweat on his forehead with his wristband. "We'll see how this novel shapes up before we start making grand statements about the greatness of your voice. Your serve."

It lasted a further ten minutes. Mani had been toyed with on the squash court and gratefully shouted the juice and coffees when they retired to the café. His intention was to procure some guidance on the next steps for his novel, so he was justifiably eager to do what it took to get any sort of feedback.

"So, give me the synopsis, Alves. First point of getting published. Have your pitch ready. The ten second version, a one sentence pitch, a one paragraph alternative and an extended one page version."

Mani fumbled over his plot, knowing from the experienced writer's raised eyebrow that this would be something that needed to be whipped into shape.

"Hmmm," Tony said staring off away, his mind absorbing the plotline. "Good story. Tell me about the characters."

This was where Mani sprung to life. These people he had imagined, built from air and knew so well. He gave a quick background on his protagonist, his gang of miscreants and the antagonist he had pictured making the task of his hero so difficult.

Tony listened in, nodding mostly, frowning other times. "The story appears sound, though a little far-fetched at times, though that's just my own personal view. There seems to be a good array of characters. I already know you write beautifully, Mani. What is it you want from me?"

"Just some feedback from someone who's done it before. I write a lot but I still can't believe I'm any good. And I'd like to know what I need to do to get it published."

"How much have you written," Tony queried.

"It's all done. Finished."

"Finished?"

"Yeah."

The older man's eyes widened. "You were still planning it when you finished uni last year. And now it's complete two months later? Have you been possessed?"

Mani pulled a little face, not knowing what else to do. He was proud of his hard work, but uncertain of his place. Unsure of the quality of what he had produced and nervous to be offering it for appraisal.

"I'll read the first three chapters as well as your synopsis. Get your synopsis in order, Alves. I'll make some scratches on it over the next two weeks and tell you what I think. And if I ask you for the rest of the story, you'll know you're onto something."

It didn't take that long. Mani had delivered a printout of his story to Tony the next day, leaving it with him while he continued his own editing. Within two days, Tony had rung to arrange another coffee, his shout this time. "Bring the rest of the book, my friend. I want to know how it plays out."

They met, this time, at Mani's direction, without the exercise. "There is little I'd change," Tony stated. "Maybe some more description and background on your main man. Humanise him a bit, but otherwise it is pretty tight."

"It's my first draft. I acknowledge that I need to tidy it up some more," Mani said. "Impose my unique touch on this ubiquitous blaze of eloquence."

Tony smiled, shaking his head at the growing assuredness of his young student, now seemingly destined to make his way in his chosen field. He spooned a half sugar into his coffee. "Don't get ahead of yourself. Granted, though, it is an exciting story."

"Glad you like it," Mani replied. "It means a lot to me. In your esteemed and experienced opinion, is it publishable?"

"More than that. It's a best-seller, Alves. You lucky so and so. A first time author and you hit the mark. That rarest of beasts. If it's okay with you I've already lined up a meeting with my agent and my publisher. Are you ready for the ride of your life?"

****

Graham Bedser dabbed his thick fingers at the buttons on his desk phone. A short, balding man with a rotund build that belied the physical effort that he put in trying to keep his weight under control, Graham had these same stubby fingers in a variety of pies, chief of which was book publishing. His numerous contacts from university days and through the growth of his management business had him representing a wide selection of individuals as their manager. He booked media types for public appearances, represented sportsmen in their contract discussions and was the agent for a few well-received, successful authors, one of whom, the academic Tony Morwell, had demanded he take a punt on a protégé of his, a young uni student who'd drilled out a novel of high quality and more importantly great marketability, in just a couple of months.

Graham had met Mani Alves after reading a selection of his work and agreed to represent him. Now, just eight weeks later, Graham's reputation, along with the esteem in which he was held within the industry had combined to kick a serious goal. Young Alves, his new client, had been offered a lucrative offer for a first-time author. Graham waited for the phone to answer.

There was no answer. He gave it fifteen minutes and tried once more, again with no result. He was meeting with one of his Channel Nine celebs for coffee soon at Paddington, just a short drive from his Milton office space. He would drop by Mani's unit on the way back to the office to see if he was there, not wanting this news hanging on him for too much of the day. Graham Bedser preferred sewing up deals and moving to the next opportunity.

He rapped on the door of the unit several times, knowing the sleep habits of young people could have Mani still under the covers at this time of day. Graham had already had two business meetings and punched four coffees into his system this morning before 11am. He banged on the door again then pulled out his sleek new Motorola mobile phone. He flipped the earpiece up to reveal the dialpad and adjusted the antenna, enjoying the chunky weight of this new contraption in his hand. He dialled Mani's home number once again, his thick fingers squashing two numbers at once, forcing a re-dial. He waited, hearing the phone inside the unit ringing, but to no avail. He returned to his office.

He wanted this news off his chest. Graham rang Tony Morwell. "Tony, this Alves kid. Is he a big sleeper?"

"What?" Tony replied, confused.

"I'm trying to reach your mate Alves. Where might he be?"

Tony was clueless as to Mani's whereabouts, so suggested he call his father. Graham pulled out the White Pages and found a number for Peter Alves. No answer at home but the answering machine suggested contacting his mobile number.

Graham called. Peter answered. Graham felt a sense of achievement. Of progress. He introduced himself, asking after Mani.

"He's probably sleeping, the lazy bugger," Peter gagged. "Try knocking on the door until he gets out of bed."

"Tried that," Graham said.

"Well, I could ask around for ya. What's your number, old mate. I'll give you a buzz back soon." Peter hung up and looked through his little black book for his nephew Jason's mobile number. "Jason, mate. It's your Uncle Peter. There's some bloke after Mani. D'ya know where he is?"

Jason was shocked to hear from his uncle. "He's having a girl's day out with my Mum and Auntie Celia. They were going shopping at the Myer Centre then going for a boat cruise for lunch. One of those paddle steamers you see on the river. Can't remember what they're called. Kangaroo Paddle King or Queen or something like that."

Peter called Graham, happy with his contribution to the manhunt. "He's been shopping with the ladies apparently and now he's off to lunch on the Kangaroo Queen paddleboat. Have ya seen them ones on the river?"

Graham thanked Peter for his effort. He knew the boats, but the name didn't sound right. He hung up the phone and yelled out to his secretary. "Janice, what's the name of those paddle steamers that chug up and down the river?"

"The Kookaburra Queen," Janice called back.

"Kookaburra," Graham said under his breath. That was it. He swilled the last of his coffee and looked out of his window. His view looked over the Riverside Expressway and its constant flash of vehicles, beyond which was the Brisbane River and it so happened that at that precise moment on the river, the very paddle steamer upon which his client now sat appeared around the bend from its city berth. "He's on that boat," Graham muttered. He had to get on it too.

The Kookaburra Queen would lap the river from the city, southwest to Toowong, then back past the city to the New Farm reach of the river, before returning to its moorings. Graham knew he couldn't wait for three hours. He needed to get this news to Mani. He needed to board the ship.

He cabbed it into the city, leaping out at Eagle Street Pier, the high end of town where many of the major legal and broking firms had their head offices. He galloped down to the waterfront. He had to try to get the boat to stop on its journey back past its base. He spoke to the Kookaburra Queen cashier behind her window. "I have a very important piece of news for one of your guests. I need to get on board," Graham announced.

"Sorry, sir, we can't stop the boat. Unless it's an emergency."

Graham knew now he had to lie. "There are three people on that boat, members of the same family," Graham said with false solemnity. "There has been some unbelievable news. Something has happened. I'm their solicitor, and I am certain that they would not want to be having what I am sure is a fabulous lunch without being privy to this news. I really need to board the boat to break this news to them. It is an emergency." He dabbed at his eyes with his handkerchief for effect.

"I see, sir. I'll get the captain on the radio immediately," the young lady said.

"Let me speak to him," Graham said reaching into the booth. She gave him the radio, the curled cable stretching through the window. "Skipper, my name is Graham Bedser and I represent one of your guests. I implore you, sir. I need to break some news to them, three members of the one family, it's just unbelievable what's happened. I can see you coming around the bend as we speak. I am at headquarters. Eagle Street. With your permission, can I board the ship, sir?"

It was most unusual for the boat to stop mid-cruise, the gargantuan task of manoeuvring the vessel close to the pier being such a precise operation. But Graham had made it sound serious enough to warrant such an action. The ship berthed, Graham leapt on and ran to the ship's bridge. "Launch her again, skip. I'll find my client."

Graham went to the restaurant level of the boat. Guests had resumed their meals after the surprise docking. He eyed the room, seeing Mani with two ladies on the verandah. He went to the bar, paid cash for a bottle of champagne, grabbed four glasses and went to the table.

Mani was just finishing his meal while the women were mid-meal and doing most of the talking. The young man looked up as Graham approached the table. It took several seconds for the face to register for Mani. "Mr Bedser," said Mani. "What are you doing here?"

Graham shook Mani's hand and introduced himself to the ladies. "You must be Mrs Alves, Mani's mother. I'm Graham Bedser," he said, shaking both the ladies' hands. "And Mani's aunt. Pleased to meet you both."

"Mum. Auntie Trish. Graham's my agent who's trying to get my...oh my God! What are you doing on the boat?"

It hit Mani, the only possible reason Graham Bedser would be on this boat, at their table. With champagne. Mani stared. The ladies smiled. Graham popped the cork off the champagne bottle, sending it flying off the verandah into the river.

"You're getting published, Mani. I have the contract right here. But we'll sort that out later. Time for bubbles, ladies!"

They stood, they toasted Mani and drank a mouthful. Mani downed his glass, accepted a refill. He slipped off his jacket, placed it over the back of his chair, swilled another glass of champagne and then, ignoring all of his childhood warnings about swimming after eating, he climbed on the rail of the ship's edge, let out a roar, and executed a perfect bomb dive off the Kookaburra Queen into the murky Brisbane River.

As you do when you get such news.

As Fortunes Rise...

The book was released in spring to mild fanfare. Mani brought Celia along for the obligatory media calls organised by Graham, who had secured favourable reviews to kick start the campaign. Mani was required to travel to Sydney, Melbourne and of course there were a range of hometown appearances in bookstores across Brisbane.

Graham Bedser wanted to play on Mani's youth to promote the story and also his homespun writing technique. "Let's keep it under wraps that you're a university-qualified writer. It'll be better for that common connection that we let the punters hear your story about starting writing on your overseas holiday. Talk up that Barcelona bloke inspiring you and all that."

Mani was unconvinced. "Won't it turn off people who want a more high-brow novel," he argued, and then to make his point he bunged on a southern redneck accent, "if we pretend it's just a yippee-doo yarn by a slack-jawed yokel who knows how to conjugate his hick words into a less discriminatin' readin' format identifiably accommodating to the common man?"

"What are you talking about?" Graham frowned.

"You want me to dumb it down and pretend I'm not educated on one hand, but on the other you want to utilise the fact that I'm young!"

"There's no doubt you're educated. I think the story you've woven gives that away. It's about marketing, Mani."

"How about we pretend I'm actually seventy-five years old and I'm aging backwards. I've spent the past thirty years in a coma after having fallen from my treehouse where I was raised by monkeys, and now I can play classical piano, and I wrote this novel, in mirror image, in a previously unknown Amazonian jungle tribe dialect using my elbow dipped in boiling pig's blood. That'll get us some sales!"

"All good, Mani," Graham responded wearily. "We should make that your second novel. For this one, why don't we leave the marketing and promotion to me and my twenty years' experience in the industry? If I'm wrong, you still have a book and an immense talent for writing, whereas I will have made no money from this effort, no income and have one less client. You win, I lose. But I'm betting that won't happen."

It was two outspoken egos in one room awash with cheek, sarcasm and opinion. Celia smiled as she watched her son bursting out of his shell, his confidence high after this endorsement of his ability. Mani too felt a freedom unknown before and was encouraged by the unfettered banter with his agent.

Graham Bedser was opinionated, aggressive, obstinate, often flustered, borderline Tourette's and yet a success, and Mani enjoyed mouthing off in a similar way. Not in an arrogant manner, more of a confident, measured, open assessment of how he saw the world combined with a swift active mind and a sharp turn of phrase. He was finding his voice.

Graham delivered as he was known to do and had done so often. People gravitated to the big-cheeked, shaggy-haired, thick-set writer when they saw Mani, as he laughed and talked his way through his appearances. Sales emanated from these genuine touch points, books signed for purchasers with a laugh and a smile thrown in for free. A buzz began, helped inimitably by the quality of the writing and the depth and action within the story. Reviews were glowing. The first run sold quickly, bookstore demands were outrageous, saying they needed more copies, thousands more. A new contract was drawn up to account for the quick success, a shrewd component of the contract for the original run that Graham had built in just in case this sort of response ensued.

Graham didn't need to say 'I told you so'.

When Mani next appeared in his office, he dropped to his knees and shuffled to his crafty agent with arms outstretched for a hug like the monkey boy he proposed he should be. "Yes sir, Graham sir. You're the boss, sir!" Mani mocked, for which he received a pat on the head and a hair tousle.

"Arise Sir Monkeyman," Graham joked. "We've got some planning to do. They've opted to print a quarter of a million copies before Christmas and you're going on tour. How would you like a white Christmas in the UK with me as company?"

****

The UK tour was a resounding success and Mani Alves became vaunted as a fully-fledged publishing superstar. The novel was into its third print run and the press was hailing the story as an action masterpiece. The month in the UK with his agent and his mother was such a whirlwind of press meetings, book signings, morning TV show appearances and cocktail functions that Mani felt he could not leave when it was time to wind it up.

Mani bade farewell to his concerned mother and with a posse of Graham's contacts willing to show him how the glitterati perform in the Old Dart, he opted to stay on for an additional month of parties, booze, sightseeing and female adulation. It was the sort of life that very much appealed to Mani, a break he felt he deserved after university commitments flowed straight into his writing the novel and now the merry go round of promotions.

He arrived back in Australia from the Jack Frost of an English winter into a merciless February heatwave that knocked him for six. He needed to dry out, get some normalcy into his existence and think about what was next for the 'new Oz novel pin-up boy', a description of himself he read in a magazine article, prompting a self-deprecating giggle. "What a desperate bunch Aussie chicks must be if they use me as a pin-up. Imagine me, lounging luxuriously naked, like Jack Thompson in Cleo, with a quill in my mouth and copy of my novel covering my privates. Giving that lustful, come hither look."

Jason, who was visiting for a catch-up cringed. "I just had to re-eat a little bit of sick that came up with that image. Thanks Mani." Jason had given Mani several days to get over the jet-lag but now wanted to hear the stories of living large in London. His second motive, with Mani's blessing, was to display his financial skills by discussing his cousin's new-found wealth and offer his input into how he should manage the money.

Mani had yet to see his first royalty cheque, surviving on the advance and relying on the kindness of strangers willing to buy for him, but he knew a serious six-figure cheque was in the mail. "It feels weird," he said to Jason as they drank coffee on the balcony of Celia's unit. "I feel like I should be out getting a job, or writing some stories to try to get some money coming in."

"How much are you expecting?" Jason asked.

"Don't know for sure. Graham says we've sold more than half a million copies. Using our old formula for your Mum's book, that should mean half a million dollars, though you reckon the author would get a bit more recognition than that."

"So blasé. Just a lazy half mil!"

"Well, I'm all ears. What's my Bank-Johnny cuz got to tell me about finances?"

"I'm a qualified Financial Advisor and I'll do the advice for free. You won't have to squander thousands on a fee."

"Like my old man. He got shafted by an advisor years ago, I remember. You're not going to blow my dough are you?"

"On the contrary. You could lose the plot and write crap from now on and you'll still have a roof over your head, a portfolio and an income. You're set for life, my man."

Jason outlined his plan, as did Mani for his own projects in coming months. A new story was in the works, he would re-start his 'Best of Brisbane' articles and he planned to spend some more time with his father. There were university friends to catch up with. Tony Morwell had invited him to some functions and there was more media to be done for his novel. "The agent wants me to tour the book again, but I need three months to get straight. I've hit my booze limit for this year and it's not yet March."

The young men continued their conversation, their bond obvious. The child in each of them was still apparent, though they had grown from boys to men, each a product of strong family and even stronger women. Their mothers had expertly guided these men like a mother bird ought.

The phone rang as Mani told Jason about UK life.

"Mani Alves, my old friend," the voice on the other end of the line began. "Now an international superstar, I hear. Do you know who this is?"

Mani noted a tinge of recognition of the voice. He scanned his past, faces rushed by but nothing came. "Sorry, no. Who is it?"

"Seriously, come on Alves. I got you your first shag. Taught you how to party, how to drink. You could say I'm the one who cracked the egg to get you out of your shell. You might still be shagless without my intervention, Alves. And you say you don't recognise me. Please, sir!"

"Right. Chris, yeah? Crispian Childs. From uni, how are you, mate? It's been a while."

"It has and I'm well, my old mate." Crispian spoke with a refined, regal air. "And we are mates, Mani, despite our absences. From one mate to another, I'm ringing to congratulate you on your successes."

"Just lucky, Chris."

"No, Alves. Not luck. I saw this coming. I knew you had it in you, this brilliance, this vision. Though are paths crossed just briefly and I sought a different glide path to you, I could sense a greatness within you. Success was assured and I have kept an eye out, expecting this success to arrive."

Mani felt uncomfortable with the praise, then remembered that he often felt uncomfortable in Chris's presence. "How long has it been? Four years? You went and studied music, didn't you?"

"I followed where my talent urged me to go. Becoming a musician – and one of some note, I might add, though I hardly imagine you'd be one to read the local street press. It was simply a natural progression, as writing seems to have been for you, Alves. Which leads me to the purpose of my call. I'd like to meet."

"Sure. Why not?" Mani said. "Though I must be upfront and say I am off the alcohol for a time. Overdid it in London."

"This wouldn't be a social meeting. I have a proposal for you. A collaboration, a merging of our talents. I want to score your work, Alves. Think rock opera, that kind of thing."

"It's not something I've ever done before. I'm not sure I'm ready for..."

"Let's just get together and see how the discussion pans out," Crispian Childs interrupted before Mani could refuse. They made arrangements.

"OK, fine Chris. But no promises, OK?"

"Fine. And one thing. I go by the name Eagle now."

"Again, fine."

"Oh, and another thing. Did you ever find that girl you so obsessed after?"

Mani stayed quiet, but for his chest exploding apart and his face reddening as an alarm went off in his head. He turned away from Jason, shielding his call.

"What was her name?" Eagle said. "It was like a comic book name. Andrea. No, Alison. Alison Arnold, wasn't it? We thought you'd made it up."

"No," was all Mani could manage. He had forgotten that he had told Eagle about Alison when they first met. He was anxious, ashamed and still obsessed, his body racked with tension.

"You never found her then. You were nuts over her, Alves. We thought you were a bit loopy. Alison Arnold, hey? Your good sort, unrequited."

"That wasn't her name, and that's all gone now," Mani said.

"Well, what was her name?"

"It doesn't matter, Chris."

"It's Eagle. That's my name. What's hers?"

"I'm going." Mani was exasperated. He shielded himself from Jason across the table, shame glowing within him.

"Don't get bitchy, Alves. Just say her name."

"No."

"Say it," Eagle demanded, his old emotional grip encircling Mani. "Say the name."

"Alison Archer!"

"Archer. There it is. That wasn't so hard, was it? Now, I'll see you next Tuesday. And don't give up on Alison Archer. Now you're famous, your luck might change."

Mani held the phone limply as the line went dead. The past had been dredged up, bringing an old foe with it and re-igniting thoughts of his childish obsession. Mani felt hollowed out, knowing that Crispian – Eagle – had weaved his web around him once more. Mani became the nervous gullible kid from those first weeks of uni and his image of Alison Archer refreshed in his mind as he wondered for the first time in months where she might be now.

****

Holed up in his hotel room in Adelaide, Mani felt his life was on a repeat program. On his second Australian tour, he had become the 'Punxsutawney Phil' of his own existence. He went through his motions – discuss his book on a morning chat show, regurgitate the synopsis his mentor had advised him to learn by rote, discuss these characters with whom he had now grown bored, put on a brave face and tell some jokes for the audience at a reading and sit for a book-signing. This followed by lunch or dinner with publishers, have drinks, retreat to his room and let the obsession begin. Wake to a hotel buffet breakfast, the only variance to re-code his program was to fly to the same hotel in a different city and engage the set routine.

The obsession he indulged was the re-birth of the long-dormant fixation on the mythical Alison Archer. Mani knew it was foolish, saw the folly in rekindling the connection with this lass he had not seen since November 1987. Ten years. He chided himself for his own stupidity, but still he acted on his yearning. It had begun again, re-launched by his old nemesis, Crispian Childs, the dirty bird Eagle who asserted a nefarious hold over the now-mature man.

It was an injurious routine he had set for himself, a foreboding act of self-sabotage that affirmed his perpetual loneliness. Mani saw it for what it was, recognised the unhealthy pattern and its inevitable portents. He would never be able to move on into a conventional man/woman relationship until he either ended the weirdness or struck on a most unlikely success.

It would begin upon his return to the hotel room. He would start on the mini-bar while channel-surfing, a pre-cursor with which he tried to fool himself until he could hold out no longer. The miniature booze bottles guzzled, he would order a carafe of the hotel's finest house wine, flip open the phone book of whatever city he was in and start dialling all the A. Archer's in town.

As the invigoration of the project's potential wore off and his sobriety was whisked away by swilling direct from the carafe, a melancholic funk settled over Mani. He became rude to those answering his late-evening calls, demanding he speak with Alison. Occasionally, an Alison would reside in the home he called, and with his hopes raised, he would put on his most charming voice, unaware of his incoherence. It inevitably proved a false dawn.

Eventually, discouraged by the impossible odds of success and drunk to the point of passing out, he would stop the calls to flick the channels on the TV to find the stimulus he needed. He bought a movie if necessary. The night would end, as usual over the past two weeks of his book tour, with Mani crashing into slumber, his pants hooked around one ankle, having released his pent-up loneliness and male tension into the 'A' page of the phone directory.

Leaving Home – 1998

"That's a shocking hairdo," Jason said to his cousin. "What the hell have you done?"

"It's a severe undercut mullet," Mani replied, shaking his curtain of hair down the back of his head. "It's kind of a best-of do. Best of the eighties and nineties."

"Shocker. It's not a hairdo, it's a hair-don't."

"It'll catch on…"

They were at the Paddington Tavern, the famous 'Paddo', where rows of pool tables and banks of TV screens entertained the throngs while cheap drinks at the 'Sunday Sesh' lubricated the atmosphere. Jason and Mani were on the third schooner and their second game of pool, with Mani attempting to repeat his unexpected victory over the kid who was good at everything.

It was Mani's last night in Brisbane before a brief trip back to London with Celia and his agent. This trip was not about his novel, but about an opportunity to expand his writing scope by going back to where it all began – travel writing. Mani had been offered a plum role as the Euro travel editor with a swanky London mag.

"How will that work?" Jason asked.

"I'll be based in London, travel two weeks of every month to a place of my choosing to discover the hidden delights of that place and then I regurgitate what I see into feature pieces for the magazine. We negotiated to allow time for writing the next novel. And there's a weekly opinion piece in one of the large London dailies, which is the parent publication of the travel mag. It's such a great offer. I'm heading over to check it out and, if all's well, to sign on."

Jason continued the stirring about Mani's hair. "You sure they won't look at you and rescind all offers? Some countries ban looking like you do."

"At least I can fix my hair. Your face on the other hand..." It was a shallow sledge that could never work due to Jason's indisputable handsomeness.

"Will you take the job?" Jason asked.

"Be mad not to. Who wouldn't leap at a salaried position to go on holidays, with flexible hours. It seems it's London for me. You'll miss me terribly, won't you?" Mani smiled.

Jason lined up his shot. "Yeah. Who'll I beat at pool when you're gone?" He drilled his shot into the end pocket. "Your new unit. You've only just bought it. You'll be renting it out, I presume?"

"I'll check with your Mum. She's the property pro. She can guide me on the property like you guided me on the shares. How many properties has your Mum got now?"

"Twelve, I think. Just ridiculous. And she's doing training sessions now too. Teaching others how she did it. Cluey lady, my Mum."

"How good is that? Why didn't you go down that property path?"

"Shares are the way for me. I get them. And they work for me."

"I hope you know what you're doing. Shares seem risky," Mani said as he chalked his cue.

"Relax, mate. I've got you in blue chips, steady as she goes. Buy and hold, long term. I would never risk your dough in anything else, certainly not in what I do anyway. Options, now there's where some risk lies. But risk equals return. It's not for the faint-hearted."

"Options. What are they?"

"Let's just say if the market goes up, which I think it will, I make ten times the return I could on shares. It's a type of leverage."

Mani creased his brow. "I've heard that word. I've heard the old man say it. Be careful, man."

"I am being careful. I study this stuff. It's my bread and butter, Mani. I make sure I get paid upfront. Manage the risk and it's money for jam. It's called 'selling puts'. I sell puts on tech shares. I studied this at uni and it's only just gelled how it works now I'm doing it. I'm making a grand a week so I must be doing something right."

It was gung-ho Jason at his best. He was excited about the cashflow. This money appeared in his account, a couple of hundred here, a few hundred there, and he just had to hold tight and hope the market kept rising and enough time elapsed. He knew it was risky, had heard of people who had been stung through option trading when the market turned against them. But he was riding it while times were good, though it could be stressful. He hid his fears of how it would feel if things went wrong.

The cousins kept playing pool. Jason kept his exterior of calm. Here they were, two rich young guys – millionaires elect – partying, playing pool, attracting the inevitable female attention which Jason's looks invited and Mani's verbosity retained. The night would end with rounds of shots and their choice of company. The enviable lifestyle of the young and wealthy.

****

The London reconnaissance trip was a success. The job with the travel magazine was all it promised – good pay and superb benefits. Mani had signed on the dotted line the same day he arrived, encouraged by Graham Bedser and Celia. It gave them two weeks to seek out the necessities of accommodation in London for a twenty-something leaving home. It also allowed Mani to indulge his many invites to A-list parties across London. Mani could still pull an invite while his novel continued to sell well and the parent publication of his new employer was affording both his book and his arrival in London some generous paragraph space.

With Celia's eye for quality and Graham's negotiating prowess, they sourced an apartment in Chelsea, within the Knightsbridge area. It was an urban hideaway on a tranquil tree-lined street with the underground just minutes up the road. The building housed four superbly appointed apartments behind its Victorian façade and Mani was convinced that he was getting a bargain to rent it for £1,600 per week. It had an open plan kitchen and dining area, plenty of space within, a giant four-poster bed and smatterings of 1800's antique mahogany furniture and unusual appointments such as a deer antler candelabra.

The coup de grace for Mani though, was the games room. It held a pool table, pinball machine, foosball table, a sit-down arcade game emulator as well as a big-screen TV with cable and the obligatory Playstation console. It was a rich boy's wonderland furnished and designed for the rising social class of young, rich playboys, new money who wanted their large incomes to support lifestyles of grown-up hedonism in the heart of London.

There were plenty such people. Hedge fund traders, IT gurus, gun salesmen and advisors, the next-big-thing musos signed to big record deals. Mani was one amongst them and this Chelsea apartment met his needs, being three underground stops from his office in Piccadilly. While Celia spent the remainder of the fortnight scouting for nearby services, supermarkets and utilities to help Mani settle in, Graham organised meetings with contacts to ensure his trip was tax deductible. Mani spent the following days party-hopping, making himself known in the right circles, knowing he could knock back several party invites and still be at the hottest ticket in town.

This would be his life for the next few years as long as, he recognised, he kept churning out the words. This had never been a problem. Indeed his second novel was well advanced in its planning, justifying the advance the publishers had outlaid to allow him to live this life.

****

The mix of trepidation and excitable anticipation had Mani on an emotional roller-coaster. It was one thing to leave home and move to a unit in the same suburb as his Mum, but to cross oceans, entire continents and go half a world away from the safety of the home nest had Mani fending off nagging doubts.

Peter attempted to reassure him. "She'll be right, mate. Me and your Mum are just a phone call away. Anytime of the day, give us a buzz and we'll chat," he said as they lunched together. Peter was looking sharp in a suit and tie, the image matching his success in computer sales. It had been his longest stint in one job for nearly two decades, reflecting the steadiness now cradling his life. He was clearly in a good paddock though, having piled on fifteen kilograms since giving up the cigarettes.

"Thanks Dad. I'll call at 4AM on a Sunday when I run out of money out on the town. I'll beg for a loan."

"Be buggered. I'll let the phone ring out. You're the one should be givin' me a loan," he said, letting the words flow into his trademark cackle.

Mani enjoyed the family support. Celia too was accommodating. "Never, ever, feel that you're alone," she said. "Pick up the phone. I can come over if things get desperate."

"What, like if I burn the baked beans? No need for that, Mum. I'm not a mummy's boy."

"Well maybe this Mummy needs her boy. You are still keen to meet for the *Celia Italia* tours, aren't you? It's the Rhine Valley and Tuscany this tour. Three weeks."

"I'll never say not to Tuscany, mother," Mani stated, stepping in to hug Celia.

And so Mani was comforted. At home he settled into a routine of working on his second novel, knuckling down and locking himself away. Bum on seat as a writer should to focus his thoughts and create.

Late one afternoon, with Mani having put in nearly 5 hours of solid writing, the phone in his unit rang. An unwanted distraction. It was Graham Bedser. "Mani, I've got an invite for you to present at the Brisbane Writers Festival before you jet out. It's a debate between young writers and older authors. You know, knowledge and experience versus enthusiasm and fresh ideas."

"Sounds like an opportunity to get opinionated. When is it?"

"I need to confirm with them ASAP. It is on September 7, but let me wrap it up. I'll call you back in five with details."

He clunked the receiver down, leaving Mani tingling and unable to settle himself. He stood and walked to the window looking out over the hill that rose from the heart of Paddington up to Red Hill. His line of sight drew up from his lounge room over the workers' cottages and terraced yards to the fortress-like red brick of St Brigid's Church on the ridge and the blue sky beyond. Wider out, he could sneak some city views. He never tired of the view; it inspired him when the words wouldn't come.

He'd made it, he felt. A speaking role at the local writer's festival alongside John Birmingham and Nikki Gemmell. He just needed Tim Winton along to rubber stamp his arrival. His mind wandered, viewing himself on stage in front of the book lovers, the readers and aspiring novelists of the country. He would be lauded, feted. He would be...

The phone rang and Mani snatched it up. "Gra Gra mate. This BWF thing. I'm in, but I want my position clear. I want my subject clarified, crystal clear so I can prepare."

"I'll clarify it for you, Alves," the voice replied.

"Who is this?" Mani asked. The voice was vaguely familiar.

"Need we do this again?"

"Crispian," Mani drawled, shaking his head in disbelief at the attitude of this guy. "It's been so long. I wondered if you still existed."

"Glad to hear you still think of me. I'm always here, Alves. Omnipresent yet innocuous." He seemed to have refined his speech to include a hint of an English Lord's accent for whatever reason. "And my name, as I divulged to you in the past, is Eagle."

"So you're like a ghost. With wings."

"More like a God actually."

"Well, I'm omnipotent. There's nothing I can't do. And omnivorous for good measure."

"Very clever. Which brings me to the point of my renewed contact. I think I have found a little something that Mani Alves can't do that I can." He paused for theatrical effect. "That I have done."

"Right," Mani said, already bored with Eagle's wordplay. He decided to stab at the heart of his nemesis' ineptitude. "So how'd that rock opera go? Coming along, is it?"

"Off subject, Alves," Eagle seethed with a passive-aggressive snarl.

Mani stayed silent. He felt no allegiance to this guy who tried to manipulate him at uni then tried to ride his coat-tails when he had good fortune. He resolved to zip up and let "Eagle" – what the hell sort of name was that anyway and did anyone ever call him that or was it a self-appointed bad-boy nickname, like T-Bone or Knuckles? – to let "Eagle" blow himself out with his own hot air.

Eagle continued. "Now I don't have to do this. Your life is your own, you do what you do. I have such a full, busy and gratifying life of my own to live and I have so much yet to achieve. But this needed doing for your sake. I heard through my well-informed grapevine that you are leaving our shores soon. An overseas commission due to your mastery of words. Congratulations."

"Don't know how you heard, but thanks."

"There's something you should know before you leave. It would be a cruel disservice not to tell you, bittersweet as the news shall be."

Mani butted in. "Sorry Cris. Do you always speak like this? I mean, we're not in a movie here."

"A little respect, Alves! You may think you're better than your peers, but a question for you. Just one. Can you promise me an answer?"

"I can't promise anything. Sorry Hawkeye."

"Very funny Alves. Remember, I called as a service to you."

"Okay, okay. What's your question?"

"What was her name? Your dream girl."

"Ah, piss off!" Mani scowled, his face flushing red.

"You said you'd answer. What was her name?"

Mani paused reluctantly. He'd been backed into a corner. "Alison," he said uncomfortably. The name felt strange to say.

"Last name, Alves," Eagle pressed in a frustrated tone.

"I don't remember. Are you kidding Cris? What's this about anyway?"

"You remember! Say her name!"

"Whatever. It was Alison Archer. It was Grade Eight. Just ridiculous!"

"Nice," Eagle smiled. "Alison Archer. What if I told you I found her?"

Mani's stomach flipped. He was being toyed with. He hovered between dismissal of his antagonist and a feeling of hope.

"I know her," Eagle announced. "We work together. Well, let's say she recruited me. She's a muso, Alves. She's in my world. I thought you'd give your fourth novel to be in my position."

"It's probably not her, Cris."

"Please call me Eagle. And it is her. Westside State High School 1987. Went to the Sunshine Coast never to be heard of again by our Mani Alves. But now, back in Brisbane, studied music at the Con and since found my inclinations and abilities to her musical liking, and sorry to be the bearer of bad news my old friend, also to her physical, emotional, spiritual and sexual liking. I could be corny like your stories and say we made beautiful music together."

"Ha, what a joke," Mani said. "Means nothing to me anyway."

"Of course not. Why would a grown man still pine for his teenage crush?" Eagle left that one hanging there, raw on Mani's mind. "It's over now. Our professional collaboration remains but I had to end it with her. My sacrifice to preserve the obvious musical connection. She was hurt, but the music is what counts."

Mani had phased out of the conversation. He stared off into the suburban landscape beyond his lounge room, while Eagle's noise continued down the line like static. The afternoon sun had begun its descent. Paddington was partially in shadow cast by the units and trees, stretching down the sloping roads in an array of shapes.

"So that's it," Eagle summed up. "That's why I called. I thought you should know seeing you're going overseas. I can arrange an intro if you like. She doesn't really remember you from school, sorry to say. Doesn't know your books either. Did you want to meet?"

Mani mumbled a feeble no.

"Go on, Alves. Surely you want to talk to her. See how she is these days. Hey, it'd be like the old times at uni. You and me, best buds, me getting you laid. Like hands through a sourglass, so too are the lays of our dives. Ha-ha, remember that?"

Mani had heard enough of Eagle's dribble. He hung up without farewell.

He stood for a while, motionless, holding the phone in his hand. He didn't know how long he stood there. There were alarms going off somewhere close. Maybe in his unit block. Outside the day's colours shifted to pinks and oranges. The alarms were swamped by sirens.

Mani's mind raced. Confusion reigned for him as a car locked its tyres, screeching closer, the whistle of a bomb descending, a train approached, out of control. The cacophony had its own life force.

Alison Archer was in Brisbane. Mani couldn't make sense of this karmic twist.

Day turned to dark outside as the strident harmony of crashing vehicles met in his unit simultaneously, overpowered by the scream of a kamikaze jet plane. Mani dropped the phone, dropped to a knee, closed his eyes as buses, cars, trains, planes, missiles, his whole life crashed down over him. He wheezed and coughed out a nuclear mushroom cloud of despair before collapsing on the rug his Mum bought him.

Out of the Abyss - 2000

It had been a whirlwind few years for Jason Sharpe. Where Mani had done a short apprenticeship in words and hit it big to become rich and famous, Jason's own path had seen a gradual gathering of financial knowledge. Small gains flourished as his knowledge grew, becoming windfalls and a small fortune. He never wanted to be rich and famous like his cousin. Only rich. Within eighteen months of beginning trading options, he already possessed a larger bank balance than his parents.

His typical day would start at 4.30AM to brew coffee and flick on his desktop PC to watch the end of day market action in the US.

The S&P 500 had been good to him in recent months, or more specifically, the technology company-laden NASDAQ index, which was skyrocketing. The 'internet', simply a toy for boffins until five years ago, was sprouting businesses left and right. Start-up companies were promising a future of cashless transactions, shopping from home, ease of ordering and unlimited options of products and services. In short, revolution was afoot and savvy entrepreneurs were cashing in, reaping the riches as share prices blossomed on the promise of future earnings.

Jason didn't need to launch his own internet business despite the lures. God knows he had started several business plans hoping to hit on the magic formula for internet success. He chose instead to be an investor and ride the waves created by the internet phenomenon.

Options trading let him effectively gamble on the direction of the market and its underlying stocks. He could buy a 'call' option, hoping prices would rise. In this market, with prices rising steadily, he could buy a call at the current price and when as expected, the price rose, he could exercise his right to buy at the lower price, locking in immediate gains. It was a bet, but in this type of market a sure bet.

Yet this was inefficient for Jason. Having analysed the options, he realised buying calls meant tying up capital while he waited for the inevitable price rises. He could get the same effect from selling 'puts', accepting upfront payment from those pessimists in the game who thought the market would fall. It was market economics in reverse, a dangerous game of 'Pin the Tail on the Market Donkey'. But Jason knew the risks.

Knowing the risks and mitigating the risks were two different things, Jason had been taught by his various mentors. Stop losses - an automatic bail-out order – to limit losses when you picked the market wrong and a big dose of humility to accept your own shortcomings were key to being a successful trader. Jason sat at this desk this day, a steaming brew in his hands and scrutinised the previous night's movements.

There had been volatility in recent days and he was relieved to see that the market had begun positively for the second day running to recover losses from the last week. Nothing to panic over, he thought to himself. Just normal market fluctuations. After a year where the NASDAQ had leapt 70%, the recent 9% drop was just profit-takers pushing the market lower.

A 9% drop, an 8% bounce back. Things were holding nicely. With an hour to go in the day's trade, Jason liked his positions, felt comfortable in his holds for another few days. After all, he had some of the giants of the industry in his portfolio. His coffee added to the warm fuzzy feeling. He was pleased, even as the market tailed off in the throes of the day's trade.

He closed his browser, fixed another coffee and headed into work. His day job in corporate finance no longer seemed the be all and end all of his existence. He still worked hard, hitting targets and enjoying the company of his team, but his real passion and thrill came from his trading. The day's meetings flowed into one another as he churned through commercial applications and proposals. He was playing usher at one of his mother's seminars that evening, and then on to drinks with friends.

The late night gave Jason reason to sleep in the next day, missing the market close for the first time that week. He read the finance news when he awoke about another market drop. It was a concern, but Jason knew the markets. He'd mastered them in his mind, so he knew the trend would come back to him. He would hold his position and watch it this evening. No knee jerks required.

This drop was a mere blip, a fortuitous buying opportunity. It developed in Jason a classic case of Baader-Meinhof Phenomenon, where you see something once then you start seeing it everywhere. An example of this 'frequency illusion' was if you wish to buy a new Mazda, suddenly you see Mazdas everywhere. They've always been there, they just become noticeable.

There were stories warning of market doom and gloom, yet Jason's bias only let him see, and hungrily absorb, the positive spin stories. They were abundant and so reassuring. He kept trading. Even as he saw the markets tank severely that evening, his stubbornness over-ruled good sense and trading technique to build on his foundation of foolishness.

A cocky young trader, having made close to a quarter of a million dollars for the year had thrown out his trading rulebook and thought himself too clever to continue with stop losses. As the market losses ticked over 20%, far beyond where good trading methods would have had him out of the market and on safe ground with minor losses, Jason started enacting the torturous close of his trades.

But it was too late. The trades were being closed for him automatically as the former market pessimists grabbed at their paydays.

Bang! Apple Computers, a $17,000 obligation. Pets.com - $15,000. Yahoo - $14,000. Geocities - $11,000. Dell Computers - $21,000. The carnage went on, as technology stocks, the former darlings of the stock exchange came under heavy fire from sellers.

It was brutal. Having received close to $14,000 for selling this round of puts, Jason's trades closed with obligations to pay unknown intercontinental traders over $240,000, with just two days to settle through his broker.

An overwhelming dread enveloped him, clawing under his skin, tightening his chest and wearying his legs. His neck became stiff from tension. These stresses could take a man down. He sat back at his desk, his shaking hand guiding his mouse, looking for a way out of what he made for himself.

"Christ," Jason said. And as Harry Chapin famously sang, it was funny how he named the only man who could save him now.

****

But there was someone else who could save him. Someone close to Jason who would unconditionally support him. What else could a mother do?

Patricia had opened her door to a defeated-looking young man. He'd had no sleep, looked dishevelled in an old T-shirt, shorts and thongs. It was most un-Jason like. He stepped in wordlessly and hugged his mother. Her alarm melted away to a loving hug as his body shook with sobs in her arms.

Jason squeezed Patricia. He'd rehearsed what to say over and over, knowing his parents might be his only saviours. He knew his Mum would know what to do and he felt foolish for allowing his trading to crash like this, particularly after boasting about his successes and ignoring the warnings from family and friends alike. Now the words wouldn't come, just tears and hurt and shame.

Jason was coaxed to the couch by his concerned mother. He explained the mess he had created.

"Oh, Jason," Patricia groaned. "I worried about this. How bad is it?"

"Bad, Mum. $250,000 bad."

"Two-hundred and fifty! You told me it was quite safe. I wondered how you could make $10,000 with no risk. It was too good to be true."

"I don't need a lecture, Mum. I feel bad enough."

"I'm not lecturing. I feel bad for letting you go on like that. For not guiding you. It hurts me to see you hurt."

Jason cried again, thumping the arm of the couch, then his own head, berating himself. He could barely believe the scenario. In dreamy hope, he wondered if this was just a cruel lesson that brokers teach young traders to humble then and that he might go back to his computer and the debt would be cleared with a warning not to get in above his head again.

"So how do we handle this?" Patricia asked. "How much have you got? Haven't you made about that much in the past year? You can pay what you've made back."

"Not quite, Mum. I've been pulling out my profits and re-investing them to buy shares. Now they're down too."

"But not gone completely, I presume. So you sell those now. Wear the loss on them and settle up."

"Well, I'll still be short. They're off 20% too. Plus I've spent some, bought some things. The car, stuff for the house. For me."

"What are they worth if you offload them right now?"

"One-twenty, maybe one-thirty."

"So how short does that leave you?" Patricia's accounting side was kicking in, assessing the alternatives.

"About that much again. One-hundred and twenty K."

"And what will you do?"

Jason's face burned with shame. His teeth clenched and the anguish rolled out once more, the tears coming again. "Bankrupt," he bawled.

"No," Patricia said. "My son is not having that stain and my son is going to learn a lesson from this. If you declare bankruptcy, it's the easy way out and nothing will stop you going through this again. You are going to pay for this, meet your obligations, fight through it and learn a lesson."

"How can I pay?" Jason whined, his dignity shattered, his calm exterior forfeited. "I'm gone. They want the money tomorrow. Tomorrow night, our time. They're US brokers."

"I'll go to the bank today. I'll speak to your father."

"Don't tell Dad. I don't want Dad knowing."

"You have no choice in this," Patricia said, her hard side emerging. "I'd rather you learn from your mistakes owing me money than some greedy broker on the other side of the world. You played a dangerous game Jason, and someone always loses. We can get you out of this but there will be repercussions . I need to talk to your father to work it out."

Over the coming days the stress shut Jason's body down. He fell ill, vacillating between delirium, sweating until the bed was soaked and moments where he felt so feeble he could barely lift himself off the couch. It seemed that the past several years of intense focus on his own betterment, early mornings, late nights and driving his mind and body to learn and achieve had finally taken a toll.

Patricia, meanwhile, kicked the rescue plan into gear, with her and Graham going to the bank to draw back $150,000 from the equity in their property portfolio. They contacted their real estate agent to list one of their properties for sale. Patricia spoke to Celia for some sisterly advice and sought out Mani for his opinion. She had a plan and needed moral support and guidance for what she would request as a condition for bailing her son out.

It was close to a week before Jason righted himself and was healthy enough to address the partially solved problem. Patricia assured him that the debt was paid as Jason readied himself for a severe dressing down. His Mum had promised some sort of redemption would be required and he feared he would be cleaning their investment properties for the remaining weekends of his life.

He sat with Patricia and Graham at the kitchen table. A folder was on the table between them. "Your father and I believe in you, Jason," Patricia started. His father remained staunchly silent. "We also believe that you will grow from this calamity and part of that growth is to ensure restitution is made to your father and I."

"Absolutely, Mum," Jason said. "However long it takes."

"There are some additional conditions." She looked across to Graham who put his hand on her back, smiling in support. "You should keep trading the markets."

Jason sighed in relief and disbelief.

Patricia continued, opening the folder. "We trust your lesson has been learned and that there are ways to mitigate your losses. It is obvious you are born for this world of finance and that it is an absolute passion. And your father and I recognise you need some capital to get you re-started. To that end..." She drew out a cheque from the folder.

Jason stared at the crisp paper in his hand. "Twenty-five thousand," he said, stunned.

"It's to replenish your trading account, but also as a down payment on the next condition." She turned a single sheet of paper around to face Jason. "You will learn from this. We are confident of that. So too was your Auntie Celia. Mani too. They agree with this plan of attack."

"They know about this?"

"I needed to square up my thoughts and make sure I was doing the right thing. I needed some advice. Don't worry, they all love you and support you. We all agreed you will learn and grow through this. But you also need to teach others. Use your experience to educate others so they can learn from your mistakes."

Jason's head swam as he looked at the proposal on the paper in front of him. "How do I do that?"

"Seminars. Classes. Education. Part of this money is from Mani. He is very excited to be your business partner. Just as your father and I have taught hundreds of people now about the path to financial freedom, you can be the guiding light for people in the trading world. Mani believes in you. So do we."

****

It was right there in front of Jason but there had been no noticing it. The idea of being an educator had never occurred to him, but it resonated with him. His own learning had been piecemeal, picking up bits and pieces of information about how to trade, but there was no system. Just a hit and miss approach through which he had got lucky at first. This meltdown in the markets had proven to him he was flying blind. "This is just so amazing, Mum. Thank you, Dad. I can't believe that you would do this for me." He was overwhelmed by the love and belief they were showing him. He accepted this as a warm embrace of support, a galvanising moment of spiritual edification. He cried again, the tears from a different source to those of days earlier.

The noise of chair legs scraping on the floor preceded a family hug where the tears flowed. Graham squeezed his son's shoulder. Jason buried his head between his parents. He was filled with a new determination, a powerful self-affirming belief, sensing not just that he had been blessed and endorsed, but that his direction in life had been unearthed. And with that, a business was born.

****

AllOptions became the registered trading name of the new operation. Mani had pledged $25,000 to become a one-quarter owner in the business. Graham Bedser drew up the contract and established the rules of incorporation. Now that the path had been set, Jason moved to bring it to life.

He had whipped up an extensive business plan with the basis of this being his mother's condition of education for the people. It was a grandiose vision that made perfect sense to Jason. Not only could he trade the markets using a self-built system of trading knowledge and secure back-up plans, he would in essence be an education company. His own experiences were then the core of his ambitions. He could teach the fail-safe methods he would personally adhere to and be the ongoing proof of the success of his system.

The following weeks saw Jason throw himself into writing a trading plan, manuals and presentations, gathering examples of high probability trades and putting into print everything he knew to be relevant about trading the markets. AllOptions would be ethical, it would assure success, allowing his students to build a base of wealth and a future income that could never be compromised as long as his rules were followed. And he would talk freely of his failures as a forever warning to his students of the perils should cockiness or laziness intervene.

As the program came together, the possibilities expanded. A Lismore uni friend now based in Sydney working as an accountant and trading in his spare time begged to be involved. Karl had been seeking a business and saw a future in Jason's venture. He fronted cash to secure the Sydney arm of AllOptions. Mani introduced Jason to a neighbour in his Chelsea street, an investment analyst named Eunan looking for a change of pace and his own project to run. Suddenly, AllOptions had the potential to go international, though some water had to pass underbridge before the London office would be approved, not least that Eunan had a further six months of his present contract to fulfil.

Just weeks later, Jason's visionary work saw the AllOptions 'bible' ready to launch. Premises had been secured in Brisbane and Sydney for training and administration. They were ready to advertise. Jason had built a 'turn-key' business in less than three months thanks to the generosity and belief of his parents and his cousin in London. The market malfunction that changed his life now stood Jason on the brink of a most fulfilling achievement. All that was left to do was to secure his first students.

He rang Mani with news of his first success. Mani had been Jason's support through this time. He was well established in London by now, having had eighteen solid months of working and partying, living lavishly and taking his pick of London's female populace. "I want to thank you and congratulate you," Jason said. "Your investment just got its first bit of revenue.

"Great news," Mani exclaimed. "So you got a class together. You should celebrate and, as I'm about to head out to a party in Soho, I will do the same."

"If you call two people a class. Now I know my ad actually works. And it feels real now."

Mani was effusive in his enthusiasm and praise. "It is up and going now. You need to make it more real. It needs a launch.

Like a ship needs to be launched, christened, a bottle broken across its bow as it is introduced to the world. Organise a party for AllOptions. Put on the drinks – people love a free drink – and raise its profile. Then, when Eunan wraps up his analyst work we'll do it again in London. I love a launch, an opening. Any excuse for a party."

After Mani hung up to go to his Soho party, Jason thought about the prospects of AllOptions. This first class would lead to referrals. The advertising would continue to bring in interested students. It would grow. Not too quickly, but organically. He felt a surge of confidence, seeing a future in education. This was real now. He could see his path. He would have his launch.

Music & Lyrics

It had been quite a ride for a twenty-five year old. Jason had gone from carefree young adult dabbling in the investing world to high-risk high-flier rolling the dice and coming up trumps to the tune of a quarter of a million dollars. The progression continued to being a destitute and desperate potential bankrupt and now, within the same year, he had a business that would have multiple offices in Australia with the possibility of a global presence.

And he was back in the markets. Admittedly, he was still being bankrolled by his parents. That could take a couple of years to settle the score but he was using his own new trading discipline and turning steady profits with minimal risk. He also had some small classes booked for the weeks ahead to whom to teach his strategies. Things were looking up and, encouraged by his mother who agreed with Mani that an official launch party would help the business make a splash, he now had a venue and a date for AllOptions' big coming-out party – March 1, 2001.

He was relaxing on the veranda of his rented Karana Downs property, looking out over the pitched yard dotted with waving gumtrees down to the river farther down the slope. He had always loved this area of Brisbane ever since the times they visited Mani and his family when they lived here by the river. It relaxed him, made him feel grounded in the big wide world that he felt could sap his life-force as he negotiated the self-perpetrated rat race.

Now, chastened by his failure and having re-assessed his lifestyle, he chose to live on acreage, alone, away from the city's temptations. He was using this chill time to tie up the entertainment for the launch. He held his mobile phone and perused the venue's band list and the Yellow Pages on his laptop. It was proving tricky to source.

The first call was answered by a sly-sounding guy with a minor lisp who became pushy to try to secure the business. He offered a variety of song-lists and was more than willing to cut the price at the first sign of hesitation from Jason. He was a solo show using backing tracks. As Jason offered his thanks and said he would consider it, the singer spat turgidly, "Good luck finding anyone who's got moves like I got, buddy!"

He worked through a list, getting more and more deflated with the quality of acts on offer. There was a Hall & Oates tribute band, a smoked-up dude trying most politely to book his grunge covers band in, signing off with a laid-back "Let me know, bro, OK. Take it easy, dude." There was a rockabilly show, a reggae band, an Elvis impersonator, the Burt Bacharach show, a Stevie Wonder look-a-like singing the hits of the Beatles. Jason started feeling he might need to outsource this job.

He felt he might be near a breakthrough when he rang a listing from the Yellow Pages. "Thanks for calling Funktopia. DeeDee speaking," the sweet voice sang in welcome. DeeDee then proceeded to sell the merits of Funktopia's groovy dance-oriented set-list. It sounded appealing compared to the other dross he had trawled over, and reasonably priced. He delivered his stock reply of "Thanks, I will get back to you."

He swung himself to his feet and collected a beer from the fridge, heartened by a feeling of progress. He sat down and dialled again, now having a benchmark upon which to base his decision. A familiar voice answered. "Hello, you've got Deanne."

Jason baulked before continuing. "Yeah, hi Deanne. I am looking to book a band for a function I am holding. I got your number from the venue. Is this Eclectic Pop Machine?"

"That's right," she replied, before launching into a spirited run-through of Eclectic Pop Machine's song menu. "And we are the ultimate party floor-fillers, playing the best dance hits of the 70's, 80's and 90's."

Jason felt he'd heard the spiel before. He had to ask. "Deanne, did I just call you a few minutes ago?"

"No, I don't think so," she fibbed.

"I just called and spoke to someone who sounds remarkably like you named DeeDee. DeeDee runs a function band called Funktopia. You don't know DeeDee, do you?"

Deanne fought tooth and nail to deny she was DeeDee playing the market under different pseudonyms according to which ad was responded to. Jason was dubious and ended the call with his standard "let you know..." response. This band search was getting more and more bizarre.

It was draining and Jason was ready to quit the search. 'Music & Lyrics' leapt out at him as an interesting name for an act. The words 'high-class' in the blurb also helped. He dialled for the final time.

"Hello," a confident voice answered. A nice voice. A female voice.

"Hi. I'm holding a launch party for my business and I need some entertainment," Jason said in a dull voice.

"Well, thank you for calling," the young lady said with such genuineness, substance and passion that Jason was taken aback. "And what is your name?"

Jason stammered "Um, AllOptions."

"Your name is AllOptions?"

"Oh no. My name is Jason. Sharpe. My business is AllOptions. It's new."

"Congratulations, Jason Sharpe. Getting started is hard, but hopefully we can get you off to a great start with a great party. So what would you like to know? Or, would you like me to give you everything I've got?"

"Um, well. This is different," Jason mumbled. She had thrown him off kilter with her efficient enthusiasm.

"Is everything OK?" she asked.

"Yeah great. It's just...you're not a freak."

She was quick with a reply. "Firstly, I agree. This industry is full of freaks. Secondly, you don't know me. I might well be a freak."

"Well, are you?"

"Oooh, direct. So Jason Sharpe, what sort of business is your business?"

"A training business. Education."

"Interesting. What do you teach?"

"I teach people not to make the same mistakes I made."

"Smart and ethical. I like it!" the young lady affirmed.

Jason was overwhelmed by this dynamo on the phone. He needed to take back some control, as males tend to need to do. "You didn't answer my question," he said.

"Which one?"

"Are you a freak?"

She laughed. "I'm not a freak. Freakish, maybe."

Jason also laughed. "That's clever. So your band is Music and Lyrics. That's a great name, by the way. What sort of show do you do?"

"Tailored to your needs. It's a four-piece, we do covers with a wide range of tunes. Off the beaten track covers, you know. Not your normal belt 'em out covers that you'd see on a Sunday at the Victory Beer Garden. Songs with style that bring back good memories. Think Tears for Fears, Mercury Rev, Pat Benatar, Edie Brickell. We can move from dinner music to background tunes to dance, all customised for your party. And I promise, no ABBA. But you might get lucky and get one my own songs."

"Sounds ace," Jason proffered. "How do we work out times, dates, costs?"

"We get together, Jason Sharpe. I'm full tomorrow, but Thursday, I have some spare time, unusually. I like to meet at West End. It's handy to everything and I love the coffee at Café Tempo. Is Thursday OK?"

"Thursday's great. Anytime. Business is not through the roof just yet so I have plenty of time for party planning in lieu of actual work."

"Great. I say 11AM, Café Tempo, Boundary Street. Do you know the area?"

"I'll find it, or wander aimlessly for days."

"All set then, Mister Jason Sharpe. I'll have all the information you need. See you Thursday."

"One other thing," Jason said. "Unless the place is otherwise empty, it might be hard to spot you. I might need, oh, like your name."

"Oh yeah. Do you ever do that?" she asked in a disbelieving voice. "I do that a lot. Mind going a hundred miles an hour. Always busy. I wonder how I get by in the world, honestly. But remember, I'm not a freak, OK?"

"OK. So your name?"

"It's Alison Archer. See you Thursday."

****

Normally an emotionless type, preferring the hard-edged seriousness of the financial world to fanciful thoughts and actual feelings, Jason had found his mind wandering amongst the realms of romanticism. The interaction he'd shared with Alison Archer had picked loose one of the strings in his tightly bound existence.

She was just so unusual. Not a freak, as he ascertained, but certainly quirky. Yet she was confident, focused and so very personable. She ran a band, only took on high class functions and was assured in her dealings. And she had a nice voice. It was all he could grasp to, without the visual. More than once did Jason find his thoughts drifting to how their meeting might play out, imagining a further connection, maybe some romance and even pictured he and this unknown image of a girl as a couple.

He shook his head to dismiss the notion and got back to the business at hand. It was a most un-Jason like reaction to what should have been just another three minute phone call to get business done, like the many he'd made over the years. A faceless voice at the other end, an anonymous liaison for the purpose of business. It got Jason thinking that maybe he had closed himself off from such feelings for so long, existing in the solitary world of finance markets, trading and making money, that maybe his subconscious was telling him it was time to seek more from life.

Then of course his business brain took over, convincing him that her quirky, sweet, exciting voice and easy rapport was just a ploy on her behalf to ensure she got the deal done. That was what Jason would do. Anything to get the deal over the line.

Either way, his drifting thoughts had another effect he was not prepared to face. It placed a whole lot of importance on their upcoming meeting, just in case the romantic sub-conscious feelings were the true lay of the land. Jason became pre-occupied with what he should wear and overtly aware of how he would present to this unknown attractive quantity that was Alison Archer.

He arrived right on time, a sentient effort to be neither late nor early. It took a slow walk of the bustling Boundary Street to ensure his eagerness was not apparent with an early arrival. There was the usual array of unusual sights in West End's main street. A busker on guitar earned his money while a rag-covered lady begged for hers. The bookshops were full of well-to-do retirees who could afford to live in the area, students and hippies. Aboriginals drank wine in the sun, Asian store-owners swept their steps. The butchery and fruit-and-veg stores emanated spruiking of salesmen, giving a true market feel. Across the populace of West End, bare feet were the norm and Jason calculated that every eighth person had dreadlocks. It was such a unique part of Brisbane, where tolerance and community were to the fore.

And in the centre of all this hub-bub, Café Tempo awaited his arrival. He entered, noticing a dozen or so people spread out within the café enjoying coffees and focaccia, reading the newspaper or just people-watching. A quick scan narrowed down the field of potential Alisons; two young ladies sitting alone. One was a dread-locked teenager wearing jeans and a loose singlet which struggled to contain her large, unfettered breasts. She read a Wilderness Society magazine and drank a mugaccino.

The other candidate was a spike-haired blond, nicely made-up and dressed in black skinny jeans, a stud belt and a glossy bone-coloured top. She wore dangly ear-rings, was partway through a long back coffee and was making notes in her Filofax on the table. Beside her, within her eyeline, was a mobile phone. Jason immediately knew who he would prefer to do business with.

He approached tentatively, passing dread girl to the table towards the rear of the narrow room. He waited for her to look up. The vibrant smile she presented when she did acknowledge Jason hit him hard inside his chest. Lovely white teeth, red lipstick and eyes glinting like the azure waters of the Great Barrier Reef. This girl knew the meaning of 'smiling with your eyes' and grasped the concept of first impressions.

Jason was stunned as those feelings re-emerged. Open-mouthed but no greeting would come.

Alison paused waiting for an introduction, then laughed. "I hope you don't freeze up like this in your classes."

Jason straightened himself out. "I'm Jason. Are you...?"

"I guessed who you were. You are exactly..." She rotated her wrist to look at her Swatch watch. "..on time! And there doesn't seem to be any other prompt, well-dressed, motivated business owners in the café at the moment."

"I heard that," came a voice over the bar counter.

"No offence, Angelo," Alison called. "You're all that and more. You know I love you for your coffee."

Jason sat. He was enamoured. It had taken just one phone call, twenty seconds and two witty comments. She was unbelievable.

It was straight into business after Angelo brought coffee. Alison buzzed with enthusiasm as she outlined the entertainment philosophy that her Music & Lyrics project adhered to. From a folder she drew paperwork – a song list with several variants, a résumé of previous gigs, testimonials from previous clients, costings and an agreement. She was funny, chatty, cool and super-efficient. Jason tried to match her witticisms but he was failing badly, trying too hard to appear cool.

Music & Lyrics were a four-piece band. Alison sang and played keyboard. They had a bass guitarist, lead electric guitar and drums. All trained and experienced musicians. "And we play it pretty cool on stage. We dress money, you know. Good clothes, very cool and aloof. That's the persona," she said. "We know the entertainment reflects your business' attitude and you want to project a good image. Funky, cool, cutting edge. That's the beauty of the right entertainment. It's memorable so people relate an enjoyable night with your business from that point on."

"Savvy."

"I like to think so," Alison said with a confident smile. "It's up to you now. Do we get to do your show?"

"Music & Lyrics, you had me at 'hello'."

Alison laughed again but Jason promised himself an upper-cut for his lameness.

Thereafter, there was more chat, stories and flirting. Jason wanted to prolong the meeting so he ordered a pot of tea and a plate of bruschetta. He never drank tea, but reasoned it would take at least twenty minutes to drink and he didn't want the meeting winding up too soon.

She was incredible. He had not met anyone like her. He needed to find out more about her. He built questions into the conversation to get some grounding on her past and to hear her exquisite voice. "So how did you come to be a musician?" he queried. "Was it Young Talent Time that inspired you, or famous parents?"

"Ha ha. No nothing like that," she said. "Just a kid who walked around constantly humming and singing tunes. Mum tells the story I would literally sing for my supper. I would give a little performance each night before dinner."

"I'd go hungry. Barely a musical bone in my body," Jason said. "But I did play guitar in a band at uni."

"Are you serious? Well, that's musical."

"I guess. Three chord songs, I had rhythm but nothing fancy. We had three guitarists, me and another guy on rhythm guitar and a fierce lead guitar guy. He held us together."

"Maybe I will get you on stage for a song during your launch," Alison said.

"No chance. I recognised my limitations. Saw that I was the background noise between our superstar's lengthy solos. I retired the borrowed Strat, with a career high of being runners up in a Battle of the Band comp in Lismore. You might have heard of the winners. A little band called Grinspoon."

"Oh my God, what? That is the bomb!" Alison was wide-mouthed in awe. "I'm supposed to be the 'cool muso' and you have the coolest music story. I feel dudded."

Jason shrugged, blew his knuckles and shined them on his chest. He got another of her brilliant smiles. "When did you realise you had to be on stage?"

"At school. It started with bit parts in the school musical, but I was the lead role for my senior years. I was so into it, I would work on the sets, do extras on the choreography, coaching. It was like I had to have it perfect. The control freak I am."

"The star of the show," Jason mused. "Which school was that?"

"Westside High."

Jason pulled his Russian Caravan tea away from his mouth – he wasn't really enjoying it anyway – when he heard that little morsel of info. "Westside High. You'd know my cousin. His name's Mani. Mani Alves. He went to Westside too."

"I drifted around a bit," she said. "Wasn't all that close to many kids. Too into my music."

"He's a pretty big name. You might have heard of him since. He's written a book and it's a best-seller. He would have been in your grade too. Mani Alves."

She was evasive. "I don't know the name. Sorry. There were other schools too. So many kids. And so much has happened since school. Uni. Singing. I manage some bands too."

Jason was disappointed. The 'Mani at Westside' connection could have been the key that locked in another date. He always had the launch, he supposed. "I just thought you might know him."

"Nope. Not familiar." She had a sip of water, placed her phone on her Filofax and announced that it was time she got going. Jason sensed mild irritation, though she flashed her gorgeous smile. "Well, I guess I'll be in touch. The gig will come around quick. Was great to meet you."

And with that she was gone, leaving Jason with his mild, nutty tea and confusion over where he stood and what he'd achieved from the morning. He was consoled by the lasting touch of her farewell handshake and the view of her lithe body as she left.

****

"How good were the Doves the other night? That's a seriously good band. They blew Alex Lloyd's tepid effort off the stage." Alison was being entertained on the rear deck of the home of her neighbour, best friend and fellow music buff, Sally. She topped up each of their wine glasses. "True musicianship!" she summed up.

"Agreed," Sally said. "They are my new favourite band. And they've earnt themselves a favourable review. I just wish I'd got to interview them."

"They'll be back," Alison reassured. "Just keep tabs on them so you can get a story and us some free tickets."

The two girls did this often. When Alison didn't have a show of her own, she and Sally, a music journalist who had as deep a passion for music as Alison, would catch gigs and then have a Sunday night de-brief over several bottles of white. They loved the music and the nightlife, were best friends and neighbours. True soul sisters!

And they were savvy too. Career-minded girls, they each saw that the best way to make a living in the cut-throat world of music was not necessarily by putting all your eggs in the 'make it big as a rock star' basket, it was about the industry as a whole. Sally realised she could fulfil all her gig desires with free entry as well as getting paid to review gigs and do interviews. Alison still pursued her musical dream, still had flesh in the game, but she had diversified and ensured she would have a lucrative career in her chosen field regardless of whether she made it big.

It had started for Alison in school. Her two senior years saw her land the lead role in the school musical. Self-taught on guitar and tutored to a high level on piano, Alison had been writing songs since the age of fifteen. She parlayed this love of music into a place at Brisbane's Conservatorium of Music – the famous Con –not only cementing her talents with expert tuition but also the relationships that would get her started in the industry.

It was only when she got out into the big, wide world and was looking to record, release and promote her own music that she twigged onto the relevance of the 'Business' portion of the Con course. She soon realised an indisputable truth about the music industry. The only ones who got rich or made a consistent living were those with the smarts to set themselves up to get paid regardless. Singers, talented musos and so-called artists rarely broke through. The odds were astronomical. It was the promoters, managers and venue owners who sold alcohol to lubricate the industry that made the money. The artist was the means, the ones with no personal end.

It prompted Alison to re-invent herself. She began tutoring kids for regular income. She took on the management of several bands, including her brother's metal band. She wrote songs for others and now had royalties flow in from writing credits on two early successes. All the while she continued with her own musical dream in an original indie pop band, as well as establishing Music & Lyrics after stealing the disaffected bass player from her brother's band.

She and Sally were on their second bottle, deep in conversation about the merits of the Oz music scene when Alison's phone rang. She snapped up her mobile. "This will be Sony offering me that long-awaited five-album deal," she joked. She answered in her usual bright voice.

"Alison. Hi, it's Jason Sharpe. I met you last week about doing a show for my business."

"Well hello, Jason," Alison said with an emphasis on his name so Sally would twig who she was talking to.

The girls shared everything about their personal lives, the ups and downs of romance, business and their hopes and dreams. Naturally, Sally knew who was on the phone. There had been banter between the girls about this handsome young businessman named Jason who had booked Alison's band. Sally was beside herself, grabbing at Alison's arm in mock horror, squirming and mouthing her excitement to her friend.

Alison kept her composure, holding up a hand to settle Sally before continuing. Inside she was tingling, her heart thumping nervously. She tried to keep her voice level. "Good to hear from you," Alison said. "Everything OK?"

She could sense the nervousness at the other end of the phone. "Everything's great," Jason replied. "Thanks for the other day. I just wanted to confirm that I feel really good about your band doing the launch."

"That's good to hear, Jason. But I have to stop you there and say we don't do discounts for flattery."

"I'm not after a..." Jason started before realising he'd walked into a joke.

"I'm kidding, Jason."

"I get that now. What are you up to then? Haven't interrupted anything, have I?"

Sally was leaning in, trying to listen. Alison shooed her away. "No, I'm with my friend Sally. She and I are discussing music of course. I was hoping you were the record company calling to offer me my worldwide deal."

"Sorry, just me. Though I will buy your CD when the deal comes off."

She loved how polite he was. And she was enjoying this little game she recognised they were playing.

"Anyway," Jason continued. "I just wanted to check if we needed to get together again before the gig. You know, to confirm anything. Songs or food or band rider."

"You're wondering if we should we meet before the gig?" Alison repeated for Sally's benefit. Alison was smiling, enjoying the tease. Sally was off her chair now, dancing around her deck in raptures, her wine sloshing from her glass. "Umm, look, I think it wouldn't hurt. The show is in four weeks so we might need to check some details together."

"That's what I was thinking, yeah," Jason said, sounding too professional.

"Maybe I should bring the whole band to introduce you."

"I don't really need to meet them do I, unless..."

"Again, I'm joking Jason."

"You do that, don't you?"

Alison gave a cute giggle. "Seeing it's just you and me, maybe we should eat. I know how busy you are. We could have dinner while we talked about the show."

"Great."

It was a slow-burning, teasing control of the situation. Alison knew why he was calling. But she decided to test his resolve, rein in his obvious enthusiasm.

"To be honest, Jason, there's no real need to meet about the gig. Everything is in order. I'm sure it'll all be fine. You're busy, so to save you some time..."

She was teasing again.

"I've no doubt the gig will be fine," Jason stated, finally sounding more confident. "Truth is, I didn't want to wait four weeks to see you again. I hope that's alright."

"It's perfectly alright, you perfect gentleman. I promise not to be such a stirrer."

"It's cool. I think it's funny. Let's meet Thursday. I'll call you."

"OK then."

"OK. Bye," he said and hung up.

Sally had been hanging on every word and it was obvious there was a date organised. Alison decided to have some fun at her friend's expense, continuing to talk into her phone.

"What am I going to wear?" Alison said into her beeping handset. "I think I'll wear something low-cut and revealing for you, Jason Sharpe. I want you to get a real good look at my body."

She filled her fake conversation with some 'Uh-huhs' and sensual 'mm-hmms', noticing Sally's heightened attention before continuing. "Oh, yeah, I think we will. Even if it is our first date. And I like it rough and dirty."

Sally was gobsmacked. She was paused in a quarter turn-half turn as though someone had freeze-framed the scene. Her arm still held her wineglass near her mouth but her head was turned in shock towards her foul-mouthed friend, mouth agape.

Alison continued. "I bet you are. I can't wait to see it. Yes, I do that...and that. Seriously, I do everything!"

Alison could see Sally freaking out, having never heard such talk from Alison let alone to speak like that to a guy she hardly knew. Alison quit Sally's misery. "I'm joshing you Sal. What sort of girl do you think I am?"

****

Jason was nervous. He was going to be judged on the quality of the launch. He had complete faith in the entertainment, being provided of course by his new girlfriend. And the venue was ideal, being city-based looking out over the river with views to the Story Bridge on the left and along to the lights shining up at the Kangaroo Point cliffs.

Deep down he knew he had nothing to worry about. He'd recruited some noted socialites and bizzoids from the big end of town who knew how to do launches. It was a guest list suggested by Graham Bedser who knew who needed to be seen to be supporting AllOptions to ensure the party had cred. Selected media would be in attendance to gain some mileage in the papers.

Business had been slow for the first six months, a steady, low-flow stream of clients rather than a torrent, however this suited the needs of the business. It gave Jason the time to not only perfect the course but also to dedicate time to trading using his system.

The profits from trading were consistent. He was tentative, erring towards caution. He was also proving fiscally sensible in that profits were re-directed out of the trading account to repay his parents and to bolster his personal finances. Jason reflected that here he was just short of a year since his epic trading failure and he was now back on his feet. The power of his parents love strengthened him and provided the fuel for the motor of his ambition.

He was to meet Alison Archer in the afternoon as she and her bandmates set up. There was three hours to the launch. Jason was excited about seeing her again, yet nervous to meet the rest of the band. He and Alison were something of an item now, still finding their feet as a couple after two dates and he felt they were testing the limits of what their relationship might be. It remained polite and platonic to this point, with neither party rushing forward to over-commit.

It suited Jason. He enjoyed the nervous giggles and insinuative gestures of early courtship. This was the magical period in a relationship that can only be experienced once, so he was happy to have it last and enjoy the mystery and refreshing alchemy between them. He remained enamoured with this vivacious wisp of a girl with the dynamic constitution.

Jason had checked into the Hilton mid-city, arranged his suit and shirt for the night and now, dressed in civvies, he walked to the venue on the riverfront near Eagle Street Pier. He had booked the hotel room for convenience. He knew he had a late night ahead of him, whatever may come.

The band was already inside setting up and loading in their gear. He saw Alison and his heart leapt. The automatic response shocked and excited him. He watched her for a few seconds as she cabled up her keyboard, his eyes moving over her fit body and strong arms, before entering the room. He glimpsed the power in her supple body as she lifted her keyboard to its stand, before she resumed her feline grace. The bandmates were just shadowy shapes behind this beacon of rock goddess loveliness.

"And welcome to the stage," Jason said as he entered the room, using his best ringmaster voice. "This fine young band from Seattle - Music & Lyrics!!" It was a big entrance to break the ice, however nerdy his Nirvana reference sounded.

"Oh, yeah!" Alison blared as she turned around, her easy smile displaying her white teeth. "I've already told the guys that if Dave Grohl moves to Brisbane, I'm leaving the band. He and I will do acoustic Foo Fighters covers and live happily ever after. Sorry guys," she said as an aside to her bandmates.

"I quit," the big guy setting up the drum kit whined.

Alison laughed and grabbed Jason's arm. "Come and meet the band."

The big guy was Arms, the drummer. Jason could work out the reference, as his biceps would give the skins a fearful belting.

He met Break, the guitarist, a muscular, fit, tattooed guy with dark, flicky hair that made him look as much surfer as muso.

Finally there was the bass player, dressed very rock and roll in skinny jeans, Doc boots and a black shirt over his emaciated body. He had a wispy fringe that dangled down to a set of seedy and beady eyes. He approached and grabbed Jason's hand in a passive aggressive handshake. Jason noted the sparse stubble on his gaunt face and his pointed nose.

"Hello, sir," the bass player said, stepping in too close, invading Jason's personal space. "My name's Eagle. Thanks for the gig, man. I hope you're a good payer. Most new small businesses are on their bones for cashflow. Ha ha."

"Never mind Eagle," Alison said in open frustration. "He's a little socially awkward."

He frowned as he was about to defend himself.

"But what a bass player," Alison added.

Eagle demurred to his employer and stood down.

"Nice to meet you, guys," Jason said. "Thank you for doing this show. I'm real excited to hear you play live. Alison's sold you with quite a rap." He was genuine and friendly. "And Eagle, I've already paid Alison. She charmed the fee out of me early, so you can focus totally on the show."

The drummer and guitarist nodded to Jason and went back to their setup. Alison began taping down the cabling. Eagle stood his ground.

"Let me get how this works," he said, closing his eyes and pinching the bridge of his nose for theatrical effect. "So you're a self-employed..." He paused for extra drama. "...sharemarket expert with plenty of cashflow and you're throwing a party for the bigwigs around town. Sorry, but am I incorrect in thinking that there could be something illegal going on?"

Eagle glared at Jason with his fake friendly smile.

Jason could only offer stunned silence, bemused by the verbal attack.

"Eagle!" Alison scolded. "Don't be pathetic. What is wrong with you?"

"Nothing wrong with me. I just like to be aware of where my paycheck comes from and not be implicated in any illegalities. No offence, my man," he said.

Jason opted to play it cool, take the high ground. "No offence taken, Eagle."

Alison jumped in apologetically. "I'm sorry about this, Jason. He's unbelievable."

"Forget it," Jason said. "Sorry to hear you're concerned, Eagle. But I paid Alison and as far as I know the payment hasn't bounced." He looked to Alison who nodded her confirmation of this fact. "And fear not anything illegal. I'm small-fry in the bigger scheme of things. It's a new business and I'm just trying to make a go of it. Speaking of that, why don't you come and see what I do, Eagle. No cost. I can show you what AllOptions offers. You never know. It might just suit a clever fellow like you."

"I'm most interested. I'd like to see what all the fuss is about. You've certainly got Alison's attention with whatever it is you do."

Alison gave Eagle a fierce glare before turning back to her task.

Jason maintained his composure staring icily at Eagle.

Eagle stepped in close with a menacing whisper, "I wouldn't celebrate getting the girl, mate. She's flaky. I can confirm that for you."

Jason weighed up the hostility, guessed that Eagle felt Jason was on his turf. There had been no indication from Alison that she and Eagle were involved. Yet this guy had a wicked side, he could tell. He flipped out a business card, telling Eagle he was in the morning class for Monday the following week.

Returning later suited up and feeling ready to party, Jason greeted his guests. He looked around to catch a glimpse of Alison but the band was out of sight, preparing. Finger food circulated, drinks flowed and Jason received positive feedback from some important guests.

At the specified time, the band came out and Jason saw why they got the big bucks. They looked sharp, but it was Alison who grabbed his attention. Dressed in a fitted black suit with a big collar, cut-off gloves and high heeled boots, she emanated sexiness as she led the band straight into Pat Benatar's moody rollicking ballad 'We Belong'.

At the end of the song, she introduced the band, welcomed the guests and congratulated AllOptions. "And here's one for the host," she said demurely. "A little hit by Tears for Fears."

The crowd seemed to turn as one to witness this entrancing image on stage. A silky talented and gorgeous singer backed by supreme musicians, holding the attentions of a crowded room with their passion and delivery.

> *Welcome to your life; there's no turning back*
> *Even while we sleep we will find*
> *You acting on your best behavior*
> *Turn your back on mother nature*
> *Everybody wants to rule the world*
>
> *It's my own desire, it's my own remorse*
> *Help me to decide. Help me make the most*
> *Of freedom and of pleasure*
> *Nothing ever lasts forever*
> *Everybody wants to rule the world*

Alison's eyes secretly met Jason's. He couldn't move, transfixed by her as she sang...

> *There's a room where the light won't find you*
> *Holding hands while the walls come tumbling down*
> *When they do, I'll be right behind you*
> *So glad we've almost made it*
> *So sad they had to fade it*
> *Everybody wants to rule the world*

Her body swayed and arched as she powered out the notes, her legs flexing as she worked her keyboard. Such a passionate delivery. Jason felt the words drill into him. He stared, oblivious to all else but the glorious stage presence of this unique lady. It was as though a portal was channeling her joy, love, hope, her very life force, direct to him through these words...

I can't stand this indecision
Married with a lack of vision
Everybody wants to rule the world
Say that you'll never, never, never, need it
One headline, why believe it?
Everybody wants to rule the world

All for freedom and for pleasure
Nothing ever lasts forever
Everybody wants to rule the world

****

He felt uncomfortable. Out of his depth, like he had to prove something. His outer bravado despised that inner feeling. Eagle felt he was the one holding the power, passing judgment, and Jason Sharpe was the one who should be on trial here. Yet here he was, feeling inadequate for no reason, as though he needed to prove that burgeoning rock stars should also be business-savvy investors, able to switch their creative mind to logical processes. He maintained his front. There was little else he could do.

It was only exacerbated when the very person he was here to expose demanded that Eagle should reveal his true self. Part of the sham, Eagle decided. Strip everyone back and equalise individuals. Neutralise them. Remove histories, personas, the enigmatic differences of the populace so that he could apply his brainwashing, until they were all just bricks in the Wall. Carbon copy puppets to mould to his theories.

"We need to record identification of students, Eagle," Jason explained. "It's an ASIC requirement. Do you have licence or passport?"

Eagle opted to comply. He needed to get in to the class as part of his research, to build his dossier on this charlatan sharemarket quack. He handed over his licence, a sceptical look conveying a message his acquiescence did not. "I guess this sort of 'investor education'..." – he gave the famous two-handed inverted commas gesture – "is fairly heavily scrutinised by the powers that be."

Jason shrugged. "Partly. More that I need to prove class numbers versus tuition income. Still, it is the government who wants your ID. Not me." He looked at Eagle's drivers licence, mocking by taking a second look to make certain the photo of the stubbled, wild-haired rock type on the identification matched the stubbled, wild-haired rock type before him.

"Thanks Christian," Jason said reading from the document.

"Crispian," he corrected, frustrated.

"Sorry. Was that Crispian?"

"I...am Eagle." Eagle used two crooked, pointed fingers and a resolute tone to get his message across. "Let's see what you've got, Mister Sharpe."

Eagle was here to unnerve this sharp-dressing, upstart, start-up entrepreneur who threatened his position in the mind and heart of Alison Archer. He kept clear of him while Jason greeted other guests. He scooped up the paraphernalia on the tables, before sitting over to one side of the rows of chairs. He wore his Skechers shoes, skinny jeans and, despite the March heat, his leather jacket which he hung over the rear of his chair.

Much of the presentation went above Eagle's head, not because it was too complex for him but due to his deep distrust of what was being shown. Jason told his story, a magnificent yarn of his highs and lows in the markets and how he now had a failsafe system to limit loss and maximise gain. Eagle was disgusted, seeing a formulaic approach to brainwash and swindle people who would fall for anything, pay their money and then do nothing. There were six others attending and Eagle felt sorrow for their naivety. He sensed corruption. He would let this Sharpe guy shoot his own foot and deliver the autopsy to Alison personally. Eagle felt assured in his ambition, despite his awkward entry.

The big winner from where Eagle sat was the smooth-talking, neatly-groomed host smiling at the front of the room, blithely encouraging wide-eyed hopefuls to part with their dollars. Eagle kept notes, a record of his thoughts so as to build a case against Jason Sharpe to present to Alison. He hoped to win her favour so she at least saw him as an option in the romance stakes. As it stood, he realised, Jason Sharpe had swept her off her feet.

He'd been following Alison Archer since their days at the Con. Eagle had switched courses from QUT to follow music and one of his early assessment pieces was to construct a business plan for a music band, being paired with Alison and another dreamy lass, one of the myriad idealistic music types at the Con.

Eagle had initially played it cool to her friendliness though inside he churned. His tactical approach to this vibrant bombshell was to not try to score the girl in the early exchanges with a view to a later pay-off. Nearly ten years later, he was still waiting.

They remained in each other's social circles and it was Alison's brother's metal band where Eagle saw his first opportunity to break. They had moderate local success and record label interest, but after several near breakthroughs, Eagle tired of the cock-rock skullduggery of this band of boozing wild men and he left to pursue his own brand of more cerebral musicianship.

At this career juncture, Alison had come calling. She recruited Eagle to her flourishing function covers band. These were not just the lazy 'hunjy' gigs he was used to. There were serious dollars and perks, like travel, quality food and riders. Never mind that the old metal band, now managed by Alison herself, went on to score their signing, recorded and toured Australia and Asia, Eagle had musical integrity, freedom to pursue his stylings and a well-paying gig on the side for cash-flow. All this, but not more, for despite his constant Alison Archer connection, despite being part of her inner sanctum, there had been no romantic headway.

By the end of the seminar, which ended with an offer to attend a series of classes at a cost of $550, Eagle had his argument locked in. He just needed to clarify and embellish the main points for Alison's benefit. She could then see the folly of her infatuation and move on, back to her ordered role in the world of music. Eagle's world.

Eagle finished his notes, packed his notepad and brochures into his leather manbag and sought a hasty retreat. He hoped to avoid the obligatories with Jason Sharpe. He missed his chance.

"How did that go, Eagle?" Jason asked, intercepting Eagle as he strode towards the exit. "Nothing illegal going on, as you suggested?"

Eagle decided to humour him. "Truly inspirational," he stated. "I'm man enough to put my hand up and acknowledge hard work and good intentions. But I must decline the gracious offer of further education. The black magic of shares is far removed from my specialties. I have too many irons in the musical fire to keep me busy."

"Thanks for the feedback. And please, spread the word if you know anyone who might benefit."

Eagle noticed a line had formed to sign up for further education. This free session would make Jason Sharpe over $2000. Eagle winced. "I'll be on my way then. Thank you for the kind invitation."

"Listen, we're about to wind up here," Jason said. "A couple of us are heading off to Fridays for lunch. You're welcome to join us." It was an attempted olive branch.

Eagle wondered why Jason wanted him close but knowing that Alison was their commonality, he suspected Jason Sharpe was trying to garner information on her. "Maybe another time. There's too much in my world demanding my attention right now."

What commanded his attention was being the fly in the ointment of this blossoming relationship. Eagle was patient yet determined, knowing the removal of potential suitors as pivotal to his chances of persuading Alison Archer to succumb to his charms.

Later that week at their regular rehearsals, Eagle arrived earlier than the other band members to speak with Alison. He had dressed in his new brown canvas trousers, applied a hint of cologne, just in case today was the day. He was nervous as he waited for her to finish a phone call.

"G'day, Eagle. That was about a new gig. Some mining company has booked us to do a show at their awards night at

Hamilton Island in September. I accepted. I hope you're keen."
She slapped her Filofax shut and checked her watch. "You're
here early."

"There's been some developments and it would be remiss of
me to allow them to escape your attention."

"What sort of developments," Alison asked.

"Well this is awkward, but I shall persevere. As you know I
visited the offices of AllOptions during the week at the invitation
of your friend Mr Sharpe."

"Oh great, don't tell me you're leaving the band to trade
shares."

"Far from it Alison. It appears that this Sharpe fellow has a
well-suited name. These training courses he runs are official
shams. It pains me to reveal this, as I know you two have
something of a friendship going."

"So, tell me more," Alison said with rising concern.

"From what I can gather, he comes from money, Alison. He is
no self-made man as he insists in his shady seminar sessions.
His parents are hot-shot property moguls, quite a big deal
apparently. The mother has written books on property investing
and they run dodgy seminars to rip dollars out of people's
pockets. Precisely what Jason Sharpe is now doing."

"Hang on a minute Eagle. That's a pretty big allegation you're
making. You don't even know the guy."

"It's not my business to interfere with your personal goings-
on, Alison. But I do care for you. We have had a long association
and I cannot let you get in deep without this knowledge. The
man is running a Ponzi scheme, a rip-off, a racket. He spends his
days preying on the weak of mind and the vulnerable, looking to
purloin and pilfer at every opportunity."

"Oh, Eagle. You didn't like him from the moment you saw
him. I saw how you were when you met him."

"As I said, I care for you and I'm a good judge of people. He is
hardly your type either. Don't you normally date the cool rock
types?"

"He was in a band at uni," she defended before realising how
lame that sounded. "What the hell does it matter what he does?"

"What he does and what he is," Eagle said. "There's more."

"There's no more, Eagle. I've heard enough."

"He hit on me."

"That's ridiculous."

"You know me, Alison. I'm pretty free and easy. I've been around and I know when I'm being hit on. I'm not doing this to hurt you, Alison. I am revealing this because I care about you. I tell you, there is a dark underside to this Mr Sharpe and you need to be careful."

There was just silence from Alison. Eagle stood and watched her as she glared at him. Eagle misread the glare for a cry for help. He stepped in to embrace her, but she pushed him away.

"Set up your gear Eagle."

****

Jason's eyes followed the curve of her back, tracing the line of sight from the perky mound of her behind, over the fabric of her singlet stretched over her fit torso to her strong shoulders and slender neck. She lay on her stomach on the rug as they talked. She was a sight to behold and Jason felt the emotion well up in him. Theirs had been a swift ride from meeting to becoming inseparable.

They were enjoying the April sunshine from the bottom of the Kangaroo Point cliffs by the river. Cyclists trundled by and rock-climbers whooped and grunted, their gear clinking as they fixed their anchors on the hard climbing up various routes. A Citycat ferry surged by, people on the front deck with wind in their hair taking in a new perspective on the city which rose up on the opposite bank. The whole scene resembled a fitness camp as walkers and joggers followed the path past boot camp devotees doing push-ups and boxing class.

Jason had invited Alison to lunch in the park. They set up a rug on the grass in speckled sunlight filtering through the trees. They had spent much time together in recent weeks, each entranced by the other. Their easy conversations and corresponding outlooks intimated something of a future as a couple.

"Did you know it is two months today since I took your booking," Alison said. "And look at us now."

"I'm looking and I like what I see," he said. "Are you happy with where things are?"

"Why do you ask?"

"I haven't had much to compare with but it seems we have moved quickly to where we are now. In a good way. Don't get me wrong," he said, putting a hand on her shoulder. "It's like we have known each other for so much longer."

"Maybe we have, Jason Sharpe."

"You're not going to get all new-age, past life on me, are you? That's a stretch for someone like me who deals in facts and numbers and details."

She rolled on to her side, ran her fingers through her short, blonde hair. "You are in your head a lot. But if you open yourself up, new things make their way in. Your heart can accept regrowth, rebirth. A new business." She smiled and gestured at the two of them, lying around as lovers might. "New friendships! Keep yourself open."

"I am wide open to you, Ms Archer! I can't believe someone like you actually exists."

She laughed. "I'm real." Their fingers intertwined, still polite and nervous as new couples are. She continued. "But really, it is not up to us how things work out. Yes, we strive to be better, to live a life of our own choosing, but we don't know what the universe wants for us."

"Like, who would have thought that I would teach?"

"Exactly. And who would have thought I would meet you. I had consciously stepped back from relationships. I didn't need the grief. So for more than a year, I have had my friends, my music, my work and it's been enough."

"What was the grief, if you don't mind me asking?"

"Oh, you know. There are guys out there who talk smooth. Act all confident, like, 'yeah, I'm the bomb and you're the one', but there are just too many assholes. Immature, insecure. But then when I was least expecting it, you come along and rock my world!"

"You're the rock star," Jason laughed.

"No, Jason Sharpe, you are...some kind of saint. Can you imagine how you appeared? Sharp talker, excuse the pun. Money guy. But that's not you. You're gentle, respectful, from a wonderful family and grounded. And you weren't trying to rush our relationship. So much so, I thought you must be religious. Or as Eagle suggested, maybe secretly gay."

"Eagle said that?" Jason asked in shock.

"He did."

"Good old Eagle. He doesn't like me much, does he?"

"He's different," she said.

Jason scooped up some cheese, gathered his thoughts as he looked off towards Mt Coot-tha behind the city, where the TV towers stood tall against the sky. "Hey, there's no rush for any of that. This time right now, for us, it's magical in a way. We're getting to know one another, there's excitement and a bit of tension. We don't get this feeling back once we go to the next step. It's a courtship. It's cute, and I think it's cool. And I'm not religious."

"See. A saint."

"Hardly."

"See. Humble, and grounded."

"OK, OK."

"What I meant when I said open yourself up was that we were ready for each other," Alison stated. "You asked me, am I happy. My answer is yes, because I was ready to be happy. Have you ever burnt candles?"

"Sometimes," he replied. "At dinner or in blackouts."

"I use them differently. I see a candle burning as passing a message. Burning a candle can release your desires into the atmosphere. Put it out there. It can help you to let go of something or to have the universe know you want or need something."

"What is it you need?" Jason asked. "What does burning candles do for you?"

"Well, I wanted my musical break. I thought I wanted to be a rock star, so I burnt a specific candle. I burn coloured paper, too. Notes asking for what I wanted."

"Coloured paper? Why coloured paper?"

"Different colours for different things. Green for prosperity, red for love. At the start of this year I wrote a note asking for a kind, genuine man to cross my path. I lit a candle and burnt the note. I watched the smoke curl around and rise into the air. It was my message being carried out into the world in the smoke."

"Has it worked?"

"It seems it has," she smiled and touched his hand tenderly.

He didn't need more invitation, leaning in to press his lips to her lovely mouth and staying there, eyes closed, just letting the feeling pour through him. They lazed longer, enjoying the company and the warmth of the sun. He made her a morsel from the small tray of antipasto and biscuits they were sharing.

"I guess I don't have any sort of religious or spiritual following like that," Jason said. "I don't pray or burn candles or worship any particular deity. I live by the mantra of facing forward, not dwelling on the past, trying to improve myself and my world and building my future."

"Ambition. Or maybe perfectionism," Alison suggested.

"No. Not trying to be perfect but always learning or seeking knowledge. So many of us live in the past. We're guided by past experiences, good or bad. I think it's a cop-out to say 'that's how it's always been' without addressing if there is a better way."

"Doesn't that do your head in, always striving?"

"Not at all. People always talk about the good old days. How it was always better when we were younger. Old blokes say, 'Not in my day'. Our young years shape us more than we know and people are always reminiscing."

"One of my favourite bands, Mercury Rev sang a lyric, 'How does that old song go?' How many times do you hear that sort of harking back?"

"Right! I think we limit our growth by holding up the past to be glorified. I consciously address my life and if I'm going the right way for me. I heard it said, 'If you keep doing what you've always done, you'll keep getting what you always got'."

"You've obviously thought about this stuff."

"I have. I'm not burning candles or going to church but I am worshipping a way of life."

"I applaud that. It's incredibly brave to do anything new. Do it in a different way than how it's been done before. Taking a step out of your comfort zone is a big effort. Challenging the way you look at the world, your relationships, no matter how dysfunctional they are, changing your belief systems to look for something more or better can be quite frightening. Career, love, food, music – people may have good intentions but they always find it easy to revert back to what they know."

"And by holding onto the past, they don't make room for anything new in their life. Right?"

"I feel like you get me," she cooed in delight. In relief.

"I get you! We seem to get each other."

"Jason Sharpe, you are a saint. I am so lucky!"

"Hey, I'm just me. And I'm the lucky one."

They lounged and laughed, looked at the clouds and kissed. Together they silently urged a wiry climber to overcome an apparently featureless wall of rock. They held hands and talked, they threw pebbles into the river and Alison gave Jason a shoulder massage. Time went by effortlessly.

Jason wanted to gush out his feelings, to reveal how deeply he cherished her very presence, her form, her mannerisms. Her. He knew where this was going, but good sense told him to hold back, to control his urge to blurt out words. Instead, he revealed another thing he had thought deeply about.

"You know I am helping a finance colleague set up an AllOptions office in London, as a partner."

"With your cousin, right? You did mention this."

"Well, he is ready to go. He's got premises sorted and his other contract is up. It's time to open London."

"You're going to London? When? How long?"

"I need at least a month there. In the northern summer. June, July."

"That'll be a test. You'd better call me. A lot."

"Well, that's just it," he said. "I don't want to have to call you." He saw the colour drain from her face. Her cute toothy smile faded. "I mean I don't want to have to call you, because I want you to come."

She punched his arm. "Don't do that," she squealed.

"Sorry, I just like being dramatic."

"Aaarghh!! You freaked me out." She gathered herself, rolled her eyes and smiled. "You want me to come to the UK with you?"

"Well, it'd be a working holiday. AllOptions London needs a launch party of course, and you seemed to know what you were doing, so I want to hire you. Just you, though. Can you do solo shows?"

"I can. It'd be a changed set list, but yes, I can."

"So I can book your flight?'

"You can. But I insist, I'll pay my way."

"Well, you will need to get paid. Should I assume the same fee?"

"I think we can arrange some sort of discount, Jason Sharpe," she said, leaning in to indulge in the resumption of their now frequent kissing.

****

Most days started like this, with some subtle differences connected to the fact that today was his twenty-seventh birthday. Mani Alves extracted himself from the warmth of his bed, today being shared by a gorgeous and witty brunette he'd met the previous night while celebrating. She'd dazzled him with an intellectual argument on the reasons Australians should be eternally grateful to the English for settling Australia. She was funny and had to be bedded. It helped that he could point to it being his birthday to convince her he needed her company.

He left her to sleep, it being 4.30AM and still dark. This was his customary hour of rising, regardless of the lateness of the previous evening's ructions – in this case after midnight – or of his inebriation. More often than not Mani had social functions that required the consumption of free alcohol and his mornings were always rust-filled due to the after-effects of the booze.

He was unconcerned about his drinking. He'd seen his Dad drink every day and it only became an issue when his life hit the skids. Anyway, your twenties were for this kind of partying. He could handle it. Mornings always got off on the right foot after a large swig from a bottle of juice.

The socialising had begun to become evident in his appearance. A big fleshy boy at the best of times, he was now positively chunky. His posture still bore the disciplines of his youth instilled by his father, but he had added layers of padding. His sedentary choice of career augmented the image. It seemed that as his profile in the writing world grew, so did his body. And so did his attractiveness to the ladies. Girls loved a substantial man, particularly a successful one with a tonne of mojo.

His early mornings were to maintain discipline in his writing. He would write for four hours head to the office for a solid half-day organising his stories and future travel destinations. The afternoons were reserved for his customary siesta, after which he would return to the office to complete his day's work then move on to the 'parti du jour'.

The frequent days that Mani woke with company changed his schedule little for he made certain his guest knew of his routine. Mani's live-in maid would facilitate a hearty breakfast and a private limousine for the lady in question. It was a routine that had been practised often in the nearly three years since Mani had moved to London.

The writing discipline had paid off, for his second novel, a two-hundred thousand word blockbuster in a similar vein to his debut, had become a best-seller in the first days of hitting stores. It only served to raise interest in his first novel so that he saw a fresh burst of sales. Having two books in the UK top ten as well as sales recognition in most Western countries meant that Mani Alves was very well known, very wealthy and a bona fide London celebrity.

The entire concept of living in London remained a surreal dream come true for Mani. He mixed in the circles of the young rich. Doctors, lawyers, finance guns, entrepreneurs, musicians and artists. All were in his social coterie and he utilised these contacts to their extremes. He would often be seen on the town, in the gossip pages of the local press and amongst the first invitees to parties, launches, functions and events. He was a big name around town. But it was the smaller, more subtle aspects of life in London that really held him here. Those moments of belonging to a place, to being part of what makes that place appealing. The soul food of a neighbourly society.

Being his birthday did not release him from his personally-imposed obligations. Writing was his life, words his passion. He had three or four projects on the go to keep him sharp and fresh. Occasionally the importance of a particular task usurped the others so that he would steam ahead, making great progress – eight, sometimes ten thousand words in a day.

He was at his desk at a quarter to five, arranged his documents, got his head back to where he was when he left off by reading back several paragraphs. It got his creative juices flowing. A large coffee with cereal and toast was brought at 7AM by his maid so he could continue writing. It was a familiar, comfortable and productive routine, but this day was broken by well-wishing phone calls. One after the other they flowed in from 7.30AM. Graham Bedser, his mother, friends and finally the one he looked forward to – contact from his much-loved cousin, Jason.

"Morning Jas," Mani crowed.

"Afternoon, Mani. Happy birthday, mate. How's your day going so far?"

"Well it's barely daylight here, but let me tell you, it's been a hell-ride this week! Fitting for a birthday boy. I've had a TV slot, been interviewed for a magazine, three parties this week, I've enjoyed the company of a youthful brunette and a mature blond, both gorgeous, written two chapters of novel number three and to top it off, I spent Sunday night as guest of honour at the heathen Feast of Ostara followed by a Druid ceremony in full robes at a mini-Stonehenge in Essex as part of the Spring Equinox. Oh, yes and I'm off to Paris this weekend for a debaucherous night in Pigalle. Rather run of the mill week for me actually. How about you?"

Jason was laughing. This was the sort of nonsense he always got from his larger than life cousin. "Me? I'm in the process of booking a flight. I understand our man Eunan is ready to launch AllOptions London. I feel it's a good time to get over there, train Eunan up and find some students. So here I come."

"Jolly Ho!" Mani said. "I'll finally see some return on my investment. Great news!" The fondness between them was innate, almost brotherly. It was little wonder as it was similar to that which their mothers enjoyed. "And of course, we will have the launch party. I've enjoyed more parties than a political campaign, so I will be the self-appointed party planner. The only straight one in all Europe."

"Sounds good, Mani."

"So what are the dates?"

"It'll be early June, for a month," Jason replied. "One other piece of news that relates to my trip and also the launch. I have arranged the entertainment."

"Or part thereof, Jason my dear fellow. You see this launch is going to be bigger than a three-ring circus and one entertainer is not going to cut it. It might go on for four days," Mani joked.

"OK, part of the entertainment," Jason conceded. "A young lady who did the Brisbane launch and who will also be travelling to London as my companion."

"You've got yourself a girl? Great news again! About time too. I was starting to think you were a workaholic, sharemarket-obsessed gay man. So tell me, who is this femme fatale that has usurped your love of money?"

"Well, you might actually know of her. It's bizarre. She went to Westside High."

"That does seem a lifetime ago, the old Westside High," Mani mused. "Well, what's her name?"

"Alison," Jason said. "Alison Archer. Does the name ring a bell?"

Ring a bell? Mani gagged as though he'd swallowed the bell, the cathedral and little Quasimodo too. This kept happening but he was learning to control his reaction. There would be no meltdown at this news as he'd had several years ago. Eagle had shaken his core when he disclosed his little Alison Archer gem before Mani came to London, almost causing him to cancel the whole trip.

Now he brought himself under control, flattened out the spines and hackles that had raised down his back and calmed the bellringer in his chest, though his forehead had become a film of sweat. His shock turned to exultation in knowing that Alison Archer still circulated in his world. A sure sign. It was soon replaced however by the horror of this latest revelation. A red mist crossed his eyes as he battled to absorb this. Alison Archer was dating his own flesh and blood.

"Do you remember the name?" Jason asked.

Mani attempted to cover his agitated reaction. "Just trying to recall. Not familiar I'm afraid. As I said, so long ago. So many people. She might have been in a different year."

"Didn't you have a thing for a girl named Alison? I hope it's not the same chick."

"No that was an Andrea. Pffftt! How funny we were as kids," Mani said dismissively. "How is this new lady? A good sort, I presume."

"Just gorgeous, Mani," Jason gushed. "Smart, pretty, athletic, fit-looking. And a brilliant musician. Switched on too. She owns property, runs her own business. She's pretty bloody great."

Mani's mind drifted back to the Alison Archer he remembered – the ponytails, the bouncy walk, the long legs and tennis shoes. He welled up, wistful for this glorious vision of the past. Again, the adult Mani had to battle to regain control of his emotions. "You'll stay with me. I have plenty of room. I live in the heart of London. The new AllOptions office is two streets from my work, three tube stops from my home."

"Aren't you living the life?" Jason joked. "Very generous of you, cuz. I can assure you we'll take up that offer."

"It's going to be good to see you, Jas. It's been too long. And great news about you and this Alison. I can't wait to lay eyes on her."

The Dizzy Heights of a Downfall - 2001

Mani slumped into his leather lounge. He stared up at the ceiling, stunned and confused by the news. There would be no more writing today. The news swirled inside his still foggy mind, processing and churning, filtering through the sting of his now sharply-enhanced hangover. After several minutes he began to laugh out loud. What news! What a birthday! The little boy in Mani wanted revenge, a jealous rage that reared when someone else possessed what is yours. But this soon passed as the writer in Mani reflected on this marvellous piece of life-scripting that was in motion and about to play out in his own backyard. His cousin, his muse, a story of love, betrayal and redemption set amongst the world of the arts and big business. Mani laughed again at the movie voiceover inside his head. He would ensure some intrigue was written into the script as well.

He needed to clear his mind and think. What did this mean? On the one hand, Jason and Alison could only be a relatively new couple or Jason would have mentioned it by now. Their bond was fresh, possibly tenuous and there may be a chance for Mani to intervene and win the girl. However the way Jason had spoken of her indicated a healthy appreciation and a tight accord. Mani was well aware of the strength of feeling in the initial throes of a relationship. They could be loyal, unswerving in their commitment to each other. The fact they were travelling across the globe together ratified some certainty of a future in their eyes. You don't travel with someone you don't like or expect to be with when you get back.

Mani could see he had a dilemma. For fourteen years he had obsessed over a fantasy and for so long he had doubted the true existence of the source of this illusion. Eagle discovered her and the upheaval from that was enormous, re-opening the wounds, propagating the frenetic fixation.

Now this dream was coming to fruition, only not for him but for just about his favourite person in the world. He pondered how he could create a positive for himself without it proving a negative for Jason. A monumental heist with no victim. A battle victory to rival Agincourt yet without the body count.

He understood he could not be the instigator of this relationship demolition. That would be too forward and obvious. Jason might never forgive him. He needed someone to run interference. But who? He racked his brain.

The other necessity was to present to Alison Archer the very best version of himself. No girl would throw in a promising courtship to be with a fat guy, no matter how rich, famous, charming or connected. Mani would get in shape. He had six weeks. To confirm his good intent he dropped and eked out a push-up, then another, strained as it was. The effort collapsed him to the floor where he rolled onto his back and drew in half a dozen deep, desperate breaths. Wow, this will be hard, he thought. He launched forward to complete a sit-up. A solitary sit-up. It was evident a personal trainer was required.

Putting more thought into his options, Mani decided he should carefully orchestrate their trip so that he got to spend maximum time with Alison. Jason would be working so this part would be easy to arrange. As he sifted his memory for a plan to encourage Alison Archer in his direction, Mani arrowed in on the perfect solution. The ideal man on the ground, someone who would love the subterfuge and deceit in this plan. He stood and snatched up his deskphone.

****

Eagle pretended to be annoyed by the distraction, but deep down he welcomed the ring of his phone. He was charting a difficult section of his rock opus, now a five year, still unfinished project. The timing of this particular section was proving difficult. It was a labour of love while being a painful journey, but he was committed to see it concluded.

"Yes." He answered his phone arrogantly, caring little for graces or pretention.

"Hello, Crispian. Did I interrupt you?"

"This would be Alves," he guessed. Mani was the only one who used his Christian name. "This is a first. To what do I owe the ignominious pleasure of a call from Australia's finest young author?" His delivery hinted sarcasm.

"Well, Cris, I think I've finally found something we can collaborate on."

"I really would prefer you called me Eagle. I may have mentioned this once or twice," Eagle said in a bored tone. "It's been nearly three years, Alves. What bothers you enough to want to call me? Something's up, isn't it?"

"Something has just come to my attention," Mani said. "Are you still working with Alison?"

"I am. And it continues to be most lucrative," Eagle added hoping to gain credibility with the millionaire on the phone.

"Good for you," Mani said. "And is there still a...bond between you two?"

Eagle sensed some panic, some vulnerability in Mani's voice. "Why do you ask, Alves?"

"Well, let me be honest. I have just discovered that Alison Archer is dating, of all people, my own cousin. His name is –"

"Jason Sharpe is your cousin?" Eagle scowled.

"You know him?"

Eagle laughed. "Yes, I know him. I wasn't aware you came from such low stock, Alves."

"Meaning?"

"I've had interactions with Mr Sharpe. He's a shyster, a low-life from what I can tell. Runs a dodgy seminar business in case you weren't aware. And yes, he is quite the item with our Ms Archer. She's taken his slimy bait, hook and all."

"Thanks for the Eagle update, Cris, but I think I know my own cousin better than you do. And that dodgy business - I'm a part owner."

"If you know him so well, why didn't you know about his burgeoning love interest? And why are you calling me, Alves?"

"I don't think either of us are happy with the situation. You and Alison have history and it sounds like you don't exactly click with Jason. I would rather their friendship was curtailed, not because I can make a difference over here, more to preserve my fond memories of young Alison Archer. Her being involved with family is just too close to the bone."

"Understood," Eagle said. "So again, why call me?"

"I want you to be my agitator. Get the lovebirds offside. Rekindle your relationship with Alison. Do whatever you can to split them up. I'll make it worth your while."

Now Eagle was pliable, willing and interested to get involved in Mani's scheme. He felt a sense of validation in that he was at last of use to this writer with the over-sized ego. And he sensed opportunity. The tables had turned. Where in the past Eagle pursued Mani for the leg-up he so desired, now it was Alves who had a need for Eagle.

"How so?" Eagle queried.

"How about I send you some cash. Or an open airline ticket. Have a holiday on me, Cris."

"How about cash and a plane fare? What are you offering?"

"A couple of grand should do," Mani said.

"Five grand should do the trick then Alves. I'm not going to risk my neck for anything less." Eagle assessed the pause at Mani's end of the line, nervous he had pushed too far. Or too little.

"OK Cris. But not a word that I'm involved. And you will keep me updated. I'll call in a week. Same time. Your payment is in the mail."

Eagle hung up the phone without farewell. He leaned back in his chair, arms behind his head. A smile spread over his face as he reflected on a good day's work. He had found himself a nice little earner. Those phone calls over the years were starting to pay dividends.

He pushed his chair back from the desk, leaving his rock opera for another time. He had a relationship to dissolve and thanks to Mani Alves, some considerable means with which to do it.

****

Mani was amazed at how positive he now felt. The news of Alison Archer's discovery, espousal and ultimate delivery to him in London had sparked a burst of vital energy in him, so much so that he felt there was nothing beyond his capability or control. His writing in the days after Jason's call had become prolific and varied. He had started a magnificent love story, based on his and Alison's long-running saga. He had been drinking less, sleeping more soundly and had fought through the early intensity of his personal training sessions with London's premier celebrity Personal Trainer, a former SAS soldier with a serious sergeant-major philosophy.

This glamorous honeymoon period slowly but surely ebbed the closer the arrival of Jason and Alison drew. His motivation to be humiliated by his demanding trainer waned to where he had to trade the big-name for a softer, prettier female version. His two weeks of reduced drinking instigated a catch-up period to ensure his alcoholic intake equalised at a level of daily lonesome boozing.

Mani's sleeping had also become erratic as he fretted over his impending re-introduction to the girl of his dreams. He put excess thought into how he would play it. A plan was formulating and he woke often during the night with an idea that had to be mentally played out to its logical conclusion, costing him precious sleep.

This lack of sleep was affecting his writing. Everything he wrote was turning into lovelorn crap, though Mani remained unaware of its lame quality. The travel stories now came from the perspective of the romantic getaway, prompting a request from the senior editor for Mani to revert to what worked in the past. He occasionally had to be awoken from desk slumber by his maid, a drool pool having formed on his notepad, after tumbling off to sleep during his early morning writing sessions.

But by far the most humiliating aspect of his Alison Archer pre-occupation was his newly-apparent habit of committing serious social faux pas. Normally Mani Alves was the epitome of fun and laughter on the social scene, a larger than life figure always in the centre of the action at the very coolest places in

London. But what were appearing now were more than cracks, they were full-on fissures.

It was a four-pronged failure. The stress of knowing he would be meeting Alison Archer in a matter of weeks had him on edge. The interrupted sleep of recent weeks had him in a zombie state as he tried to maintain his high-octane social presence. His drinking was more intense as he tried to both settle his jangled nervous system with alcohol and simultaneously tried to counter his sleep debt with high-energy, high-alcohol mixes to keep him up for the party. And his judgment became impaired by his single-minded preparations for Jason and Alison's arrival, causing Mani to become dismissive of those not valuable to his plans and vindictive to whoever seemed to be acting counter to his plans.

At one party, he absent-mindedly offended a big-name book publisher and instead of apologising, Mani got into an intellectual battle complete with abuse and putdowns which climaxed with a swaying, frothing Mani spitting his drink over the publisher. One very big bridge burnt.

Mani's strike rate with the ladies dissipated too. While partly attributable to Alison Archer being front of mind, he was also finding new ways to make himself unattractive to females. His boorish behavior and slurred speech from over-imbibing had potential bedmates backing away slowly, retreating from this car-wreck waiting to happen. Mani's maid never had so little to do in the mornings.

It was a slow, graceless decline and Mani's soft skills degradation was complete on a balmy, sun-drenched Tuesday morning in mid-May. It was this day he encountered his much maligned ex-trainer sitting in one of the many very funky outdoors restaurants in the Soho district.

Mani was strolling back to the office, returning from his daily wander to a local pub where he had enjoyed an early lunch and a couple of vodkas. He spied the trainer, buff to the extreme, his biceps bulging from the short sleeves of his rayon T-shirt and sporting his customary military buzz-cut and dark glasses. He was enjoying lunch with a group of similarly handsome humans.

Mani had chosen to ignore him, but it was two simple words – "That's him" – that Mani heard as he passed by.

Mani paused mid-step. The trainer and his friends were all gawking at Mani. "That's who, big guy?" Mani snarled.

The trainer had a smug smile. "Just pointing out the subject of one of my finest stories," he said in his thick Scottish brogue. "The one about the soft, flabby writer with the red cheeks who couldn't stand the heat. So how's the heat, Mr Alves?"

Mani waited for the tables muffled laughter to die down. "It wasn't so much the heat, old chap. It was more the lack of cool. And my new trainer has a bit more going for her than a hack, ex-military grunt with no personality."

"A female trainer? So if she trains you right, you'll have a lovely female's body. Correct?" Again his table laughed.

"Oh very funny. Please excuse our little tiff, people," Mani said to the people at the table. "I'm sure your friend is very good at training civilians for those top-secret, covert missions to the Middle East that everyone needs to be trained for." Then he directed his words to the trainer. "Not really in touch, are you my friend. This whole popularity thing will blow over, I assure you."

"And I am sure your new lady trainer specialises in training programs for expectant mothers. That is why she took on the famous writer who looks like he's about to produce a baby!"

This got a great laugh from his companions. Mani went red-faced after this slight. "Stand up," Mani demanded. I challenge you to a wrestle! We'll see how brawn with no brains goes against this flabby writer. Up you get! Mano e mano."

"Go away, Mr Alves. I am having lunch," the trainer said.

This infuriated Mani even more. "Here's your lunch," he growled. Mani stepped in and picked up a plate from in front of his ex-trainer's lady friend. He tipped the half-eaten ragu over the Scotsman's head.

The trainer rose, all six foot four inches of him, steam rising from the hot sauce dripping down his shoulders and a red-eyed anger evident on his face.

Mani slipped his jacket off, folding it over the back of a chair. He removed his shirt and singlet, rolled up his suit pants. His large lily-white torso bulged over his belt as he prowled awaiting the attack of the ex-army goliath.

"You are ridiculous, Alves. Please leave."

"You are scared. Please fight. No hitting, only the wrestle. Don't let fear deny this."

Mani recalled afterwards several things about this battle. The trainer's ripped body as he removed his shirt. He recalled holding his own for several minutes as his high-school wrestling practice came back to him. He remembered a crowd building up around this battle, yet no-one intervened. And finally, Mani remembered seeing his own shoe in front of his face and thinking that his leg shouldn't be able to reach up that high as searing pain shot through his leg. What Mani didn't recall was his vagus nerve in the side of his neck being gently pressed, the SAS instruction of body pressure points allowing the trainer to subdue Mani and put him to sleep.

****

Often in life, small victories can mask major deficiencies. Just when you think you are on the right path, feeling confident in yourself and carving great inroads to a glorious future, a moment in a single day, a single action or event can reveal the repulsive truth. It can be ignored, or recognised as a nadir, a turning point towards redemption. Maybe even salvation.

Mani's public meltdown had shed light on his behaviour and the glare of personal scrutiny prompted immediate changes. He had seen the effect of drinking to excess in stressful times. His father had reduced their home to ashes ten years prior, his judgment impaired by the booze. Mani heeded the lesson, resolved to get himself in order. A twinged hamstring from having his leg bent to such an extraordinary angle by his nemesis ex-trainer was a small price to pay for such insight.

And so, Mani's yo-yo existence resumed. His very best intentions were on display in the several weeks after the showdown. He was back to a routine that involved writing, getting fit, drinking less and ensuring his gossip page mentions were positive. It was a tritely manageable existence that bolstered his image while he craved Alison Archer. She would arrive in just over twenty-four hours and Mani had perfected his plan. He wanted to be good, but he wanted her so bad.

Having nailed three thousand words to the page in the morning, Mani headed out of his apartment for his twice-weekly walk to the office. It was part of his self-improvement, a health habit encouraged by his trainer. The day had begun well, with him waking up next to a pretty young thing he met at a book launch and party the previous night. He'd had some drinks but apart from the standard fuzziness, he didn't feel ill and after such a prolific outpouring of words, he was quite keen to get started on his walk to the office.

Most days the walk took thirty minutes punctuated by pauses at traffic lights as heavy morning traffic crawled along the Piccadilly A4. He wandered by the Roman columns and arches of the Hyde Park Gates and continued on the opposite side of Piccadilly with the verdant Green Park on his right. Halfway in to the office, Mani realised something. He'd not had to stop. He had moved without interruption, the lights changing precisely upon his arrival, allowing him to glide in some sort of perpetual motion.

He passed a man in a suit with a monocle and this English gentleman doffed his hat at Mani as he passed. Partway along Piccadilly as he neared the French chateau-style Ritz building, a gleaming red Ferrari with its top down eased alongside him as he walked. The car's stereo blared Mani's favourite song, Anastacia's 'I'm Outta Love' which Mani got to hear in its entirety as the Ferrari stayed at his walking pace while negotiating the traffic snarl. Even the blonde girl in the passenger seat gave him a smile and held his gaze for several seconds.

This is a particularly good day, Mani thought as he approached the café strip. His phone rang. He answered it.

"Mani Alves, good morning, my name is Petra. I spoke to you last month at the London Gallery fundraiser. I am the PA to the chief of programming at So Television."

"Yes I recall," Mani said. "How are you, Petra. We talked about the time you skied in a bikini on the Val d'Isere."

"And you said you would wear a bikini skiing if I got you on Graham Norton's show."

"Ah, yes. I make some interesting promises when I'm socialising."

"You'd better get your bikini sorted, Mr Alves. He would like you to appear on 'So Graham Norton' in November. I presume you would like us to negotiate with your manager? You provided his card when we spoke, if you recall."

"Petra, my darling. Let's do it! Please send my manager the details?"

The day had just got better. He passed a café with flower boxes teeming with red petunias. The comely young maitre'd, armed with a body to die for and eyes you could fall into smiled at him and offered him to enjoy their hospitality. Out of habit, Mani left with both his coffee and her number, as the brilliant day neared perfection.

At his desk in his Piccadilly Circus office, the first indication that this heavenly day was soon to turn was the panicked email from his mother. It arrived late morning just as Mani's concentration was flagging and last night's drinks were starting to haunt him. He called Celia.

"What's up, Mum? Your email sounded urgent."

"You might want to call your father. I still speak to him once a week and he's not been well. They've found a lump in his armpit, but as he always does, he's brushing it off."

"Jesus." Mani felt a surge of worry. He thanked his Mum and hung up the phone. His Dad, the bulletproof Peter Alves. He'd never been sick, but Mani's mind drifted to the years of drinking and the smokes. He tried to picture the call he needed to make, all the while imagining life without his father, not knowing how serious this might be.

His senior editor rapped on his door, looking down over his glasses at a report. "Might I suggest you tone down your travel expenses while on tour Mani? It has been noted by the bean-counters that your costs are often excessive. I can't imagine the owners looking favourably on three hundred quid for..." He pushed his glasses up his nose for a better view of the report.

"...relaxation expenses, whatever that might be. I assure you, they'll be watching."

Mani was now feeling the full effect of his hangover. The magical start to his day had dimmed, even more so when his publisher rang to say they were rejecting his sappy love story and they were also demanding a re-write on the three chapters he'd submitted of his new novel. How the day had turned. He needed lunch. He needed a heart-starter.

He left his desk, ambled downstairs and outside, where the sunshine and the fresh air seemed to revive him. However once he started walking, the activity loosened up his insides, creating some urgency. He would need to search for a toilet.

Just two blocks from his office the St James Tavern offered a good option. A toilet, a beer and a reasonable counter meal. It was just what was required for his hangover, a roast meal with lashings of gravy. He entered, sought out the lavatory, clenching his buttocks and keeping control of his under-siege sphincter. In his haste, walking on tippy-toes in his discomfort, he violently swung open the entry door to the gent's room. Something blocked his advance and the yowl of pain from beyond the door suggested why. He opened the door more gently to reveal a baldy, frail pensioner grimacing in pain, reaching into his pocket for his handkerchief.

"Sorry mate," Mani said. "Didn't know you were there. Are you OK?"

"You bloody got me, fella. But I'm OK," the little man squeaked magnanimously as a little trickle of blood emanated from an angry gash on his forehead. He dabbed at the blood with his hanky.

"You're bleeding," Mani announced, stating the obvious. "I'm really sorry."

It didn't feel good to injure a senior citizen. He's probably a war veteran, Mani thought, before the emergency of his own rear end returned.

As bodily functions tend to do, the closer you get to the possibility of relief, the more urgent the need becomes. Mani yanked at his belt, tore at his zipper, hauling his shirt up and his trousers down as his bowels railed against his own will. He let a bit of wee go in his boxers in the panic before he sat and exhaled audibly as last night's indiscretions gurgled out of him, making his eyes water.

After he caught his breath from the physical effort of what he'd just done, Mani realised how polluted the room had just become. Rich food and alcohol made for potent patties far removed from the fluffy floaties that health experts advocated for such ablutions. A film of sweat had broken out on his brow and his head was spinning. Cleaning up, his declining day got worse as his finger slid through the cheap thinness of the public toilet paper.

Sweaty, irritated and disgusted, he cleaned up as best he could with one fouled-up finger. He stood and pulled his trousers up in anger with such force he not only gave himself a partial wedgie but also caused his wallet, sitting comfortably in its regular back pocket position to leap from its station, backflip once with a twist, then at the peak of its flight, open up, hover momentarily, then career downwards towards the bowl. It landed with a splat upon the previously deposited foulness.

Mani cringed. Could the day have turned worse? He left St James Tavern without his beer or his beef and gravy, passing a concerned huddle as the barman tended to the injured pensioner. Mani would have to find another watering hole nearby to sate his increasing desire for a beer.

He knew just the place and only a block or two away. He strolled up Shaftesbury Avenue past the Apollo Theatre. He passed a plump lady in her fifties with too much make-up walking her dachshund. She smiled at Mani, who shook his head to himself. Getting eyed up by old birds now, he thought.

He turned the corner into Rupert Street heading to Waxy O'Connors and of course he then stood in a neat little pile of dog shit, previously belonging to the old girl's puppy. "Of course," he said out loud. He stepped out of his shoes at the entrance, leaving them in the street and entering in just his socks.

Waxy O'Connors was an iconic old pub with an internal maze of rooms that served as a multitude of separate bars. The place was all rustic timber and rough-hewn brick, some rooms with stained-glass windows and church pews. One of the bars amid the labyrinth even featured a petrified tree and the place was always reliable for an eclectic crowd and a cool, but not cold beer. The room Mani chose for his refreshment was the Cottage Bar, which had a reasonable crowd in for this time of the day as people flocked in for their meals.

After three beers and still waiting for his meal order, Mani was approached at the bar by a young lady, an Aussie who recognised him.

"I know you. You're Mani Alves, aren't you? The writer, right? I'm reading your book," she said in a familiar drawling Australian accent that had been tinged British by her stay in the UK.

"Nice to hear," Mani said without enthusiasm. "Thanks, but yeah, not a good time."

"I'll grab my book. You have to sign it for me."

"No, really, love. I tell you, I'm not in the mood to sign a book. Sorry."

"Oh come on, it'll only take a second."

"And it'll only take you a second to go away and leave me alone. I'm sorry, OK."

She was taken aback by this. "A bit of fame has turned you into an asshole, I see."

Mani did not want to be seen in that light. "Look, I'm sorry. I just haven't had a good day," he said.

The girl retreated, scowling.

Mani ordered something stronger. His scotch came. His meal was still being farmed it seemed. He felt bad about the brush-off. He should really look after his fans, he thought. But it had been such a shift in his day, he had no energy for anyone else. He turned and looked to the table where the girl sat with several others.

"Turn your face away, fat boy," a fellow with a Brummie accent amongst the girl's group called as Mani peered over. "Rude bastard. Think ya too big for ya boots, mate?"

Mani turned away. He didn't need the grief, but when another snipe came from the same chap he could not keep his tongue. "Wassa matta, guv'nor?" Mani mocked. "Havin' trubble undastandin' ya!"

"Ah, you're a smart-arse, mate," he called back. "You'll get a punch in the nose if ya ain't careful."

"That'll fix everything, won't it?" Mani retorted. "Seriously, are you sure you're in the right place? Shouldn't you be back at the factory, mate?"

"Ah, you're cheeky! Big name writer, hey?" he said, then to his female friend. "Here, give me the book. This bastard's signing it for ya."

Mani felt all his old bullying fears rise up within him as the wiry man strode towards him, book in hand. He hated confrontation and he silently cursed his loose mouth after several drinks.

"Here y'are, mate. Get signing and stop bein' so rude."

Mani took the book and the pen being held out by the girl behind him. He didn't need to be treated like this, he thought to himself. He was a wealthy, famous writer, part of the new elite of London. He wasn't going to be held hostage by these tourists. What were they even doing in his part of town?

It was sorrowful that Mani did not even realise how he had changed, how he had developed such a status-defined attitude. He took the book, turned to the back pages and tore out the final two pages of the story and stuffed them in his mouth and chewed them up. "Enjoy the book," he mumbled through the wad in his mouth as he handed the defiled book back to the man.

All manner of name-calling and caterwauling came back directed at Mani, who in his half-drunken state and arrogance spat the chewed up pages at the duo as they retreated. The Brummie man flicked the book at Mani. "Have ya flamin' book back. You're a loser, mate!"

Mani wore the book in the chest. Anger rose up and he clutched the book, wound up and grunted in effort as he threw it at the man. The Brummie ducked. The woman turned when she heard the grunting. The book cannoned into her face, causing her to collapse and her eye to close over as though a purple egg had formed on her face. Her three friends rushed to her aid.

Mani stared bug-eyed at what he had just done. This was not good. He imagined the payout he would have to offer to sweep this one under the table. He stood and hurried to where the group tended the girl. That's two people Mani had damaged in under an hour. He shook his head in bewilderment, trying to figure out what he'd become.

"Piss off, mate!" the second man in the group growled. He shoved Mani out of the way with more force than either of them expected, causing Mani's socks to slip on the tiled floor. He stumbled sideways then backwards, his calves hitting a chair. Horribly off balance and falling backwards, Mani reached out for anything to arrest his tumble. The Brummie was nearest and by reflex Mani grabbed his shirt collar to right himself, to no avail as they both careened into the table.

Mani slid over the tabletop as it tipped covering the two men in beer, ashtrays, cigarette butts and glass. Lots of glass. The Brummie was a passenger in Mani's frantic grip and he ended up under the tipped over table, as glasses shattered and the sharp edge of the glasstop table pinned his hand to the ground.

It was pure bedlam as Mani rolled over to see blood spurting from the Brummie's hand. As Mani went to lift himself to his feet, spitting a soggy smoke butt from his mouth, he saw a pinky finger on the ground. He picked it up, stood and stared at the severed digit.

"Give me ma finger back, bastard!" the Brummie yelled, turning pasty white.

"No," Mani yelled in equal amounts shock and disdain.

The Brummie let out a fierce but frightened yell. He was not coping with seeing his disfigurement. "You really are a right prick, mate! Someone call the coppers! And call the bloody paramedic!"

A London Summer - 2001

Jason and Alison arrived in London, the very image of the happy, successful couple and quite inseparable. Mani arranged for them to be collected by a driver and delivered to his apartment where Mani's maid ensured their comfort. With Mani at an afternoon meeting, he would greet them later at a dinner he had organised to welcome them.

Mani was excited for his reunion not only with Jason, but also the myth turned reality that was Alison Archer. The dinner was to celebrate their arrival and this was his first opportunity to enact his plan to win over Alison. Mani had hand-selected the guest list to ensure he would be shown in the manner in which he was esteemed by his associates in London. He had some powerful friends attending, including a well-known actor and a famous singer, with the sole aim of presenting to Alison the sort of privileged life that he led.

Mani had spent the previous afternoon at the police station giving statements about the events leading to the patron's injury. All pointed towards Mani being absolved of blame, it being recognised as a freak accident. With that concern lifted from his thoughts, he was able to switch his thinking to Alison. His stomach was turning flips in nervous excitement. The thought and effort he had put into his plan rivalled the planning he devoted to his novels. He hoped for the same immediate success.

Mani needed to be there when the couple arrived at the restaurant. He'd devised a specific seating arrangement and another notable guest, a former flame of Jason's named Jenny, now travelling Europe from her London base, there with the express instruction to flirt outrageously with Jason. Alison would sit next to Mani with Jason next to him. This would give Mani optimum opportunity to talk, laugh and promote himself to her throughout dinner.

He had booked a private room at the restaurant, with guests to meet at the bar. Mani socialised while keeping one eye on the front door, longing to see his cousin and their girl. At last, they arrived and he laid eyes on Alison Archer for the first time since the days of spitballs, crowpecks and ignominy. This time things would be different, he convinced himself.

She was perfect. Just lovely, as he expected her to be. A swell of emotion twirled through his body, as he tingled with adrenalised excitement. He tried to reconcile this elegant vision with his memory of her from school some fourteen years before. She was tall and thin as he remembered, yet muscular and toned. Her beautiful blond hair was these days worn short and funky. Her face had matured, the little girl now a grown woman, a gorgeous specimen.

Excusing himself from his conversation, Mani went to them and embraced his cousin. "So brilliant to see you, Jason. It's been too long!"

"I can't believe I'm finally here. Awesome to see you, Mani, and can I say, I love where you live. I think I need to start writing books for a living."

"It's a life of solitude that chose me," Mani said with a slight bow and a smile at his beloved cousin. He then turned to Alison. "And please introduce me, Jason. This must be Alison." He hesitantly stuck out a hand for a formal greeting, remembering the result of having leaned in for a more personal greeting on stage at Westside High.

She took his hand in an awkward touch, but for Mani, a touch nonetheless, before she threw caution to the wind and stepped in for a brief hug. "Hey, we're all friends here. What the heck," she said putting one arm around Mani's shoulder and kissing the air by his cheek.

Drinks were ordered and introductions abounded, but Mani was in a bubble, smiling and laughing by rote while keeping a surreptitious eye on Alison Archer. She was here! He was equally in disbelief and awe. And she was every bit living up to the expectations of Mani's long-held fantasy.

When they sat down at a table for their meal, Jenny began her flirting in earnest, clinking her glass with Jason's all too often, giggling and cooing about the old days when they were a couple. Mani could tell that Jason was uncomfortable as was Alison, but he kept her occupied with the strategically placed intellects around the table. Mani's actor friend kept the conversation ticking in a lively manner with his insights while Mani was certain Alison would be impressed with the big-name indie rocker who had joined them.

Through it all, Mani noted how composed Alison was, more than holding her own in discussions and venturing her own opinions. She was proving herself the confident and articulate individual that Mani expected her to be. He settled in the moment, savouring this coveted individual in his immediate presence.

Later at a nearby bar and with the new arrivals fading in line with their Australian body clocks, Mani had to withstand the inevitable query from Jason about the odd presence of Jenny at the dinner.

"It just seemed a strange decision to have her there," he stressed.

Mani leaned his large frame against the bar. "I didn't do it to make you uncomfortable," he said. "I apologise if it did. Alison, you weren't distressed, were you?"

"No, to be honest. Why would I be? She seemed a nice enough girl."

"Precisely," Mani said in vindication. He signalled to the barman for a follow-up round of drinks, noting the distrustful look he was receiving from Jason.

"In case you didn't notice, she was all over me, Mani. Alison, I apologise. I'm sure it must have been awkward."

"Are you sure?" Mani asked. "I just saw her being friendly with everyone at the table."

"I don't think there was anything sinister in it, Jason," Alison said.

"I just can't pinpoint why she was there, considering our past."

Mani proffered further explanation, sensing a backfire in his plan. "Simply put, Jas, I wanted a little flavour of home for your first night here. Jenny's a great girl, we keep in touch with us both living in London. Us lonely Aussies have to stick together." He laughed and gave his cousin a jostling man-hug and hoped that Jason's doubts would slide away along with his jet-lag.

****

A crucial element built into Mani's plan was to ensure he was available to host Alison while Jason committed heavily to the setup of AllOptions' new office. Mani had requested leave from work for this period and gave all assurances that Alison would be well looked after. He would show her the sights, the best shopping and make his driver available at her beck and call, giving Alison full authority to utilise his limousine account.

The days settled into a rhythm of Jason heading into the Piccadilly Circus office while Alison and Mani would choose their adventure. Mani showed Alison Harrods department store in his neighbourhood, they drove by Big Ben and Westminster Abbey, wandered in Trafalgar Square and by Buckingham Palace. Mani watched her, enjoyed her movement and her style while asking questions in getting to know her all over again.

"The problem with England is there are too many English," Mani pronounced while they strolled the aisles of Selfridges. "I just wish I had more of an Australian connection here. That's why I had Jenny at the dinner last night. She's a reminder of home. It's not easy being an Australian in London."

"Like the laments of an Englishman in New York perhaps," Alison smiled.

"Everything can be referenced by music for you, I see. Very clever." Later he ventured a comment on her and Jason. ""You two seem happy."

"Yeah, I guess. It's early days, but it's going well."

"Good to see. Jason seems much more relaxed than his normal wound up self. You must bring out the best in him."

This was Mani's first foray into planting little seeds of doubt without appearing too disruptive. He noted her look as she processed the comment.

While the days were Mani and Alison, the nights were reserved for the boys. As soon as Jason arrived home, Mani had a drink in his hand, a bottle of wine open and dinner plans made. Dinner would often be the three of them plus one or two of Mani's friends, after which Jason would be dragged to a local pub or one of Mani's customary parties.

It suited Alison as she had continued rehearsals to master her solo style for the launch and having researched gigs around London that had to be seen, her nights were similarly occupied. Mani had helped in this regard by being able to source tickets to several high profile shows. This agenda was also part of Mani's scheme to keep the couple isolated from one another, thus testing their relationship and allowing him to identify any cracks he might exploit to win Alison Archer over.

For Mani and Jason, it was like old times. They laughed and kidded around as though they were once again teenagers back in Brisbane. Though Mani was such a different person these days – worldly, wealthy, well-travelled and socially a tour de force – he could lapse back into his younger role as Jason's second. It was his comfortable place with strong links to their youth and Mani embraced that old feeling. Yet while Mani was happy to play the quiet cousin when it was the two of them, he was also eager to display his social status for Jason at the soirees they attended.

On their fourth day in London, with Jason again at the office, Mani had his driver whisk Alison around the never-ending sights and shopping of London. Mani tagged along though he could have used some extra sleep after prodding Jason into a large night on the town. Mani nonetheless fought through his own seediness, for he had more seeds to plant.

It was she who broached the subject of their nocturnal endeavours. "You boys were out late last night. And noisy on the way in. Bit of a big one, was it?"

"Oh yeah," Mani replied. There's always a party on offer in London. Some just escalate to full-blown rampages more than others. This was a launch for a new magazine called Moment from the same stable as my own rag. Bit of a big deal apparently."

"You live a surreal life, Mani. Mixing in the circles you do - celebrities, parties."

Mani took this as praise from Alison. "I knock back more invites than I accept. I couldn't possibly maintain such a pace," he fibbed. "If it wasn't for Jason urging me on, I think I might have missed this one. He was keen to push on."

"He was, was he?" Alison said. "Jason doesn't strike me as big on parties."

"Yeah, well I thought he had outgrown that side of him. He can get rather loose when he's drinking. It only happens now and then, but when he's in the mood, he's hard to keep pace with." Again Mani saw the doubting look as she stayed quiet for several minutes.

He applied further needle, initiating a pre-designed conversation while inserting his customary charm. "You're different to the girls he's dated in the past."

"He's probably not my standard type either," Alison replied. "Not that I would pigeon-hole myself or anyone else."

"He is different, that cousin of mine," Mani said. "He worries me sometimes with this whole business thing, trading and being pre-occupied with making money."

"He's ambitious. Nothing wrong with that," she defended.

"You know he lost the plot a year ago." Mani noted her quizzical look. "Oh yeah. Went big on the trades and came out second best. His parents had to bail him out. I lent him money to get AllOptions started. I love him but I just worry about the direction he's taking."

With that, he ceased the conversation, changing the subject as they entered the terrific space that is Hyde Park. Job done, he thought.

Later, strolling the park on their way home from Notting Hill, they chatted easily. Mani remained at his charismatic best, playing the tour guide while all the time his eyes adored her. He was enchanted with her knowledge and outlook on life.

"So you went to Westside High?" she asked.

"I did. Great memories. Seems so long ago."

"Doesn't it? Sorry to say, I don't really remember you. I don't remember much about school though," she added laughing.

Mani didn't want to reveal much. "I was a quiet kid. Kept to myself mostly."

"I spent just as much time at other schools."

She didn't need to tell Mani that. He knew it already. He felt he knew her well. They exited the park at South Kensington and the subject of school was soon changed. "Oh wow," Alison said in amazement. "What is that building? It's just incredible."

The tour guide also moved on from the school discussion. "Royal Albert Hall. It's a masterpiece, isn't it?" Mani said, though he sensed some discomfort from her about Westside High School. Maybe she did recall him, Mani thought in horror as they circumnavigated the domed hall and admired its architectural beauty.

When they reached Mani's apartment, he retired to rest, not wanting to swamp her. He sensed a connection had built between them and he'd gained her trust. He would let his disclosures sink in and fester before producing more insights to rock the boat.

He was single-minded in his ambition, almost bloody-minded considering the damage he might be causing Jason. Yet Mani justified his deeds with the assertion that such a handsome and charismatic man as Jason should be able to take his pick of females, so why should he have Alison Archer when Mani had such a history and self-appointed right to her? His next move was to test the waters; actually more of a massive leap into the churning, murky unknown depths.

The morning had begun with early drizzle but improved to a clear bright day perfect for viewing London from the famous London Eye. Mani had his driver deliver Jason to the office before Alison and Mani continued on to the giant wheel on the banks of the Thames. Mani squirmed when he witnessed the soppy farewell between the two lovebirds before Jason alighted. His nerves only intensified the nearer they drove to their destination. If what Mani was about to do received a favourable response, it would all but seal the deal, a coup to rival the Ayatollah Khomeini's Iranian revolution.

They rose up slowly in their roomy capsule on the enormous wheel. They were alone in their carriage and the clear day gave them a view over London and miles beyond. Mani watched Alison scoot around from one side to the other in her excitement. She pointed out sights she recognised, prompting interested utterings of agreement from Mani.

"It's a beautiful place, London," he announced. "I can't think of anywhere else I'd rather live. She's a grand old dame."

"The view is stunning."

"I think everyone should live in London once," Mani said. "It's the heart of culture, art, history, literature, music. A travel hub to the delights of Europe. Just glorious!" He was leaning with his hands against the glass, drinking in the view as he spoke. He turned to her then. "Would you live here?"

Alison thought for a second, then nodded in the way you do when an internal decision is reached. "One day, maybe," she said.

"You should get over here while you're young. There are opportunities for you here, particularly for your music." Mani wanted a response from her, waited. Slowly, their eyes met. Mani felt his desire for her well up within him. This was his moment. "Listen, I want to ask you something," he said.

What followed was one of the most unlikely and ambitious proposals ever extended by one person to another, as Mani poured years of pent-up yearning into a string of carefully selected words with which he hoped to win over his Alison Archer.

****

"But I hardly know you, Mani. I mean I only met you this week."

"It feels like I've known you much longer than that." He stood close to her, posed as if delivering a Shakespearian performance. He thought a knee drop might have been a little excessive.

"I don't think it would be right. For now."

"I know it's unexpected. I know it seems rushed. But I know what I feel and it feels right."

Alison looked upon the pleading man before her, the city of London a sprawling backdrop beyond the glass enclosure. "So you're asking me to give up everything I have back home. My work. Jason as well."

"I'll make it worth your while. We will have a brilliant future together."

"I am just flabbergasted. I can't think straight. How can I answer such a thing?"

"Just say yes," Mani said, spreading his arms theatrically. "Make me the happiest man in the world."

"You would have to pay me well."

"I would. Whatever it took."

"So what would you pay?" Alison asked. "Not that I'm saying yes."

Mani shifted his gaze, deep in thought as she watched his response. He hadn't put thought into this sort of detail. "How about 100,000 pounds every year?" he said. "Plus costs to move over. But remember, it's more than the money. It's the life you would then be able to lead. Travel. Contacts for your music. Anything you wanted."

"This is too surreal. I can't think!"

"Take your time. Weigh it up."

"Why me?"

"I see what I need in you. You're smart, you're savvy, quick thinking, you've got your stuff together and it doesn't hurt that you're also very attractive."

"Not that that should be a pre-requisite for a job."

"Of course not, but it opens doors, there's no doubt about that. So what do you say? Will you come and work for me?"

Alison was overwhelmed. She had been shadowed by Mani over the past several days. It hadn't bothered her as he was a friendly and engaging host and Jason had rarely been available as he tried to set up the business. Deep down, this was a bit embarrassing to be asked to move to London to work for Mani as his personal assistant within three days of meeting him. She sensed a sadness and loneliness in him. A firm but kind repudiation was the only valid response.

Regardless, she was thrilled to be in London, not least because of the choice of gigs that were on offer. Having scanned the local street press – the ultimate source of local goodness in any city around the world – she had pinpointed gigs by Manic Street Preachers, Sophie Ellis-Bextor, Zero 7 and a breaking band called Muse who were playing at the legendary Brixton Academy. This was an opportunity that her friend Sally the music journalist would die for.

Between her tourist adventures with Mani and her downtime when she rehearsed for the launch show, she had still managed to spend time with Jason. These moments together were rare thus far on tour. Jason had indulged in big nights of drinking with Mani and the negatives that Mani pointed out about his cousin had her finding difficulty in marrying the conflicted messages she was receiving.

It was concerning for Alison that Mani, who clearly revelled in his cousin's presence, had continued to denigrate Jason in front of her. It was all done in his cheery way and laughed off as though Jason were just an untamed but lovable rogue. This was far from the Jason she knew, the guy she had fallen for. She began to worry that maybe the gloss was coming off their romance.

But by buying Alison a sapphire necklace and an enormous bunch of flowers, Jason had managed to get his message across. That and the looks he gave Alison, those looks of such intensity that he made her swoon like a giddy schoolgirl. It left her in no doubts about his feelings.

The remainder of her first week in London saw further destabilising of her confidence. Jason, recovering from yet another big night with Mani, had initiated a romantic day for them. But once again AllOptions took precedence and Jason had to withdraw. The business was behind schedule.

Alison had been bereft after this, feeling as she presumed those do who have spouses so married to their job. She told him she understood, made all the right noises, but the disappointment cut deep. Mani must have noted her moroseness for he was quick to intercede.

"Hey, let's go to Soho," he said. "There's a music shop there, highly eclectic, full of rare and vintage music, bootlegs, underground stuff and up-and-comers. My friend, an author and an ex-rocker with numerous stories to tell runs the place. You'll love it."

"That's OK," Alison said. "I need to rehearse."

"Nonsense, young lady. You've done nothing but rehearse. Let's get out and get groovy in the grooviest place in London. You can update my taste in music."

"Why not. I could do with a laugh."

"Clearly," Mani said.

"That noticeable?" Alison turned up her lip, despondent

"Sorry to say, it is. Look Alison, he's a busy guy. Don't get too down on it all."

"He did invite me over here Mani. And I know it's for business. It's disappointing, that's all."

Her shoulders slumped, but Mani seemed to want to genuinely console her.

He placed a hand on her shoulder. "Jason's a great guy but he's very self-motivated. Maybe self-interested. It's not you. It's just that he would never let anyone get in the way of his goals."

The Lengths We Go To

Mani passed his credit card across the bar. "Two cognacs on ice and a couple of Flying Dutchmen thanks. Oh, and keep the tab open. We'll be having a few. While you're at it, a round of drinks for the table of ladies over my right shoulder. Anonymous, of course."

It was after 10pm and the cousins were situated in a quiet, classy bar in Shepherd's Bush. After dinner they had delivered Alison to the gig she was seeing and circled back to find this bar, one of Mani's favourites. It featured a solid oak bar with glasses hanging over the counter, bizarre chain mail chandeliers and an unused fireplace over which hung framed artwork, while a collection of memorabilia adorned the walls. A piano man played for the small crowd of twenty or so patrons.

"You left me hanging last night, so tonight you drink with me," Mani said.

"You set a cracking pace but I have a lay day tomorrow, so I can let my hair down a bit."

Mani swilled his ice around with his yak. "The business is on target then? Our business, should I say." He laughed.

"In good hands, Mani. And in good shape. Eunan's a cluey guy. I daresay I won't need to return for more training. He gets it."

"So you'll not be back to visit?" Mani enquired in a pleading tone. "You're leaving me all alone in London?"

Jason flinched from the strength of the cocktail Mani had ordered. "You're hardly alone. You have more friends, contacts, associates and acquaintances then anyone I know." He smiled as he counted this list out on his fingers.

"Then why am I so lonely? This place eats me up."

"You're kidding right?"

"No. I'm struggling with being here when all the family's back in Australia. I'm burning myself out. Boozing too much. I might be forced to come home soon anyway. Back to my old life."

"I didn't realise," Jason said. "You always seem so up."

"There are pressures. Most that I have brought upon myself."

"There's pressure everywhere, whatever you do. You're not alone there. It might not be so different at home."

"Granted," Mani said, unsated in his emotional duress.

The conversation ebbed and flowed and was swallowed up in reminiscences. The two men, comfortable in each other's company, continued drinking. Behind his façade of quips and zaniness, Mani felt he hadn't vented adequately. He wanted more sympathy. Empathy. Anything.

He held up his drink, stared through it and pulled a face at his cousin, causing Jason to laugh. "This drinking is out of hand, Jas."

"Well, you do have guests. And it is summer."

"Ha ha. Sound reasons," Mani laughed. "Any reason seems to work. How about this? The reason I drink is to celebrate Tony Blair's Prime Ministership. Every day, here's to the PM."

Jason joined the mirth. "Big Ben tolled its bells. Cheers." He raised his glass then emptied it.

"St Pauls Cathedral remained upright today. Where's that bottle?" Mani stated in triumphant tones. They laughed at the ridiculousness. "The truth is Jason, I'm not in control of it. I'm on it every day and it starts earlier and earlier."

"Just stop."

"Not that easy. The temptation is always there. And I feel it's expected of me to go to these parties. This is my life. All I've known for three years."

"Maybe you need to change it up. Come home maybe. The good thing about being a writer is you can do it anywhere, right?"

Mani drained his glass and in an absurd paradox signalled to the barman for another round. "Again, not that simple," he said forlornly. "I've lost it, Jas. The words elude me."

"What do you mean?" Jason was concerned about his cousin's low state.

"My book deal is being reviewed. The last six months work has been rejected. My most recent story idea scrunched up and binned."

Jason put a hand on Mani's shoulder in support. "I feel ignorant coming here, imposing on you while you are having troubles."

"I wanted you here. Alison too. It's good to see you happy." They clinked glasses. "How's Alison doing? Is she enjoying her trip?" Mani asked.

"You've spent more time with her than me. But I think she's OK. She knew I was coming here for work. She's just doing her thing."

"She's a nice girl. And seems to be enjoying London. One thing came up when we spoke though," Mani frowned. "I don't want to be the one to pry. Your decisions are your own."

"What do you mean?' Jason asked.

"She seemed a bit put our about the launch."

"As in...what? She doesn't want to do it?" Jason was incredulous. "It's one show and she's got four weeks leisure time!"

Mani tried to appear diplomatic, but he sensed he'd raised the tension perfectly. "Not that she doesn't want to do it. From what I can tell, she'd do gigs every day she loves music so much."

"So, what is it?"

"It's more about her doing it solo. Without her band. She seemed a little put out, that's all."

"Is that right?" Jason vented. "Wow, I never got a sense of that."

"Please don't disclose that I betrayed her trust. I just thought you might want to consider that and decide how you'll handle it."

Jason was bristling. "Of course," Jason said. "In perfect confidence. It's interesting to know."

It was precisely the response Mani aimed to achieve.

Later, the boys rolled home to Mani's apartment in quite a state. A bottle of Hennessy was opened and duly depleted. Alison would not be home from her gig for several hours and the cousins were beyond composure as the evening's drinking took full toll on their senses. Jason lolled on the sofa in Mani's writing room as background chill music played. Mani alternated between leaning back on his desk chair as they spoke and upright animation as the lads laughed and talked.

"Remember this?" Mani said, holding up a black device. "The dictaphone your Mum got me ten years ago."

Jason strained his blurred eyes. "Wow, you've still got it! Does it work?" His head was spinning widdershins.

"Yes, it does. Of course I've bought newer models since, but I always kept this one. It changed my life. It made me a writer. And it still works a treat. Here, say something."

"What do you want me to say?" Jason mumbled through his drunkenness.

"Just tell me your name."

"It's Jason."

"Speak clearly. Are you drunk or something," Mani laughed.

"I don't know what's going on," he gibbered as he sat splay-legged and over-affected.

"And what are you doing in London, Jason?" Mani asked holding the recording device under his mouth.

"Visiting you, ya big nutter."

"And you are partying hard in London, I can see. What will the missus say? What's her name again, this lovely new spouse of yours?"

"Alison. She's awesome. It's alright, she won't mind me drinking with you, but gee I'm going to be sick tomorrow," Jason garbled. "This night's just been over the top."

Mani then launched into a diatribe about drunken Aussies in London giving ex-pats a bad name, all in jest of course, as he taped the whole thing. He finished up talking in a female voice to his subdued cousin, strutting around effeminately, pretending to be Alison. "Jason, you sexy little Aussie boy. You want to show your Alison some love?"

Jason giggled at Mani wiggling his hips. "Nutter!"

"You want to take me on a date, hey handsome. How about you take this sexy she-male to the Jay Kay gig with you, huh?"

Jason shook his head, disbelieving the stupidity he and Mani were engaging in. "I'm not going to the Jamiroquai gig with you. You're not as pretty as my real date."

Mani pouted theatrically. "Well, say goodbye then, my drunken Aussie friend." He continued to hold the dictaphone under Jason's face.

"Goodbye and good luck. I hope we wake up feeling better than I expect we will," Jason slurred.

Mani clicked off the recording device, looked at it fondly. "She's a trusty old friend, this recorder. I could never thank your Mum enough."

****

Jason had arranged a lunch date for him and Alison, and of course Mani presided over the occasion. Alison had got quite a laugh out of the gibbering carcasses she encountered two nights earlier upon returning home from her gig. Jason and Mani were giggling and incoherent playing Snap with a deck of cards after having tried and failed at playing Jenga. Scattered wooden blocks had suggested such dexterity as Jenga demanded was beyond the skillset of inebriated men.

Jason had been sheepish about his state so had chosen to delay his entry to the office this day to dedicate attention to Alison. They had spent the morning strolling the parks and spending quality time. Now for lunch, Jason had chosen an outdoor restaurant.

When Mani arrived he was bemused to discover that Jason had chosen was the same café at which Mani had disgraced himself by wrestling his trainer. He recounted the story with its inevitable sorry end. Alison and Jason both got a great laugh out of this.

"So that's why you had a sore hammy the other week. Because you got owned by a Scottish personal trainer," Jason said.

"Involuntary contortionism is my preferred description," Mani declared. "Even though he subdued me, it still satisfies that I poured a plate of pasta over his head."

"You get yourself into all sorts of crazy situations Mani," Alison chipped in, giggling. "Your life is quite mad."

Mani watched her laugh, enjoying her natural easy responses. Even though she was laughing at him, he still sensed an admiration of the outrageousness of his lifestyle. She could laugh at him, with him, however she wanted. For Mani, it was a joy to watch.

And she was laughing a lot more in recent days. Maybe she was more relaxed in Mani's apartment as a visitor, and now more as a friend. She was getting to know her way around London, seeing her bands, getting into the scene and maybe feeling better about her solo show.

Possibly, Jason was showing her more affection and Alison was responding accordingly. Mani's carefully placed suggestion to Jason must have triggered a flush of emotional tenderness from him to her. That was OK, Mani reasoned. He had ways to counter this obvious response.

After lunch, paid for by Jason and punctuated several times by introductions to acquaintances of Mani's, Jason had to bid them farewell. The office beckoned, as there was work to do. Mani watched their public display of affection as he was leaving, amused and annoyed at the way two people he loved in differing ways showed off their obvious ardour.

Mani sat enjoying his coffee after Jason left, soaking up the brief stint of sunshine and waited for Alison to initiate a conversation. Mani had an hour before he was due to meet his publisher in Central London. He leant back in his chair, serene as he watched the passing crowds, a hint of a smile on his lips.

Finally she spoke. "You seem to know everyone around here. Or should I say, they seem to know you. It's like you're some sort of royalty."

"No, no," Mani said modestly before smiling at Alison and adding, "Not everyone. Just the wealthy and important ones." They both laughed. "To be honest Alison, I just try to be friendly with everyone I meet, interested in them, do the right thing, be kind and it's just amazing how that comes back to you."

It was Mani showing himself as he'd like to be, for Alison's benefit. Deep down he knew this self-description was not accurate. But if he couldn't push his own barrow, who would?

There must be some reason for his evident popularity. It was better that he had a creed to describe his popularity.

She nodded as she processed his words, and again Mani felt the admiration, that things were turning his way. He decided to press home the advantage. "I thought you and Jason were having a full day together."

"He granted me the morning and then lunch. But the business needs him. He said he is close to tying it up but there are some last touches that he needs to oversee."

Mani gave her the 'I told you so' look.

"He promised me a weekend in Dublin after the launch," she said with a mix of defeat and hope. "Once the business settles into a rhythm."

"It's a lot of work to set up a business," Mani empathised.

"Evidently."

"He's a perfectionist. He wants things done right. Been like that since he was a boy. He struggles to let go and lets the stress get to him occasionally. All his worries about the new office, the launch and trying to keep trading all the while. He's stressed!"

Alison sat forward in her chair, the sun across her concerned face. "The launch. What is stressing him about the launch?"

Mani gestured as though calling for calm, went to speak, checked himself, then said, "Nothing at all. I shouldn't have said anything." It was a beautifully choreographed and delivered piece of acting.

"Mani, you have to tell me," she said. "Why is he stressed about the launch?"

"It's nothing, Alison. I reassured him that all would be fine. It's just Jason being a perfectionist."

It was time for Alison to play Mani to get him to talk. "I consider us to be friends, Mani. We've gotten to know each other. If there's something I should know, I'd expect a friend to tell me."

"Don't get offended. Don't jump to conclusions. And most of all, don't hang me out to dry for reporting this," Mani said, pained.

"Reporting what?"

"Jason revealed some minor, very general concerns about the launch."

"And specifically?" Alison pouted.

"Well, he wants it to go well, naturally. He wants it to reflect the status of AllOptions in London. This is not Brisbane you know."

"Meaning?"

Mani acted flustered. "It might be Eunan, not Jason's doing, but he is concerned that more star power needs to be present for the launch. A bigger performance."

"He doesn't want me to do the launch!" Alison muttered, stunned.

Mani could not tell if it was a question or a statement. "Not at all, Alison. Just a minor, as I said, very general concern. Don't take it to heart. I'm sure it's only Jason being pedantic."

"I'm shocked," she said slumping back in her chair.

"Please don't disclose that I betrayed his trust. I shouldn't have said anything."

But Mani was glad he did as he watched her sulk.

****

Pleasantly surprised to see the number display on his phone, it was with some anticipation that Eagle answered Mani's call. It could only be positive news for him and he could use a boost to his coffers. He had stagnated over recent weeks with little in the way of gigs or income since Alison had decided to go overseas. She had declined gigs before and after her absence so that it would be a full two months without a payday for Eagle. He'd kept himself occupied with seeing gigs around Brisbane and working on his own music in the meantime.

He steadied himself before answering, in an attempt to control his excitement.

"Good afternoon Alves. How are things shaking in the Old Dart? Won any hearts of note recently?"

Mani let out a truncated laugh before responding. "I guess you know why I'm calling then, Cris. As a matter of fact, the happy couple are teetering and I'm not certain I want to be the one to catch her fall. But you are a different matter."

"Do explain."

"I need you over here, post haste. There's a little window of opportunity for you on two fronts that I am certain you will want to be part of."

"You're getting awfully needy here, Alves. All of a sudden I seem to be indispensable to you."

"Hardly. This isn't for me. This ball is now in your court, to use sporting parlance."

"You're not the sporty type, Alves. Sporting maybe, considering how generous you were on your last call. Should I assume you are to be equally generous this time around?"

"You'll be looked after. But here's what I need you to do."

Eagle listened intently while Mani ran through the details of his meticulous plan. Eagle was to leave for London in the next 48 hours, Mani told him. He should bring any of his musical equipment necessary for he would be a late addition to the musical line-up for the AllOptions London launch. He should also polish up his presentation skills, for he would be bestowed a gold-plated opportunity to make his grand play at Alison Archer.

"I thought this entire charade was around you enticing the girl of your teenage dreams over to your camp. Now you want me there to muddy the waters. I don't get it, Alves."

"I think I might have been wrong all along. My crush was sheer folly. The reality not living up to the fantasy or something like that. But I still cringe at the thought of her with my cousin and that's why you're required here to cash in when I end it."

Eagle smiled as it dawned on him what was really happening. "She's rejected you! And there you are being all high-minded and altruistic while I bet inside you're burning up. Am I right, Alves? You've been given the flick!"

Mani dismissed Eagle's goading and laid out the terms of Eagle's employment, including a demand for absolute secrecy regarding their involvement and an odd demand for Eagle to ignore all phone calls from Alison, the bandmates or Jason Sharpe, only answering to Mani.

"Why would Jason Sharpe be calling me?" Eagle queried.

"He won't be, but I want to maintain control and I can't have you shooting off at the mouth, Cris."

"Whatever you say, Alves. And each time you ignore my demands to call me Eagle, my price increases. Are we understood?" Eagle felt he could assert himself with Mani obviously in need of his services. He pressed for upfront payment and a business airfare of course. Mani complied, and though Eagle could not see the point of his going to London to help Alves with his plan, it was an overseas trip. He would get to do the gig and maybe make his final pitch to usurp the other two in Alison Archer's thoughts.

****

Having met, then been employed by Jason Sharpe, flirted, been pursued then romanced and invited overseas all within the space of three months, Alison wondered if it had all been too rushed. She was feeling dejected, her confidence having seeped into the mild air of this English summer. This latest piece of news became another brick in the London wall that was building between her and Jason.

While he was at work building his empire, Alison felt abandoned. Mani was an OK guy, she thought, but he had low self-esteem and an obvious drinking problem. Too much fame and money too soon perhaps. Despite Mani's foibles, it was his stunning insights about Jason that had her concerned as to the health of her still budding relationship.

Between her happy moments amongst the sweat and exultation of the shows she had seen and the moments of solitude when Jason was working, leaving her in this enormous yet empty city, Alison wondered why Mani would relay to her such negativity about Jason. They were very tight as cousins, enjoyed each other's company. It couldn't be financial or status jealousy, as Mani had much more of both. Maybe a long-denied feud or family grudge, but that seemed unlikely. Jason's family was nothing but nice. So it could only leave one reason for his doubting words and criticism of Jason.

The truth.

How could he not want me to do the launch, Alison lamented. The Brisbane show was a blast and it was Jason's idea for her to do the London show. She concluded the only course of action that seemed reasonable and would cause the least damage to both her holiday and her relationship. In the early afternoon, with Jason at work, Mani locked away writing and the run of the apartment, Alison delved around, located the Yellow Pages and started dialling.

The following day, with Jason again dedicating a half day to spend with Alison, she raised her concerns and presented her solution.

"I've been thinking about the launch," she began, soon after they exited the matinee performance at the historic Richmond Theatre in London's inner west.

Jason, clasping her hand as they strolled, appeared positive. "What are we now, ten days out? How are your rehearsals going?"

"As I said, I've been thinking. I have watched how hard you've worked to set up your business and how important it is to you."

"Look, Alison. I'm sorry I haven't been as available as we thought I might. Please be patient with me. I'll make it up to you."

They exited The Green up a cobbled laneway toward the retail strip. "I completely understand," Alison replied. "I think it's awesome what you're doing. You should be proud of what you've achieved. But that is what has got me thinking. Maybe AllOptions needs to make a bigger deal of the launch. A bigger show. Drop a bomb on these Londoners!"

She watched for his response, to see if she had jabbed at a sore point. Nothing. The only response confusion from Jason.

The street bustled around them, as people with fistfuls of shopping bags scurried to their next purchase. Finally Jason responded. "I'm not sure what you mean."

"I've been ringing around and a bit like when you rang around for bands in Brisbane," – they smiled in acknowledgement – "there are some freaks in bands in London too. But I've found two that are quality, experienced and most importantly available for next weekend."

"Why did you do that?" he asked, perplexed.

Alison's response was upbeat, despite her wounded soul. "AllOptions needs to put on a big performance. This is the business hub of Europe. You want impact and U2 and Coldplay were unavailable, though I called Chris Martin personally and of course he wants me to duet with him."

"But you're doing the launch."

"I don't think I can pull it off, Jason. It needs more than me."

He was bewildered. "I think you're enough. More than enough."

This prompted tears from Alison as the pain of having to confront this met with his denials. She sensed Jason covering his tracks, yet he was being nice. Maybe this was his way, an act to smooth things over as he got his way. Alison's heart drooped to her stomach, her feelings jumbled as they leant against the brick wall beside a book store.

"I always felt so confident in Brisbane," she moaned. "But London is just too big, too humbling. It puts my little musical ambitions into perspective. It strips away my hope and makes me feel small."

Jason moved to her and put an arm over her shoulder as he faced her. His other hand lifted her chin so he spoke to her face. "Not at all," he said. "Not to me."

Alison smiled and shrugged, tears ambling in crooked paths down her cheeks.

He continued. "AllOptions doesn't need to be enormous in London. I don't want it to be. But because London is so enormous, a small AllOptions can thrive. You should feel the same about your music. In fact, I have more belief in your artistic ability, your quality and uniqueness than I do in my business ability. There's no-one like you Alison. I hope I haven't put pressure on you by asking you to do this show because that's the last thing I intended. I think you are more amazing than amazement itself."

She laughed and sniffled her runny nose. "That doesn't make sense."

"Exactly, my beautiful girl. You are so amazing you make me say things that aren't even sentences." He hugged her in, her tears dampening the shoulder of his blue shirt. "Please don't get down. It's difficult being away from home. It's daunting."

"I think I just miss my life back home. I miss my band. They make me feel like a bit of a star."

"Well, we've got Jamiroquai this weekend. We'll grab some of their band members. They've got plenty."

This made her laugh. As his firm backing soothed her they held hands, standing close. They kissed and her tears rubbed away on his skin, joining and cleansing them. It felt better for Alison, this feeling of reassurance as though her fuel tanks were replenished.

****

It had come as a shock to Jason when Mani brought out in the open Alison's concerns about doing the launch as a solo act. Jason was hurt that she would not be up front with him and that she would choose to discuss it with Mani rather than with him. He had barely believed it when Mani told him, as there had been no indication of her displeasure. Nothing but positive vibes about being on stage and no mention whatsoever of missing her bandmates.

He could not fathom Alison being low on confidence either. This was a girl who seemed to have an unlimited supply of confidence, not just in how the world received her but in her ability to offer something to the world. Jason only saw zest and zeal, a passion for her music and an over-riding ambition to make the most of her life. But there it was, direct from her mouth. She didn't feel she was up to the launch by herself.

Jason had cajoled her as best he could, disbelieving such a dilemma would be reality. In his mind there was no question as to Alison being up for the launch. AllOptions should be honoured to have her perform. But Jason knew that he should oblige her request, out of respect for this marvel of a girl for whom his feelings had grown in recent months. The words had not been said, but Jason presumed what he felt was love. What he saw was their future. But he would accommodate her misgivings in his own way, rather than have her bow out altogether. That would denote consensus and in no way did he think she was not up to the requirements of the launch.

Jason took it into his hands to correct the issue. He took Alison's research and scrapped it. The two bands she had short-listed may have been of high quality, but they would not be doing the launch. Alison would do the launch, Jason decided. And her bandmates would be there by her side to refurbish her confidence and bring out her absolute best. He would, as the Blues Brothers said, put the band back together.

It might prove difficult, he realised, considering he didn't know the band members by any other than their unofficial monikers of Eagle, Arms and Break. He would have to secret their numbers from Alison's phone without her knowledge. It had to be a surprise for her. He would continue to encourage her and build her up as his launch entertainment and then have the band arrive with days to spare to give her a lift.

Jason asked Mani if he could intervene to gather the required phone numbers in the necessary clandestine manner.

"I don't know any of them either but why don't we search through her phone?"

"Risky," Jason replied. "What about you get into a discussion and find out their names. I know that one of them, the bass player Eagle is her close ally. Apparently they have spent a lot of time together over the years. What his real name is, I wouldn't know though."

"Who could possibly know that?" Mani wondered aloud. "I'll give it a crack and report back ASAP."

"It's time critical, big man," Jason said. "I need these guys to agree to an immediate trip to London."

When Mani came back to him it was with mixed news. "Her phone is locked by password. I found out her drummer Arms has a real name of Bevan Snodgrass. No wonder he's gone with

Arms. Fractionally cooler, don't you think? No word on the other two jokers though."

"One name is enough. We can look him up and he can tell us the others," Jason said.

"The online White Pages could be an option," Mani said, excited by the chase. "But wouldn't most musos not have a listing. Don't they sleep on friends couches and live in the backs of vans? No fixed address and all that."

"Well, we get someone in Brisbane to chase him up."

"Hunt him down, Jason. Make no mistake, this is a manhunt. I'll get Graham Bedser to sniff him out. I know as my manager he's uncovered some good deals for me, so I know he'll enjoy the hunt."

Jason shot a quizzical look at his cousin as Mani flipped open his laptop and logged on to the internet. He noted how Mani was switched right on to anything with a bit of a thrill. His enthusiasm was admirable. Together they sought out the Snodgrasses of Brisbane to find the musical member known as Arms, to no avail.

Mani was immediately onto Graham Bedser. "Grazer, get your dirty little black book out and hunt down a fellow named Snodgrass. First name Bevan, musician and drummer by calling and goes by the moniker 'Arms'." Mani noted Jason's gesturing and added, "Big arms, apparently."

As expected, Graham came through with a number. Mani assured him Arms didn't owe them money, they just needed to make contact.

Jason dialled and put his proposal across. It was favourable. He was free and easy and able to jump a plane tomorrow if it meant getting paid. He was also forthcoming with a number for Break. Again Jason dialled.

"Alison feels the show would go much better with her compadres at her back. I support that and I want to ask you to come to London for the launch," Jason said. "It will be $2,000, a plane ticket and a room at the Novotel in the heart of Hammersmith. Arms is already committed. What do you say?"

"Dude, I am in!" he replied in his slacker drawl. "When do I leave?"

"Tomorrow night, your time. I will arrange Qantas tickets and call you back. But before I do, I need the final cog. Your mate Eagle. How do I find him?"

"Whoa, just a minute. We're not mates. Between you and me, the guy's a bit of a freak. But he's in Alison's pocket somehow. He's like that. Sad to say, but I don't keep his number, bro. Alison would be the best bet there. But, I know, secrets and all."

Again, Graham Bedser was consulted. Again, he came through. "That one was easy, Mani. This guy is a serious self-promoter. Seems Eagle is a bit of a personally proclaimed star. Good luck!"

For the third time, and with his hopes high of pulling off this masterstroke of planning, Jason dialled. The phone was off, with no option to leave a message. Jason gave it a few minutes, tried again and fretted that his plan was going awry.

"As my Dad used to say, Jason. She'll be apples," Mani said. "This Eagle guy is probably stroking his ego at a gig or studying music theory in a library or getting a naughty massage. He'll switch on the phone sometime soon."

Jason hoped so and was encouraged by Mani's optimism. He needed this last piece of the puzzle, as much to satisfy his own ego as to rescue his battered relationship. He would re-try the number throughout the evening, knowing not that the phone was under instruction not to be answered.

Big Day Out

He wasn't able to pinpoint what made him feel so, but Jason was feeling intimidated this day. It could have been the weather, which had a foreboding menace in the skies and the chill and texture of leftover soup. This after a long run of mild, even balmy days since he arrived only emphasised the contrast.

Or it could have been the company that was causing him unease on this day of Ashes cricket at The Oval, a day which also doubled as his birthday. Mani's choice of allies were a varied and unusual mix of professions; two doctors, an engineer, a builder, a gym owner, a semi-pro boxer, an architect and a bakery store owner. Yet each shared a common trait – an intensity of personality that bordered on fierce antagonism. They were, to a man, hard-core sports fans, all Chelsea locals and ready for the spiritual and verbal battle that was an integral part of their primal patronage whether it was Premier League football, Six Nations Rugby or cricket Tests.

Just how Mani became involved with these fanatics was beyond Jason's comprehension. He rarely showed interest in sport growing up, but had become as one with this rapscallion gang. Mani looked different from most of them, Jason noted. There were bald heads, tattoos, hard, muscled bodies moulded by discipline to match the fervour of their team support.

Jason fitted in more than Mani from a bodyshape perspective, his naturally fit angular body, toned from tennis and summertime water-skiing back in Australia was in sharp contrast to Mani's slobbish frame and long hair. Yet neither Mani nor Jason seemed a match for the Chelsea boys' shaven pates, threatening eyes and unsmiling faces. Jason resolved to fit in and enjoy the day.

"Here, mate. Drink up. Mani's bought the bar tab before play," one of the lads urged Jason, offering a pour from a jug of beer.

"I'm keeping a lid on it, thanks mate," Jason said.

"Coupla jars won't hurt ya!"

Jason accepted the drink. He felt the discomfort of overly close perusal, feeling boxed in by Mani's friends as though they were guarding him. He'd resolved to keep the drinking to a minimum. He had agreed to the day out to experience the Ashes in England, but the main event for his birthday was the Jamiroquai concert that evening with Alison. She was beside herself with excitement. She seemed more relaxed since AllOptions had demanded less of Jason's time.

Faithful to their traditions, the Chelsea Boys had a meticulous routine in their preparations for the day's play. It was accepted that the first hour of play could proceed without them. The bar held more allure as they primed themselves with beer for the Ashes battle. It was a gradual build up so that by the time they reached the ground, the group were well hydrated and eager to bellow their support.

Having been to Brisbane's Gabba ground once or twice for a day of cricket, Jason found the English atmosphere and its cooler weather much more conducive to an enjoyable day of cricket. The chants of the crowd, often launched by Mani's friends, kept the throngs entertained and surely lifted the spirits of the under pressure English cricketers who again chased leather against the Aussies.

The late afternoon gloom spurred a return to The Beehive pub. Here again some pressure came to bear from Mani's Chelsea boys for Jason to drink. He'd managed to extract himself from the round of shouts prior to being at the ground but back in the bar he was again included. He could handle himself though and knew the tactics he should employ. Beer in hand at all times, half full, presenting himself as getting amongst it rather than being empty-handed.

"Just taking it easy, mate. I've still half a pint to go," he would deflect when offered another.

It seemed an unusual battle of wills as the crew tried to ply him with ales. Jason was up for the tussle though and put on an impressive display of stonewalling that the English batsmen would have to duplicate if they hoped to keep Messrs McGrath and Gillespie at bay.

****

Mani retreated to a back room of the Beehive to confirm a pair of reservations. He needed the quiet and privacy to ensure the rest of the day would proceed as smoothly as his mind's vision expected. He dialled.

"Good afternoon. Excelsior Hotel. How may I help you?"

"My name is Mani Alves. I have a deluxe suite booked for this evening. I wish to confirm both the booking and the late check in time. I require the key available for collection from 9pm."

That's correct, sir. And we have the late checkout and buffet breakfast as part of your package. Full privacy on the room and several names authorised to collect the room key. Is that all correct, sir?"

"Perfect, thank you," Mani replied, ending the call.

The day had gone according to plan thus far. He knew Jason would not be a big drinker considering his evening plans with Alison. Mani's friends had played their role perfectly, giving Jason the authentic English experience of sports barracking while maintaining a safe haven for him. These were hard boys he had enlisted; not Mani's typical socialising group but their spiritual leader, Mani's good friend Dr Scott Raymond assured him that anyone who was included in his party would be safe and protected in their ranks. Things could get rough in the hurley-burley of the stadium outers, as Mani had found out once at a crosstown Premier League derby. However Scott confirmed that his boys would be a powerful ally for friends of friends and maintain the strictest confidence.

The second call Mani made was to confirm their early evening booking. The Velvet Pluto Gentlemen's Club reiterated the booking of their private area, with plates of finger food and Mani's generous bar tab to cater. Mani figured Jason might appreciate some eye candy as a postscript to their day of cricket.

He returned to his battle-hardened party team who had raised a chant from the afternoon's cricket to lift the spirits of the Beehive's patrons. The atmosphere in the bar was at its rollicking best as the day's light faded to a murky dusk outside.

Mani had a quick word to Dr Scott before calling for quiet amongst their crew. He had an announcement to make.

"Gentlemen, I thank you for your efforts today in introducing my beloved cousin safely and securely to the indisputable pleasures of home team support, Chelsea-style."

There was a loud cheer from the lads.

Mani continued. "It's just a shame that once again the local heroes could not produce anything to match the Antipodean might of the irrefutable goliath that is the Australian cricket team.

There were pantomime boos and hisses.

"Jason, my friend, my business partner, my blood. Happy Birthday to you. It is a massive pleasure having you stay with me in London. We've shared so much of our lives growing up, so for me, it's an honour to share the finest experiences that the UK has to offer."

There were ayes of acknowledgement as Jason held up his nearly-empty drink to his cousin.

"Now I know you have a prior engagement for later this evening and I know that most of us in attendance may find producing and receiving intelligible words difficult later on, so I thought a birthday toast before we move on to the next establishment might be in order. Dr Scott, I think, has organised some drinks."

Dr Scott duly obliged, delivering a tray of Black Russians and dispersing one to each in attendance, firstly to the birthday boy guest of honour, then to Mani and the thirsty group.

"Here's to you, Jason," Mani cried. "May your future be one of success, joy, love and lots of money. I love you, my brother."

Mani held his drink up in a sincere gesture of love and respect for his cousin. Even with his heart heavy with the knowledge of his own input into the rest of Jason's night, Mani felt things were progressing as expected.

He watched Jason lift the drink to his lips as he sipped from his own. The Chelsea boys urged Jason on, taking turns at encouraging by example, pushing in close to Jason in some form of tribal initiation, each downing their drinks in turn and cheering as Jason drained his own.

"On we go, gents," Mani decreed launching into a freebasing flow of words to rally his men. "To the Velvet Pluto for manly pursuits. Let us carve a swathe through the night, swords drawn, nostrils flaring. Want not for pleasures of the eye, the mind, the flesh for we select our own true life course and the shadow we cast alludes only to our comings and not ever our goings. We are liquid knights, formless, floating through battles indeterminate, but brave to the bitter end. Let me hear you roar, Men of Chelsea!"

****

Far removed from his regular comfortable life back in Brisbane, Jason had succumbed to pressure and endured more alcoholic days over the past several weeks than in the entire past year. Typically allowing himself a couple of beers once or twice a week, perhaps after a hard game of tennis, his consumption had multiplied due to Mani's social extroversion and ever-present encouragement. Jason, normally so balanced in Brisbane was proving quite a lout in London.

He could not quite pinpoint when in this latest bout of drinking he fell off the rails, for as far as he could remember he'd maintained strict control of his intake. Yet here he was, drifting in and out of consciousness in a darkened room. There was loud music, cheering male voices, flashing lights. A niteclub, he wondered, unable to focus or lift himself.

Flickers of memory snapped back at him as he floundered. The birthday toast he presumed would be a heavy shot of vodka. He was prepared for that, knowing his own alcohol capacity. He was under control but his trip to the gents before leaving The Beehive had him light-headed and shaky. He reasoned the crisp evening air on the walk to the next venue would right his ship. He needed to be in shape to meet Alison later for the Jamiroquai gig. The cool air outside only served to worsen him and send him deeper into his fuzz-walled mental abyss.

Since then, he'd lost all memory, hauled along stumbling, incoherent and unaware. From the outside, he would appear as just a wobbly wheel amongst a rowdy bunch of revellers, being encouraged along to the next watering hole. However, within his group he was being cared for via a strict protocol of duties. Mani remained close by Jason talking him through his vague stupor, an arm around his shoulder, under his armpit or around his back, nursing him along.

The others in the group had words of encouragement and close eyes on his care. "You'll be right soon mate," the muscular builder said. "Coupla waters and you'll be fine."

"Deep breaths, friend. We'll sit you down at the club and get you back on track," offered the moustachioed engineer.

Jason did not recall coming inside, being sat down. He did recall an olive-skinned brunette wearing tassels on her nipples and little else giving him a glass of water and wondered in his next coherent moment why he was drinking another beer. Flashes of cognition, grabs of dialogue, faces he recognised swinging by, whoops of laughter, naked girls, Mani cradling his head. Time was immaterial, the weight of his head a church bell on his shoulders as his mind made images of downy pillows and deep slumber as his reward to succumb.

At one point he thought he saw Alison in among the crowd, expected her to come back to rescue him, revive him. He wondered if maybe they were at their gig together, if he'd had a great night with his lady and this was the aftermath. Nothing was clear, he could not judge time. He felt for his phone but the pocket was empty. He reached for his wallet in another pocket but only retrieved a beer coaster.

Then he was moving, not under his own steam but he felt the motion and it strangely revived him. He was lying back, looking into the eyes of a pretty blond girl.

Alison!

Alas, no. She was unfamiliar. She was naked. She gyrated over Jason's limp prone body, pinning him down. Jason was aware of chants and cheers nearby. He was on stage, the lights burning his eyes, being used as a prop for this sexual show. The stripper's mouth locked to his throat, sucking intensely but briefly before she raised herself up straight-legged to a full standing position, generating a roar from the lascivious male crowd. Jason rolled away, was gathered up and returned to his private couch, his neck scarred by a lovebite, his dream state resumed.

At some distant point – it could have been anytime soon or never, such was his removal – Jason felt Mani shake him, checking on him. "What's happening?" Jason croaked.

"You just drank too much, Jas. We're looking after you."

"Get me out of here," he pleaded. "And Alison..." He trailed off.

Mani gestured and the next phase of the plan was enacted.

The Chelsea boys stood Jason up. "Drink this," the Doctor ordered.

Jason yanked his head back. "No more!"

"It'll help. I'm a doctor, Jason."

He drank, the fizz and bubbles prompting an immediate lift in his constitution enough to walk, to leave. Jason staggered to the door, surrounded and supported by his protectors. As he neared the exit of Velvet Pluto he saw a face from the past, possibly, surely, a dream.

"Eagle," Jason grunted, looking into the narrow face of the bass player who stood at the doorway. "This is London. What are you...?"

He couldn't finish as a cough emitted a trickle of vomit. Jason lurched forward, freeing his arms and only just reaching the footpath before unleashing a foamy, ferocious vomit. Unknown hands steadied him, a towel across his mouth to wipe him clean and then he was moving again, drifting back to his comfortable submissive place. The imaginary doona and pillows welcomed him in a soft embrace and Alison sat over him, stroking his forehead.

****

Mani watched his cousin leave, confident in his security as his minders gauged his health. A wave of regret rolled across his mind as he felt the pain of Jason's demise. It was sad to see him in such a state but at least he would sleep it off. Mani gave himself a minute before re-aligning himself with the present.

Returning to the club, he laid eyes on Eagle for the first time since uni nine year before. Their eyes locked on each other, each man assessing the other for signs of familiarity and weakness, comparing themselves against the other. Dress sense, hairstyle, body shape, muscle tone, panache and general carry. It wasn't only women who did this.

Eagle spoke first as they came face to face in the muddled light of the club's entry. He wore his trademark rock star uniform of skinny jeans, leather jacket and Doc Martens that looked too heavy for his thin legs to carry. "Mani Alves." It was a kind of half question greeting. "The Eagle has landed!"

"Are you serious, Cris? The first words after nine years are 'The Eagle has landed'. I'm a writer, you know. I seek originality in the world and you come out with that."

Eagle bit back. "The way I see it Alves, I get to say and do what I want. You've paid me, flown me over here to do a job. If you get mouthy, I take flight and you're no better off."

"Take flight? Like a seagull? A London pigeon? No, that's right. Like an Eagle."

"Enough Alves!"

"OK, OK. Just teasing Cris. I gotta have fun, you know," Mani laughed. They shook hands and each managed a smile, recognition of the likenesses between them that instigated this tension. "Good to see you. And thanks for coming."

"All part of the crazy life of a muso," Eagle responded, prompting a raised eyebrow from Mani. "And what did you do to Sharpe?"

Mani ignored the question. "OK, at this stage Alison doesn't know you're here. Have you been absent from contact to all in your band?"

"Affirmative. It's been a nice break from my normal hectic existence."

"Right, it's time to make the call. Do you remember what we discussed? We need to get this right or you and I both miss the boat." Mani handed Eagle a phone and his dictaphone.

"I think the third time you told me was overkill."

"It's important. One more time," Mani said.

Eagle replied in a bored tone. "You give me the signal, I dial, press the play button, hang up, then the phone goes off. Got it, Alves. Not the most elaborate of plans but well within my capability."

Mani decided not to say anymore. Eagle would only bite back as he always did. Moving to a quieter corner of the strip club, Mani pulled his mobile phone from his pocket, held it pensively, mentally rehearsed his lines and pressed in the numbers. There was no turning back.

****

She stood against a stucco wall on the street outside the venue. Inside, the first support band had fired up and Alison could hear the muffled energy of their music. The wall loomed over her. She felt anxious as she waited, her leg bent so that the sole of her shoe pushed against the wall behind her knee. It was as though the black wall might swallow her up. Every few moments she would pull back her coat sleeve to check her watch then dig in her pocket for the Jamiroquai tickets. These tickets were a big deal.

Where is he, she fretted silently. Time was getting on. They were due to meet half an hour ago and he wasn't answering. She knew he'd had a long day at the cricket but assumed he would place a certain level of importance on this engagement. She hoped he had. She shifted her weight, switched feet against the wall, checked her watch again, then the tickets like some sort of nervous tic.

The past week had been such a volatile time and her emotions had leapt to extremes like the violent pumping of a piston. On one hand Jason was being so much more attentive, spending less time on the business, but Mani's disclosure about the launch had ratcheted her emotions. It was difficult to figure out particularly as he was a no-show thus far.

She felt her phone vibrate against her thigh and she fumbled for it.

"Alison, its Mani. Is everything alright?"

Her heart sank a little. "Well, yes, except for Jason not being here."

"He should be there by now. I lost him two hours ago and I've been trying to reach him. I presumed he bailed out to meet with you."

"Well not yet," she said.

"Has the show started?"

"The doors are open, but not the main band yet. I'm outside." She was even more anxious now. It shouldn't have taken an hour or more, the trip being a simple walk-tube-walk that would take no more than a half hour.

"Look, Alison. He wasn't in the best shape, I'm sorry to report. He was getting into the spirit of things, despite my reminders about your function," Mani lied. "I feel bad that he's not made it there. I don't think..."

Alison's phone beeped during the call. She cut him off. "Hold on, Mani. There's a call."

Mani was swift to deflect. "Wait on, Alison. I think I see him. He's here. I'm sure it's him!"

"Let me check this call, Mani. It might be him." She looked at the screen of her phone, but there was no number display.

Again Mani was swift to assert himself. "I'll get you to speak to him before you hang up. He's just here. If he needs to get there quick, I can arrange transport. It's busy here, so many people."

"Is it him?" she agonised. The phone had stopped beeping, the other call terminated.

"Actually, shit, no. Not him. Just a look-a-like. Sorry. Let's talk again soon and I'll keep looking, OK?" He'd stalled her for a handful of seconds.

Alison looked at her phone. The missed call awaited her. She chided herself for not taking it then dialled her message bank, praying it was Jason. She impatiently pressed the numbers of the menu, her pulse quickening and her chest tight. A feeling of dread swept over her. It was Jason. She pressed the phone hard to her ear trying to hear over the street din and bass hum from inside.

"Alison, its Jason. This night's just been over the top. I don't know what I'm saying. I don't know what's going on. I'm not going to the Jamiroquai gig with you. It's alright. Gee I'm going to be sick tomorrow. Goodbye."

The slurred words were like a sword slicing into her, splitting her hams. She wobbled momentarily as her legs weakened, her stomach queasy. Feverish, she dialled his number but there was no answer. Again she tried but it went straight to message bank.

How could he do this, she wondered, a distasteful blend of shame and disgust burning her insides. And who did he think he was? She was fuelled with anger at this treatment, the sheer disrespect. She thought back to the charm Jason had displayed during their courtship, compared it to the meek affront he had offered tonight. Alison made her decision right there outside the club, spare ticket in hand. This was unforgivable. It was over.

Into The Fog

As Mani strolled through streets teeming with people utilising their Saturday night to hit the town, drink, mingle and meet new and old friends, he reflected on what he considered the piece de resistance of his plan. He was drunk, having shared some time with Eagle before they tired of each other and went their separate ways. For Mani, his way was to the Excelsior to check Jason's welfare.

Far from being guilt-ridden or regretful, the sociopath in Mani Alves considered the plan had gone perfectly. With Jason out of the way and his phone and wallet in Mani's possession, Mani was able to deliver his masterpiece. Eagle had arrived and hovered inside the club, an eye on Mani's group but silent and unknown. It was an unfortunate error that Jason had encountered him in the doorway, however Jason's state was such that the meeting could be attributed to drunken hallucinations.

As Mani neared the Excelsior he had replayed the evening's events in his head to ensure nothing had been overlooked, right up to the final piece. The phone call. It was a cruel act towards his own cousin, but Mani had goals and he was willing and determined to do whatever it took to assume Alison's virtuous love.

The words from Mani and Jason's drunken conversation the previous week had been spliced together using his two dictaphones, taping back and forth to create a seamless intoxicated tirade. The call to Alison was then timed to allow Eagle to play the ten second message while Alison's phone was otherwise engaged. All the while Mani played the charming knight showing concern for the desired damsel. Mani rejoiced that he could comfort Alison in her time of need and things could progress from there to their natural, rightful conclusion.

His mind's eye witnessed a brief image of his mother with Aunt Patricia at her shoulder, a premonition of sorts. Celia was scolding Mani, dismissing him from their midst, from the family, for his disgraceful deed. But then he imagined his Dad leering in the background, laughing at the sting, appreciative of the lengths an Alves man would go to get his way. He wiped the vision from his mind, as swiftly as he might have wiped regret, for his actions were justified.

Mani pushed open the door into the warm surrounds of the hotel's lobby, went to the eighth floor and tapped lightly on the room door. Dr Scott answered.

"How is he?" Mani asked, business-like.

"He's stable," the doctor replied. "I managed to get some fluids into him. I'm sure he'll be fine after a normal night's sleep. A bit fuzzy but nothing else."

"What will he recall? Did he ask what happened or why you were here?"

"He won't be able to piece it all back together. Rohypnol does that to you. He'll be dreaming and seeing a lot of things without knowing what was what."

"As long as he's safe," Mani said with erroneous compassion.

"No-one's ever really safe when you drug them, Mani," Dr Scott said sternly. "But he'll have no ill-effects."

"Thanks, Doc. I guess we can leave then." Mani pulled a folded note, written the day before, from his jacket pocket and left it on the bedside table along with fifty pounds. Jason would be fine, he figured. Breakfast at 9am followed by the fallout.

Mani and Dr Scott left the room, shook hands in the foyer and left separately. The night had turned chilly so Mani, confident in Jason's welfare, sought a cosy bar where he knew the regulars and the staff. He would drink some more and mull over his plan.

Returning to the apartment soon after 2am, Mani first checked Alison's room. She had been home. Some of her gear was missing, the rest of her bags packed and piled with her keyboard. She had left. A note explained her decision to Mani. A separate note was sealed in an envelope for Jason. Mani decided to leave it unopened though the intrigue of its contents ate at him. She had booked a hotel for the night. She would take a couple of days to think about things and then be in touch. She asked Mani not to call her. She was hurting, from the tone of her note.

Mani poured an unneeded nightcap, attended his toiletries, set an alarm and then ploughed into bed, exhausted. Before sleep came, he thought again of his plan and how it had run. Surely there would be no comeback for Jason. Mani's planted trilogy of misdemeanours – the launch blight, the missed gig and the phone call – will have cleared the way for Mani to provide solace, then strength, then love to Alison.

His mind traced back to the cute little blond girl at school and to how she had morphed into this wonderful strong beautiful woman. Her confidence was there, just temporarily misplaced. It would thrive again once Mani proved there was hope that a man can provide a solid base to a relationship. He smiled a contented, replete smile and then he was out.

He slept. And slept. He awoke only when the phone rang which he answered in a funk, certain it would be Jason.

"Over the infidelities and indiscretions of your night, Alves?"

"Cris. Why are you calling?"

"Eagle," he stressed his preferred name, "is doing today what you brought him here for. I plan to speak with Alison today to arrange a meeting. Is she there by chance?"

That didn't suit Mani. "For a thousand dollars, can you leave it for a day? She's moved into a hotel room, so she's not here anyway."

"A grand! Done!"

"And not a word Eagle. Remember our deal."

"Oh Alves. Why would I rat on you? You've cleared the way for me beautifully with your schemes. Alison will, I am sure, appreciate the comfort of a shoulder from home."

Mani took a second to judge the potential repercussions of Eagle's efforts. He decided that any sort of healing, even if instigated from Eagle, would aid Alison at this time. And Eagle hardly represented a true threat.

"Well, good luck, Cris. But do remember she is wounded. You might want to..."

"I hardly think I need advice about the ladies, Alves and certainly not from you," Eagle hissed.

Mani withheld a laugh. "OK, OK. You know what you're doing. As I said, good luck."

With Eagle off the phone, Mani lounged back and stretched, grunting like an animal as he yawned. He paged his maid for breakfast to be sent in. He needed sustenance to right his ship, rid himself of his hangover. He had another important call to make.

****

Jason thought he heard a door slam. It could have been far off or in his space. It was hard to tell. Either way, it roused him only minimally. One eye flickered open, only to re-close involuntarily. The other eye seemed glued shut. With some effort, he levered them open and tried to focus.

He was in a hotel room. This came to him as a revelation. Grateful he was secure, it also generated a rueful concern as to how he arrived here. His hands told him he was fully clothed. Relief swathed him. Without moving his body under the covers, he listened intently for any company, shifted his eyes to search the room. It was almost completely darkened, thick drapes drawn to reveal only a sliver of light, enough to discern the layout of the room. The bathroom door was open, the small room empty. He was alone.

With weak arms, he lifted the covers off himself, leaned up on an elbow with some effort. He felt lethargic, like he'd had a legitimately heavy night and little sleep. Trying to stand, he stumbled forward as a combination of loss of balance and fatigued legs failed him. He caught himself against the bedside table, shook his head to clear the infernal fog shrouding his brain. His eyes were misted, like he'd spent too long in the chlorine of a pool.

He saw a note, recognised Mani's hand. Simultaneously, the room phone behind the piece of folded paper rang, as though it was booby-trapped. He took the note in one hand and scooped up the phone, knocking a glass of water off the side table.

"Hello," he answered in a croaky voice.

"Jas, it's Mani. You're awake."

"How'd you know I was here? And where am I?"

"You lost it last night, buddy. We got you a room. You were in bad shape."

"I was barely drinking," argued Jason, his voice steeped in doubt. "How did I get so blind? It doesn't make sense."

"Dr Scott looked you over. He said it was probably the first wave of a virus and combined with a couple of drinks, you just took it badly. He said you'll be pretty fried for a couple of days unless it gets worse and you might need complete bed rest. How you feeling?"

"Tired." Jason had a defeated tone to his voice, reflecting his physical state. He suddenly sparked to attention as he remembered the other by-product of his downfall. "What about Alison? The gig!"

"You went AWOL for a period of time. I rang her to see if you had managed to meet up. She's annoyed, as you'd expect. Only later we found you out in the street, crook. That's why we got you the room."

"Who's we?" Jason questioned forcefully. "It sounds sus, Mani."

"As I said, Dr Scott looked you over. Look, I'll send my driver over. We arranged breakfast so I'll call reception and have them send it up. Best you eat."

"Forget the driver. I'll make my own way home," Jason grumbled. "Tell Alison I'll be there soon. Actually, I'll ring her myself."

Jason hung up and switched on a lamp. The whiteness stung his lazy eyes. He read the note. It was legible, easy enough to read. How, Jason thought, could Mani write so neatly after a full day and half a night of drinking? His suspicion mounted. He searched for his phone, his wallet. Nothing. He found the fifty pounds with Mani's note.

He dialled Alison. No answer

Again, he dialled. This time there was a tentative hello.

"Alison, it's Jason."

"Now your phone works," she said sarcastically. "I don't think there's anything to talk about, Jason."

"Hold on," he pleaded. "Look, I'm sorry. I can't explain what happened yesterday."

She broke in. "I know what happened. It's been happening since we got to London. You are all charm and then once you feel you've done enough charming and impressing, you can go back to being the selfish, money-obsessed party boy. Well, you've had your chance with me. I think we need some time apart."

"Alison, please listen. I think Mani's up to something. I think he or his friends did something to my drink."

"Yeah, they kept filling it when you held it out for more!"

"I wasn't drinking much. But I went downhill. Mani's doctor friend said it was a virus or it could have been tampering. I don't know."

"Convenient. Blame someone else. Your cousin has at least been a gentleman, despite his insecurity and his obvious alcoholism. You. You're just sneaky and self-interested. It's not the first time you've left me stranded, but it will be the last. You can be sure of that."

Jason had no defence. He admitted to himself that it didn't look good. "Don't make hasty decisions please Alison. Not straight away. Let's just get together. Give me a chance to explain. And apologise."

"I think your message was quite clear. You didn't want to leave the party and go to a gig with your girlfriend and then you ignore my calls. It's low!"

"I lost my phone. I think I was drugged."

"Self-administered, I'm sure. And you managed to ring me before you lost your phone. Your message was blunt enough. I doubt you ever planned to come to the gig with me."

"Message?" Jason said, confounded. "What message? Look, I'm coming home to talk."

"I won't be there."

"What?"

"Jason, just don't ring me OK. I'll call you to finalise the gig, but otherwise this trip is no longer about you and me."

She hung up, leaving Jason aghast. He collapsed back onto the bed, his eyes battling to stay open. He rolled onto his stomach, bit his lip to keep himself awake, but his low energy levels would not let him stand back up. He only found an inner effort when there was a knock at the door. Breakfast.

Sufficiently invigorated after the food to leave the hotel, Jason arrived back at Mani's Chelsea apartment soon before midday. He felt no hangover from the alcohol, just a mist that dangled through his viewpoint and combined with a lethargy that demanded sleep. He entered. Mani, who'd been writing and drinking coffee, was soon aware of his arrival.

"What the hell happened last night, Mani? I need an explanation," Jason said with a firmness that normally lay dormant.

"I wasn't in the best shape myself, cuz. It was a big day. One minute you were as good as gold, the next you were a swaying carcass like someone had stolen your spine."

"Things don't add up mate," Jason said. "Now Alison's barred me for missing the gig and she said I left an insulting message for her. I'm bloody wild about this. I purposely didn't drink at the cricket so I'd be right for Jamiroquai and next thing I wake up amnesic in a hotel room."

"With a lovebite on your neck," Mani pointed out.

"What!"

"Mate, I can't explain it. You were loose as. Coulda been the drink, the doc said it could have been a virus. I mean you look terrible. Maybe you should sleep it off. Alison will come around."

Jason ran his fingers through his hair, exasperated. He felt terrible. "Apparently I left a message. So where's my phone?"

Mani produced a scribbled note from next to the phone. "This would explain that. The Velvet Pluto just called. Your wallet was found under a couch in our private area. They rang me to ask if you were part of my group. A phone was also handed in. No doubt it's yours."

Jason glared at his cousin, dubious.

"Look, how could I have done something to you?" Mani continued his defence. "And why? If anything, you should be grateful I was still around. I made sure the doc stayed with you in the hotel room. The main thing now is you're safe. Rest up and then speak with Alison again. She'll come around."

Broken Hearts & Revelations

There is an actual medical name for what she was feeling. This hollow, dull ache that caused her throat to tighten and her shoulder to only feel OK when she slumped one side of her body. This lack of appetite, a stabbing under her fourth rib, the clawing emptiness ripping open her chest cavity. It was Takotsubo cardiomyopathy, where the brain, in reaction to a traumatic incident, distributes chemicals that weaken the heart tissue.

It was otherwise known as Broken Heart Syndrome.

Alison had self-diagnosed and tended to her own medical needs through a pragmatic mix of inner strength and getting on with the things that she knew made her happy – namely music. A couple of days had passed since Jason's relationship misadventure and his calls had slowed to an irregular trickle. He was getting the message after bombarding her with texts and calls and thanks to Mani's big mouth revealing her new temporary digs in Hammersmith, flowers and a card.

She held firm, the damage he wrought with his lack of consideration irreparable to her. To forget the pain, she shopped and locked herself away from the world to rehearse, though this had its moments when she thought of him as she envisioned the AllOptions launch gig.

All in all, Alison managed this upheaval the same way she had always managed in her life; by getting on with her love of music, not letting her emotions out and generally being all business. The gig would be difficult but she had to treat it as just another well-paid job. She could then fly out, get home to the cradle of her existence and rebuild her trust and joy in the world. Without closing the door on a future, she considered now that she and Jason were no longer an option. What hurt the most was the loss of those early moments of promise and the affection of blossoming love; the real shame being a relationship unfulfilled. She was sure they could eventually be friends. There was no reason not to be.

The phone had been off all day as she detested interruptions when she was working. She also desired a freedom and anonymity when out of the house. Now, in the late afternoon, she switched it back on and the regular ding and buzz of the missed calls and messages made her think it could have made for a groovy sample to back some of her original lyrics.

She listened to the messages. There were the expected pleas from Jason to woo her back, apologetic and pained. He alluded in one dispatch that Alison would hear from some special visitors soon and so it proved as Arms, then Break left messages to say they were in London, at the behest of Jason Sharpe, to do the gig. This at least made her smile.

Inevitably then, and unmentioned by the other bandmates, she had heard from Eagle. He too was in London for the gig as well as some other business, he let on. He wanted to meet, so coffee was organised for the following morning. With the launch just days away there were rehearsals and set lists to arrange.

When she ventured out to meet Eagle, the city had presented a real London scorcher, the sun blazing down on the pasty, reddening faces of the locals. People sought shade where they sat fanning themselves, while wearing perplexed looks at this meteorological aberration. For Alison though, it represented a strong reminder of home, of the warmth and glow of the sun that even at this time of year meant most days were best greeted with short sleeves and sunglasses. It also reminded her of how close she was to going home and how soon this deteriorating tour of the United Kingdom would be over. Seeing Eagle too would instil how much she was missing her life.

But when she met him at a local café, it was not the rock and roll version she knew, but something altogether different. Gone were the skinny jeans, Skechers, leather jacket and stud belt. No more did he sport the greasy, dangling mop of hair in his eyes or the unkempt facial hair carved into a goatee. Alison noted an entirely new persona had replaced the bass-playing slacker his previous look embodied.

He now wore an English wool suit, good quality and well-fitted. It was grouped with a tie of private school stripe and matching hankie, a lilac shirt and cuff links, and high gloss Alfred

Sargent dress shoes. A pencil thin moustache was all that remained of his grungy facial hair and his carefully manicured hair was short at back and sides modelled with hair product into an impressive quiff. The man who had come for coffee was Corporate Eagle, funded by Mani Alves' generous payoffs.

"Wow, Eagle. You look so different," Alison complimented. They kissed by each other's cheeks.

"A true gent will match his look to the environment. I thought a more cultured look would suit the gentrified climes of Old London Town."

"Well it looks great. I've never seen you wear a tie."

"I like to think I can still surprise, even after how long we've known each other. It's a Windsor knot, by the way," he said, proudly jiggling the bulge at his throat.

"I'm sure the Windsor's would approve," she joked. "Seeing they live just up the road." The joke sank.

They sat, ordered coffee, then another as Alison vented about her holiday travails. The conversation led back around to the upcoming gig.

"So after all that's happened, I am so glad it's worked out that you're here for the gig. And the other boys. We'll be able to rock the joint properly."

"So, I'm confused," Eagle said. "You're doing the gig for Jason Sharpe, but clear it up for me. Are you or are you not a couple?"

Alison squirmed in her seat. "Well, no. It's worked out that he and I are not really suited."

"I told you so," Eagle said. Alison noted he straightened in his chair.

"You're not supposed to say 'I told you so'. More of a 'there, there' is what I need," she joked.

"What you need - what you deserve – is a genuine person to share your time with. Someone who will cherish the very person you are, Alison. Someone respectful."

"Men are just too hard, Eagle," she said, oblivious. "I'd give up men for my music. At least music feeds me, coaxes me, lifts me up. No need to try to work out double meanings and sorting lies from truth. Music is my new boyfriend!"

"I'd support that. I can be right by your side, in life and in music." Eagle's eyes fixed on her with a determination previously unseen by Alison.

She rolled his comment around her mind. There were a few seconds of silence between them. Eagle was resolute in his gaze, his eyes locked on her. Processing his words, it became apparent what he was doing.

"Eagle, why are you dressed like that?" she asked.

"I'm dressed to impress."

"Impress who?"

"Who and what. Let's talk about the 'what' first. What I am trying to impress upon you, Alison, is that not everyone is what they seem. Just because I normally swathe myself in the robes of a musician, it does not preclude me from fitting other images. I share the chameleon ethos, and I wear it well. So if it's the corporate look that's required, it is no great leap as such. If we were off to Twickenham for the ruggers, I would pop the collar and dress Country Road or even go the tweed jacket with elbow patches. I would make it work."

"Why do you feel you need to change?" Alison asked him with a growing awareness of what he was getting at.

"I have at least one very powerful reason to change, Alison," he replied with stoic defiance of the odds. "Similarly, a man who wears sharp suits, again with the intended pun, doesn't necessarily fit the image of goodness he might try to portray."

"What are you saying, Eagle?"

"If it's the corporate look you want, I can be your man. You didn't ever need to seek out the Jason Sharpes of this world. I can be everything you need and I offer myself to you Alison Archer. You would never again be put upon by distrustful underhandedness like you have seen on this trip. That is my promise."

"Are you making a pass at me?"

"This has been coming for a long time, Alison. I've known it and I think you've known it."

She looked sadly at her long time musical collaborator. He was a good guy, but this feeble approach was misplaced and the last thing she needed in her current state. Even she could tell his heart wasn't in it. But there was no way Alison could dump on Eagle. He didn't deserve to be hurt.

"Eagle, how did I meet you?" she asked.

"You headhunted me," he replied.

"Specifically. From where?"

"Through your brother and his incongruous metal band."

"That's right. You came from my brother's world, but you were and are different from that world, to that type of music."

"No doubt."

"Well, please understand, that's how I see you. Like a brother for my musical world. I do love you Eagle, but not in that romantic way. It would only ruin what we have musically. Please don't be offended."

He wasn't. Alison had let him down gently and that pleased Eagle. Relieved him, it seemed to her. They could go on being bandmates.

After Eagle left, she got to thinking about how it all came about. Above all else, Mani had been ever-present during this trip and he had managed to keep Jason well occupied. They were family, so this was understandable. She thought over the problems she and Jason had had. She imagined how it would have been without Mani's influence. Would Jason have really acted like this?

Back at her room, she thought further down this path, seeking a meaning, a reason for the breakdown. Without Mani's inducements, how bad had Jason's deceit been? How horrid his behaviour? It occurred to her that without the Jamiroquai gig fiasco, most of Jason's behaviour was harmless fun coupled with an admirable dedication to his business. A few shenanigans on the drink, coupled with being late to a couple of lunches. She wondered what else she should have expected.

To top it off, Jason had actually done a quite thoughtful thing. He had invited, and more importantly paid for, the band to come over to London. That could only have been out of care and concern for her frail state of mind. It was she who went to him with her doubts, those fed to her by Mani. Jason had been nothing but supportive to her. She mulled these elements over but soon dismissed them as her damaged inner romantic pining for the hope of a good outcome. He still stood her up for the gig and as she had determined, the combination of issues was unforgivable.

She resolved to speak with Mani to air these grievances. Nevertheless, she was firm of mind as to what had to be the indisputable truth – she was single Alison Archer, a whirlwind love affair behind her and the glorious days of her life and career ahead of her. Life would be as she would make it. She fell to sleep dreaming of the positive experiences she could have in music, life and maybe one day again, love.

****

Lazing about his apartment on a Thursday morning, Mani was well in his male comfort zone. Feet on the couch, Dido's latest album playing on his surround sound system and a small jug of coffee, some water crackers, chorizo and a lump of cheese as big as his fist from which he sliced odd-shaped hunks with a heavy-bladed, stubby cheese knife. This was his new routine for mid-morning since he'd made the decision to hand in his notice at the magazine. The editor-in-chief at the magazine had granted Mani immediate leave and he finished up the same day. Mani needed time to dedicate to writing his novels and had also decided to head back to Australia, partly to snap his drinking problem and dry out, but most importantly to continue his pursuit of Alison Archer.

The past weeks had been emotionally wracking yet despite the undoubted pain he had inflicted upon both Alison and Jason, Mani could not turn away from his goal. It had been such a focus for so much of his life to consummate those early feelings. Now he had gone to such depraved lengths he could not retreat. With Alison in London for just a few more days and the groundwork laid, Mani planned to lay bare his feelings for her and display his commitment to her by uprooting and re-emigrating home. Jason might never forgive his execrable pursuit, but their brotherhood had to be collateral damage in Mani's grand plan. It was after all, Mani's love story.

So Mani relaxed. He had the apartment to himself in recent days. Since Jason's birthday night, they'd barely spoken as Jason committed to long days at the AllOptions office. Mani had only heard him come and go without conversation. Things would be terse between them for a while, he realised, maybe forever. And with Alison holed up in temporary accommodation, Mani was enjoying the run of his own apartment for the final month of his tenure in the United Kingdom.

He carved off a large corner of cheese, partnered it with some sausage and with his coffee depleted, he wondered if 10am might be time for a wine. The harsh squeal of the house phone startled him back to sober thoughts.

It was Alison.

"It's really good to hear from you Alison. I've been concerned about you but I knew you wanted your space," Mani said in his most sympathetic tones. "How are you?"

Her manner seemed to be relaying her troubled state of mind. She was reaching out, he sensed. She was needy. "I'm confused with everything that's been going on, Mani. But I'm hanging in there, trying to make the most of these last few days."

"Good for you. If you ever need someone to talk to..." he offered.

"Well actually, are you free now? I just need to get some things off my chest. I need to say some things to you. And hear some things. Can I come over?"

His pulse leapt. Surreal opportunity glowed before him. Alison Archer, his decade-long fantasy now desired a one-on-one meeting with him. He felt this was his moment. She would be there in half an hour.

Mani gathered up the remains of his high-fat man-feast and delivered it to the kitchen. He needed to tidy up before Alison arrived. He perused his apartment with an analytical eye. Ten minutes of tidying should do it. He sniffed his armpits. Normally fastidious about his personal hygiene – big guys needed to be – he had not showered the previous night or this morning. There was not time now, so a spray bottle shower - a quick spray of underarm deodorant - and a fresh shirt would have to suffice.

He was in a pique of excitement, the anticipation of her arrival too much to bear. He realised he could seal his destiny in the next few minutes. Jason would be at work for at least another few hours. Mani had a free run at conquering the doubts and false starts of all these years. He straightened the cushions on the couch, did the same to his hair and smiled to himself as the realisation washed over him. Alison Archer was coming and in a matter of minutes Mani's life may well be about to peak.

She arrived and immediately took the lead. It was out of Mani's hands where this interaction might go, for Alison had things to say.

"So much has been going through my head the last couple of days," she said, wrought with emotion. "I had to talk to you because you just might be the one who can help me get through to making sense of all this."

Mani's hopes soared. These were his sentiments too. He was here to get her through and get through to her. He looked at the blond goddess before him. She'd had her hair punked up, clipped on the sides, wispy tails clinging to her graceful long neck, her fringe defying gravity and carrying a yellow highlight. He drank in her loveliness. He had made coffee and offered her a cup.

"When I came here Mani, I thought Jason was just heaven sent. He was gentlemanly, charming, so bloody handsome I had to pinch myself. But I don't know what's happened. I am seeing through his good points to all this laddishness and carry on. I mean you're his cousin and you said he used to be like this. But even you can see how he's been, can't you?"

Mani nodded mutely.

"I've had more quality time with you since I've been here than I've had with Jason. You and I have really talked. We've connected Mani. It's like you're the real one out of you and him. You're flawed like we all are, but that is so much more of a lure than being led on."

Mani's mouth dangled open as she delivered her words. "I was just being friendly, Alison, being available. You are a wonderful girl and you're right. We have had quality time."

His comment passed through the conversation unnoticed.

"You've had some less than savoury points of view about Jason. And I listened to you but didn't take notice. I thought what you were saying was unusual at first. What I knew of Jason was nothing but positive."

"I wasn't trying to be negative," Mani interjected, trying to rescue his image. "Just throwaway lines."

"Well, he got the benefit of the doubt. But then I saw the real him. All the drinking and selfishness. I realised I was just a miniscule part aside from his real drive and passion. He runs his business, trades the markets and no-one is going to eclipse that in importance."

"You deserve better. You deserve a pedestal, Alison." Mani wanted to slap himself for his lame cheerleading.

"Damn right, I deserve better. I'm no dizzy blond. I am unique, I am a woman with unlimited possibilities and no man should treat me with anything less than the full respect that this powerful, independent female deserves. Demands!"

"Too true," Mani agreed. She was winding up, an obvious anger building as she vented.

"Jason can suffer the consequences of his actions. He can look back in two, five, ten years and say 'I let a great opportunity go. I lost a kind caring, ambitious and talented girl'."

"Add beautiful to the list too."

Alison looked at him oddly, feeling the nervous energy of Mani's excitement. Something about it made her uncomfortable. "It's his list, Mani."

"Of course."

She softened then as her anger receded into distress. "Why did he have to let this happen?" she lamented, welling up. "It was going so well. Positive at every turn, romantic to the max, fun and light-hearted. But then we came to London and it turned on a penny."

"As these things tend to do." Mani had been listening to her vent and noticed her angst turn briefly to softness and melancholy for what might have been.

"I just wonder if it can be the same," she whined. "Once we're back in Brisbane, I mean."

She was showing signs of vulnerability. Mani sensed his opportunity but he knew he needed to cement in her psyche the unshakable foibles of Jason. He had a desperate, distraught and lonely girl before him, out of her comfort zone in a foreign land, mixed up by a man who duped her and crying in his apartment, the home turf on which he rarely lost.

"After betrayal, there can be eventual forgiveness but it can never be forgotten," Mani pronounced. "And you are a proud person, Alison Archer. It should only be the longest of roads back for him."

"I know," she wailed, tears flowing now. "Listen to me, I'm a mess. I don't know what I want. And to make things worse my bass player even hit on me yesterday and I'm in such a state, I nearly considered it as a good option. I mean that would be plain wrong."

Mani knew what she was talking about. He couldn't believe that Eagle had mounted any sort of reasonable case to win her affections. If so, it proved Alison's fragile state and Mani sensed his odds shorten with her now so vulnerable.

"Taking Jason back would be absolutely the worst decision," he declared.

This was the cue for her tears to become sobbing. She rubbed her eyes, mascara staining her cheekbones. Mani saw her blow a little involuntary bubble of spit.

"Do you need a hug?" he asked. She nodded.

Mani stepped forward, the prospect of physical contact titillating his every nerve. He wrapped his arms around her slender shoulders, gently drawing her to him. Problem was, he didn't know when to stop, where to draw the line between supportive hug and domineering squeeze. He felt her struggle against his strong grip.

"Cry, baby, cry," he said soothingly. "When you've got to get it out."

She was tense and quivering with her distress.

"I'll be your shoulder, you can tell me all," Mani cooed, patting her back. She relaxed into him, burrowing into his shoulder. "Don't keep it in ya. That's the reason why I am here."

He held this pose, the girl of his dreams ensconced in his loving arms, giving her the support she lacked elsewhere. Mani had found his nirvana. Her crying slowed as they nuzzled together, he cherishing the touch and Alison yielding to his sympathy. His own feelings welled up. All the years of desire, the unknown whereabouts, the stunted emotional growth that came with being stuck on someone you never really knew.

She pulled back, lifted her head from the embrace. He didn't let go. "Mani," she began. "Did you just say the words from a song to me then?"

"No."

"You did. I know those words. They're lyrics. What is it?" she asked herself.

Mani kept his head down, tucked into her, not wanting to relinquish the gains he had made.

She pulled further away, wriggling her shoulders from his grip. "♫ That's the reason why I am here ♫," she sang in her flawless voice. "Michael Hutchence. You just comforted me with the lyrics of an INXS song, Mani. What the hell is that?"

It was as if a plague had been disseminated for as Alison ceased her tears, so Mani, the big, strong comforting male still maintaining his desperate iron grip around the shapely blond in his loungeroom, burst into tears of his own. This was a grim image as his thick torso convulsed and all the shameful remorse of his pathetic obsession rose to the surface. He blubbered like an inconsolable child.

"What's up, Mani?" she queried, mystified.

"I done vuddy subleg dank sitty toop idit...aaah, aaah, ah!" he wailed, incoherent with guilt and grief.

"What," Alison asked, confused but aware of his snot and tears against her hair.

"It not his...I made...told that stuff..ooh...aahhahaha," he bellowed with ridiculous fanfare.

Alison was now composed even as she was confused. Her face smudged with its own sadness, she had now been usurped by this horrific embarrassing outburst of which she understood nothing. "Settle down," she said. "I can't understand you!"

Mani drew in a deep breath to control himself. It was confession time. "All of those horrid things that Jason has allegedly done. It's my fault. I'm to blame. I set him up!"

"I don't know what you're saying."

"Jason didn't miss the gig. I took him out. I had a doctor drug him and take him to a hotel. He didn't know what was happening. He had no chance." Mani held out his arms in some sort of feeble plea for forgiveness. Alison's anger returned, her eyes glowering at the pathetic, over-wrought man before her. Mani thought she would hit him at any second.

"I can't fathom that someone would do that. To their own family much less."

"I did some bad things."

"What else did you do?"

"The gig. Jason wasn't concerned about you and the gig. I made that up."

"You asshole!"

"I know," Mani bayed, crying again.

"What else?"

"I invited his ex to dinner on purpose?" Mani said in an out of context questioning tone. He kow-towed to her, caught out.

"And he's a cleanskin. I made up stuff. He's never done a bad thing in his life."

"What is wrong with you?" Alison paced now, fired up, her mind racing. "The phone call from Jason? How did he make a call if he was drugged up?"

"Me," Mani confessed. "I recorded a tape of him blabbing on during one of our drunken nights. That was part of my plan too."

"Your plan? What plan was that, Mani?"

"To keep you two apart."

"Why?"

"So I could have you," he blurted.

She needed no words. The look she gave Mani struck at the deepest part of his soul. It was one of such distaste, such contempt that he felt he could never recover. He'd been looked upon as a leper by the woman he loved. His blubbering re-started as he attempted to justify his heinous acts.

"Alison Archer. I love you!"

"What the...?"

"I always have. Ever since the day I first saw you at Westside High School, I've been infatuated with you, Alison."

She attempted to deflect. "How could you know me from school?"

"Grade Eight, I saw you at school and fell in love with you," he gushed. "We never spoke except one time for about a minute. Oh, and of course you assaulted me when we won the essay comp. But that has been enough to sustain me. I have spent my life searching for you, dreaming of you and pretending that one day we would get together. Can you imagine how it felt to realise my best friend – my own cousin – was dating the girl I had always wanted? He'd found what I had been looking for."

"That's just sad."

"I know!" The tears came again for Mani. "All the bad reports about Jason, all his bad behaviour, it was all of my pathetic design, a ploy to turn you from him to me. You were mine. You were my fantasy, Alison Archer. The coolest, prettiest girl in school and I have spent my entire pitiful life seeking you out."

She bowed her head. "I don't remember you from school. Sorry Mani."

"We talked in the tuckshop line."

She shrugged.

"The essay comp. We were joint winners."

"Too long ago."

"We kind of hugged. You kneed me!"

"I'm sorry. I don't remember."

This provoked a fresh wave of grief for Mani. He shook with sobs, wiping away snot with his sleeve. All the well-cultivated visage of the urban legend of the literary world had vanished. He looked up at her, depleted of pride having admitted his deceit, only to see Alison whimpering and holding her arms around her body.

"Why are you crying?" he gargled through his own distress.

"I'm not crying," she lied.

"Well there's water on your face. What is it?"

She clenched her fists and whipped her arms downwards in frustration. "Because I'm sitting here judging you for holding a candle to Alison Archer for half your life and I'm no better than you. Worse probably."

"How could you be worse," Mani said. "That's impossible."

"No. At least you sought the truth. I'm just an impostor!"

"How?"

"I know exactly what you meant about your feelings for Alison Archer."

Mani ceased his tears and looked at her. "Why are you using your own name in the third person?"

She didn't answer, just raised her eyebrows, gestured as though it was obvious and cried some more.

Mani didn't get it. "Yes, what?"

"Oh, geez, Mani. Alison Archer was the coolest, prettiest girl in school. The blond hair, slim body, popular, gorgeous. Boys wanted to be with her, girls wanted to be her. Let's just say you weren't the only one to have a crush on the image of Alison Archer."

"So you did go to Westside High, but I don't understand."

"My name, before I changed it, was Hilda Harper, she of moderate grades, low popularity, thick glasses and inappropriate comments. And the possessor of fantasies to be like Alison Archer. To be Alison Archer! So as soon as I was legally able, I killed off Hilda Harper and became who I always wanted to be."

"Hilda Harper." Red-eyed Mani shook his head in disbelief, ran his fingers through his moppy hair. "Sorry, I don't remember you from school."

"I went out with one of your friends from the brainiac study group."

Mani shrugged.

"Parker! Callum Parker, the fat kid!"

"I'm sorry Alison. I mean, yeah...Alison. I don't remember."

This prompted more sobs, tears mixed with makeup and now all Mani saw was some dorky kid from school crying in his apartment. It also meant there was no Alison Archer. He was no closer to his goal and this made him cry some more as they held each other, two pathetic infatuates from Westside State High School.

****

"Maybe it would be best if you delegated some of this stuff that needs finishing. You need to get yourself freshened up."

Eunan was making good sense, for Jason had just blanked during a dummy run of an AllOptions sales presentation. He was fumbling over important terms and completely hashing the layman's explanation of call spreads and butterflies. It was tiredness rather than nervousness. He needed more sleep.

After the bust-up with Alison he'd been committing to sixteen-hour work days and now with the launch just two sleeps away and the schedule tight, Jason was exhausted. The ache of his separation from Alison gnawed his innards like an ancient torture. The hollowness that settled over him affected his daily actions of eating and sleeping, his deprivation such that he felt he may waste away to dust. The hard work, stress and lack of both rest and sustenance amplified his fatigue.

He would mull over the scenario, make his nightly call to her, rejected and ignored, and ponder his options to right this terrible wrong. As far as Jason was concerned, what he and Alison had was far more than a casual dalliance. Her presence provided to him an excitement that single men could not imagine or fathom. That is why he needed her on this London trip. That she was now excommunicated from him was nothing short of utter devastation to him.

Knowing his own fragile state and the higher importance of the following days, he saw the sense in Eunan's urgings to abdicate for more rest. An afternoon at the flat to rest and read would be the ideal tonic. He would pick up a takeaway burrito and then tube it the three stops to Knightsbridge.

Arriving home, he slid the key into the lock and thought he heard speaking inside. It only then occurred to Jason that Mani might be home. He normally had vacated the flat by early afternoon after having written during the mornings. When he entered, Jason was shocked to witness the scene before him.

Seeing his girlfriend and cousin locked in a passionate embrace was more than his frazzled state could endure. In that instant, all the frustration of this trip combined to a focal point behind Jason's eyes. His suspicions of Mani's motives and behaviour, his mistreatment, the blitzkrieg of benders and his subsequent existence on the wrong side of the wall Alison had built. Jason was poised to launch into a malevolent outburst as the blood rushed to form a spiralling headspin.

Before words could be formed, something about this scene appeared less sinister. Jason noticed the apparently unfaithful duo turn their faces to him, the mess of tears, stained makeup, saliva, running noses and red puffed eyes sold him on something different. There was no sexual electricity here, not with so much snot and drool between his estranged lover and his bawling cousin.

Jason's anger turned to shock, then concern. "What's up with you two? And what's going on?"

Mani spoke first, his voice shaky. "This must look weird, but I can explain. I should explain. And apologise. Jason, I'm sorry."

"Apologise for what?"

"Well, this trip hasn't worked out as you thought it might, has it?"

Jason looked at Alison, whose head was bowed. She didn't look up. He longed to sweep her up and hold her. "Well, no, far from it," Jason answered.

"There's been a reason for that, Jason," Mani admitted with quivering voice. "And I've been explaining that to Alison. In summary, I'm behind you two breaking up. I've been setting you up, playing games with you. I am so sorry. I feel disgusted at myself."

Jason's eyes bulged, his mouth dropped open. He watched Mani. Alison started to cry softly. "Please stop crying, you two," Jason scolded. "Can you explain what you're talking about?"

"Alison is crying because she actually loves you and I'm crying because I've been trying to break you two up since you got here. You see, Jas, I am just so completely pathetic, I've been infatuated with Alison Archer since Grade Eight in high school. I've been behind all the tension, keeping you separate, feeding both of you lies and stories. I even drugged you and faked a phone message on your birthday." He began to whimper.

"You did what?" Jason growled. He took two strides towards his cousin. "I should bloody belt you!"

Alison piped up. "Don't Jason. That won't solve anything. There's more to tell anyway."

"For the record, Alison, I never did anything to consciously hurt you," Jason stated. "I've been an absolute mess the past few days. But first, what more is to tell?"

Mani cowered, hopeless and defenceless. "I am so sorry Jason. I can't believe what I've become. I'll understand if you never speak to me again. But I had to do something. I've been besotted with Alison for so long that logic just went out the window. I was desperate."

"I thought you had to have known each other," Jason said.

"That's the worst part," Mani howled, the waterworks restarting. "She doesn't even remember me. I mean she might, but she doesn't." He pointed accusingly at Alison.

Alison stood, retaining her grace despite her tears and emotionality. "The other thing that needs explaining is that I don't remember Mani from school but he also doesn't really know me from school either."

"I'm getting confused," Jason said.

"Mani thought he found Alison Archer, but he hadn't because I'm not Alison Archer."

Jason spread his hands wide in front of him, frowning. "You guys are acting strange. What does that mean?"

"She's not Alison," Mani said.

"I'm not Alison. Well I am, but not the Alison that Mani has gone to so much deluded effort to pry away from you."

"This is nuts! What do you mean you're not Alison?"

"Please forgive me, Jason," Alison said as she took a tentative step toward him. "I'm just as bad as Mani. I was also infatuated with Alison Archer at school and as soon as I was old enough, I changed my name from Hilda Harper to Alison Archer."

"Who the hell is this Alison Archer girl? Is everyone obsessed with her?"

"I am," Mani said forlornly. "But now I've got to find her again."

"I was, so I just became her. Will you forgive me, Jason?"

"You have to forgive her, Jas," Mani said. "She's blameless. It's all been my doing. Take it out on me."

Jason glared at them both. They'd begun to cry again. He let these revelations roll around his mind. Alison was still Alison even if she grew up under a different name. She was still the gorgeous and hypnotic girl he coveted. Mani was another story. This was pure selfish deceit. The lengths he'd gone to in his quest to destabilise Alison and Jason went against everything their families stood for. They were meant to be blood, growing up virtually as brothers, sharing everything from books to toys and dreams and successes. It was nigh on unforgivable for that bond to be snapped with such a cold, cruel act. Jason could not conceive of anyone drugging a relative to get a girl.

He harked back to their days growing up in Brisbane when they would spend hours talking, relying on the other to provide a sympathetic ear and reciprocal conversation. Jason knew of Mani's struggles, he catered to them, providing support and encouragement against the difficulties he faced from bullying and social awkwardness.

He also had a sense of pride in Mani's achievements, unsurprised that they came from his imagination. It was this very imagination, borne of the hardship of school, which guided Mani's decisions, Jason knew. It had fed his infatuation with the blond girl from school and inevitably led to this point. Mani's actions were not vindictive or personal, but a despairing act perpetrated by a man who hadn't learnt how to behave, who'd been showered with fame, money and influence where it didn't fit his ability to cope.

Why should Jason blame Mani for it wasn't Mani that did this. It was Mani's father; it was Jason himself; the education system and the machine of money that had corrupted his decision-making. Mani was holding onto the past and in consequence, the past was exerting a hold over him.

With all this analysis in a few seconds, Jason responded to the damning actions.

"Mani, your quirky ways have been what's kept me close to you. You live a mad, mad life, we all accept that. And I see this wasn't you against me. I understand and I forgive you. You're family and while you do now owe me a few years of favours, I can't be angry at you. You're my nerdy cousin made good."

This prompted an emotional reaction from Mani. The tears began once more. "I'm distraught. I'll never forgive myself," he bellowed.

"You will," Jason said. "And Alison. Whoever you were, what is important to me is you, now, as the person you are. You're Alison Archer, the only one I know and the only one that counts. I beg you to forgive me. I think it's now apparent that I'm not a selfish as you thought. I had some assistance."

She peered up at him doe-eyed, a rebel with a messy face. "I can't help but feel this is all my fault and I'm just some sad little girl pretending my way through life."

"Nonsense, Alison. I love you both." Jason stepped in to Alison, hands on her shoulders, looking into her eyes. "But you, I especially love. I am so sorry this mess came about. I just hope we can resume what we had. I promise you my absolute best."

He drew her to him. She snuggled in as his arms went around her, back in the mutual comfort of their embrace.

"But I must say," Jason added. "This has been weird."

Mani was staring off into a corner of the room, his mouth turned down sadly. "I guess this means I haven't blown my chances with Alison Archer. I mean the real one." He gave a nervous, guilty laugh.

"I'm real, Mani," Alison said.

"You know what I mean."

"She's out there, this mystery woman," Jason said. "And she's waiting for Mani."

"Big chance I'd have after this debacle," Mani said. He walked to the sideboard, fetched a decanter of Scotch and three glasses. He deemed lunchtime most suitable to start drinking. "She's no doubt some supreme high-flying goddess. Well-heeled with a male model husband. I might as well become a monk. Serve penance for my crimes."

"Definitely, she'd be in the lap of luxury," Alison chimed in. "In Europe in a country mansion or the Hamptons in New York. Somewhere unbelievable. Maybe Hong Kong with a millionaire husband, her own fabulous career and a nanny for her beautiful children."

"Listen to you two," Jason said. "Starstruck!"

They laughed, the tension in the room relieved.

"Well, it's true, Jason," Mani offered. "You never knew her. She was something else. She was beyond me. Beyond all of us. What was I thinking?"

Jason shook his head in disbelief. "She might be selling drugs in Woodridge. You don't know. Or she might have married an old rich guy, poisoned him and is now the archetypal black widow in jail. Either that or she is still trying to pass grade 12 at Westside High on her tenth attempt. Get over her Mani, look what she turned you into when you thought Alison was the Alison. That's what happens when you idolise the past."

Alison offered her view. "No, you don't understand. Not a chance that would be her."

"She'd be a supermodel," Mani predicted.

"That's ridiculous," said Jason.

"No really. I mean, look at all the supermodels with matching initials," Mani said getting into an excited stride. "It's a thing, I think. Some sort of ancient code of glorious beauty that lures men. Think of Cindy Crawford, Paulina Porizkova, Stephanie Seymour, Rebecca Romijn. And don't forget Melinda Messenger!"

"Farrah Fawcett," Alison joined in.

"Graham Gooch," Jason said emphatically. "He should have been a supermodel."

Alison nodded her head, as much to confirm to herself as to verify for Jason. "Alison Archer was beautiful."

"It's entirely feasible, almost a certainty that she became a model," Mani declared. "She was that good, Jason."

"Maybe she grew up to be Naomi Campbell." Jason flashed them a cheeky grin.

Mani shot a playful look at his cousin. "Now you're just being ridiculous."

Sea Salt & Lines in the Sand

Home to some of Australia's most beautiful beaches, the Sunshine Coast managed to temper the hot Queensland sun with a permanent flow of cooling sea breezes. The type of zephyr that dries the saltwater on brown arms and sends a tickling shiver along sunburnt backs. A series of gorgeous sandy beaches, inlets and coves stretching over sixty kilometres from Noosa in the north to the southern hamlet of five distinct beaches at Caloundra, the coast sat as a jewel, an hour north of Brisbane.

The bluest of water and banks of identical waves made this heaven for surfers and families alike, drawing visitors with its laidback vibe. As the swells rolled in from the Pacific, so the population swelled. As the saltwater spray from the crashing waves lingered as a permanent mist, people shifted here in droves, some after cheap housing, others the lifestyle, but most after having fallen for the region on a holiday.

Mani Alves, famous writer, former London socialite and now back in Brisbane living in his Paddington unit and enjoying Mum's home-cooked meals thrice a week, was on the Sunshine Coast after a bout of research led him to these idyllic surrounds. He was re-imagining an old theme and the Coast presented the ideal location for the climax of his story.

He was holed up in a low-end surf shack he'd paid up to lease for a month in the sun. He'd been out drinking with the locals, listened to local bands at the Sol Bar in Coolum Beach, sipped coffee on the Maroochy River and eaten out at riverside restaurants in Noosa. He was getting a feel for the place and getting to know how the natives lived.

This particular day had led him back to the beachside Bi-Lo supermarket for more research. He felt the shock of the overly cold air conditioning as the shop doors slid open. A cashier's shrill squawk of "Price Check" pierced the muzak from overhead and lean, bare-chested, barefoot men bought chicken and breadrolls, while girls in short patterned skirts, bikini tops and thongs shopped for juice and snacks.

He'd been in this supermarket just the previous afternoon, purchasing a token pack of razors when he'd had a cheeky, cheerful interaction with the attractive checkout chick who served him. After spending a distracted morning trying to write, interrupted by a late morning dip in a cool water cove by a jutting headland near his rental house, Mani's thoughts had turned back to the cute smile and body-hugging uniform of the girl at the counter. He decided he would drop by for another viewing.

He enjoyed this more flexible routine he'd adopted since returning home from London. There was no need to force words or meet deadlines. He could write when the words came and live a more relaxed life away from the constant lures of big dangerous London.

He stood at the end of the aisle, out of the bustling market walkway. From here he could watch the girl, unseen by her, as she deftly scanned and bagged goods. She had an easy smile and a conversation for each of her customers, though she operated methodically, almost by rote. Like so many, she was here for the money but being pleasant maintained her sanity in a repetitive role.

Mani stepped into the aisle, dodged a trolley and lined up at her checkout. He realised he had nothing to buy so he grabbed a bunch of gerberas. Watching her, he noted the familiar smile and the blond hair, though the face was over-tanned and hard-lived. He leant left to scan the view up and down her body. The red uniform displayed obvious fitness and delightful curves and those legs, thin and athletic and beachcomber brown. Though not able to see her feet, he wondered if she still wore her tennis shoes and rainbow laces.

What Mani couldn't tell from this external view was the life this young girl had lived. How she'd given less than her best to her studies, preferring beach time, and now regretted those choices. How she'd chosen the wrong type of guy again and again and had borne a beautiful daughter to one of these now absent losers. And how her mother and retired bank manager father cared for her daughter while their own daughter worked. And that she was ambitious and on the cusp of starting a career now her little girl was beginning school.

Sidling up to the checkout, Mani watched her tidy up and accept payment from her customer, before absent-mindedly greeting him. He felt the fluttering thrill of hearing her voice and seeing her name badge.

Alison.

She responded playfully to his presence. "You again," she smiled.

"I told you I'd be back," Mani responded confidently. He gave her a smile, that of a man at ease with himself.

"What's a fella like you doing hanging around in a supermarket?" she teased. "Shouldn't you be getting back to work?" She was referring to Mani's dress sense, the habit of wearing a suit jacket whenever he left the house.

Mani noted her admiring look, not knowing that she gravitated naturally towards big guys. "I work when I want. I'm a writer," he said, handing over the flowers for scanning.

"Lucky you," Alison said. "And who are these for?"

"They," Mani replied, "are for my latest muse."

It was impossibly obvious flirting.

"Who might that be, Mr Writer?" she asked, raising an eyebrow.

"Well that is a very long story. It's funny you know. When I saw you, I had this feeling like I'd known you for a long time."

She tilted her head, her curious, teasing smile remaining. "You're new to me."

Politely, with all the manners and mannerisms of a man ready to invite someone to join him as an equal, to wipe away the doubts and illusions of all that had past, Mani Alves asked if Alison Archer would like to meet after her shift. "Maybe get coffee," he said, "and get to know each other."

Finally, deep down within himself, he felt whole as though it was he who had control of his future and yet owned his past. Like he had conquered the obsession, brought a sword down on the throat of the strangulating beast he'd fought for so long. Mani Alves had drawn a line in the golden coastal sands to bury the saga that had held him back from the crystalline, mysterious future he had in store.

###

Thank you for reading my book. If you enjoyed it, won't you please take a moment to leave me a review via my website.

Thanks!

Mat Murphy

****

Connect with Mat Murphy

Website: www.matmurphy.com.au

Follow me on Twitter: http://twitter.com/matmurphy88

Friend me on Facebook: http://facebook.com/matmurphy

Connect with me on LinkedIn:
au.linkedin.com/pub/**mat-murphy**/3a/b94/70

Via Smashwords and Amazon

****

Mat Murphy lives in Brisbane, Australia.

A fully qualified financial planner, beach nut and sports encyclopaedia, Mat enjoys travel with his wonderful wife Kim, epic bushwalk adventures, hanging with his tribe of kids and playing soccer.

This is his first novel.

Made in the USA
Middletown, DE
20 June 2015